# The Weave

# The Weave

## Nancy Jane Moore

Aqueduct Press

Aqueduct Press, PO Box 95787
Seattle, WA 98145-2787
www.aqueductpress.com

ISBN: 978-1-61976-077-6

Library of Congress Control Number: 2015936644

10 9 8 7 6 5 4 3 2 1

Cover design: Kathryn Wilham
Cover illustrations: Mayan observatory tower "El Caracol" (the snail) at Chichen Itza, Yucatan, Mexico, © Can Stock Photo Inc./janniswerner; Snow scene, © Can Stock Photo Inc./fbxx; Unidentified flying object, © Can Stock Photo Inc./andreacrisante; PIA02923: Mosaic of Eros' Northern Hemisphere, NASA/JPL/ JHUAPL; Star-Forming Region LH 95 in the Large Magellanic Cloud, NASA, ESA, and the Hubble Heritage Team (STScI/ AURA)-ESA/Hubble Collaboration

Printed in the USA by Thomson-Shore, Inc.

# Acknowledgments

Over the years, many people helped me with this book. Early on, my sister, Katrinka Moore, lent me her cottage in the country, where I banged out most of the first draft.

More recently, three people helped me develop more probable means of interstellar travel and communications: my brother-in-law Michael Lawrence, my Aikido colleague Matt Fisher, and my Clarion West classmate Alex Lamb. Their combined efforts made me smarter, but, of course, any errors—not to mention flights of fancy that may make physicists cringe—are my own.

The complete and thoughtful editing by L. Timmel Duchamp and Kath Wilham at Aqueduct improved my original story markedly. Having been raised by a brilliant editor, I am deeply grateful for the effort involved.

Robert Freeman Wexler, Diane Silver, and Anne Sheldon have provided ongoing support for all my writing.

Special thanks are due to two people. Therese Pieczynski, also a Clarion West classmate, read the first draft of this novel and told me it was good. Whenever I was about to give up on it in despair, I reminded myself that Therese liked it.

And Jim Lutz put up with me through the last two sets of revisions, plus a round of substantive edits. His patient—but daily — inquiries as to how the novel was going kept me on track even when I was in the depths of angst.

*For everyone who stares at the sky on a starry night and wonders who else lives in the universe.*

# Prologue

## I

A small girl—maybe five years old—walks along a pedestrian lane in Demeter, the main city on the asteroid Ceres. Her left hand is firmly attached to her father; her right trails along the handrail, and she wears gravity boots. She is not native to Ceres and will not be there long, so she needs the boots most of the time to counteract the muscle decay that comes from living on a low-gravity asteroid. She doesn't argue about the boots, although they are clumsy and ugly and she much prefers the sensation of floating around she gets without them: her daddy told her to wear them, and she always obeys her daddy.

The father who walks beside her is not a tall man, but he has wide shoulders and powerful legs. His hand dwarfs his daughter's, but he holds hers gently. His skin is light brown, as is his daughter's, though her face shows more traces of Asian heritage than his. He, too, wears gravity boots, but they look less clunky on his feet and go better with his Marine uniform than they do with her shorts and t-shirt.

As they walk down the street—it's their first visit into the city since they arrived at the military base two days ago—several Ceresians float by. They use the handrails to pull themselves along. They are young people, their hair cut and dyed in the furthest extremes of this year's fashions, their bodies showing implants chosen with care to shock their elders, their legs dangling. Their feet are bare, the toes curled under.

"Look, Daddy," the little girl says, staring in fascination. "Aliens."

Her daddy laughs. "No, honey. They are people, just like us. They just aren't wearing their boots right now." She isn't old enough to be told the whole story: that these people have adapted to the low gravity and their muscles have atrophied. In some ways, the father muses, they are becoming a new species. But that's too complex for a five-year-old, who means "non-human intelligent life forms" when she says aliens, even if she doesn't know it yet.

The child is disappointed. She very much wanted to see aliens. She tells her father—in that deadly serious tone young children use when they've figured out something important and need to educate their parents—"Someday I'm going to meet aliens."

And her father—to his credit—does not say, "There's no such thing as aliens." He says, "You bet you will, Caty. You bet you will."

## II

On the fourth planet from a bright yellow star, a being sits staring at a small pane of ground glass, watching the night sky. Stars and planets abound: the night is clear, as it often is on this planet.

The pattern is a bit blurred. The being holds the piece of glass firmly with two hands, reaches down with a third hand, and up with a fourth, adjusting two knobs. The focus improves; the image clears.

The being recognizes the layout of the stars and planets, for it has watched this sky many times, knows the different ways it looks at the different times of the year. In one corner of the sky, it sees something that moves, something that does not belong. It watches the object for a while, notes its path and trajectory, and then sits quietly, eyes closed, in deep concentration, reaching out to others in the weave.

As the being sits, a younger one comes into the room and climbs into its lap. This one looks like the telescope watcher in miniature: both are covered in fur evoking the pale gold of dawn or sunset. The first one does not open its eyes as the newcomer wiggles around to make itself comfortable, though it strokes the small one as a parent strokes a child.

The small one leans over the ground glass. The object that does not belong is still there, moving across the sky. From the child's mind flow images of fantastic beings: wide fat things, with no arms or legs; horned creatures twice as tall as any being ever seen.

The father is amused by these images. It strokes the child again, untangling a knot in its fur. But it can feel nothing from the sky object, and neither can the others with whom it is connected. Nothing with a mind. Nothing alive.

A debate—of sorts—begins to rage within the weave. An image of some kind of beings—like them but not like them—sending the object. Another one of rocks and matter, nothing tied to life. A protest that this object appears different from the meteors and bits of asteroid that they know. And from the small one—insistently—constant images of unusual beings, each one more improbable than the last. The debate continues without resolution.

A last image is introduced, one out of ancient history: many objects similar to the one in the night sky and beings landing, creatures that look neither like them nor like anything in the child's imagination.

The child can feel the adults' fear, but is more excited than afraid. Other worlds exist beyond this place; other beings populate the universe. Then and there it resolves to meet these others one day.

The father is engrossed in the discussion of what should be done, but spares a moment for the child's thoughts. And pats the small one gently, encouragingly, as if to say, yes, my dear one, yes, you will.

# BEFORE

# 1

Sanjuro was heading for a post-work drink when her com sounded. The Colonel said, "Sanjuro, we've got a riot in progress in Demeter. I need your company in the city fifteen minutes ago."

The war on Ceres was supposed to be over. The rebel leadership had surrendered a month ago. Some mop-up remained, but that was work for peacekeepers and military police, not combat marines. An Army peacekeeping division with an MP component had recently been deployed across Ceres and the smaller asteroids of the Belt. About half the marines who'd fought here were already gone, and Caty Sanjuro's company had been doing routine standby work at the small base a few klicks outside Demeter for the past two weeks. The base—a small facility set up for low-grav training that had become the surface headquarters—was gradually shrinking to its pre-war size, with most of the temporary structures removed. Their next orders were supposed to be for home and some down time.

"Excuse me, sir," Sanjuro said. "But isn't that an MP assignment?" Before Ceres, she'd have simply said, "Yes, sir" and hit all-call to get her people together. But this war had altered her in ways she'd never thought possible. Combat always affects people—killing leaves few human beings unscathed, despite the violence that permeates history—but before this operation she'd always been able to put her job in context. Sometimes there were no good choices; sometimes war, ugly as it was, beat the alternatives. This time, though, she felt like she'd been fighting on the wrong side.

The Colonel said, "You're reinforcements. There's only a small force of MPs in Demeter, and they're still struggling with the low grav. The whole thing's veering out of control. They need backup. I'm sending details now."

That wasn't as much information as she wanted, but the tone of the Colonel's voice made it clear that the Q&A period had expired. "Yes, sir," she said, and hit all-call.

Sanjuro looked out at her company. They were packed in the briefing room. Like most buildings on Ceres, the ones on the Marine base were made from local rock. They might have been nice if they'd had windows and been painted something other than utilitarian grey, but those in charge had deemed artificial light more practical, given the short lengths of Ceresian days and nights. The lousy decor added to the feeling of depression that had settled over her troops—seasoned fighters all, but sick of this war. No professional soldier likes fighting amateurs, particularly amateurs who believe in their mission. More than one of her people was struggling with the same conflicted emotions she felt. She knew these people, knew the last thing they wanted to deal with was a riot.

Sanjuro needed to inspire them, and she needed to do it quickly. So she said, "The Army can't hack it."

"So what's new?" someone yelled out. Someone else said something Sanjuro couldn't quite catch that drew loud laughs. She didn't have to hear it to know it was at the Army's expense.

She said, "The MPs they put in Demeter don't even know how to handle a riot."

More laughter.

"They need marines."

That drew a few cheers.

"We're the closest backup, and they know we can do the job."

"You bet we can," somebody said, and there were more cheers.

"Anybody got a question? No? Get your armor on. I want you on the transport in five minutes."

"Good job," Lt. Gloria Elizando said as she and Sanjuro left the troops to their sergeants and moved into a private room to suit up. "You almost got me to cheering, too. But then I remembered we were going out to deal with a fucking riot, which is not supposed to be our job." She grabbed her hands behind her back and leaned forward to stretch. "Kuso! I'd hoped we'd seen the last of battle armor for a while."

The armor was a metal-cloth alloy, flexible, but a lot heavier than the heat-regulating graphene body skels they wore on ordinary duty. It was worth the extra weight—it would block most projectile weapons, diminish the effect of explosives, and, when the headgear was in use, filter out gas—but no one liked wearing it.

"Me, too." Until the captain had been shot, she and Glory Elizando had each run a platoon, but now Sanjuro was technically in charge of the whole thing. Six months' worth of seniority had given her the nod, but Elizando hadn't resented it. They got along okay.

Even in uniform they didn't look alike: Elizando exceptionally tall, with dark brown skin and bright gold hair, Sanjuro short only by comparison, with thick black hair, light tan skin, and the wide Japanese eyes that went with her name. Her father had insisted she use her late mother's name.

"Guess this is why they left us on the base, instead of moving us up to the station," Sanjuro said.

"Too bad they didn't leave one of the other companies down here." Actually, they both preferred being on the surface. Being on the station that moved in geosynchronous orbit around Ceres meant making polite with the brass, and both of them had the line officer's contempt for those who made battle decisions from afar.

The transports ran on mag-lev lines between the base and Demeter. They were utilitarian, but at least they had windows. Through the mild distortion of the arched cover that encased the transport line, Sanjuro could see sunshine filtering through the mass of tree-like plants that covered all parts of the asteroid that weren't under a dome. The astrobiologists said those gene-modded plants would give Ceres a breathable atmosphere so that people wouldn't have to live in sealed domes forever. Once that change happened, more settlements would be built, and eventually the workers who'd completely adapted would be able to make real lives here. Another fifty years, the biologists said—soon, but not soon enough for the people taking part in the riot.

Sanjuro knew the history, but until she'd arrived on the asteroid she hadn't thought much about it one way or the other. The war on Ceres had started as a miners' strike, and workers in the Asteroid Belt's other main industry—tourism—soon joined in. No one had expected two such diverse groups to get together. The miners were people who couldn't pass exams for most types of work, while the tourist workers included the kind of thrill seekers who liked to lead extreme expeditions as well as aspiring actors who flocked to the Belt's low-grav theme parks. But, as it turned out, they had key things in common—poor pay, safety issues, and atrophied muscles that kept them stuck in the Belt.

When she'd been a kid, Sanjuro's dad had run low-grav training at the base for a couple of years, so she knew that most long-term workers sooner or later stopped doing the exercises that kept their muscles in shape for higher gravity. Their hours were long, the exercises took lots of time, and most found their work easier to do if they adapted completely to low gravity. Unlike the Marine brass—who simply ordered their people to the do the exercises—company execs weren't displeased if their workers didn't bother. Lack of muscle definition meant they had no place else to go.

The strike was illegal—the contracts that got workers the fare to the Belt prohibited unions along with requiring people to work for their initial company for a set number of years. The Ceres government, at the request of the corporations, sent local soldiers out to break it. Some of the local troops were retired members of the systemwide Combined Forces run by the Solar System Union, but most were soldier wannabes who couldn't pass the exams for enlistment in the interplanetary forces. A small troop, they had only one advantage over the strikers: weapons. They broke the picket lines.

The strike ended, but the leaders quietly began to organize something more deadly. Two years later they announced their resurgence with a bomb attack at the adventure park on Vesta. Killing tourists got them labeled as terrorists, and allowed the Ceresian government to ask for SSU military help. Combined Forces sent in marines— Sanjuro and her people had come in with the first division. One division hadn't been enough, and more people soon joined them.

The outcome had never been in doubt—the rebels couldn't get their hands on enough money or weapons to win—but nothing about it had been easy. A year of effort had brought the war more or less to a halt, but the cost in lives and injuries had exceeded projections by over a hundred percent. Every time Sanjuro looked at her troops, she remembered the ones who weren't there.

Sanjuro's father, Jake Horner, had died on one of the outlying asteroids. He shouldn't have even been out there. He was in his early sixties, the highest ranking enlisted marine on Ceres, and his assignment was admin. But the colonel in charge wanted to be a general. When he got intel that some of the rebels were holed up on that rock, he'd led a raid, bringing along Horner and some other experienced troops as a squad. It had been a trap—a mine buried deep inside had taken all of them out along with the asteroid itself.

Confusion greeted Sanjuro's troops as the company poured into the former corporate offices that served as military headquarters in the city. Like the buildings on the base, the structure was a series of interconnected domes made from local soil and rock. But the walls were painted bright yellow. It might have even looked cheerful, if the windows hadn't been occluded and the room rearranged to serve as a command center.

"Dios, I'm glad you're here," said the captain who appeared to be in charge. He was staring at a holographic projection of the city outside. A line of words flashing in red drew Sanjuro's eye to the key in the upper left hand corner of the holo: "True Visibility at 5%." The image itself was crystal clear, showing a mass of rioters running in all directions, with soldiers bouncing around trying to keep order. A couple of soldiers were hunched over workstations, probably running the holo.

"We got a bomb threat at the high school about fifteen minutes ago," the Captain said. "I sent the bomb squad over to check it out, and now I can't raise them on com or get a scan reading. Meanwhile we've got one hell of a situation out in Governor's Circle, so I can't pull any people out of there." The Captain's headgear was open, and his right eye kept twitching.

"What's going on in the Circle?"

"Rioters everywhere. We used gas, but they must have been expecting it, because they just keep coming." He waved his hand at the projection, which did, indeed, show people constantly materializing. Or rather, a simulation of that—they were running a comp program based on scan data, Sanjuro realized. The Captain saw the look she gave it and said, "Vid's not working. The gas made it bad enough, but then the rioters set off some smoke bombs. You can't see a thing out there except by using scan. And since everything doesn't register on scan, we thought we'd better get the comp to run some projections."

*Great*, Sanjuro thought. *Made-up data.*

"I've got three squads out there trying to round people up, plus one in the council building protecting the politicos. But the baka Ceresians just move too fast."

*Four squads should be enough*, Sanjuro thought. "How many rioters are there?"

The incredulity Sanjuro felt must have been obvious, because the Captain's reply sounded defensive. "Probably about a thousand." He waved at the projection again. "We're real short-staffed. Everyone figured any trouble would hit the mines, not downtown Demeter. We've just got a company of MPs down here, plus the bomb squad."

Sanjuro looked at Elizando. The bomb threat at the high school was probably a hoax, but nothing was certain in this kind of chaos. Adult rioters probably wouldn't target the school, but kids might.

"We better check out the school," Sanjuro said to Elizando. "Take one squad over there—leave me the rest."

"Right." Elizando gave an order and a dozen people headed for the doors. Sanjuro hit com. "And Glory, stay in touch, okay?"

"Yes, ma'am." Her tone wasn't quite sarcastic.

"Who's in charge out there?" Sanjuro asked the Captain.

"I'm trying to run things from here," he said. "Usually it's better when I can see the big picture."

"Well, tell your people we're on our way. And make sure you let us know what you see."

The rest of the company moved out at the lope that was standard fast pace on Ceres. It made them look like a troupe of oversize ballet dancers doing a series of grand jetés. Most people picked up the lope fairly quickly; it took longer to figure out how to turn or stop. Sanjuro's company had spent close to a year on Ceres; they knew how to move.

Demeter, like most domed cities, had been laid out in circles rather than right angles. Governor's Circle was the city's only real park; open space came at a premium. The council chambers—another series of interconnected domes—were the main buildings on the circle. Other government buildings took up about half the circle's circumference, with the rest of the space given over to high-end retail and upscale offices. Even an outpost like Ceres has an upper class.

Sanjuro wondered why the Army hadn't called in the troops at the mines. They weren't as close as the Marine base, but they could still get here fast. She let the thought slip away; right now her attention had to be on her job. By her reading of scan, there were considerably fewer than a thousand rioters out there; the Army Captain's comp projection had distorted the situation, even if some rioters weren't registering. The readout showed MPs foundering around, trying to catch Ceresians and falling as they turned too fast or reached out too far. They bounced back up just as fast, but by then the Ceresians were gone. The MPs' actions lacked rhyme or reason.

Even her people couldn't move as fast as the Ceresians. The only way to develop perfect movement on a low-grav world was to give up high-grav muscle definition. "Circle your people around in the passways one block off the park," she told her sergeants. "Once we control the perimeter, we'll trap the protestors in front of the Council building. I'm going to check in with the Army people holed up in there, see if I can get their people organized so that they're helping rather than hindering. Keep your weapons on disable. Doesn't seem to be anything more vicious than rocks out there." Though a few people probably had something more lethal. They always did. "And no more gas. There's way too much of it now."

She ducked into the Council building the back way, reassured the sentry who blocked her path that the Marines had come to save his ass, and found a full squad in the front part of the building, where a barricade with gun turrets had been erected during the war. This wasn't the first battle for Governor's Circle. A lieutenant paced around behind them, alternately checking scan and com.

"Lieutenant, you've got more people than you need in here," Sanjuro said, not bothering with the niceties of introduction. "Two sharpshooters can keep the front steps clear. We need to put all the troops we can out on the streets to round these people up."

"Who…oh, you're the marine the Captain said was on her way. I don't know if we can—"

"I do. Put your two best shooters there, and there"—she pointed—"and get the rest of them out on the streets. We'll hook 'em up with my sergeants out there; they'll know how to position them. Hell, you'd think you people never dealt with a riot before."

"We haven't," the Lieutenant said. "Most everybody in this company is fresh out of training. All the experienced troops are over at the mines. Nobody expected—"

"Anything to happen in Demeter. So I've heard. Well, let's try to fix this mess so that your first riot won't be your last one."

The Lieutenant stared at her. She didn't have her headgear on, so Sanjuro could see the tension in her face. She hesitated for a few seconds and then used vocal on her com. "Captain, the marines say we can hold this building with a small force, so I'm sending most of my people out to help with the round up." A pause. "Yes, sir." She turned to Sanjuro again, "He says we might as well follow your directions, because nothing else is working."

"A real vote of confidence," Sanjuro said, without bothering to hide her sarcasm. "Let's get moving." She headed out the back door, into the block behind the chambers.

It was slow going. The borrowed soldiers stumbled as they moved. Sanjuro wondered what all these inexperienced troops were doing here. Surely the Combined Forces brass had known they'd need peacekeepers and MPs once the war was won. With all the hot spots on Earth, the Army had to have plenty of people with substantial post-war mop-up experience. They could have sent some of the pros for low-grav training six months ago and had the right people here.

Relying on scan was becoming a real pain in the ass, especially since it didn't seem to be registering an accurate number of rioters. Even granted that Ceresians moved fast, the constant up and down of the numbers couldn't be right. But as near as Sanjuro could guess, given the state of her data, most of the rioters were actually in the Circle, not on the side streets.

Sanjuro sent the soldiers around to the blocks outside the park to mix in with her marines, and pulled the MPs who were roaming around inside the Circle back out to the edges. The maneuver took longer than she wanted, but after fifteen minutes she had the perimeter, with troops spaced evenly around. Now all they had to do was walk in, herding protesters as they went. It ought to work. They moved toward the Circle.

Com beeped. Elizando. "Hey, Sanjuro, we're at the high school. Looks copacetic. Bomb squad found nothing. Hardly anybody here anyway—looks like the kids are all out your way. Teachers, too, probably."

"Great. Come on back. We could use the help."

Elizando didn't answer.

"Glory? Elizando, stay online." No response. "Come on, Glory, talk to me." She tried their private channel. Still no response. "Oh kuso." She hit all-call. "I've lost Elizando on com. Is everyone else here?"

The reassuring sound of voices reporting in was interrupted by a thundering explosion that momentarily deafened her. She switched from local to wide area scan, and saw red alert alarms about where the high school ought to be. Double kuso. Without com there was no way to know if Elizando's squad was outside the damage area—and therefore able to bring things under control—or blown to Pluto with the building.

The Army Captain's voice was hysterical as it came over com. "The school blew up."

"I know, Captain. It was hard to miss. Stay calm," Sanjuro told him. Her own mind was racing. Should she pull everyone out of here and head for the high school? That didn't feel like the right choice, but she couldn't figure out why. Go on your instinct, Sanjuro, she told herself. She spoke to the Captain. "Send someone over to the school area and find out what's going on."

"I don't have anyone to send."

"Pull one of those people off your sims. They're not doing us any good. Or go yourself. We have to know what's up, and I need to get this situation under control."

She continued leading her troops in. Rioters screamed and cursed, and threw rocks and worse at them. The smoke began to clear in spots, showing her angry people waving signs, nothing more. Their faces were contorted, and they were screaming and throwing things, but they were moving forward under the pressure of the armed soldiers. Sanjuro's people could get this under control, assuming that whatever had happened at the school didn't ignite more trouble.

A fresh wave of gas blew across the protestors. "Goddamn it," Sanjuro said, "whoever set that off is looking at a court martial." Now she couldn't see anything again. She called up scan, and the number of enemies doubled before her eyes. Damn it, scan had to be malfunctioning. Otherwise, where had those people come from?

Sergeant Begay's voice came through com in a shout. "The new ones got live weapons, Captain." She heard shots ring out, saw flashes register on scan. Somebody screamed through com, and the sound almost pierced her eardrum. If the sound came through com, the screamer had to be one of hers.

It didn't make sense. Another scream. More explosions nearby. She knew they'd never caught all the rebel leaders, had never rounded up all their weaponry. If her people were screaming, somebody had to be firing armor-piercing rounds. Something still felt wrong, felt off, and she didn't trust scan, but she'd run out of time. She brought up all-call. "Reset your weapons for kill. Fire on any target firing at you." That last point was a brief curtsy in the direction of standard operating procedures; she knew damn well that once they started firing live rounds people would be shot regardless of whether they were holding rifles, rocks, or babies. But she couldn't let her people die without fighting back.

Sanjuro reset her own weapon and fired in the direction of one of the flashes. Eighty-odd troops let loose a barrage. She began to hear lots of screaming from the people in front of her. She realized she wasn't hearing any more screams through com.

Begay's voice again boomed through all-call. "Stop the firing. Tell them to stop, Captain, tell them to stop." His voice cracked. "Scan's wrong. They aren't armed. Stop the firing. Please stop it."

Her scan was still registering enemy fire, but she had been in too many battles with him to distrust Begay. "Cease fire," she said, repeating the words as she moved toward Begay's location until she heard the shooting taper off, stop. "Sergeant, what's happening?" She stumbled on something, recovered, leaped over it, and then turned back. On the ground lay a teenager. His eyes were wide open, but he stared at nothing. The gaping hole in his chest told her all she needed to know.

Begay said in her ear, "Scan lied." He was crying.

Sanjuro left the boy's body, thankful to get away, and connected up with Begay. He knelt in the street, cradling the head of a dead man. The deceased had the same kind of broad, brown face as the Sergeant. She put a hand on Begay's shoulder.

"Madre de Dios, we killed civilians." The Sergeant wasn't even trying to stop his tears.

Sanjuro knew how he felt. Com buzzed in her ear. "Captain, Lt. Elizando sent me over to tell you that things are fine at the school. We've got some kind of com glitch." Another voice cut in, "Captain, I got to the school and everything's fine there. Nothing blew. I don't know what the explosion was, but nothing blew. Just some kind of com problem. I had to come back halfway to get through."

The explosion. She hadn't felt it; just heard it. Probably through com, now that she thought about it. It had been so loud she'd assumed it was an outside noise, but something that big should have shaken the ground. She called up the Army Captain back at the Combined Forces headquarters. "Captain, get medical out here on the double."

"But scan's still showing—"

"Scan's chingado, Captain. Along with everything else. We don't have anything out here except dead and dying civilians. Get medical here now."

# 2

Sanjuro was surprised that the Colonel suggested they meet in his quarters. She'd been there once before, for one of those parties people went to for career, rather than personal, reasons. The accommodations were spacious, particularly for a space station; they had been designed on the assumption that an officer might bring a spouse and children to a posting, though the Colonel had neither. He took her past the formal room meant for social occasions, back into a small den, the room where he really lived. One corner held a desk messy enough to show that someone worked there. Several comfortable chairs were arranged in another corner, and the Colonel had set out a bottle of wine and a couple of glasses on the table between them. The walls were covered with masks from a variety of Earth cultures. Sanjuro recognized the ones from Noh theatre and some others that appeared African in origin.

The Colonel noticed her looking. "I collect," he said, in a slightly apologetic tone, as if hobbies were a weakness. "Please, sit over here. I've got some Europan wine. Their grapes aren't quite up to Earth-standard yet, but they'll do. They'll do."

Sanjuro sat, took a sip of the wine, which was much better than that offered in the officers' mess.

"I thought we'd be more comfortable here," the Colonel said. "No recording devices. And the place is swept regularly to make sure no one else is listening."

Sanjuro nodded. Even if he were telling the truth, it didn't matter. She wasn't dumb enough to say anything to a superior officer that she wasn't willing to have on the record.

"It was a terrible thing, that riot in Demeter. We've done some digging into it. Scan was hacked, of course. And the com glitches turned out to be a nasty little worm. The explosion and gunfire were just playback devices built into com after the worm opened the door. You probably heard about all that."

"Yes, sir," she said. "Though I haven't heard who did the hacking."

"Neither have I. If Intel has figured it out, they aren't telling me."

Sanjuro assumed he was lying.

"I've read your report. The second one. The one addressed to the Marine Commandant."

Sanjuro stiffened. Her wine glass wobbled, but she managed not to spill anything.

"It's all right, Captain. I understand why you tried to go around me. You must have assumed that I knew the facts and was doing nothing. No hard feelings."

She didn't believe that either, though it sounded sincere. "I should have copied you on that, sir." She set her glass on the table between them.

"Well, it would have made things a little easier when the commandant asked me about it, but no harm done. He sent it back to me."

Sanjuro looked at him. He hadn't said, "sent me a copy;" he'd said, "sent it back to me."

"The brass want to keep this whole thing on Ceres, Captain."

She'd never heard a colonel refer to "the brass" before; in her mind, a colonel was definitely brass. "I guess that's why I haven't seen anything about it on any of the newservs."

He nodded. "And you won't. Unless you're planning to send your report to them."

Sanjuro was glad her wine was sitting on the table. She was pretty sure she'd have spilled it if she'd been holding the glass. "And why would I do that, sir?" The calmness of her voice amazed her.

"Because you're not going to be happy with what I'm going to do with it."

"Which is?"

"Nothing."

Sanjuro heard a hint of disgust in his voice. She looked at him. He was grimacing.

"Someone set this up, Sanjuro. Someone who wanted to make very sure that not only did the rebellion fail, but also that no one would start another one for a hundred years. And they succeeded. A massacre..."

Sanjuro winced at the word.

"A massacre like that early in the war would have given the rebels more to fight for. At this point, though, it just drives a stake through their hearts."

She nodded.

"I don't know who set it up. I wasn't party to it. You may not believe that, but it's true. I'd like to think no one military was, that it was an outside deal, but the fact that the Army set inexperienced people down in a situation that called for real pros makes me think someone was bought off somewhere. I'm pretty sure there were even plants among the Ceresians to set off the riots." He finished his glass of wine, poured another. "But I have nothing resembling proof of anything, and the resources that should be able to give me proof aren't cooperating."

This time he refilled Sanjuro's glass to cover his pause.

"Your report's been purged from the system, Captain. Not just deleted; purged. Except for the copy that I'm sure you've kept. And you'd be wise to purge that one, too."

"Why, sir?"

"Because all you've got are allegations. You can't prove any of what happened."

"I can prove that people died, sir."

"Yes, but you can't show who set them up. Maybe you can stir up trouble and be seen as a hero. Or maybe they'll just hang the whole thing on you and shut you down. Never think they can't do that, Sanjuro. They might even use your father's death to argue that you were out to get the Ceresians."

"What?" Though it shouldn't have surprised her. So obvious—her father's death gave her a reason to hate Ceresians. The fact that the person she hated was the bakatare colonel who gave her father chingado orders wouldn't make sense to anyone except a few sergeants. And no one would understand the sympathy her father had with the rebels. Not that it had kept him from doing his job—from dying because he was doing his job—but a man like Jake Horner who knew how many opportunities he'd missed in life because his genes weren't considered good enough couldn't help feeling sorry for the workers who were stuck on Ceres. And all that was too complicated for most people.

"Whatever happens, odds are the guilty parties will never be found."

"Are you ordering me not to talk to the newservs, sir?"

He smiled. "No. If I did, you'd probably call them up just to spite me. I'm trying to explain to you that it won't make any difference. It might just be news for a while and then blow over. Worst case, they'll need a scapegoat. And that scapegoat will be me, or you, or, just possibly, the Army captain who was running those incompetent MPs. But it won't be whoever actually pulled this off."

Sanjuro nodded. She got up to leave.

"By the way, Captain, your promotion's been made permanent. Congratulations." He held out his hand, and she shook it.

Prof. Andrea Bogdosian replied promptly to Sanjuro's message.

"Captain Sanjuro: I am sorry to hear that the Marine Corps refuses to allow you to attend graduate school as part of your military duty. However, as you know we are very impressed with your credentials and would still like to have you in the xenology program. So long as you are leaving the military on good terms, I am sure we can find a fellowship to support you during your studies."

She looked at the words "So long as you are leaving the military on good terms." She wondered what Bogdosian had heard. The professor was reputed to have major connections throughout the System. Though maybe she was just guessing, based on Sanjuro's sudden request for a fellowship following close on the heels of a messy war. The hell of it was, the Marines would probably be willing to send her to school at this point; she was pretty sure the Colonel would recommend it if she asked. He'd know it meant she wasn't going to tell the newservs anything. But she obviously couldn't tell them anything if she wanted Bogdosian's fellowship, either.

And what good would it do to tell the newservs? They probably wouldn't have any more luck at digging out the whole truth than she'd had. She'd tried—she knew people in Intel, had friends who were better hackers than she. Everything had come up empty. The Colonel was probably right: if she did go public, someone would be made a scapegoat and the truth would stay hidden.

She wrote Bogdosian back, assuring her that she was leaving the Marine Corps on good terms, with a recent promotion. Then she carefully composed her letter of resignation. Her reenlistment date was coming up; she doubted they'd hold her to the absolute minute of it.

She purged the report from her private comp. A complete delete was a simple hack. If the Colonel or the commanding general had kept a copy despite what the Colonel had said, she doubted they'd do anything with it. Even Intel wouldn't, so long as she cooperated. And she was cooperating.

Cooperation left an ugly taste in her mouth. As soon as she finished she went next door and woke up Elizando. "Hey, Glory. Let's hop the elevator down to Demeter and get drunk."

## 3

The observatory was at the top of a tall hill on the outskirts of the village where Sundown lived. The path to it was steep and rocky, impossible for wheeled vehicles. The climb to the building that housed the telescope required a couple of hours. Despite the effort, Sundown made the trip several times each week during the warmer seasons, usually arriving just before nightfall and spending the night. In the winter, Sundown came whenever the weather permitted, staying in the hut for several days. The observatory had been built to withstand the winter storms, so while the accommodations were basic, there was no risk of freezing to death. Solar panels set into the roof provided more than enough energy to heat the building and power the telescope.

Studying the skies was Sundown's primary work, along with teaching astronomy. Sundown had learned the work from its father, who had been the leading astronomer for the Golden Mountain region. Sundown's friends joked that it had become an astronomer while still in the pouch, for its father had climbed to the observatory—at least during good weather—while the baby was still nursing. Of course, Sundown did not remember that time, only the stories about it.

What Sundown did remember was that, when it was out of the pouch but still quite a small child, it had demanded to know where its father went so many nights, and when sent an image of the telescope and the view of the stars it gave—so much more detailed than could be seen standing out in the garden—had begged to go along. After repeated requests, Sundown's father had consented, though it must have known it would have to carry the child part of the way. On the first trip, Sundown had fallen asleep clinging to its father's chest as they climbed and had been hard to wake up to look through the scope when they arrived. But all tiredness fell aside when Sundown took that first look through the scope. From that day on, Sundown had come to the telescope as often as possible.

Climbing the path on a day in late spring, Sundown missed its father, who had been killed fighting a fire that had swept through their village during a particularly dry summer eight years back. The wind had suddenly changed directions while the crew was digging a fire break, sending the blaze their way and trapping them all. Smoke inhalation had killed them before the fire burned their bodies, so the healers said, but many had felt their suffering.

Sundown's mother had been among the healers helpless to do anything except bear witness. It had retired to a contemplative community after the deaths.

Sundown's own child only visited the observatory as part of school work—students of all ages came up on a regular basis. The child had never shown any particular inclination to study further. Sundown supposed it was time to look for an apprentice with passion for astronomy so that the knowledge would be passed on. None of the older students had shown much more interest than Sundown's child had. Sundown might have to seek farther afield, perhaps among the amateurs who gathered to share telescopes in parks on clear nights.

The previous winter had provided more snow than usual and had been succeeded by a wet spring. Making a way up the trail, using a stout walking stick and occasionally bending over so that the lower set of arms reached the ground, affording more stability, Sundown rejoiced in the riot of colorful flowers that lined the path. Rare yellows, greens, and blues joined the usual purples and reds, and every plant that could possibly flower seemed to have done so. Most years—dry years—the flowers were scattered, duller, and quickly gone.

A bouquet of odors accompanied the colors, as many varieties of smell as there were colors to see. Each tiny flower had its own fragrance, a hint of fruit here, a touch of musk there, all laid over the rich, earthy smell of soil that has received enough water to ferment below the surface.

The flowers not only brought beauty and fragrance, but also provided the promise of fruit to come. But pleasure in this bounty was tempered by regret that Sundown's father could not be here to see it. Their treks to the observatory had included lessons in botany, another passion Sundown had come to share. Soon Sundown would be gathering berries on the way back down the mountain and ranging off the trail to search out good fungi; a damp spring meant more of those as well, more than enough for the family. The excess could be sold in the market or traded for other delicacies.

Sundown made it to the top in time to watch the sun set in a spectacular burst of oranges and golds. The last fading light reflected the pale gold color of its own fur, a sight that always made it feel tied to the universe, if only by color. As the colors faded away, the first stars began to appear, accompanied by a sliver of moon. But the air had grown chilly with the disappearance of the sun. Even in summer it was rarely warm at night anywhere on the planet, especially at higher elevations. Sundown moved inside to make dinner and wait for full dark.

The sky was very clear, and the waning moon gave off little light. Sundown set the telescope for continuing observations of one of the other planets in the system, now at the closest point to theirs in more than a hundred years. Sundown carefully memorized the images, storing them to share with the weave of minds that held knowledge in their community and with the planetwide network of astronomers, and also made notes on a mathpad, calculating distances, refining earlier determinations.

Abstract concepts such as math required notation, and Sundown was fortunate to have a computing device that made it easy. The mathpads were expensive to make. Had Sundown not had the financial support of Golden Mountain's ruler, Sorrel, who believed strongly in the importance of study and discovery, it could not have afforded either the device or the telescope. Astronomers in some of the other regions were not so fortunate.

Not long before dawn, calculations completed, Sundown reset the telescope for a larger view and watched the sky in hope of seeing the unusual. In years of watching, Sundown had seen many fascinating things: stars streaking across the heavens, meteors striking one of the other planets, eclipses of the sun. Sundown had carried on its father's work, cataloging many more planets and stars.

But Sundown had yet to see another image like that of the dead ship its father had observed so many years ago. That ship had stayed in their sky for a little over a year and had twice orbited the planet. Discussions still went on among those interested in astronomy and history about what it might have been. Some still contended that it might be a prelude to invasion, even though nothing had yet happened. Others dismissed it as an aberration in the sky, something unknowable.

Sundown was hoping it meant company.

# TRANSIT

# 1

The auto-cab stopped at the front gate of Combined Forces Headquarters. Caty Sanjuro pulled out her bags and queued up behind a Space Corps pilot checking in. Twenty years had passed since she'd last seen Brussels, when she'd served a brief stint in the Marine Honor Guard here at headquarters before reporting to the Academy in Hokkaido. It didn't look as if much had changed. She noted with approval that they still used marines to guard the gate. Not that they needed a human guard; it was just one of the little perks of headquarters.

The gate corporal gave her a snappy salute, and she returned it with equal crispness. Something about his manner hinted that he held her in higher regard than the pilot ahead of her. She smiled to herself. Intramilitary rivalry would never die, no matter how many official orders instructed the troops to the contrary.

Sanjuro gave him her code, and he ran a quick retinal scan while calling up her assignment. She eyed his service ribbons while she waited. He'd served in the peacekeeping operation on Titan. A nasty job by all accounts, since both sides had declared war on the peacekeepers, who'd still had to follow limited rules of engagement. He must have done well; guard duty at Combined Forces counted as a reward assignment.

"Here we go, Captain Sanjuro. You're billeted at the Sci/Tech Corps Officers' Barracks." A brief look of surprise came and went on his face. "Do you need help with your bags, ma'am?"

"I can manage them, Corporal." Marine pride. She still ached from the long shuttle ride in coach from Luna, but was damned if she'd show it.

He nodded, as if she'd just passed another test, and showed her a base map. "We're here," he said, pressing spots to light up the points she needed to know. "Sci/Tech barracks are there, officers' mess in this area, next to the admin building."

"Thank you." She picked up one of her bags with her left hand, leaving the right free to return a salute. Ten years might have passed since she'd last worn this uniform, but some habits die hard.

He hadn't started the salute. "Ma'am," he said. A couple of things clearly puzzled him, and combat experience had given him the arrogance to ask.

She knew that a cold *Thank you, Corporal* would bring rigid attention and a fast salute, and if he hadn't had the battle ribbons, she'd have done it. Instead, she raised her eyebrows at him. "Yes?"

"Pardon me, ma'am, but we don't get a lot of marines with Mars and Ceres combat ribbons assigned to Sci/Tech Corps."

She knew what he meant. People got assigned to Sci/Tech for their knowledge, not their military background. Most Sci/Tech officers had PhDs and demonstrated their own kind of arrogance.

Sanjuro decided she didn't owe the Corporal an explanation of how she got to Sci/Tech. She said, "Well, maybe it's time they got a few of us."

"Yes, ma'am." He almost grinned as he saluted.

The barracks also rated a human clerk, though the corporal at the desk wore Sci/Tech whites instead of Marine blues. She gave Sanjuro a perfunctory salute and said, "Can I help you, Captain?"

"Sanjuro. I'm assigned here."

The Corporal called up her records. "So you are, ma'am. Part of the Cibola Expedition." She looked a little envious. "Room 25. A package came for you. We put it in the room." The Corporal looked at Sanjuro's uniform, and then back at her projection. "Uh, supply also delivered a couple of Sci/Tech uniforms for you,

Captain. Records show you coming from a university. They didn't tell us about your other service connections."

The glitch didn't surprise her. When she'd sent the re-enlistment forms back after being chosen for the expedition, she'd indicated that she wanted to come back in as a marine assigned to Sci/Tech, rather than straight into the scientific and technical forces. The comp probably had it right, and some human had figured she'd marked it wrong. "Could you get them to straighten that out, Corporal?"

Sanjuro phrased it as a request, but her command voice must still have come through. The Corporal reacted quickly. "These uniform specs right, ma'am?"

Sanjuro nodded.

"They'll have you something in a couple of hours, ma'am. You need anything else?"

"Is Major Kyo billeted here?"

"Yes, ma'am. Room 32. But she went to a meeting about an hour ago. Should I tell her you're here when she gets back, ma'am?"

"Please."

Room 25 didn't differ much from typical base accommodations. A narrow bed, built-in cabinets and closets, and, due to her status as an officer, a bathroom crammed into one corner. She queried the net for her access parameters as she unpacked her full dress uniform and examined it critically for wrinkles.

"Full net access: military, academic, and civilian."

She whistled. Sci/Tech Corps had privileges indeed. No ordinary military comp allowed full access, even though virtually every soldier knew how to hack the system to get into forbidden realms. Sanjuro could do her own work here easily.

Not that she'd be here long enough to do any work. The expedition crew had come to Brussels to be paraded before the Solar System Union Secretary General and Assembly, a less than subtle political reminder of who paid the bills. Sanjuro and two or three other last-minute recruits were joining up here. Two days from now they'd take off for the Asteroid Belt and a final month of preparations before they shipped out on the *Mercator* for the first human-crewed extra-solar expedition.

The next stop would be Cibola. Sanjuro felt excited, like a small child the night before her birthday. A hell of a birthday present: a trip to a planetary system forty light years away, which, because of the Alcubierre/Nguyen Drive, would only take five years. The drive was based on Miguel Alcubierre's whimsical twentieth-century theory that a spaceship could cross space at greater than the speed of light without violating general relativity if the space in front of it contracted and the space behind it expanded. The ship, ensconced in a bubble between contraction and expansion, would not travel faster than light, but the contraction of space would reduce the distance dramatically. A/ND had become a reality when Kel Nguyen had figured out how to create the negative mass required to make the contraction and expansion happen without destroying the sun in the process. Engineers and physicists had taken fifty years to turn Nguyen's theory into a working spaceship drive, but now the human race had the technology to explore beyond the Solar System.

Research dating back to the twenty-first century had given them some place to go. The probe ship *Copernicus*, dispatched in the last century to explore the parts of the galaxy first highlighted by the Keplers, had sent back data on the Scorpius 41 system. Sanjuro'd followed the reports on the net with everyone else, reading about the mineral wealth of the system's planets and asteroids, the power of its young sun, the atmosphere and biological life signs of the planet they'd taken to calling Cibola, all so similar to those of Earth.

When the SSU space exploration department had started planning the Cibola expedition, she became so jealous she could hardly stand it. She began to regret leaving the Marine Corps when she learned that the expedition would include some fighting forces in addition to scientists. Their wanting a xenologist seemed past wishing for. And then, a month ago, they'd invited her to join the expedition.

Sanjuro didn't bother to unpack anything except the uniform. Instead, she opened the long, skinny box she had shipped from Luna. Her dress sword. An archaic weapon, of course. Only marines affected them these days. She doubted she'd be allowed to take it on the expedition, but she wanted it for the formal dinner tomorrow night.

She picked the scabbard up with her left hand and drew out the blade, executing a sharp cut as she did so. The blade whistled through the air.

A knock sounded at the door. "Come in," she said, quickly sheathing the sword. It wouldn't do for someone to find her playing.

"Aha, just what I needed. An armed escort." Sumi Kyo stood there.

Sanjuro snapped a sharp salute, and Kyo returned it with an even bigger grin. "Lord, Caty, you're in Sci/Tech now. We don't do that sort of thing." She opened her arms and they hugged each other with enthusiasm.

"It's so good to see you, Sumi." Sanjuro pulled her head back, and Kyo took advantage of the opportunity to kiss her on the lips.

"Likewise, I'm sure. Kuso, you haven't changed at all. The old uniform still fits, and you're as spit and polish as ever. Your hair's even regulation length." Kyo ran her fingers over Sanjuro's short-cropped black hair.

Kyo's hair was equally black, but longer on one side than the other and flecked with gold. Her ears sported gold filigree earrings that resembled tiny spider webs. Nothing prohibited by regs, but flashier than the average officer. She'd always dressed that way.

No one had expected them to be friends, back at the Academy, when they'd met as first-years assigned to the same squad. They seemed complete opposites, Kyo forever being gigged for smart remarks and minor violations of the dress code, Sanjuro with creases on her creases; Kyo the scion of a family that ran a powerful biotech in Korea, a family that disapproved of her decision to follow a military career; Sanjuro the upstart child of a Marine sergeant, a rare working-class element in the privileged world of Earth's leading military academy. But they shared something that most of their classmates, fresh from school, couldn't understand: they'd both served on Mars, Kyo in the Space Corps, Sanjuro a marine, fighting the rebels who wanted to break off from the System. Both had postponed the Academy and enlisted when the war broke out. Their styles differed, but they agreed about the degree of real respect due to senior cadets.

Sanjuro, who almost never earned demerits, irritated her seniors as much as Kyo did because they could sense something disrespectful under her *yes, sirs*. The situation came to a head the night of their first formal dinner, when she'd worn her battle ribbons and medal on her dress uniform. A cadet captain had jacked her up, demanding to know what gave her the right to wear those items. And she'd responded, "Rule 27 (b) (3), sir. 'A cadet with previous military service may wear…'" He'd told her to shut up, she'd said, "Yes, sir," and no one mentioned it again. Kyo had sat next to her, grinning at her at every opportunity. On the next formal occasion, Kyo wore her own service ribbons, and they became good friends.

"Old habits," she said to Kyo, and got a laugh. They stared at each other for a minute, in the way of old friends. It had been too many years since they'd seen each other in person.

"I owe you big time for this," Sanjuro said.

"They'd have picked you anyway. I just gave you a little advance warning, that's all. Once they finally reviewed that *Copernicus* data showing intelligent life forms on Cibola, they had to get a xenologist. And, let's face it, a lot of your colleagues seem a tad strange, at least to the military mind. Even the Sci/Tech military mind. They couldn't understand why someone would want to study intelligent alien life before anyone found any intelligent aliens."

Sanjuro knew all too well the prevailing attitude about xenology. While the discovery of life—along with its precursors and remnants—throughout the Solar System had built astrobiology into its leading role in space science, the xenologist focus on intelligent life was still derided by some as science fiction. The centuries devoted to the SETI project had turned up a few signals that indicated the possibility of intelligent life, but they had come from so far away that no one had been able to follow through to determine if they were more than noise.

Professor Bogdosian had dismissed the skepticism of her fellow scientists with her famous answer to the question of why study aliens when we haven't met any. "Because we're going to," she said, and she'd convinced the University of California at Berkeley to establish a xenology division inside the School of Astrobiology. But neither Bogdosian's forceful personality nor the connection with astrobiology had given the field complete respectability. The presence of intelligent life on Cibola changed that.

"So what's the rest of the Sci/Tech group like?" she asked.

"Well, as you might expect, it's heavily weighted toward people who know how to exploit the wealth of the new system's asteroid belt. Sci/Tech is headed by Colonel Rao. She's an astrogeologist, though she's more invested in the economic impact than the scientific one. You should salute her, by the way. She's more military than your average Sci/Tech."

Sanjuro smiled.

"There are several more astrogeologists, plus some astrophysicists and a bunch of chemists, all with a bent toward applied science. They don't want no damned dreamers on this trip. They probably would have rejected Einstein, or even Alcubierre and Nguyen.

"Plus ten astrobiologists, including me. They want to be sure we have enough people to study the microbial and plant life, see what can be modified for human use. The brass wants more than scientific papers out of all this." Kyo's tone sounded a little harsher as she said this. She cleared her throat.

"At least one of every kind of engineer you can think of. A good statistician to make sure we can all run our data properly. Some skilled support types among the enlisted personnel. And you, the sole xenologist."

"I could use a little help. From what I could tell from the *Copernicus* data you sent me, there could easily be millions of Cibolans."

"Yeah, but how many people can it take to study them? They don't seem to have progressed very far beyond the agricultural stage. A few major concentrations of people—*Copernicus* estimated it at seven—but that's about it."

Sanjuro frowned.

"Sorry. That's the official point of view, not mine. But even you have to agree that the Cibolans don't resemble the omnipotent aliens of fantasy."

"Okay, so they haven't reached our stage of evolution. We can still learn much by studying them," Sanjuro said.

"I know, I know. But while you and the likes of Bogdosian are chomping at the bit to get your hands on real, live, intelligent aliens, the government didn't fund this expedition just so you and I could do a little research. We need those minerals, those energy sources out there. For that matter, given the population pressure in the Solar System, we need the living space. If we can colonize Cibola without having to bioengineer it, we can build a base in nothing flat, do further exploration from there. A/ND flight has opened the universe for our use."

"Are you still giving me the official point of view? The Cibolans might disagree."

Kyo made a face. "Yeah, they might. But it's not like we're going to destroy them."

"Just land on their planet and modify it for our own purposes. We don't have any idea how that will affect them."

"You know that, and I know that. Of course it's not the way things ought to be done, but doing science—or even diplomacy—properly is not a priority of the System government. If it's ever been a priority of any government."

"Don't those bakatares in government realize how much of our progress comes from doing the science right?"

"No. They never remember that. Maybe if the Cibolans seemed scarier, they'd let us do it our way. But these aliens aren't even responding to radio signals." Kyo held up her hand to block another torrent of words from Sanjuro. "Look, you know I agree that we need to study them thoroughly, figure out how they evolved so we can make intelligent guesses about other species. It's vital to learn how life develops in different places. But we're going to have to do it around the margins. Once again, bad economic policy trumps science. It was ever thus.

"I know you could use help, but at least you can send stuff back for others to work on. We'll be using the A/ND system to ship reports, including sound and holos, back on a regular basis—they've been testing it as a communication device by sending tiny capsules between here and Titan, and it seems to work well. It'll take months for the capsules to travel back to Earth once we get out to the new system, though, so they're also sending us off with beaucoup de entangled particles. We'll have ETQ for daily check-ins and immediate response via written reports. I'm sure Bogdosian will see everything you send back through both processes."

ETQ—built on the principles of quantum entanglement—had been used throughout the Solar System for a hundred years. Sanjuro knew this from her time in combat. It wasn't used in ordinary situations, since an abundance of communication satellites made it possible to keep in touch via the System Net on most of the planets and moons. That system even allowed live talk for those who could tolerate the lag time. It didn't work everywhere; ETQ had made it possible for those exploring Pluto and Charon to stay connected.

Once they left the Solar System, *Mercator* would be far out of range of satellites, but with ETQ the crew would always be in touch with home.

"Look, get cleaned up, whatever you need to do, and let's go to dinner. You can meet the rest of the crew there, including the military types. I'm curious to know what you make of Admiral Vargas. You ever meet him?"

"Just briefly, right after the Academy. He hadn't made admiral yet, but everybody assumed he'd get the first real expedition. I always heard he was a sharp guy, very cool under pressure."

"There are those who add the word 'arrogant'—he's famous for preferring his own advice to other people's. But he's been right most of the time. He's the one who named the planet Cibola, by the way. He's something of an historian. I've taken to calling him Coronado."

"Not to his face, I hope."

"Oh, hell no. He probably knows about Coronado. Nobody else gets it," Kyo said sadly.

"It's been a long time since I took ancient history, but if I remember it correctly, Coronado went looking for the seven cities of Cibola—and their gold—but never found them."

"Exactly. He almost died looking for them." Kyo grinned. "Damn, I need you on this trip. No one else ever gets my jokes."

*And a good thing, too,* Sanjuro thought as Kyo left, *or you'd be court-martialed out of the service. Even in Sci/Tech.*

## 2

Sanjuro thought about her fellow xenologists as she stripped for a shower. She hoped she'd be able to send real data back to them, things they could work with. Hell, Bogdosian expected her to bring back Cibolans—she'd told her that when Sanjuro'd stopped at Berkeley on the way to Brussels, in part to get her blessing.

Just looking at the place had made her homesick. She had loved Berkeley when she'd done her graduate work. The old trees, the shingled buildings that appeared to be made from redwood shakes (even if most of the seemingly natural materials were now generated via nano), walls covered in ivy dating back to the twenty-second century when efforts were made to deal with plants lost to the droughts of the twenty-first, and the Campanile, which was almost as old as the university itself. The old universities paid tribute to their heritage in a way that made the more modern institutions like Sanjuro's own Neil Armstrong University look like warehouses.

Of course, NAU was on Luna, where there were no old foundations to imitate. But the buildings could have been less sterile and dull. That they weren't spoke to the restrictions placed on universities by their corporate donors, who didn't want to see their money wasted on frills, despite the fact that their own headquarters used the hottest architects and flashiest designs. The companies that funded Berkeley and even more ancient institutions like Oxford and the Sorbonne were more willing to put in a little extra for "front" than the people behind NAU.

That they funded frills didn't mean the big corps didn't interfere in the old universities in the same way they did with the new ones. They just did it with greater elan. Andrea Bogdosian would never have been able to establish a xenology program at Berkeley if she had not first spent years developing corporate support. People like David Mitchell, founder of the company that built the first working A/ND, and Alexis Wang, CEO of the leading nanotech company, listened to Bogdosian when the academic world was still making fun of "alien hunters." The university had wanted their money bad enough to establish the Mitchell-Wang Program in Xenology.

It had been penny-pinching support. Bogdosian's charisma had been enough to suck in Mitchell, Wang, and other CEOs, but she couldn't convince them to give her an unlimited budget. Even executives who sought immortality for themselves and their companies by grabbing naming rights weren't willing to put a lot behind an ephemeral program.

Bogdosian had made xenology into a rigorous academic discipline, drawing from astrobiology and merging in ideas from anthropology and linguistics. Nobody knew what intelligent aliens might be like, but theories could be developed by comparing the evolution processes of lower life forms on other planets with human history, and Bogdosian's theories had a spark of genius that set the stage for change.

She made use of course offerings from related fields, requiring substantial work in astrobiology and anthropology before allowing students to take xenology seminars. The money she saved went to fund scholarships for the students she really wanted, the ones who would be able to continue the field and give it greater respectability.

On her visit to the Berkeley campus, Sanjuro found Andy Bogdosian in her office looking at a large holo of Cibolan cities that had been published online. "Caty, my dear, so very good to see you."

Bogdosian had grown noticeably older in the last five years, her thin hair now completely white, a stoop to her shoulders Sanjuro'd never seen before. She gave Sanjuro a peck on the cheek, cleared the nearest chair, and told her to sit.

"They've asked me to join the Cibola expedition."

Bogdosian nodded. "Yes, we've heard. I'm sure you'll do an excellent job."

"I know some people here must be disappointed."

"Oh, not that you're going. But we do think they might have included a few more xenologists."

"It should be you. You know more than anyone."

She shook her head. "I'm too old. Likely the trip would kill me. My heart isn't what it used to be, and even transplants can only do so much. Not that I wouldn't like to go." She looked wistful. She'd spent fifty years planning for the possibility of intelligent life on other worlds, and now Sanjuro rather than she would reap the benefits.

"They sent me copies of the significant *Copernicus* data and gave me permission to share it." Sanjuro forwarded the old professor a file packet as she spoke. "I'll do what I can to get more data back to you when we get there. There's no way I can analyze a whole culture on my own. Perhaps the brass will realize it once we start work, and we'll be able to bring others on once I get established."

"I hope so, Caty. I hope you'll bring some beings back to study— I do want to meet a few of these Cibolans— but we need many people in the field studying them in their native habitat to really understand them."

"Yeah," said a bitter voice in the doorway. "But they're sitting on a planet highly suitable for human habitation in a system with an asteroid belt that's going to make a lot of people rich. If they don't turn out to be all that smart, who's going to care? Besides us, that is."

Sanjuro knew Derek Li well enough to recognize that his belligerent tone was a cover for jealousy. If the only consideration in staffing the expedition had been academic work, Derry would have given her heavy competition for the job. And he might have won out. They'd been going head to head since the first day of grad school—

Bogdosian believed in pitting her brightest students against each other—and the won-lost record was mostly tied. But Li didn't trust the government and really didn't trust the military. They didn't trust him, either: his name had made it onto lists during his college days, when he had acted out his rebellion against his father, CEO of the weapons manufacturer Bearco, by getting himself arrested for protesting military intervention at every opportunity.

Sanjuro said, "Well, they wouldn't be sending anybody if they didn't intend for us to study these aliens."

"Oh, yeah. I'm sure they'll let you do a little study. But if they decide the aliens are too much trouble, they're going to expect you to just step aside and let them take over the planet any way they can. That's why they want you, isn't it? They know you can be trusted to follow orders."

His comment hit too close to the mark to be considered just a cheap shot. *Never confess your sins in bed,* she thought, regretting for the nth time the personal things she'd told him during the few months when they'd thought they were in love.

"At least this mission isn't corporate funded," Sanjuro said. "Didn't I hear you'd made peace with your father and convinced him to contribute to Mitchell-Wang?" She smiled at Derek, who gave her a dirty look in response.

Bogdosian frowned. "Caty, you know we could never have developed this program without corporate support. The government, the military—neither was willing to see the potential like some of our leading entrepreneurs did."

Sanjuro was startled. Her comment had been aimed solely at Derek; it hadn't occurred to her that Bogdosian would see it as an insult as well. It dawned on her that the professor had chosen Li for the program not just for his brains, but because of his father. Andy had assumed—rightly—that Li would reconcile with his father and bring his share of the considerable family assets and political clout into the xenology fold. Why else give a scholarship to a man who came from such stunning privilege?

Sanjuro'd always known Andy Bogdosian never did anything without at least a couple of reasons, but this particular insight bothered her. Still, there would have been no preparation for meeting new intelligent species without Bogdosian's efforts. What the professor had done was vital no matter what compromises she'd had to make to develop xenology into something more than speculative science.

Sanjuro could afford to be magnanimous: she was going on the expedition because of Bogdosian, and she'd won big time in her ongoing war with Derek Li. "I'm sorry you're not coming too, Derry. I lobbied for more xenologists, and I'm going to keep pushing. With luck we'll be studying Cibola and its people for a very long time." She tried to make it sound sincere; she did want more xenologists, and Derek knew his stuff, though his renewed corporate ties might cause even more trouble than his abrasive personality.

"I don't know whether you're lying to yourself or just being a complete jopa. Nobody gives a fuck about the Cibolans; they just want what that system has to offer. They're taking you just to make it look good."

Andy said, "Derek! Even if the commanders of this expedition turn out to be so shortsighted, you know full well that Caty believes in this work as much as you or I. She'll do everything in her power to protect the Cibolans."

Li turned toward her. "Will you, Caty?" His tone said he didn't believe it. He turned on his heel and left.

Sitting on the edge of her bed, polishing by hand boots that only a drill sergeant could have found fault with, Sanjuro found herself wondering if Li were right.

# 3

Kyo introduced Sanjuro to most of the mission scientists at dinner. For the most part, they seemed like any other group of researchers. Two geologists at one end of the table were arguing over the meaning of a certain mineral discovery on Pluto. A physicist was picking the brain of a chemist.

But even though, as Kyo had observed, they didn't appear to take their military status as seriously as the Space Corps officers at the next table, Sanjuro found them different from the university-based academics she was used to. Perhaps it was only that they were practical scientists—more like their cousins in the corporate world than the ones in academia. But she suspected that military mindset played a part as well.

In a university, you could—at least to some degree—pick your own area of study. A military scientist worked on whatever the commander said to work on. And while both institutions were highly political, the nuances that got you ahead differed a lot.

Sanjuro had learned to navigate academia. She'd spent the last five years trying to develop the xenology program in the astrobiology department at Neil Armstrong University on Luna. A shaky proposition: NAU set up shoestring operations for lots of developing disciplines, but jettisoned projects if they didn't pay off fast. Sanjuro had fought hard to keep her program going, petitioning corporations for funding and using Bogdosian's clout to keep things on target.

Now, of course, NAU would get the benefit of their investment. Students would be signing up in droves, and the administration would be able to pick and choose its funders. Other schools would be playing catch-up.

Sanjuro, too, would prosper. She would be able to come back and waltz into a job anywhere she chose. Being the only xenologist with field experience would ensure that.

Although she remembered how to act in a military environment, she doubted she could fit completely into one again. In combat, you couldn't question; as part of a new discipline, you did nothing but question. A military scientist had to bridge those contradictory methods. Sanjuro suspected that most ended up as either good officers or good scientists, but few as both.

The woman sitting next to her, a captain like herself, though perhaps ten years younger, said, "You know, I've always wondered why someone would decide to study xenology. Before now, I mean. I imagine it's about to become a very popular course." The captain was one of Kyo's astrobiologists.

Sanjuro shrugged. She'd stopped trying to give a serious answer to that question years ago. "Lucky I did," she said, "or I wouldn't be going on this expedition along with you folks."

One of the majors said, "I wouldn't have thought a marine would go in for something quite so, uh, esoteric." It wasn't quite a taunt.

Sanjuro had also stopped explaining to people in other fields that the rigor of her training would match theirs. She said, "Well, they work together well. If someone makes fun of my academic work, I can always kick their ass. Sir."

Her comment drew a laugh, though she caught a few raised eyebrows.

Kyo said, "She can, you know. Kick your ass. She fought on the ground on Mars and Ceres. And has the medals to prove it."

The table got quiet.

"She can probably even go head to head with Colonel Masire," Kyo continued.

That got a laugh. Someone said, "Hell, I'd pay to see somebody kick his ass," which got another.

"Who's Masire?" Sanjuro asked.

"Marine commandant. Got a troop of around eighty. Seems to think he could take over the whole Solar System with them."

"Eighty marines. I wouldn't think it would take that many," Sanjuro said.

Kyo pointed out that the marines couldn't get there without the Space Corps, and someone else observed that marines weren't the only combat troops around. The conversation degenerated into good-natured interservice rivalry; it seemed as if about half of the Sci/Tech contingent came originally from other services. Though no one else had been a marine.

Back at quarters, some of the younger officers had started an impromptu party in the common room. Several people joined it, while others went off to their own rooms. Sanjuro stayed outside, sitting on the porch. It was early October, and the air temperature was just cool enough to suggest that winter wasn't far off.

Sanjuro took deep breaths, enjoying the real air. She knew that, chemically, bioformed air and the real thing were the same—both had the same amounts of oxygen, nitrogen, and other elements—but like everyone else living on Luna, she swore she could tell the difference. In a couple of days they'd be on shuttles to the space station and the big ship, and she wouldn't breathe any more real air until they got to Cibola. And Cibola's air would not be Earth's.

A man in a marine uniform strode up the path toward the barracks. Sanjuro caught the flash of a colonel's eagle and jumped up to salute.

The colonel returned it. "At ease."

Sanjuro found herself looking at a man perhaps five or six years older than her own forty. His face showed African ancestry—his forehead sloped up toward his hairline, and his skin tone was a dark brown. Nice brown eyes.

"I wasn't expecting another officer," he said, looking a little confused.

Of course. The marine commandant. "Oh, I'm not in your troop, sir. I'm detailed to Sci/Tech. Caty Sanjuro."

"Ian Masire." He stuck out a hand, and she shook it. "Didn't know we had any scientists in the Corps." He was looking at her badges.

"Well, I've been out for a few years. But when I was asked to join up for this trip, I couldn't see wearing any other uniform."

He grinned. "So, what's your specialty?"

"Xenology."

"Ah, you're along to make friends with our aliens."

She thought she detected a bit of mockery. "You got a problem with that, sir?"

"No, Captain. Should be interesting to see if you can do it. I'm pretty curious about the Cibolans myself." He nodded, and walked in.

*Attractive man.* Sanjuro wondered if they were going to be friends.

# 4

Sanjuro didn't have to wonder whether she was going to get along with Col. Lakshmi Rao. Thirty seconds into her meeting with the Sci/Tech head, she knew it was a lost cause.

"Frankly, Captain," the Colonel said, leaning across her desk and scowling, "I don't see why we need an alien anthropologist on this mission."

Sanjuro had enough sense to keep her mouth shut, though the term "alien anthropologist" was considered an insult by everyone in xenology.

"Once we inventory the asteroids and get the planet ready for human settlement, we can send shiploads of you people up to wander around on Cibola and write turgid essays on the noble savages or whatever it is that you do. But first we need to do the important work."

Sanjuro continued to say nothing. She knew Rao wanted an argument, and she knew it wouldn't do any good.

The Colonel wore her hair in a no-nonsense cut. An expensive, no-nonsense cut, Sanjuro knew; she went in for quality haircuts herself. She might even use a real person to cut her hair, or at least a first-rate salon AI; the Colonel came from a wealthy family. Rao was only a few years older than Sanjuro, at best: young to be a full colonel in Sci/Tech. Political clout, Kyo had said. Sanjuro reminded herself that she was back in uniform. Rank mattered.

Rao sighed. "But I'm stuck with you. I'm going to put you in with the astrobiologists who'll be studying the planet. You'll be under Major Kyo's command."

Sanjuro said, "Yes, ma'am," and suppressed a smile.

"That's all."

Sanjuro stood up to go.

Rao said, "Oh, and Captain. I'm not quite sure why you're here as a marine detailed to Sci/Tech. I understand you resigned from the Marines some years ago. Surely it would make more sense if you just signed on as Sci/Tech."

It wasn't an order—Rao didn't have the authority to tell her she had to make the switch—just a broad hint: your career is toast unless you switch services. Given the reception she was getting from Rao, though, she wasn't likely to build much of a military career again, regardless of what uniform she wore. The only way she was going to make a reputation was by doing good work among the Cibolans—and that would do her more good in academia. She gave Rao an apologetic smile. "Both my parents were marines, ma'am."

Rao's frown deepened. "Just remember: you're under my command. Don't think you can go running to Col. Masire for help if you don't like it."

"Yes, ma'am." Sanjuro let the ice show through in her voice. Not arguing didn't mean not making it clear that Rao's remark was insulting.

"Rao hates my guts," she told Kyo when she ran into her on her way back from the meeting. "How the hell did I get here?"

"It's not personal. Rao hates the very idea of xenology. She's convinced it's just social science, no matter how much biology it applies. She's opposed to anything that could distract the mission from the exploitation of resources."

"Even study of the evolution of other life forms?"

"She doesn't see the practical benefit of that."

"Seriously?"

"That's why she's in charge. Most astrobiologists wanted to see Colonel Volokhonsky lead the expedition. He's the guy who led the expanded research into the bacterial life on Titan and got a lot of acclaim for his insistence on setting aside an area of Charon to see what happens to the microbes on their own. But the powers-that-be in Brussels found him 'too controversial.' They figured he'd spend too much time doing science and not enough developing commercial potential. Rao was more reliable. Worked to my advantage: I get to run astrobiology."

"So how did I get here?" Sanjuro repeated.

"Bogdosian called in a few chips."

That made sense. Bogdosian had always chosen her students with long-range goals in mind. "I don't think Rao likes marines, either."

"Well, that shouldn't surprise you. No one likes marines except other marines. You could still come over to Sci/Tech."

"I don't see much point in it. From what you say, I'd have to ditch xenology to get on Rao's good side, and without xenology I wouldn't be here. Anyway, I'm not looking to build a military career again. I just want to meet some aliens."

"Well, at least wearing that uniform keeps you from looking flaky. No one ever accuses marines of being flaky."

"Not if they want to live. By the way, I'm under your command. So you can run interference for me." She said this lightly, as if she were just kidding around.

Kyo made a face. "That should be great for my career. Which, by the way, is Sci/Tech." Her face turned serious. "Are you okay, Caty?"

"Yeah, sure. I'm tough. I don't expect everyone to love me." That wasn't exactly a lie.

"It'll work out," Kyo said. "Anyway, she can't fire you, not out on Cibola."

"She can keep me from doing my work."

"She won't. She'll be too busy micromanaging exploration of the asteroid belt."

Sanjuro laughed.

"I've got to go. Another damn briefing. As if I really knew anything to brief all these civilians on."

"I'd better run, too. I've got a meeting with Vargas."

The meeting with Hernando Vargas went better than the one with Rao. The Admiral was pushing sixty, with just enough grey in his thick black hair to make him look distinguished. A handsome man, one who kept himself in shape.

He'd troubled to look up her records, knew something about her military career. "I can't believe the Marine Corps let you get away, Captain."

"Well, I wanted to study xenology, and they thought that was kind of odd."

"Lucky for us you did. I can't wait to see what you discover about the Cibolans. Should make fascinating reading for everyone."

His enthusiasm made her bold. "Sir, we could still bring a couple more xenologists on board. I know of several who should have no problem passing the health and fitness tests."

He gave her a smile full of regret. "I'm sorry, Captain. But, frankly, we stretched the budget to get you in. We couldn't pass up the opportunity to study a sophisticated life form. But the other work has to take priority. You understand."

Sanjuro understood. He had no more interest in her work than Rao did. He was just nicer about it. She stood up to go.

"By the way, Captain. We'll need you at the press conference tomorrow morning. The newservs are full of questions about the 'Cibolans.' I'm sure you can give them some interesting speculations."

Sanjuro bit back a sarcastic reply. The leadership didn't care enough about intelligent life on Cibola to give her the proper resources to do her work, but they wanted her to feed the public's appetite for aliens to beef up support for the mission. It rankled, but it didn't matter. Whatever else, they were going to let her go meet aliens.

"Certainly, sir," she said.

# 5

Another dry year. Nothing unusual: dry years outnumbered wet. Places prone to flash floods from violent storms set up drainage systems to collect and save that water for future use. Food plants received water; ornamentals had to survive or die on their own. All the planning in the world could not produce water in those years when it simply didn't rain.

Although the current drought had not been particularly bad in Golden Mountain, other places on the planet were suffering. The Bronze Forest region had declared a famine, and the Silver Skies region, which usually scorned contact with the rest of the world, had joined the planetary weave to seek aid.

Many in the Golden Mountain weave were critical of those in Bronze Forest because they tended to have a lot of children. In most regions on Cibola, one or two children was the norm, but in Bronze Forest people often had three or four. Bronze Forest was also known for its frequent weather extremes, putting it at greater risk for disaster. With a smaller population, they would suffer less, the argument went.

Why the people of Bronze Forest had let their population grow so much provoked much speculation. Some thought they were building a force to attack their neighbors to obtain a more stable source of water; the region to the west, Copper Water, included at least two rivers that had never run dry in the worst droughts. Others thought it was sheer foolishness.

Sundown, though a strong proponent of feeding the hungry, agreed with those who feared the Bronze Forestites had grown their population for warlike reasons. An increase in population could not be accidental; the art of controlling conception went back many centuries, and children in every region were taught the mental skills necessary to prevent pregnancy before they reached puberty. Both parties had to consent before sexual activity could result in a child.

Back before the planet had reached its current status, with seven regions of reasonably equivalent populations and resources, chaos had ruled. A leader in one village who craved power might bring together a force of enough minds to overpower a neighboring one and build a power base from that. The historians remembered that time and reminded everyone else on a regular basis. All feared any return to those warlike times. Balanced populations among the regions were considered an element of security. Except, perhaps, by the people of Bronze Forest. Or their leaders.

But allowing people to starve to death was as horrific as war. Requiring concessions of the Bronze Forest leaders in return for aid was one thing; refusing it altogether was another. We could need help, Sundown argued within the weave. Sundown told Sorrel, hereditary leader of the Golden Mountain Region, that one of the things the Bronze Forest leader had to trade for aid was the ability to make superior telescopes. The one Sundown now used had been purchased from Bronze Forest when Sundown's father was the regional astronomer.

Sorrel took the proposal one step farther: in return for food aid, Sorrel obtained not a new telescope, but detailed instructions on how to build one and how to construct the superb Bronze Forest microscopes as well. In the worldwide astronomy weave, Bronze Forest astronomers expressed their bitterness with this agreement, and Sundown also heard that those in the region who manufactured telescopes, microscopes, and other optical devices were deeply resented the damage done to their business. Their leader seemed to have little regard for science and technology and to consider trading their business away a small price to pay for aid.

Sundown would have been equally angry had Sorrel done something similar. But Sorrel was unlikely to do that; their ruler's vision for the region was too all-encompassing. And if the Bronze Forest leaders were indeed considering war, much knowledge could be lost in the ensuing chaos. Best that it be preserved in more stable regions.

The need for aid in Silver Skies did not produce such a tangible result, but it did start a thaw in that region's relations with the rest of the world. To negotiate for food aid, their leaders found it necessary to participate in worldwide talks. As those discussions grew profitable, their scientists, engineers, and artists began to communicate with their peers in other regions.

Even disasters can have their uses. Sundown and a team of engineers worked to build a larger and more accurate telescope. The observatory building was expanded to house it, and once the new scope was in place, Sundown began to encourage more students and amateur astronomers to spend time at the observatory. Several times astronomers from other regions came as well. Sundown still had not found an apprentice, but several young people showed promise.

# 6

Sighing, Sanjuro closed the file she'd been reviewing. In the nine months since *Mercator* had left the Solar System, she'd gone through every scrap of the *Copernicus* data, examined all the pictures in blow-ups of every square millimeter, looked at all the life-sign readouts, even created a three-dimensional holo globe showing the Cibolan settlements, all of which appeared to be no further north or south than forty degrees of latitude, counting from the planet's equator. But all she really knew about the beings on the planet was that they had developed agriculture and built cities.

*Copernicus* had come close enough to take readings on atmosphere, water, and gravity, and had sent out smaller flying vessels to collect more information about life on the planet at closer range. All that data showed signs of biological life and that humans could likely live on the planet without bioforming. However, since there had been no response to a bombardment of communication signals directed at the planet—not a major surprise, since the SETI project had never received any response to signals sent in that direction—the probes had not done more detailed surveys, and no rovers had been deployed on the planet to document the life-sign findings in depth. Instead, *Copernicus* focused on the other bodies in the planetary system, particularly the asteroids, documenting their significant mineral wealth. The probe ship had taken millions of photographs of the planet and done many scans, but the computers and techs reviewing those items had found no evidence showing intelligent life until long after plans were underway for the *Mercator* expedition.

When the *Copernicus* and related missions were being developed, astrobiologists had argued for a more detailed analysis of any planet that showed life signs. But the push for the probes had come primarily from factions looking for Helium-3, other energy sources, and rare elements, and the *Copernicus* programming had been structured around finding locations that had those things in abundance.

Sanjuro was glad that the exploratory vessel had not set rovers down on the planet. Machines would not have a been a good way to introduce the Cibolans to human culture. But the lack of data was frustrating. Even with magnification, the pictures they had were tiny and devoid of helpful info. The inhabitants seemed to come in a variety of colors and to have six limbs, but the *Copernicus* had not collected any information about the genetic structure of either plants or animals. Sanjuro included more detail than that in her reports, and she transmitted lengthy speculative messages to Bogdosian, who replied with speculations of her own. But that's all they had: guesses.

*Four years and change before I get to do my work*, Sanjuro thought.

She wasn't alone. The astrobiologists felt the same way. Kyo regularly cursed the *Copernicus* designers. "Those bastards knew that if we found a planet that could support human life we would need more detail about it, if only to plan for human settlements. Why couldn't they have given us more data? As soon as we land, the brass will pressure us to prepare for bioforming. They're not going to give us any time at all to figure out what the planet is really like."

"Even back then they knew how to give AI room to make judgment calls on its own," Min Chang said. "But they set it up with strict parameters: 'If X, then Y,' with no room for deviation." Chang, a second lieutenant, was one of Kyo's astrobiologists.

"Well, uncontrolled AI can be dangerous," someone else observed. "Look at the disaster on Venus." Given the greenhouse effect on that planet, an early twenty-second-century effort to settle Venus had employed AI. Left to their own devices, the AI had created a society that the System determined posed a major threat to human life—one that human forces had just barely been able to defeat with the help of controlled AI forces. Since that time, the System had not permitted unfettered AI.

"Worth the risk forty light years from Earth," Chang said. "We might have real data now instead of a bunch of photographs and long-range scans."

"Unless we had a new system being run by AI." An old argument.

"They wouldn't have had to run unfettered AI," Kyo said. "Just provided a few more options in the *Copernicus* program. Given that one of the things we're supposed to do is analyze bacterial and plant life to see if it can be adapted for other uses, they could have at least have put some rovers down so we could do some of that work in advance."

The geologists and physicists had more to work with. *Copernicus* had taken detailed readings among the new system's asteroids and moons, putting rovers down on the largest ones and producing thorough analyses of their elemental makeup. The data was sufficient for those in charge of its extraction to plan a mining schedule. Several geologists had been heard to complain about the large amounts of iron. While that would be useful for the eventual settlements, it was far too heavy to ship back to Earth.

The SciTech crew maintained an Earth-centric work day and -week, and that pattern led to another one: they gathered weekly in *Mercator*'s officers' club after work for a traditional post-work happy hour. The club had been designed more for efficiency than comfort: there were no chairs or barstools, just elbow-height tables. At maximum capacity it would accommodate about half of the two hundred fifty officers onboard. But despite its bar-like physical intimacy, it lacked the decadent ambience of a real tavern. The lights were too bright, the walls were the same institutional grey as the rest of the ship, and the piped-in music was too bland—chosen to offend no one, it irritated everyone.

The club was located on the same deck as the two mess halls—one for officers, the other for enlisted—and the enlisted crew's club. As near as Sanjuro could tell, the two clubs were exactly the same size, which made sense because there were about the same number of enlisted as officers. Sci/Tech was officer-heavy, and the Space Corps crew included a full complement of pilots. Running the ship took a large enlisted crew, even though most systems were robotic or AI: farmers to run the hydroponics, techs to manage the nano- and other machines on board, food-service workers, and general clerks. Plus the marines, who only had a few officers.

Since all food and drink service came from the same kitchen, both clubs and mess halls offered the same fare, though only the officers had human service staff. Sanjuro asked one of the bartenders why they'd bothered setting up separate spaces and received a shrug in reply. Just the military, his expression said.

"You know," Chang said one day as they stood around drinking bad beer—the nanobrews tended to be mediocre at best— "by the time we get back to Earth, the flight to Cibola will probably take a year or two max."

"Yeah," somebody else put in. "The experimental ships they're testing out past the belt would cut our flying time in half."

"The ones that make it," Kyo said. "Seventy-five percent of them burn up."

"Engineering problem," Chang said, waving his hand in the air. "Engineering problem."

"An academic engineering problem," Major Andrew Case said, "until we can do something with all the Helium-3."

The *Copernicus* data showed that solar winds were much stronger in the new system, resulting in a high concentration of Helium-3 in the asteroid regolith and on the moons orbiting several of the planets. Further exploration—and even transit back and forth to the Solar System—required that Helium-3. A/ND used other power sources as well, but a fusion reaction was necessary to initiate it and to run the ship's operating systems. While the Solar System had some Helium-3, there wasn't enough to power more than a few long-range exploratory missions.

The presence of Helium-3, along with evidence of a large concentration of platinum metals and a number of other rare elements, had led some wag to name the prime star El Dorado—replacing the numbers given the system in the twenty-first century. The name had taken hold, and now the place was officially called the Doradoan System.

The asteroid belt back home in the Solar System had once been well-stocked with platinums, too, but every year, fewer and fewer new veins were located. Human ingenuity had bioformed most of the suitable locations in the System, but human population had continued to grow faster than places to live. By the time bioforming produced a real atmosphere in the Belt, it would already be overcrowded. Luna wouldn't be, but only because the Lunaians put strict controls on immigration.

Population growth was most rapid in the poorest regions on Earth, but it was not inconsiderable among the upper classes, despite the amount of money required to make sure each generation got the gene tweaks to keep up. Without expansion, all those smart new generations weren't going to have enough opportunities. The *Mercator* crew consisted largely of people who wanted to make new discoveries or just explore the universe for the fun of it—they had planned their careers in the hope that they'd get a shot at the first out-of-System expedition—but they understood the significant economic push behind the expedition. Still, like most smart people who weren't in charge, they questioned the wisdom of those who were.

Case said, "I wish they'd take a little more time in their design work before they test the ships. Every one of those burnups wastes limited resources."

"Well, that's what human beings do best," Kyo said, an edge of bitterness in her voice.

Sanjuro knew what Kyo meant. Anyone who studied Earth's history—and Bogdosian had required that, too—knew about the species that had disappeared before anyone realized their value, the minerals depleted by prodigal use.

"We'll find plenty," one of the younger geologists said. "The Doradoan System is full of untapped resources. And there's a whole universe out there."

Case gave her a look. "That's no excuse for waste, Lieutenant."

She wilted under his gaze.

Case was the crew's senior physicist. A slight man, with dark hair and pale skin. A major who should probably be a lieutenant colonel by now. He was older than Rao and had been in Sci/Tech longer.

"He did all his education at Cambridge. He didn't even do undergrad at Hokkaido, like most of Sci/Tech did. That tends to get you passed over for promotion," Kyo had told Sanjuro. "Plus he has a bad habit of not keeping his opinions to himself."

"He's mostly right," Sanjuro said.

"Surely you know that doesn't make any difference."

"Too bad he's not in command instead of Rao."

That sentiment was widely shared among a lot of the junior Sci/Tech crew. But Case had laughed it off when someone suggested it to him. "Not the job I wanted."

Life on *Mercator* wasn't boring. With a full complement of Space Corps crew, plus the marines and Sci/Tech, it housed a community of some five hundred people. Regular transmissions via the A/ND com system from back in the System (as they had begun to call home) sent them music, holos, interactives, books, and professional journals only a few months after they were published. Some of the scientists found they could finally catch up on their reading.

A shipwide choir was organized, one of the few activities that mixed officers and enlisted. Dances were scheduled regularly. Gym space was limited, which prohibited large-scale team sports, but competitions were set up for boxing, wrestling, judo, and handball. In addition to formal training classes—the military always emphasizes regular training—impromptu language classes and book discussion groups cropped up. Some ambitious souls even tried their hand at theater, with only moderate success. Or, as Sumi Kyo put it, "I never knew 'Hamlet' was a comedy."

Only Sanjuro and the planet-bound astrobiology staff felt the frustration of marking time. The Space Corps crew was doing its job. Captain Adam Marley, the lanky, dark-skinned man who ran *Mercator*, rotated his large complement of pilots through the various jobs involved in flying the ship. These really weren't their jobs: like the marines, the pilots—outside of the few actually needed to fly *Mercator*—had primarily been included as a small fighting force in the event of trouble. But as Marley said, "If this trip is successful, we're going to need plenty of pilots who can fly ships using A/ND. And since we've got time, we might as well train the ones we have available."

Space Corps morale stayed high. Each week brought them the mini-crises common to all workplaces. Space Corps crew in the mess hall could be heard telling near-miss stories, complaining about others who screwed up, and—on occasion—talking about the sheer pleasure of making the job go well. And Space Corps parties were the hottest ones on board.

As for the marines—well, combat troops are used to waiting around for something to happen, alternately hoping that it will and praying that it won't. And they worked the hardest at staying in shape. Everyone was required to get regular exercise, but the marines drilled constantly to maintain their ultrafast reflexes and high endurance.

*Mercator* had been designed as a working science ship as well as for extra-System travel, so it came equipped with substantial comp power for running simulations, several labs (not currently in much demand, since they had no samples to analyze), and meeting rooms ranging from a large auditorium that could hold the entire crew to conference rooms that seated a dozen or so. Like most other rooms on *Mercator*, the conference spaces were painted grey and lacked personality. While the living quarters had been designed with the same lack of creativity, most crew members put up wall hangings and pictures or encouraged plants, giving their rooms some color and individuality. No one did that for the meeting rooms.

# The Weave

The Sci/Tech crew spent a chunk of their working hours in meetings. Rao required weekly reports from all the scientists and technicians, most of which entailed constant reviews of the *Copernicus* data and any papers sent from the System about it. The repetitious nature of this work irritated everybody, but at least it gave them something to grouse about and helped build a sense of community. Sanjuro didn't think Rao intended that outcome, but even the Colonel had to find the regular reports on things everyone already knew boring.

Each division held a weekly meeting—often attended by Rao. In addition, the entire Sci/Tech staff also met weekly to hear a brief talk from each specialty summarizing the latest theories. After a few months, the most interesting ideas had been exhausted, but that didn't dampen Rao's enthusiasm for the reports.

Sanjuro suffered particularly in these meetings. It was hard to form many conjectures about the Cibolans with limited data and only humans to compare them to. She spent lots of time analyzing the weather patterns and their relation to settlements, since that generated something quantifiable. Still, Rao made a point at least once a meeting about the inadequacy of Sanjuro's work.

"I don't really understand why you can't do a better job of estimating the population," Rao said at one meeting.

"Colonel, while we have some idea of building patterns, we don't know how densely Cibolans live. They may require a lot of space per individual. Or they might live packed close together."

"Can't you do more with the data than that?"

"*Copernicus* sent the small flyers close only once, for a small strip of the planet, or we wouldn't even have any idea what they look like. That area appears rural, but some of the longer distance scans indicate a more concentrated population in other locations. Any number I give you is going to be a guess."

"Guessing is what you people do, isn't it?"

Sanjuro worked hard at not losing her temper. "Why does she jump on me so much?" she asked Kyo.

"I think she likes being negative. Some people do. And she's under the illusion that sniping at people brings out the best in them. You're an easy target, because you don't have enough data to work with to do more than guess. But you're not the only one she does it to."

"I guess not. She seems to pick on people in rotation. But there's no point to it."

"No, but I don't see any way to stop her. Engaging her certainly won't work. And you need to watch your expression in there. You used to be better at presenting a placid face to idiots."

Sanjuro laughed. "I'm out of practice. It's okay to argue with idiots in academia. Anyway, she's not an idiot. She would be easier to deal with if she were. You can't read her reports without knowing she's driven by the urge to see—not just exploit, but literally see— what's in that pile of rocks up there. Why doesn't she understand that you feel the same way about figuring out the biological makeup of the planet or I do about seeing what the people are like?"

Kyo shrugged. "Damned if I know. But treat her like a bully you can't afford to punch out."

If it hadn't been for Case, likely Sanjuro—or one of Rao's other targets—would have lost it in one of those meetings. Frequently, as Rao started to pounce on a minor slip up in some hapless victim's report, Case would butt in. "Excuse me, but I didn't quite understand how those pieces came together. Could you go over that again?" And the thankful victim would restate the facts, correcting the mistake, letting them go on to more constructive activity.

His interruptions annoyed Rao. "Really, Major, must you interrupt me?"

"Oh, sorry, Colonel. I didn't mean to interrupt. I just wanted to be sure I was following the discussion. I'm like most scientists, woefully ignorant outside my own field. Takes me a couple of times to understand new facts."

"I admire the way you handle Rao," Sanjuro told him one day. "Though I don't really see how you keep your temper."

"Well, all she can do is be nasty. She can't fire me."

"Good point."

"And if she's the worst thing I have to put up with to explore a different solar system, I can deal with that. I want to find some new piece of knowledge about the cosmos. And where better than in a pristine asteroid belt?"

Sanjuro took his words to heart and reminded herself whenever she ended up on the hot seat: "You're going to get to see aliens."

＞

After about two weeks of using the regular exercise facilities, Sanjuro realized she wanted something else, so she'd gotten permission to train with the marine troop when they did unarmed fighting drills several times a week. They met in a room padded on all sides, even the ceiling, since it was also used for weightlessness training. The padding, like the walls it covered, was grey, and the space lacked any decoration. The room wasn't particularly large; about half the marines trained at any one time, and it was necessary to pay careful attention not just to your partner, but to the people alongside you.

The moment Sanjuro walked into the room the first time, she could almost hear her father, in his best master sergeant's voice, answering the whine of some young punk who wondered why they spent so much time on empty-hand fighting when no one fought a war that way. "Keeps you sharp," Jake Horner would have said. And then thrown a punch. The troop also spent time in sim weapons exercises, but it was clear that Col. Masire agreed with her father about the value of sparring drills.

The day she managed to throw Tish Montoya, Sanjuro knew she was finally getting back into real fighting shape.

Montoya was the master sergeant of this crew, the senior enlisted. A short woman, well-muscled, but not big. Somewhere in her late thirties. Compared to some of the big guys among the troop, she looked like she'd be easy. But the first time Sanjuro sparred with her, she got decked in about thirty seconds by a punch to the plexus she hadn't seen coming.

By contrast, most of the younger marines came easy, once she got her wind and some of her form back. They could, and did, out-quick her, but she could outsmart them. A small movement here, a shift of her eyes there, and they'd be off balance. A quick foot sweep or slight pull would send them flying.

But Montoya. Montoya did to her what she was doing to the others and made it look easy. So when she finally managed to drop under Montoya's center and take her legs out, it was a major victory.

"You surprised me out there, Captain," Montoya said as they cleaned up after the workout.

"About time," Sanjuro said.

"It won't work again."

"Something else will."

Montoya grinned. "My kind of challenge. But you move good, for a Sci/Tech. I guess you got the right to keep wearing the uniform."

"Thanks." Sanjuro knew an enlisted compliment when she heard one.

They finished dressing in a companionable silence. As they started out of the room, Montoya said, "Mind if I ask you some-thing, ma'am?"

"Go ahead."

"You any kin to Becca Sanjuro? There's been some speculating in the ranks."

Probably a wager, if Sanjuro knew anything about marines. "She was my mother."

Montoya gave her a look of outright awe.

Becca Sanjuro was an idol to most marines. Fifty years back, when the unrest in the System was at its peak, Sgt. Becca Sanjuro managed to get hundreds of people off Europa during the worst of the fighting. She died doing it, but that didn't hurt the legend any.

Sanjuro said, "She's just a legend to me, too, Sergeant. I'm an in vitro baby—born about five years after she died. My dad want-ed me to carry on her name."

Montoya nodded, though the awed look hadn't quite disappeared. "Several folks figured you as kin, but nobody got that close."

"So who won the bet?"

"Captain?" Montoya's voice conveyed pure innocence.

"I started out as a grunt, Sergeant."

"Oh. I didn't know that. I don't think anybody got close enough to win, ma'am. Have to roll the money into the next thing that comes along." She started to leave, and then turned around. "Ma'am? How come you were enlisted? I mean, here you've got a PhD and everything; obviously you had the smarts to be more than a private."

"The rebellion broke out on Mars when I was finishing secondary school, and the System was short of soldiers. Growing up military, I figured I had something to offer, and it didn't seem right just to go off to the Academy without doing my part."

Montoya grinned. "Guess that's what you'd expect from Becca Sanjuro's daughter."

Duty was a concept that Montoya could respect, but the undercurrent of the conversation reminded Sanjuro of her childhood. She'd been raised by a career sergeant, but due to her genetic enhancements, she'd been educated among officers' kids and others of the upper classes, people whose genes had been tweaked for generations. The schizophrenia of her upbringing had left her between two worlds, tied to neither.

She couldn't help being aware that those with money could build designer kids, while those without got children who might have some native talents but not the multiple ones of the enhanced. Or, at least, that was the conventional wisdom. The occasional super-talent might jump from the unenhanced ranks—Nguyen, who had figured out exotic matter, was reputed to be a natural genius—but for the average person, the lack of enhancements meant second-rate jobs.

Although medical tweaking had been successful at eliminating inherited illnesses caused by specific genes, the genetic basis for high intelligence had never been narrowed down. That hadn't kept people from coming up with changes that were supposed to improve brain function. In a similar fashion, numerous tweaks that were supposed to improve physical performance had been developed. Some studies asserted that improvements in both intelligence and physical skill were small at best, but they had not put a damper on the market for tweaks. Since most modern genetic alteration was set up to be heritable, it was assumed that the children of those who had enhancements started with a higher level of intelligence and skill that, coupled with their own tweaks, made them more able to handle important jobs.

Sanjuro always pushed aside such thoughts. She couldn't do much about the unfairnesses built into the system; people had been enhancing genes for three hundred years now. Even if you devoted your life to trying to expand opportunities, you weren't going to make much of a difference.

# 7

The snow had stopped. Sundown stepped out into the garden, wearing knee-high fur-lined boots, a heavy outer coat, and a multi-colored knit hat its child had made in art class. The snow was just deep enough to cover the toes of the boots. Less than they had hoped for. But the wind had also ceased, and the sky was clearing. Sundown could hear the sound of the snow collectors making their way up the street, shoveling snow from the street into wagons to take to the reservoir. People had been working in shifts since the snow had started that morning. Snow was easiest to collect before it froze solidly, as it certainly would overnight.

Sundown had done a snow shift that morning; snow removal, like fire-fighting and street-cleaning, was a community task done by all the able-bodied. Iron, Sundown's spouse, was taking a turn at dealing with the snow now, working across the street as Sundown set out.

Sundown and Iron had been enjoying a pleasant sojourn at home alone. Until this snow, brought on by a warm front, they had been housebound by temperatures well below freezing and gale-force winds. Their child was away, spending time with other children undergoing their first formal lessons in protecting thoughts that should not be shared and blocking unwanted messages from others. The young ones already knew much of this, for learning to control thoughts was as basic as learning to walk, but working in a large group made the skills easier to master. Necessity is a great teacher, and in any group there would be some with whom a being would not want to share anything but basic politeness. The training taught as much about learning when and whom to trust as it did practical skill.

The time with Iron had been delightful, but Sundown had not had the opportunity to go to the observatory for several weeks, and the work was suffering. The low snowfall might be bad for water purposes, but it meant the path up to the telescope would be passable. And the snow had stopped early enough so that Sundown could reach the top of the hill before nightfall. Winter weather rarely allowed skyviewing. Sundown sent Iron a brief message, received one in return that caused a body tingle, and then, not content with affection from a distance, ran across the road to hug Iron goodbye. Sundown planned to stay at the observatory for several days—longer if the milder weather held.

Sundown reshouldered the pack, which had been knocked askew in the hug. Walking on, Sundown heeded others on the roads: the snow collectors making their final rounds, a crew going out to help those whose homes were damaged during the gales, a group of farmers checking on the well-being of the animals pastured at the edge of town. Tomorrow the market would open, and people would gather to stock up on provisions and enjoy each other's company.

Sundown passed by one of the buildings where the young ones were grouped together for study. One group was playing outside, creating snow statues. After their play, the children would dismantle their constructions and take the snow to the storage area. No one wanted to deprive the children of a winter play opportunity, but even the young knew the value of snow. Inside, a group built machines, working in pairs, eight hands sometimes being better than four. Sundown passed a thought with the teachers. Their child was at another school on the other side of the village; Sundown sent it a message as she left town and was pleased to get a response quickly and clearly. The child was doing well at lessons.

At the foot of the hill, Sundown felt the regret at missing village life and time with Iron fade away. The universe awaited at the top.

# The Weave

About a year into the trip, Vargas came up with a plan that helped Sci/Tech morale: he offered them the opportunity to learn some of the Space Corps operations. Rumor said it was actually Captain Marley's idea. Sanjuro suspected that was true; from her observation Marley had the experienced commander's eye for potential morale problems. She had always wanted to learn to fly, so she signed up for piloting.

While *Mercator* came with a large complement of small fighters and shuttles, it wasn't possible for pilots to fly them during the trip. Only *Mercator* could be housed in the bubble that moved them across space. So the ship had been equipped with a flight simulation training space to keep all the Space Corps pilots sharp. The room was outfitted with rows of cubicles. Each cubicle was about the same size as the pilot's seat on a fighter, and each had a large screen on three sides. The controls were set up like those in a fighter. Even the pilots conceded that the simulation was close enough to the real thing to keep their skills in tune.

However, though the course had been designed to boost morale, the Space Corps officers conducting the training considered teaching non-pilots how to fly a tedious waste of time and didn't mince words in saying so. Lt. Goran Yurinko told the first class, "All we're going to do here is teach you to fly something in case there's ever an emergency and you absolutely have to. We don't expect you to learn any real maneuvers."

Sanjuro and Kyo, who'd signed up as well, reverted to the disrespect that had carried them through the Academy. Sanjuro sent Kyo a message: "Arrogant bastard."

Kyo replied: "Arrogant bastard: noun. Someone who assumes he's always right, even when he's wrong. Synonym: Space Corps pilot."

Yurinko's initial lecture seemed to focus on what they wouldn't be able to do. But finally they got a shot at the sims. Sanjuro hooked herself in and felt immediately at home. She could remember some basics from the rudimentary training she'd had early in her marine career—marines didn't do a lot of flying, but the Corps made sure all their combat officers and non-coms could at least handle a shuttle — and the moves came naturally.

Basically, the pilot was one with the ship. To guide it, you made small moves; big ones were generally a disaster.

Yurinko was walking around the room, talking each of them through the steps one by one. "Ease out of the berth. No, no, don't hit the sides. That's valuable machinery you just sheared off."

Sanjuro tuned him out. She took the fighter out of its berth into the expanse of space sim set up for beginners; avoiding collisions came later. She tried flying straight lines, found it too easy, and shifted to trying the various turns Yurinko had mentioned in his lecture.

"You jopa! What the fuck are you doing?"

Sanjuro hadn't heard Yurinko come up behind her. She was startled by his voice, but managed to keep control of the fighter. "Something wrong?"

"We aren't to that point yet." He reached toward the reset button, and then looked at what she'd been doing. "You really get this far without any problems?"

"Yeah. Was I supposed to have problems?"

"Everyone else is." He put a series of commands in. "Try this." She was suddenly confronted with a crowded sky.

"I want you to follow that red ship, without hitting anything else out there."

The red ship's first move was a three-sixty spin, and Sanjuro spun right after it. She followed as it threaded its way against the flow of traffic, between tightly spaced obstacles. The joy of maneuvering the sim fighter completely engrossed her, so that she again didn't realize that Yurinko had come back until he shut her machine down.

"That's enough." He ran the readout, and whistled. "Damn. You're good at this. With reflexes like that, you could fly anything. They must have tested you at Hokkaido—how come you didn't become a pilot?"

"I was set on being a marine. Combat skills are pretty similar."

"Not that similar." No arrogance in his voice now; mostly she heard admiration.

Given that Rao alternated between ignoring her and sneering at her, it was nice to hear a compliment. Still, there was something faintly embarrassing about being very good at what was, after all, a sideline. "Gene tweaks," she said, casually. "My father kind of went overboard on the gene tweaks." Whether or not it was true, it was the kind of modest explanation everyone took at face value.

"Whatever. I'm going to put you on the list of those who get to fly the real thing once we get to El Dorado."

"Great."

"We'll have to give you a shot at flying *Mercator*, too. Dealing with the A/ND requires regular tweaking. It's not that we need you, but if you've got the talent for flying, you might as well use it." He paused. "You'll have to put in a lot of work. Talent's great, but you have to spend time to get really good."

"I've got more than enough time. It'll be nice to have something challenging to work on."

She scheduled several hours of practice time every week. Being good at something new took the edge off of Rao's snide remarks.

Sanjuro found that her favorite time was spent in training with the marines, although it took everything she had. Masire gave her even more trouble than Montoya. He didn't always train with his crew, but he ran the occasional workout. She noticed that few people ever really got him, not even Montoya or a couple of the young guys who had real talent for fighting. When someone did tag him, he'd praise them, but leave open the implication that he'd left the opening. And then thrash them a few times to hammer the point home.

It added to his mystique: the superwarrior who could handle anything. And kept his people in awe of him. After a few weeks of watching him Sanjuro finally figured out how Masire pulled it off.

They were in the lounge drinking beer one evening after training. They'd fallen into the habit of getting a drink on the days when they worked out together.

Masire always seemed a like a big man when they trained, but actually, Sanjuro realized, he wasn't any taller than she was. His family came originally from Botswana, but he was fourth generation military, making him, like Sanjuro, not tied to a particular place on Earth or anywhere else in the Solar System. The exercise session had relaxed him, leaving a contented expression on his face.

Training had relaxed Sanjuro, too; she felt frivolous. "Impressive how you pull it off, the image of the invincible colonel."

"You mean you don't believe it?" he said in mock horror.

"I could really see it tonight. The way you set up, your opponent doesn't have a lot of choices. You leave just enough space for the attack you want."

"Hey, that's just good strategy. Besides, if I didn't, some of those folks would kill me in there."

"Like they're killing me."

"Well, you're doing okay. Better than okay. Pretty obvious you used to be damn good at this. I'd venture you're even better armed."

"My weapons work is even rustier than my empty hand. And I imagine the weapons systems are new and improved since I last fought a battle."

"New, maybe, but not all that improved. You should come train with the troop in sim sometime, get a feel for it."

It sounded tempting. "I probably can't justify that," she said. "Training with you guys meets my exercise requirement, but Rao would rather see me do less fraternizing."

"Fraternizing? With marines or enlisted?"

"Both, I think. I get regular lectures on what's expected of Sci/Tech officers."

Masire leaned forward and cupped his hands toward her ear. "I'll let you in on a secret: she's as big a bakamono in senior staff meetings as she is with her own folks."

Sanjuro grinned. "Glad I'm not the only one who thinks so. And I like hanging out with your people."

"Well, you're in good with us. You've won Montoya over, and that's important. Any new officer can't get along with Montoya, I get them transferred."

"I like her, too."

"You were serious combat once, weren't you?"

"Yeah." Images danced through her head, not all of them ones she wanted to remember.

"I thought so. You move like someone who's done it for real. Mars?"

"And Ceres. Plus most of the hot spots between."

He nodded, like a man who knew what she meant.

Just friends, at first. Sanjuro found him easier to talk to than the Sci/Tech officers. For one thing, he was genuinely interested in xenology. He'd read Bogdosian's popular book, the one designed to convince the masses that humans would meet aliens one day.

"It just always struck me as reasonable that we'd find other intelligent life in the galaxy. I can't imagine we won't find more of it as we get farther and farther away from home. All that nonsense about life on Earth being such a coincidence. The universe is vast. There's room for lots of coincidences."

"You're preaching to the choir," she told him.

"I guess that's why I never wanted to go to grad school," Masire said. "It seemed to make people too narrow-minded, present company excepted, of course."

"And besides, you like kicking butt."

"There is that. Plus sitting around waiting for stuff to happen gives me lots of time to read."

He'd read a lot more than the Bogdosian book: astronomy, physics, biology, history. And literature ranging from Homer to Le Guin to the widely acclaimed (and equally widely denounced) work of Gillian Gudridsdotter, whose language inventions included both the great dead languages and the key modern ones and made *Finnegans Wake* look comprehensible by comparison.

"I guess grad school could make you narrow, unless you studied with Bogdosian. She wanted us to know everything, because we had no idea what we would find. And I still don't. I'd like to get prepared for meeting the Cibolans, but I don't have any idea what I should be doing. So I just keep trying to read everything."

"You're calling them Cibolans, now?" Masire seemed amused.

"Well, I need to call them something until we know what they call themselves."

"I suppose so, but I'm not sure calling the place Cibola bodes all that well for the expedition. Coronado never found the gold he went looking for, and he treated the people he found badly."

"Well, I hope we'll do better on both scores," Sanjuro said. Her hand brushed Masire's as she reached for her beer, and she felt a sudden charge. The expression that came and went across his face told her he felt it, too. But she wasn't ready to deal with that. She took refuge in the conversation. "Though with our eagerness to exploit the asteroids out there, I worry a lot."

Masire glanced at her hand, but apparently decided not to push the issue, because he, too, kept their discussion focused on the more neutral topic of the expedition. "Well, our ability to explore the galaxy is limited if we can't find more sources of Helium-3. And we don't just need those platinums to make us wealthy, like the ancient Europeans: those metals make our ships and communications devices possible. Though we might not use up the Solar System's supply of them anytime soon if we didn't want to go farther afield."

"But we do want to go farther," Sanjuro said. "It just seems natural, finding out what else is out there."

He grinned. "Yeah, it always seemed that way to me, that we should explore not because of economics or even scientific knowledge, but just to see what's over the next ridge. Probably some of the conquistadores felt that way, though. I'm not sure it's any more moral than looking for gold." He reached for his own beer and managed to touch her hand, which she'd left lying on the table.

Again she felt the surge, and again she let it go by. "Even back then the dreamers probably had to make lots of practical arguments to get the money together. That's why so many who came along were obsessed with gold. Of course, it's not just wealth: Cibola looks like a nice place to put some of our extra people, which is another thing we have in common with those ancient Europeans."

"Yeah, and we've got more of a population problem than they had. I spent a couple of years trying to keep people in Southeast Asia from killing each other over food and shelter, and I gather even the off-Earth settlements are feeling a squeeze."

"Luna can't handle an increase in population until more bioforming takes hold, and that will be decades. The situation there is pretty typical, from my experience. Settling people on Cibola won't solve the problem by any means, but it will provide enough of a relief valve to play well back home." Sanjuro rubbed her forehead and made a face. "You know, I've avoided thinking about these things. I just want to explore the universe and meet aliens, and while I know there are other forces at work, I try not to think about them too hard. Here you've made me remember that it's not all just a great adventure." She reached for her beer.

Masire put his hand on hers. She felt the charge again, but she didn't yank her hand back. "Well," he said, "I guess that means we'll have to make sure things get done differently this time."

# 8

People had started pairing up despite the complexities of relationships in the military. Most of the crew had come aboard unattached — the fact that the mission was likely to last fifteen years meant people with partnerships had thought carefully before signing up — and they were eager to do something about their solitary status.

Sanjuro had let the first few overtures pass. She'd never been one for long-term relationships. Both soldiers and grad students tended to keep things light, since the odds of ending up in the same place as your sweetheart were small. That might have changed when she'd taken the job at Neil Armstrong U., except that most of the other permanent people her age on Luna were already partnered up when she got there. She'd confined herself to casual affairs with short-termers at the military base and discovered that she liked her single status. The situation on *Mercator* was different; still, she found herself a little leery of getting involved with someone who wasn't going to ship out in six months.

But the pleasure of Masire's company was undermining her defenses.

One day after training Masire invited her back to his quarters. The space was marginally bigger than hers and very tidy. Masire wasn't a man who left anything lying around. He had put up minimal decorations: a picture of his mother, a second one that seemed to be a family group, a colorful painting likely done by a child, and a star chart.

He saw her staring at the painting. "My niece," he said and pointed to a little girl in the family picture. "My sister's daughter."

*Wow*, Sanjuro thought. His family had money indeed if they could afford two children and already be started on the next generation. Masire wouldn't be a colonel without the genetic advantages money could buy, and she doubted his family would have done any less for their daughter and grandchild.

Masire had snagged some beer from his pantry as they came in. He poured it into glasses, handed her one, took a sip from his own, and made a face.

"At least it's cold," Sanjuro said.

"It would be undrinkable if it weren't. Oh, for the porter on Luna."

They were seated opposite each other, Sanjuro in the room's lone chair, Masire on his bunk. Their knees were almost touching. Masire shifted his position. So did Sanjuro. Now their knees did touch.

Her hair was still damp from the shower. Masire combed it with his fingers and flicked a few drops of water away.

She touched his short curls; they were almost dry, but she imitated his finger movement anyway. They laughed at their own silliness. He took her hand.

"We probably shouldn't do this," Sanjuro said, but she didn't let go of his hand.

"You're not in my command. It's not against the rules." He gave her hand a pull, and she joined him on the bunk.

"No. But technically I'm still a marine. Things could change."

He kissed her then, and things changed.

An hour later, Masire scrunched himself closer to the wall and propped himself up on an elbow. "So, why'd you leave the Corps?"

Sanjuro raised an eyebrow at him. "That your idea of romantic conversation?" She let her feet tangle up with his under the covers.

"You don't think wanting to know about a person is romantic?" His hand was resting on her arm. He began to stroke it lightly.

"Well, I don't think my time as a marine had much romance to it. Besides, that's what everybody asks me. Why not ask me why I became a marine in the first place, if I was the kind of person who wanted to be a xenologist?"

"Because I spent the afternoon training with you, and it's patently obvious why you became a marine. Anybody who takes that kind of joy in sparring exercises couldn't become anything else. Besides, you're a legacy: Becca Sanjuro's kid. How could you do anything different?"

"You've been talking to Montoya."

"Everybody knows. You don't have to answer the question if you don't want to." He was still stroking her arm.

"I don't mind the question. I quit the Corps because they wouldn't send me to grad school in xenology." Her standard answer. The touch of his hand threatened to seduce her all over again, but it didn't overpower her habit of keeping certain facts to herself. She liked Masire, but things were just starting between them.

"Oh. Why'd you want to study xenology anyway?"

"You mean, why would I leave something sensible like the marines for a flaky subject like xenology?"

"I don't think xenology is flaky," he said. "You know that."

"So why do you think it's odd I wanted to do it?"

"Because it's radical. And one thing I know about marines: they don't tend to do radical things."

She grinned. "Maybe they should try a few."

He laughed, but gave her an expectant look.

"Oh, well. It was a little kid thing. You know how, when you're little, sometimes something just catches your fancy and you say, 'that's what I'm going to do when I grow up.' With me it was meet aliens someday. My daddy encouraged it, probably because it got me to apply myself in school. And I just never outgrew it. Stupid, huh."

"No. Not stupid. Not stupid at all. Your dad must have been a hell of a guy, to encourage you like that."

"Yeah. I miss him."

"I suppose he's retired now."

She shook her head. "Jake died on Ceres. During the war." Funny, how it still hurt to say that, even after more than ten years.

"Sorry. I didn't know."

"No reason you would have. Just another messy death in a messy war. Lots of things died on Ceres." Her tone was bitter.

"Glad I missed it," Masire said. "I spent most of that time on Earth, running a peacekeeping project in the Southern USA. Like most peacekeeping efforts, it was dangerous and frustrating, I kept wishing I was fighting a real war, where you knew who was going to shoot at you and, even better, could shoot back. I complained a lot at the time, but in the end it was the American job that got me this one: they wanted someone who had significant experience with both combat and peacekeeping. And given what everybody says about Ceres, not being there probably did my career more good than being there would have."

"We fought on the wrong side," Sanjuro said. She sat up, pulled away from him. She couldn't talk about Ceres in the comfortable circle of his arms. "The war was a classic misuse of the military by the big companies, especially since the workers in the Asteroid Belt had good reason to rebel."

"That's what Montoya always says. She saw her first action there." He touched her arm again, lightly enough so that she didn't pull away.

"Class thing. You grow up working class like me and Montoya, it's hard not to sympathize with the workers."

"But you got out, got into Hokkaido."

That was more a question than a statement, and she answered it. "Jake got money along with my mother's medal of honor when she died. He used it to build a super kid. Without the advantage of gene tweaks, I'd be like him. Or Montoya: too smart for my job, but not smart enough to pass the officers' exam." Her muscles tensed as she felt the combination of anger and guilt that always accompanied the subject. She'd been lucky; so many others hadn't. She found herself wondering if Montoya could pass the exam, given a couple of years to study intensively for it.

"Lots of things in life aren't fair. Only so much you can do about it." He was stroking her arm again.

"I know. Still makes it hard to take sometimes." The feel of his fingers was making her feel relaxed again. She wanted to let the subject drop.

Masire must have picked up on her feelings because he said, "I still can't believe the Corps let you get away."

"Well, I'm back now, more or less."

"Yeah, you are at that." He pulled her to him again, and that effectively changed the subject.

>⇒

The officers' club was almost full, but Masire was nowhere in sight. Sanjuro made her way over to the bar. "Hi, Ginny," she said to the bartender. "A dark beer, I guess."

Ginny made a face. "You want to skip the beer this week, Captain. Something's off in the nano again."

"How's the whisky?"

"Better than the beer, but I'd mix it with something tasty if I were you."

"A Manhattan?"

"That should be drinkable." Ginny finished making a daiquiri and put it in front of another customer, replied "got it" to an order from one of the servers for two more beers and a wine at the other end of the bar, and grabbed a bottle of bourbon. "The Colonel running late?" she said as she added vermouth.

Damn. Was the relationship that obvious? Her message signal flashed in the corner of her eye just as she started to reply.

Masire's message said "Sorry. Last minute request from on high. Thirty minutes?"

"Yep," she said to Ginny as she sent back "Okay."

If Ginny hadn't been so busy, Sanjuro would have stayed at the bar to chat. But the bartender fielded two more drink orders as she handed Sanjuro hers and turned to draw the beers. Sanjuro stepped back to let someone else squeeze in and surveyed the room. Yurinko and several other pilots had taken over two tables. They were loud, probably on their third or fourth round of drinks. A little too much hilarity for her mood.

Two of Kyo's astrobiologists were at a table in the corner, but they looked to be deep in conversation. She looked around again. No vacant tables or people she knew well enough to join. Except that Rao stood at a table near the door, alone.

Sanjuro wished she hadn't taken the drink so she could just leave, send Masire a message to meet her elsewhere. She looked over at the biologists again, but could tell that one of them was very upset about something. The pilots exploded in laughter and yelled for another round. Rao was hunched over her drink.

Be an adult, Sanjuro, she told herself, and walked over to Rao's table. "Mind if I join you, Colonel? The place is really packed."

"Make yourself at home, Captain." She took a last sip of wine and signaled to the server to bring her another.

"How's the wine, Colonel?" Sanjuro asked. "The bartender told me to skip the beer."

"I've had worse, but not much. Still, it's doing its job."

Rao's face was drawn, and there were circles under her eyes. Sanjuro said, "Bad day?"

"Just dealing with a lot of nonsense requests from back in the System. I don't know why they want so many reports on our detailed analysis of *Copernicus* data. I mean yes, we do have the best scientists in the Corps up here, but they've got the brightest minds at a hundred universities looking at what *Copernicus* sent as well. Once we get to the Doradoan System we'll know things they can't get on their own, but I don't see that we can add much to their knowledge right now."

Rao's complaint reminded Sanjuro of how she felt when the Colonel yelled at her in meetings, but she decided it wouldn't be politic to point that out. "Well, in my experience, the brass who aren't on the scene always assume you're not really doing anything and have infinite time for filing reports." As soon as she said it she wondered if it sounded like she was implying that Rao wanted too many reports.

But the Colonel laughed. "I hadn't thought of it quite like that. You're probably right. They probably think we won't do any analysis unless they demand reports. As if I could keep this lot from poring over the data. I'm not sure they're always getting the right information out of it—sometimes I marvel at the dullness of supposedly bright people—but no one can say that the scientists on this crew aren't eager to find out all they can."

That was the nicest thing she'd ever heard Rao say about her people, even with the snarky comment in the middle. Sanjuro realized for the first time that the woman did appreciate her people, knew they were classic curious scientists dying to find out everything they could about this new place. "Yes. But the people back home can't see us doing that. They need reports for their accountability standards to make sure things are being done by the book."

"It's still a waste of time and money. We shouldn't be wasting our entangled particles on reports; those should go through normal channels. They'd still get there in plenty of time for all the audits and such."

"They're asking to have routine reports sent through ETQ?" Sanjuro said.

Rao nodded. "It makes no sense—surely they have no need to see it immediately—and it uses up our entangled particles. But they want us to re-send all the reports they haven't received yet that way. That's about three months' worth, given the current speed of the weekly capsule sent to Earth via A/ND."

Sanjuro shook her head. "I don't suppose it was that hard to resend, but what a waste of resources. We can make more capsules for sending via A/ND, and it takes very little power to send something that small. I know that we brought a lot of entangled particles with us, but once we're out of them, ETQ is done."

"Yes. That's what I told them, but no one listened. And you're right: resending the reports wasn't that difficult. My clerk got them all packaged and sent out in a day. But it made me think I'd better go back through what we've got, to see if I can figure out why they suddenly changed the rules. I've been staying up late, re-reading reports."

"Come up with a reason?"

"No. But it still makes me uncomfortable. Hence the wine. I just couldn't face the reading tonight without fortification. None of you are stimulating writers, you know."

Another dig. Rao seemed incapable of going too long without insulting people. But reports, even ones dealing with fascinating finds, were not novels. "Well, the scientific method doesn't lend itself to exciting language," Sanjuro said, and was rewarded with another laugh.

"Too true. And if anyone did make it sound exciting, I'd figure they were covering something up."

Sanjuro looked up and saw Masire walking across the room. He raised an eyebrow at her. "I hope it's just the usual bureaucratic love of reports and not something else," she said, downing her drink. "Thanks for letting me join you." She started to move away, but Masire had already reached them.

"No, no," Rao said, drinking the last of her wine. "I need to go. You and Colonel Masire can have this table." She nodded at Masire, then gave both of them a look.

Sanjuro braced herself, expecting some negative comment about fraternizing or worse.

"Have a good evening," Rao said. "You obviously have better things to do than read reports."

They stared after her as she walked out. "Damn," Sanjuro said. "She turns out to be human after all."

"You make it sound like that's a problem."

"Harder to hate her if she's got a decent side. No, no, don't order a beer. Ginny says it sucks this week. The Manhattan's drinkable."

Masire ordered two.

"You know, I think she's right to worry. Why would the System want the science reports sent by ETQ? It's not like anything's going to happen with any of it until we get to the Doradoan System." Sanjuro finished off her drink.

"It's not just the science reports. That's why I was late. I was setting up the system to resend security reports by ETQ. They sent an order today instructing us to send everything—even mess hall figures—that way. Vargas is livid. He thinks they're undercutting his authority."

"It doesn't make sense."

"The bureaucrats back home never make sense," Masire said.

"Could I speak to you a minute, Captain?"

Montoya and Sanjuro were the only ones left in the dressing room.

"Sure," Sanjuro said.

"You maybe know that I'm involved with somebody in the Space Corps crew. A woman in tech services."

Sanjuro nodded. She knew it, in the vague way you know things about people you work with. Was Montoya going to ask for advice? She hoped not; she never knew what to say to people about relationships.

"I just don't want you to get the wrong idea about what I have to say." Montoya took a deep breath. "I've served under the Colonel for almost ten years now. I think I know him pretty well."

"He's a good commander," Sanjuro said, still not sure where this was going.

"He's a great commander. I wouldn't want to serve under anyone else. Takes care of his people, but expects the best out of us. I don't want you to think I don't respect him."

"But," Sanjuro said.

"But he likes women, Captain. In all the time I've known him I've never seen him without one for more than a couple of weeks—usually a real babe. And never with the same one for more than six months. We've kind of had a bet going, how he was going to handle this trip."

"Oh." She wasn't particularly surprised to hear that. Masire handled himself too smoothly not to have a lot of experience. The warning amused her, but she suppressed a smile: Montoya was speaking in dead earnest.

"I'm not trying to pry into your personal life or anything. And I don't want to give you the idea he's a prick; near as I can tell, he doesn't lead anybody on. He's just not in it for the long haul, ma'am, if you get what I mean. And I thought you ought to know." Her voice trailed off.

Sanjuro could see her lack of reaction was making Montoya uncomfortable. "Does everybody know that we're seeing each other?"

"All the marines, anyway. Most of us have been with the Colonel awhile, so we know each other pretty good. And it's hard to keep secrets onboard. *Mercator*'s kind of like a small town."

Sanjuro nodded.

"It's just, well, you seem like an okay sort, not all stuck up like some of the scientists in Sci/Tech. You come in here, train like hell, even though it's not your job. I just figured somebody ought to tell you about the man. I mean, I'd crawl through hell on my belly for the Colonel, but I'm not going to cover for his shortcomings, woman to woman."

Sanjuro didn't see any point in explaining that she probably wasn't all that different from Masire when it came to relationships. "Thanks, Montoya. I'll watch myself."

# 9

All the stalls in the marketplace were staffed and doing a brisk business on the weekly market day. It was early summer, with fresh food widely available. The clothesmakers, potters, toolmakers, and artists had laid out their wares as well. Now that it was summer, the trading season had begun in earnest. While a few stalls opened on other days during the week—some farmers and other sellers had made a good business of selling on the off days—village life revolved around the weekly market.

The Golden Mountain people traded with other regions, including those of the southern hemisphere, where the seasons were reversed. But a metal-poor planet has only so many resources that can be used to construct motors for fast-moving vehicles, making transport between the regions expensive and fresh food in winter beyond the means of most. Slower vehicles also moved between regions as well as within them—lightweight sun- or wind-powered machines overland, and similarly powered boats on the edges of the ocean—but these did not travel quickly enough to move fresh products. The return of local produce with warmer weather remained important.

Sundown and Iron walked through the market. Their child had joined the hordes of children racing around, bumping into adults, crawling under stalls, making up new games to which only they knew the rules. The adults tolerated the children's rambunctious play as they filled their bags with fresh produce and haggled over a bright piece of material, a well-honed knife, a set of cups.

On a stage in one corner of the vast marketplace, a succession of performers delighted the crowds. Sundown and Iron took a shopping break and sat to listen to a musical group. The lead musician played the reedpipes, a mouthpiece attached to two tubes with finger holes, one tube longer than the other so that they produced sounds in harmony. All four hands were required to play the reedpipes, each working independently and yet in concert. The piper was backed by another musician playing a flute, a thin tube played by blowing across an air hole. Another plucked strings laid across an enormous wooden base shaped like a covered bowl, which made low sounds. Two more played smaller stringed instruments. The final performer was surrounded by large containers covered with skin heads, each a different size. The player struck them with small mallets, creating a blend of four rhythms, each hand beating out a separate pattern.

In the front, Sundown saw their child sitting with friends, eyes focused on the piper. Sundown sent a private message seeking the child's reaction. "I want to learn the reedpipes" came back. Iron and Sundown shared the message. Our child may be finding a passion in life, Iron sent. Or it may be a passing fancy, Sundown replied. Still, lessons were in order. Iron's reply showed their child practicing beginning pieces while they held their ears. They shared amusement at the image; there was no question in their minds that they would allow their child to pursue music, even if the early efforts would wreck the peace of their home. How else do people find their passions, but by experience?

As the three lingered over a meal, Sundown watched their neighbors shop and play, knowing that this market experience was slowly disappearing. As a leading scientist in Golden Mountain, Sundown often traveled to the capital city for in-person meetings with Sorrel and with other scientists. While regular communication among experts happened within the weave, it was easiest to share ideas when people were in the same room, particularly the complex ideas of science. The capital was much larger than their village, and instead of a marketplace where farmers and artisans came to sell their wares, it had a neighborhood of permanent retail shops. Separate stores sold food, housewares, clothing. Other buildings offered food and drink, and even entertainment. In the city, merchandise could be bought on a daily basis, music heard at any time.

The village marketplace would eventually give way to similar shops; already some sellers staffed their stalls with hired staff every day. When that happened, Sundown would miss the special feeling that came from the whole community sharing a physical space together, rather than only the mental space of the weave.

Sanjuro was half-awake, so she felt it when Masire suddenly sat up. She opened her eyes, saw him blink. He must have received a com message. They turned their systems off at night, but overrides existed for emergencies.

Masire crawled over Sanjuro. "Sorry, got to go."

"What is it?"

"I don't know. Vargas just called an immediate meeting. It may not take long."

Sanjuro sat up and reached for her uniform. "But it probably will. And it's almost morning anyway. I should go over my report one more time before the staff meeting."

They walked up the corridor to the lift. No one else was stirring on this wing. Masire gave her a quick kiss as the doors opened. "Later, Sanjuro."

Sanjuro's quarters were on the same level, on the opposite side. Her room was private, but unlike Masire, she didn't rate either a private bath or pantry; she shared those with five other junior officers. She took a cup of coffee with her into the shower—the ship moved so smoothly that it was easy to forget you were in space. Except that she barked her knee on the edge of the stall as she got out, as she always did. No wasted space on a starship.

Sanjuro took more coffee back into her room and pulled up a holographic screen so she could go over the report. She liked to do her writing and data analysis on a big screen so that she could see more than the few lines available in her eye lens. After a few minutes, she found herself dozing off, despite the coffee. She shook herself awake. More sleep would help, but not enough: the problem was the report. You could only spend so much time going over things you already knew without getting bored silly.

She made a fresh cup of coffee and sat down to take another stab at it. Maybe she could find some way to liven it up so it wouldn't bore everyone else to death.

Her com signaled in her ear. "Yes?"

"Captain, I need to meet with you." It was Masire.

She couldn't remember the last time he'd used her rank instead of her name. That made this official. She glanced at the time; not quite seven. Something big must be going on.

"Did you have a time in mind, sir? I have a staff meeting at oh eight hundred."

"This takes precedence. Fifteen minutes. My office."

She heard an undercurrent in his voice. Not exactly anger, but something. She gave him a crisp "Yes, sir," and clicked off.

Sanjuro tried puzzling out what might be going on as she ran a quick comb through her hair and raced off down the corridor. If it had been Rao calling, Sanjuro would have assumed she was being called on the carpet for something. But as far as she knew, she hadn't done anything wrong, much less something serious enough to be worth bringing in Masire in his role as chief of security.

She made it in ten minutes. Masire was sitting behind his desk. Lt. Commander Ariana Gervaise, the chief lawyer on *Mercator*, sat next to him. That would have told her the situation was all business, even if Masire's tone hadn't made it very clear. She snapped to attention and saluted.

Masire indicated a chair in front of the desk. "Sit down, Captain."

Sanjuro sat, seeing the desk as the barrier it was intended to be.

Gervaise said, "I need to record this."

Sanjuro waited.

Masire frowned. "Sanjuro"—and his voice almost sounded personal—"is there anything you've been keeping quiet about? Because if there is, now would be a good time to tell us about it."

She stared at him. That was an invitation to confess to a crime. The situation was making less and less sense. She bit back a sarcastic reply about having disrespectful thoughts about senior officers; whatever was going on, Masire was deadly serious, and Sanjuro didn't know Gervaise well enough to know whether she'd get sarcasm. The lawyer was young for her rank.

"No, sir."

"You sure?"

"Colonel, Commander, I assure you that I have no crimes on my conscience important enough to warrant this discussion. My word on it."

Gervaise made a note. Masire rubbed his chin. Stubble was just beginning to show; he hadn't had time to shave.

Sanjuro said, "What the hell is going on?"

Masire looked at Gervaise. She nodded.

"A starship with A/ND capacity took off from the System yesterday morning. Not a Solar System Union ship; it's owned by a consortium of systemwide corporations. They call it the *Cortez*."

"Haven't there been a couple of those?"

"Yeah, but small ones, test ships hopping to Pluto and back. This one is damn near as big as *Mercator*. It's taking our route, headed straight for the Doradoan system."

Sanjuro felt as if she'd stumbled into a surrealistic painting, one where you found yourself upside down just when you thought you'd reached a corner. She said, "What?" and wondered if her jaw had actually dropped.

The other two looked at her, their eyes saying nothing.

"How the hell did they get that kind of ship together? I know some of the System companies are unbelievably rich, but I didn't think anything short of systemwide government could bring together enough resources to build and outfit an extra-System ship."

Masire said, "Neither did anyone else. But it's a consortium of twenty of the most powerful corporations in the System, including several of the Asteroid Belt powers. Plus, the company that built the ship was the prime contractor for *Mercator*."

"How could they keep this quiet, with so many people involved?"

"Probably wasn't that quiet, except to us and the general public. I imagine people in the System power structure were negotiating with them along the way, seeing if they could head it off, or if not, at least cut some deals. They must have made some kind of agreement. It's not an official expedition, but the System isn't sending military ships out to stop them before they get to the A/ND starting point."

Sanjuro suddenly remembered how this discussion had started. "You thought I knew about it?" Her voice was flat, but no one could have missed the anger that underlay it.

"There's a team of four xenologists on that ship, led by a Dr. Derek Li. I think you know him." Masire's voice sounded tight.

"Chingado." Sanjuro closed her eyes. "Bogdosian." Then she remembered Gervaise was still sitting there. "Sorry, ma'am."

Gervaise waved a hand.

"She's not on the ship, but I gather Prof. Bogdosian had something to do with the expedition, yes," Masire said.

"Of course she did. Impressive. I wouldn't have thought even Bogdosian could pull off something like that. But you have to give her credit. She knows how to work the system."

"So you didn't know about this?"

"No, sir." Sanjuro was very angry. She wanted to tell him he should have known, that he shouldn't have had to ask. But that was the personal side speaking. Professionally, of course, he had to ask. With Bogdosian in the picture, it made complete sense. Knowing that didn't make her any less angry. "Look. I admire the hell out of Andrea Bogdosian. And I owe her for developing the field and for giving me the training that put me on this ship. But I don't have any illusions about her. Bogdosian has a dream, and everyone she works with is a tool to get there.

"She wouldn't have told me about this. She'd have done this on need-to-know, and I wouldn't have needed to know. Plus, she'd figure anything she told me would be passed on to the Admiral. Which, of course, it would have been."

"And Li didn't tell you either? I know you and he used to be…close."

She heard the jealousy there. It startled her; she didn't think things had gone so far between her and Masire that he would feel threatened by a long-dead relationship that had never amounted to much in the first place. "If you've been digging that deeply into my affairs, sir"—she bit the "sir" off sharply—"then you also know things ended badly between us. Derek Li trusts nothing military, especially me. I'm the last person he would have told. He's probably laughing his head off, thinking about my finding out."

Gervaise said, "We're going to have to go through your messages back to the System, Captain. You have the right to demand a formal hearing on that of course." She let an implied "but" hang in the air.

"Not a problem, ma'am. I don't have anything to hide."

"I think you're telling the truth, Captain," Gervaise said. "But we have to clear everybody that has any connection to these people. You understand that."

Sanjuro nodded.

Masire said, "It's particularly important with you. Col. Rao thinks there's some kind of xenologist plot here."

"There is," Sanjuro said. "But it's a lot more than a xenologist plot. Bogdosian has a lot of clout, but the people who pulled this off are much more powerful than she is. She must have found out about their plans and managed to get xenology included in them. Maybe she even planted the initial seeds among some of her corporate friends. That's how she works. It probably grew from there into a full-fledged conspiracy. But I'm not part of it."

Gervaise said, "We'll let you know if there's anything else, Captain."

Sanjuro stood up, saluted, and walked out. Masire followed her out into the passageway. "Sanjuro. I know you're mad. I'd probably be mad, too, in your shoes. But you know we had to ask. Others on board have similar connections, and they're getting asked, too." He put a hand on her arm.

She shook it off. "It was legitimate to ask, Masire. But not to start out with the assumption I was guilty." She turned to go.

"Damn it, Sanjuro. That's standard interrogation procedure. You ought to know that. Was I supposed to do it differently for you because we're sleeping together?"

"No. It's just, oh, kuso, I just figured you knew me better than that. It hurts that you don't."

"I do know you well enough to know that you're honest. I also know you well enough to know that your first loyalties lie with xenology. You wanted more xenologists on this expedition."

She gave him a cold stare. "You're right. My first loyalty is to my work—but to the actual work, not the politics of it. Sure, I think we need more xenologists to do the job properly, but I would never have chosen this method for getting them. Corporate involvement before we even finish doing a real evaluation of the place bodes nothing but disaster. I'm glad you think I'm honest, but you also must think I'm stupid. If I had known about this nonsense, I'd have been a fool not to tell someone. This was going to go public sooner or later."

"You're not being fair." His hand clenched against the doorframe.

"That makes two of us." She walked out.

Gervaise dropped by Sanjuro's Sci/Tech cubicle late in the afternoon. Sanjuro hadn't realized that the lawyer was so much shorter than she was until they stood next to each other. Her skin color was slightly darker than Sanjuro's. Gervaise still looked as impeccable as she had looked in the early hours; her curly black hair was pulled into a neat bun on the back of her head, and not one wrinkle rippled her uniform. They found an unoccupied meeting room.

"I wanted to let you know that we didn't find anything in your messages, Captain. The comp techs are still tracing unauthorized messages, and they could turn up something else. However, so far all they've found in the illegal channels is a porn ring."

Sanjuro said, "Usually there's some smuggling going on, too."

Gervaise grimaced. "I expect there will be, once we get to our destination and find something to smuggle. I hope not, though. Dealing with the porn merchants will be annoying enough. It's a waste of my time, but we can't continue to pretend it doesn't exist since we've found it."

"Nasty job, security."

"Yes, it is. Anyway, you're cleared. I've informed Colonel Rao as well as the Admiral."

"I'm sure she believed you."

"The Colonel is very angry about the *Cortez*. Clearly someone on board has been in communication with the private expedition, most likely with the collusion of someone in communications back in the System. It's not unreasonable to consider who might do such a thing."

"Very diplomatic, Commander."

Gervaise smiled. "Lots of people are angry today. I'm trying to keep the discussions civil. And it's Ari off-duty, unless you have a problem with that, Captain."

Sanjuro stuck out her hand. "No problem. It's Caty."

"Let's get an off-duty drink sometime soon, Caty." Gervaise gave her a wave as she left the room.

Maybe Gervaise was making friends so she could keep an eye on her. But something about the lawyer appealed to her. The conversation had made the last of her anger dissipate.

Still, Sanjuro avoided Masire. She liked him, liked him a lot. But the security business reminded her of how ugly things could get when the personal and the professional overlapped. Better to let things go.

She missed him, though, and was annoyed at the small flutter she felt when she found him behind her in line in the dining hall.

"Still mad at me?" He gave her a winning boyish grin.

She steeled herself to be some combination of professional and casual. "No. At least you believe me. Rao is still convinced I'm in on a big conspiracy. I guess she didn't take your word for it that I'm cleared." She was fishing, wondering if he really had cleared her.

He sighed, and the boyish look disappeared. "I can't do anything about Rao. She's the way she is. But no one else thinks you've done anything. Gervaise gave you a clean bill. Vargas accepted our conclusions without reservation. He's still pretty angry that he just found out about the *Cortez*; he isn't buying the official line that the top brass just found out."

"I guess that helps."

They ended up eating together. Masire managed to steer her toward an underpopulated corner of the room.

"So. Forgive me?" The boyish grin was back.

"You didn't do anything wrong." Sanjuro's voice sounded uncompromising, even to her.

"I should have found a better way to handle it."

That was a real apology, and she knew it. She relented. "I could have been less prickly about it." She ate a bite of food, which tasted even more like cardboard than usual. She washed it down with a slug of wine, and made a face that might have been caused by the food. "It's going to happen again, you know. We're bound to end up in touchy professional situations. That's why people who work together shouldn't sleep together."

"Kuso. Things would have been just as difficult for us if we'd only been friends. No one likes to take action against their friends. Surely you're not going to say we shouldn't have become friends?"

She laughed. She couldn't help it. He knew how to jolly people out of their bad moods. That was probably why he was such a success with women.

"So if I'm forgiven, why have you been avoiding me? And don't tell me it's because you started worrying about having a relationship with someone you work with. If that were all, you would have felt obligated to talk to me."

She knew he was right. "We've been seeing each other for a while now. I figured maybe it was time we moved on to other people."

Masire looked stunned. "Is there someone else?"

She hadn't expected such a blunt question. It forced her to be honest. "No. I haven't met anyone else on board I like as much as you. But I thought maybe you might be ready to move on, before we got too serious."

"Oh. You've been talking to Montoya."

"No, no," she lied. "We just haven't made any firm commitments, and I thought—"

"Nonsense. Someone told you I'm a womanizer, and it can only have been Montoya."

"Montoya worships the ground—or whatever—you walk on. She'd never call you something like that."

He grinned. "The hell she wouldn't. She doesn't approve of my relationships, and that's a fact. You don't have to worry that you'll get her into trouble. I'm not such a fool as to damage my relationship with the best noncom I've ever had just because she tells other people about my sex life. It's not like it's a big secret."

"So you do have a new hot babe on your arm every six months?"

He slapped the table. "Kuso! I knew she'd called me a womanizer. But she's got it wrong. I don't pick women for their looks. I like brains. Some of my exes were great lookers, some weren't. But you're far from the first PhD I ever slept with."

"But you do change them often?"

"Look, I'm combat. You were combat; you know what it's like. People in my job don't stay in one place for very long, and we rarely end up twice in the same place. I usually find a civilian in the area, and when the assignment is over, the relationship is."

"You never heard of the long-distance relationship?" She gave a little laugh, to show she meant it as a joke.

"Oh, yeah," he said bitterly. "That's the kind my father had with my mother. He used being married as an excuse whenever one of his girlfriends began to get serious. I figure it's better to do it without all the lies."

"Just being faithful doesn't enter the picture?" Damn, now she sounded preachy.

"Sanjuro, I like women and I like sex. If I promised to be faithful, it would be a lie. It just wouldn't happen. Besides, you're not going to tell me you're all that different."

She gave a real laugh. Being called on her own behavior made the situation easier to handle. "Well, I like men as well as women. But you're right; I've never been one for long-term commitments. Which is another reason to let things go now. If something happens to turn it ugly, we'd lose the friendship, too."

"I didn't think you were such a coward."

He said it lightly, but the words stung anyway. "Damn. That's a low blow."

"Sorry. I didn't mean that as harshly as it sounded. I like you a lot, Sanjuro, and I'd like to keep spending time with you." He took her hand. "The last time I had the opportunity to spend multiple years getting to know a lover, I was at the Academy and too young and stupid to take advantage of it. We've got a lot of time to spend together. Why don't we see what happens?"

"You're slick," she told him. "I see how you got that series of women." She meant it as payback for his coward remark. He winced. "But I like you, too. So, okay, let's see what happens. Only let's remember this is a small community and neither of us needs any enemies. If things start to fall apart, let's make a real effort to be civilized about it."

"I always am," he said.

"I'm not."

He laughed. "Well, then, the responsibility's on you, isn't it? Want to go dancing after dinner? Or something?"

"Maybe 'or something,'" she said.

⇒

The corporate expedition effectively shut down communication with other xenologists. Rao ordered Sanjuro to stop sending any of her reports to Bogdosian and Li, and then broadened it to include anyone else in the field.

The order wasn't limited to xenology. All of the scientists had been instructed to stop sending any reports back to non-military scientists. The official reports were still being sent to the system via ETQ, but Rao made it clear that these were to be very basic. She obviously thought everything they'd sent so far had been given to the *Cortez* crew.

"Just put down the work you've done. No frills. No speculation," she said.

For once the entire Sci/Tech crew agreed with Rao.

"Well the ship name is certainly appropriate," Kyo said. "*Cortez* was greedy, and so are these corporations. They want to come in, piggyback on our work, and make a fat profit. We're government-funded; we shouldn't hand them the keys. Let them do their own work."

"Sure," Sanjuro said. "Though it really doesn't matter much right now, when all any of us can do is speculate. I'm sure they got all the *Copernicus* data and all our reports. That's more than enough."

"It sets a precedent for later, once we reach El Dorado."

"Maybe. Though I bet you that by the time we get there, Bogdosian or some of those high-placed corporate types will have whispered in enough ears to get the non-cooperation order reversed. That didn't come from the System, after all. It's just Rao and Vargas."

Kyo looked at her. "I hope you're just paranoid."

"Me, too. But don't be surprised. It's what they do best."

"Great. We'll feed them all the raw data while they're still en route, and they'll have plenty of time to work with it."

"We probably won't even be able to get information back from them. Damn it all to hell. I was planning to ship data back to Bogdosian and company on a regular basis once we got there, so I could get some other opinions about the Cibolans. Now even if the rules get changed, I'll have to be damn careful what I send them. That could have been avoided if the System had included a couple more xenologists on *Mercator*."

Kyo gave her a funny look. "I don't follow that one, Caty."

"If there were more of us on *Mercator*, Bogdosian wouldn't have decided she needed to add others to the project."

Kyo laughed. "You're the real conspiracy theorist! I know Bogdosian's got clout, but this wasn't her plan. She couldn't have put together the kind of financing this must have taken. It's mind boggling."

"She didn't get the money and maybe she only got involved when she heard about the intelligent life on Cibola. But I'll give you ten to one she is part of the leadership now. She knows all those people."

"You're serious," Kyo said.

"She knows I'm outnumbered up here, and that xenology isn't this expedition's first concern. She wants enough people to really study them, and she'll sell all our souls to the devil to make sure that happens. For that matter, she wants a lot of other xenologists to meet some Cibolans. I'm sure the *Cortez* plans involve bringing aliens back to Earth."

"You sound like Rao."

"The only difference between me and the Colonel on this one is that she thinks I'm part of the conspiracy and I know I'm not."

Kyo laughed again, but Sanjuro didn't join in. None of this was funny anymore. Kyo said, "You're attributing too much to Bogdosian and not taking into account the way big companies think and plan in advance. More likely she just saw a chance to get more xenologists out to El Dorado when she heard about the *Cortez* plan, and took advantage of it. She can't like corporations being involved any more than you do."

Sanjuro said, "You're probably right. But you know, I'm not sure Bogdosian cares about whether the Cibolans get to keep their own lives, so long as she gets to study them. Their very existence justifies her life's work."

Kyo scratched her head and made a face. "That's kind of nasty, isn't it?"

"Yeah." But she didn't take it back.

A day later, Kyo pinged Sanjuro. "I need to talk to you. Now." Her tone was so grim that Sanjuro wondered if the Major was mad at her for something unknown. She presented herself at Kyo's tiny—but private—office.

"Shut the door," Kyo said.

Sanjuro complied. She had never seen her friend look so angry.

"I've been going over the list of corporations behind the *Cortez*. It includes a little firm called Kyo Bioformatics."

Her family's business. That didn't surprise Sanjuro. The company was a major player in bioforming and in developing products from bacteria. "You've always said your family never passed on a good opportunity."

"Oh, yeah. Including using its black sheep with the military career."

Sanjuro was puzzled. She knew Kyo had cut most of her ties to her family. She sent birthday wishes to the children of her siblings and cousins, but didn't communicate regularly with her parents or the uncle who was the current CEO.

"Don't you get it, Sanjuro? That's why I'm here. There were half a dozen other astrobiologists in Sci/Tech who could have had the job. I'd done a good job on Europa, so I let myself think it was merit. But it was influence. My uncle must have talked to someone."

"You're jumping to conclusions. That would mean the *Cortez* mission was being planned back when the SSU was still setting up *Mercator*."

"It probably was. The big corps plan in advance. I bet the group behind the *Cortez* started planning stuff the moment the *Copernicus* data came in."

That fit in all too well with Sanjuro's own thoughts. "That makes sense," she said. "But it doesn't mean you didn't get this job on your own. It's well known you don't get along with your family."

"Lots of people don't get along with their families, until push comes to shove and they have to choose. My uncle is betting I'll chose family. Or, at least, won't stand in the way."

"He doesn't know you very well, then."

"Maybe he does. If they come out here and rip things out from under us, going back into the family fold may be the only way I'll get to do work that matters." She sighed and looked up at the ceiling, as if searching for a clue. "One of my cousins—another astrobiologist—is on the *Cortez*. I got a message from my uncle, telling me there would be a spot available for me when I wanted it."

"Through the com system? Wouldn't somebody have spotted that?"

"The message was in Korean and from family. Likely nobody paid much attention. But it had to be timed right, so maybe someone at the sending end did know what he was up to. He wouldn't have wanted me to see it before we heard about the *Cortez*."

That did make it sound more suspicious to Sanjuro. But she said, "I'm sure you got the job on your own. Your uncle is just taking advantage of the situation."

"Wouldn't it be pretty to think so," Kyo said, her voice dripping sarcasm. "I know those people, Caty."

Given her own thoughts about Bogdosian, Sanjuro couldn't think of anything else soothing to say. The odds that the powerful were manipulating both Kyo and her was only too likely. "Would you really go to work for them?"

"Not if I could avoid it. But what if that's the only way I can study life on Cibola? What if otherwise I'll be sent home?"

Sanjuro didn't have an answer to that.

>⇒

Six or seven months later (relative System time), Sanjuro got a message from someone she'd known at Berkeley. "Well, you've certainly gone a long way since those old college days. First Luna, and now way beyond the System. Lots of people green with envy back here on the old home world who'd love to know the details. Why not do an update for the old alumni mag? A mutual friend of ours would be glad to whip it into shape, if you sent a rough draft."

The message had apparently come through the personal message section of the A/ND com system, and had been sent about three months back. A/ND com was one of the AI systems built into *Mercator*. Although the messages that came through it were actually sent back and forth between ship and Earth in a physical container, the humans who used it sent their messages over their ordinary com systems, just routing them to the A/ND interface. Except for the delay, it felt like normal communication.

The message sounded ordinary, forthright, the sort of thing no censor would look at twice. Except that the person who sent it had been one of her professors when she'd been in school, not one of her classmates. And since his degree was from Oxford, the odds were he didn't give a rat's ass about Berkeley alumni news. He and Bogdosian were good friends; rumor had them as ex-lovers who had broken up without rancor.

Plus, there was a line of gibberish at the bottom. That wasn't uncommon; a lot of their messages had garbled lines. But she recognized this one; a code key, from an amateur crypto program popular back when she was at the academy. Not hard to break, if anyone was looking for it. Probably no one was.

They were feeling her out, no question. The whole thing confirmed her paranoia about Bogdosian. The professor must have sold her soul to the corporate parazitks.

She deleted the message without replying. But she didn't tell Gervaise about it, either. Maybe it's just innocent, she told herself, and then—because only an idiot lies to herself—maybe you're going to need to contact Andy one of these days, no matter whose side she's really on. She knew she could remember the code.

# 10

Sanjuro knocked on the door of Masire's quarters; she had the code, but preferred formality. Some of the couples on board had arranged to share quarters, but despite the fact that Sanjuro slept in Masire's room often, they had never taken that step. When asked, Sanjuro said they both were the kind of people who needed privacy. It was a legitimate concern — only the Admiral rated two-room quarters — but Sanjuro knew they both kept up a wall for other reasons. The security flap over the *Cortez* had made the potential for conflict obvious.

Masire opened the door with a flourish. The lights had been turned low. A silver bucket sat on the desk, with a bottle sticking out of the top. Next to it sat a crystal vase, containing several roses. Two champagne flutes and a tray full of chocolate truffles completed the display.

"Dios," Sanjuro said. "What's the occasion?"

Masire's face fell. "It's our anniversary. We first slept together three years ago."

"You're kidding."

"I never joke about romance. You really don't remember?"

She hoped she hadn't hurt his feelings. "I remember the first time we slept together." She kissed his cheek, to let him know how pleasant the memory was. "This is the right month. I just couldn't tell you the actual date."

"Well, now you can. I expect you to do the elaborate stuff next year. I spent hours on those roses."

She picked up the vase and looked at them. They were silk—well, nano silk. But they'd been cut and put together by hand. "Masire! I didn't know you had so much talent at crafts."

"I don't. If I was any good at it, you'd have a dozen. I ran out of time."

She kissed him again.

"The champagne probably sucks as bad as all the other alcohol, but the truffles are damn close to the real thing. I tested 'em."

She hugged him close. "It's a wonderful surprise."

The champagne proved mediocre, but the truffles were much better than anyone would have expected. The two of them sat entwined on the bunk, feeding the confections to each other, giggling like schoolchildren. Then Masire began to undress her, taking his time. She let him get her completely naked before she started to do the same for him. Everything they did that night was slow and intense; Sanjuro thought she might die of the intensity long before they both shuddered their way to orgasm.

Afterwards, unwilling to pull apart, Masire whispered, "No one else has ever mattered to me this much."

Almost she replied with "I love you," but something held her back, and she contented herself with "Me, either."

Sundown was tired from spending several hours observing a meteor and calculating its trajectory. The findings contradicted the ones issued by an astronomer from the Cobalt Sands region. Sundown had redone the work three times, but kept getting the same answer and had finally concluded that the error must be the other astronomer's. Because neither had found that the meteor posed any risk to their planet, the differences in their results were only a matter of scientific accuracy. Efforts to contact the other astronomer could wait until the next international scientific discussions in the weave. Cobalt Sands was in the southern hemisphere; it took a lot of combined mental power to communicate at that distance.

Sundown considered going to bed, but dawn was several hours off and there was another meeting in the capital city in two days. Sundown wouldn't be able to come back up to the observatory for at least another week, and the moon would be brighter then, interfering with her work. Instead of sleeping, Sundown recalibrated the telescope for a sweep of the sky, then stepped away for a few minutes to get a hot drink and move around.

When Sundown returned to the scope, a dot was moving rapidly at the edge of the vision field. Nothing should be moving so fast in that region of the sky.

Hastily, Sundown recalibrated to focus the full power of the scope on the moving dot, but even that magnification was not enough to see what it was. It might be another meteor or the leading edge of a meteor shower, though no one had predicted such an event and failures to predict common sightings were rare indeed. More likely it was an optical illusion. But repeated recalibrations of the telescope did not take it away, nor did observing it from the older scope.

If it was neither a meteor nor an illusion, then the most likely explanation was some kind of vessel, perhaps similar to the one they had observed so many years back. Sundown watched the dot continue to move for another half an hour, and then decided that letting others know could not wait until morning. Sundown reached out and contacted the weave.

The weave was less powerful at night, with so many in Golden Mountain asleep. Still, Sundown was able to reach Sorrel and, with that assistance, the other three astronomers in their region. One of them was also at a telescope and, following Sundown's directions, quickly spotted the moving object.

The weave expanded, as more minds joined it. Astronomers from Copper Waters were now participating; they, too, had noticed the object. They had drawn in others from Bronze Forest, where it was now midday. Although the Bronze Forestites could not see anything, they added their power to the weave. Soon they were joined by astronomers and others from Cobalt Sands in the southern hemisphere. They, too, had noticed the object, and had managed to awaken enough residents to allow them to reach Sundown and the others in the weave.

As dawn broke on Sundown's mountain, most had concluded that the object in question was indeed some sort of vessel, not unlike the one Sundown's father and the others of that time had seen. By mid-morning they were making tentative efforts to scan it, to see if any life forms were aboard, but it was still too far away.

Sundown changed plans and stayed at the observatory. Iron came up in the afternoon, bringing supplies, and stayed while the world watched and waited. For all that Sundown was in constant contact with the worldwide weave—with only the occasional short nap—it was wonderful to have physical contact with another during this chaotic period.

Several days passed before they began to receive mental signals from the ship. At first just odd images, then a chaotic rush, impossible to classify at first impression, but clearly generated by minds. Likely intelligent minds, given their presence on a vessel flying through space.

*More than one. Many more than one,* Sundown thought. A community of intelligent beings, traveling here from another world. Excitement at this idea beat out exhaustion.

Even as they tried to make sense of the images, a debate began on how to respond. Should they send messages, or retreat into silence, or even attack without warning? Images from an ancient invasion—one Sundown remembered its father explaining—were evoked countless times. Fear was not an irrational response.

But there was wonder in the air as well. Flying objects, traveling from distant planets, carrying intelligent beings. Sundown was not the only one bursting with curiosity to know more about these people. More than one engineer in the weave—including Iron—wanted to know more about vehicles that could fly through space. We could learn so much, Iron's contributions made clear, an urge at least as strong as the fear.

After another day of contact—almost all adults on the planet participating, national divides forgotten—the images began to make more sense. Some were faces, others machinery, some clearly memories of other planets, another sun. Enough were images of smaller beings to make them think of their own children, and that softened the hearts of even the strongest proponents of attack without warning.

Rarely did the entire planet come together to make any decisions. Most of the time, each region handled its own affairs, and only natural disasters or strife between two regions might draw the others in. Even then, the governments led decision-making.

But something like this could not be kept from anyone, if only because of the necessity of combining so many minds in the weave to reach the ship. The planet-wide weave would make the decision on what to do.

For several days—days in which only the most crucial of ordinary work got done, days in which few adults slept for more than a few hours at a time—the debate raged: reach out to these people, or hold back and wait to see what actions they take, or try to frighten them away, or destroy them before they reach the planet. Feelings on the subject did not break down along national lines, or by any other obvious divisions. Spouses found themselves with opposing views; the Bronze Forestites, widely regarded as unnecessarily aggressive by residents of other nations, seemed least in favor of attack. The intensity of the debate destroyed more than a few friendships and alliances, and the number of duels in succeeding days was far higher than average.

In the end, curiosity—coupled with caution—won the day. Efforts would be made to contact the beings on this vessel, to see if they responded and could be brought into the weave. But these aliens would be under intense observation as well.

The various governments began to assert themselves, organizing committees to communicate and to watch, and setting up a system of reporting. Meanwhile, everyone would continue in a state of readiness and be ready to come to the defense of their families, their homes, their planet, should it become necessary.

Amidst the fear and caution and practicality, Sundown detected more than one mind in which the dominant feelings were curiosity and desire to meet these alien beings. Sundown was not alone in wanting company.

# EXPLORATION

# 1

Sanjuro's head ached. "Just my luck," she said to Kyo, sitting next to her in the shuttle, "we're finally landing on Cibola and my head feels like it's going to split open."

"I thought you got something from Medical for that. Must be some new virus. My crew's been complaining all week."

"Medical doesn't think it's a virus. Diagnostics can't find anything wrong."

"I never trust diagnostics," Kyo said. "They're never as good as the doctors who design them."

Sanjuro shrugged. Through the viewscreen she watched as the other shuttle—the one carrying the Admiral and the other big shots—landed on the planet. Admiral Vargas would step out soon, followed by an honor guard of marines and the other high-rank personnel.

Then Kyo and her crew of astrobiologists and Sanjuro would be allowed to get out and start setting up a base. The Admiral knew the value of a dramatic moment, and his landing was being holoed for shipment by A/ND back to Earth. The asteroids might be the focus of this expedition, but landing on a planet made a better show, even if no one would see if for a few months.

Kyo said, "You probably gave yourself the headache trying to get Vargas to stick around to talk to the Cibolans."

Sanjuro gave a tiny grin. "A reasonable theory. Maybe you should take up psychology in your spare time. I can't believe he won't even consider staying for a day so we can try to meet them formally. It would be good fodder for the holocam, too."

"Maybe. Depends on what the Cibolans would do if they saw him. We have no idea whether they're friendly. Anyway, he's itching to get out to the asteroid belt, figure out what can be mined."

"I know. But damn it, it's bad form, sending lower-rank people to meet the locals."

"That from the gospel according to Bogdosian?"

"Don't bait me, Sumi. My head hurts. And you know damn well you agree with me."

"Yeah, but it's not going to happen. So figure out what else you're going to do."

"I've already done that. Years ago."

"Ah, yes: five years of planning is a long time. I may agree in principle that keeping Vargas around for a formal intro is a good idea, but in practice I just want him out of here as soon as possible so I can do my work. Be grateful. Neither he nor Rao will be breathing down your neck."

"That's because they don't give a damn about my work. Or even yours."

"They care about mine. I'm in charge of making sure people can live here. And of figuring out if the local bacteria are useful."

"You know what I mean," Sanjuro said.

Kyo sighed. "Yes, I do. And no, I don't like it either. But that doesn't mean we're not going to find things out that completely differ from our expectations. And then they'll have to listen."

"Will they?" said Sanjuro.

Their shuttle put down next to the first one. Sanjuro watched on the viewscreen as Vargas walked out onto the planet surface, followed closely by Masire and several of his marines.

Vargas wanted to be the first person to plant his foot on a non-system planet, but he didn't plan to take chances. They'd spent two Earth weeks in orbit watching the inhabitants, scanning for dangerous viruses and analyzing the atmosphere.

"Today the human race takes its first step into exploration of the universe beyond our home," Vargas said.

He kept talking, but Sanjuro stopped paying attention. Vargas had spent five years working out this speech, just as she'd spent five years planning her approach to the Cibolans. There was such a thing as too much preparation.

The other commanders came out of the shuttle: Captain Marley. Commander Deirdre Pham, Marley's second in command. Colonel Rao. Major Case. A couple of Sci/Tech officers that Rao liked. Ari Gervaise. A couple of senior pilots.

Kyo was right; there were advantages to Rao's lack of interest. She'd be gone soon, and both Sanjuro and Kyo could get down to doing what really interested them: Kyo looking at the flora and fauna of the planet and Sanjuro trying to meet the "Cibolans."

On the surface, Masire and his marines formed a formal honor guard, and it gave Sanjuro a pang. She didn't want Masire's assignment: he would stay in orbit on the ship, along with Marley. And with luck, nothing requiring combat skills would happen here. Still, she remembered the small pleasures of serving in an honor guard.

Just rituals, she told herself.

She heard an order—authorization from the command shuttle to disembark.

Sanjuro followed Kyo down the ramp. Rank order. Kyo wouldn't have bothered with military formality, even on a first landing, but Sanjuro made sure they did it by the book. Ritual again. One of the reasons she wanted Vargas to stay and meet the Cibolans with her.

She took a deep breath as she stepped onto ground for the first time in five years. Real air, not canned. It didn't smell like Earth. Though, in truth, she couldn't quite remember what Earth smelled like.

A light breeze stirred the air. Sanjuro could almost taste the dry tang of dust, but the breeze also carried a sweetness that called to mind a dried potpourri of roses and a tartness that suggested overripe citrus.

Stepping on the planet didn't feel particularly different from stepping on Earth, not nearly as different as stepping on the surface on Luna or Ceres. It almost felt like coming home, to feel soil and rocks and grass—well some kind of plant life, anyway—under her feet.

But the landscape stretching before her didn't look like Earth. Or like any place she'd ever seen. The sky was blue, true, and the sun shone yellow-orange, but that was due to the similarity of atmospheres. Everything else was the wrong color, the wrong size, and in the wrong place.

A large collection of plants grew nearby. Similar to trees, except they had the circumference of bamboo coupled with the height of redwoods and were covered in magenta foliage. A short purple ground cover with skinny leaves grew in the clearing, and the ground was olive green. The stream running through the tree-like plants also looked olive green, probably because of the rocks and soil in it. Only a trickle of water made its way down the streambed.

Sanjuro stood there, awed.

"Pretty amazing," said Kyo.

Sanjuro nodded; she couldn't come up with any words that did the sight justice. She kept turning her head around to look as they walked over to join the senior crew. The cameras had been turned off.

"Fantastic view," said Vargas. Even he sounded awed. "Your people prepared to set up, Major?"

"Yes, sir," Kyo said. "We're unloading now."

"Good, good. I look forward to your reports. And yours, too, Captain," he said to Sanjuro.

"Yes, sir." She hadn't heard what he said; she was too busy taking in the new world.

"Well, time to get moving, figure out what else there is to see out here." He waved a hand, and people started back onto the shuttle. Masire raised his eyebrows at her, gave her a "what can you do" shrug as he followed the Admiral on board. Gervaise waved.

Sanjuro checked the time. Ten minutes. Five years in space, and Vargas was satisfied with ten minutes planetside. Of course, the geologists were eager to get on with their work among the asteroids, but how could they ignore an entire planet?

Oh, well. Kyo was right: at least they'd be left alone to do their work.

⤝

The images from the minds of the creatures landing on the planet bombarded Sundown and the others who were reading them. A parade of faces. A frame around a series of ordered lines of gibberish. Things that appeared to grow out of the ground and put out limbs and flowers and fruit, though they were so much wider and taller than their plants that Sundown wondered if they were manufactured rather than grown. Buildings that reached for the heavens and others that looked to contain one small room. Spaceships like the one now in orbit around the planet. Water lapping along a shore. And a continuous flow of something that had no shape, no image, but was overwhelmingly present.

The images coming through were both so diverse and so specific that they indicated intelligence, Sundown thought. But no one could find a functional pattern. Like a baby, someone sent. Babies, once their eyes began to focus, typically sent a steady stream of everything they saw, experienced, or remembered.

But it was only a short time before babies—even ones still carried in their fathers' pouches—began to order their thoughts and their sending. It was a natural process, coming well before they reached an age where they could be taught control.

These people—clearly adults from their size and their purposeful action—had no obvious structure to their minds. And no control whatsoever. Sundown and the others scanned every individual mind in range, and found none to be any different. It seemed impossible that such disorder could be communication, yet surely these beings communicated in some way. They had traveled through space, after all.

We need to go deeper, Sundown sent. We need to observe them more closely.

Not yet, came back from Sorrel and others in the leadership. Not yet. Let us continue to observe from a distance. We still do not know how much of a threat they represent.

>≔

Ian Masire watched on the shuttle viewscreen as the people on the surface began to set up their station. He envied the marines he'd left down there; after five years in space, he was more than ready to live planetside for a while.

But as the commander, with part of his troop on Cibola and another chunk of them accompanying the asteroid expedition, his best location was on the orbiting *Mercator*. It gave him the flexibility to move wherever he might be needed. He'd left Montoya down there to shore up the lieutenant in charge.

Duty, damn it. Duty. Had he taken charge of the Cibola group, everyone would have known his reasons were personal. Including Sanjuro. And while he thought she might want him down there, she wouldn't have respected his choice.

He'd already compromised enough. He'd agreed to let Sanjuro set up her station without a marine guard. They'd argued about it for months.

"How can I hope to establish a relationship if I come with a troop of soldiers?" she'd said.

"What if the aliens come with weapons?" he'd answered.

"Lots of ways to deal with that, without fighting back."

"But suppose they've got a military culture. Suppose they don't respect someone who doesn't come with force."

"Well, then, it's a good thing I'm a marine," Sanjuro told him. "Or don't you think I can project a military presence by myself?"

He'd had to laugh. Besides, the scan they'd run from orbit before landing showed few items among the Cibolans that could be classed as weapons and nothing that resembled guns or artillery. Still, she would be alone, putting her at significant risk if the Cibolans came in numbers. Sticks and stones there were in abundance, and those were the first human weapons.

Masire didn't have to talk her into it, of course. As chief of security, he could just order a small crew to go with her. He had decided not to for a purely personal reason: he knew she wouldn't forgive him. He tried to console himself with various facts. Sanjuro's desire to set up alone wasn't foolhardy; she had given careful thought to the best way to approach the situation. Masire trusted her judgment. And the size of the crew he could have assigned wouldn't have made much difference. The whole situation was inherently risky, and always had been. He didn't think she was in more danger without guards; he was simply scared of losing her. The token gesture of a few marines would have helped him pretend that her job wasn't risky.

He tried to tell himself he'd have worried about any crew member sent out on their own, but he knew this situation was different. When had he and Sanjuro crossed that line to the point where she mattered more than anyone else? It scared him, to think how much he'd come to care.

He switched off the viewscreen. Quit agonizing, Masire, he told himself. That's Becca Sanjuro's daughter out there. She can take care of herself.

# 2

"This looks like a great place to start," Kyo said enthusiastically. "Lots of plant life. And I imagine we'll find some animals or some such over in those—do you think I can call them trees?"

"Careful before you assume too much. Too easy to think that what's here is like what's on Earth."

"Astrobiology one-oh-one."

"I took that, too. Maybe you'll find something alive that doesn't fit in our neat categories," Sanjuro said.

Kyo grinned. "My goal in life. Be careful out there."

"Always am."

"No, you're not. But it occurs to me that, in spite of all the kidding around you've had to put up with, all xenologists should have experience as combat marines."

"You're assuming that the Cibolans will be unfriendly to aliens because humans would be."

"Just considering the possibility. Don't shoot anybody you don't have to, Caty, but come back alive. Okay?"

"Yes, ma'am." Her tone was gently sarcastic.

They'd landed the shuttle about a hundred kilometers from the nearest city. Sensor data from sweeps run by the survey systems on board *Mercator* when they first arrived confirmed the information from the probe *Copernicus*: Cibola seemed to be sparsely populated, a handful of cities spread around the world in the temperate zones within forty degrees north and south of the equator. Both polar regions covered more than half of their respective hemispheres.

Smaller settlements ranged outward from the cities, but there were still vast tracts of land unpopulated, and not only in the colder regions. An argument had raged among the astrobiologists about whether the expanses of unpopulated land indicated something in the unsettled areas that was inimical to the Cibolans or simply reflected the planet's low population. Other data showed a dearth of mineral resources and water, another factor that might have affected population patterns.

Sanjuro had found the arguments interesting but had thrown out another possibility: perhaps the arrangement of cities and wild lands was cultural. The biologists had rejected that out of hand. The Cibolans were primitive; therefore, they must be driven by biological imperatives alone.

One of the reasons Sanjuro had taken up xenology rather than astrobiology was that she never believed things were as simple as that. Biology was an important factor, and she had a thorough grounding in it, but it seemed likely that any group of sapient beings would be ruled by more than biology. Humans were.

But again, she tried to keep an open mind. Don't assume the Cibolans are like humans. Or like Earth animals, she told herself. There might be an explanation you haven't even considered.

She set the landcraft on its lowest speed so that she could take in the landscape as she moved past. It was a boxy vehicle, with windows on all sides, allowing the occupant to see in every direction. The star around which Cibola orbited shone brightly. The landcraft power source was fully charged, but the windows also drew power from the sun. (Sanjuro couldn't help thinking of it as The Sun, in capital letters; the light was too similar to Earth's.) She reset the landcraft system to solar; might as well save the reserves for a cloudy day. Though what data they had suggested Cibola didn't have many of those.

She intended to set up a camp about ten kilometers from the nearest Cibolan town, one of the smaller communities that encircled a large city. That distance should be close enough for the locals to check her out, but far enough away to not appear as a threat. She hoped. She would sit and wait for the Cibolans to come to her.

She hadn't wanted to do things this way, but it seemed to be the only option left. They had beamed messages—mathematical patterns, music, simple spoken language—toward Cibola for several weeks before they arrived. They sent them again from orbit while they launched several communication satellites and ran scans to confirm the original analysis of the planet's atmosphere. But nothing had come back in reply.

Why was heavily debated among the scientists: the Cibolans didn't have receivers; they had receivers but lacked transmitters strong enough to reply; even if they got the messages through some natural phenomenon that acted as a receiver, they were too primitive to recognize them as communication. The theoretical debate had been intense enough to have given everyone the headaches.

The area where they had landed the shuttle had looked wild and uncultivated, but as Sanjuro got closer to the city, the surroundings started to change. A subtle difference at first: just a perception that the plants were growing in more orderly rows.

Sanjuro was traveling overland; her craft was a hovership and needed no road. She had programmed it using coordinates developed from their orbital mapping, setting the alarms for the possibility of trees, hills, and other obstacles. However, about forty kilometers from the shuttle landing spot, she came upon a road. Not a paved one, but a cleared and graded one. She reset the program to track the road.

The fields alongside the road now showed signs of cultivation. The first had pale purple shoots poking up out of the olive-green soil. The second had bushy maroon plants, each with a tall stalk in the middle that appeared to be setting fruit.

She negotiated a curve and spotted a group of what must be a form of animal life—about twenty creatures gathered around a shallow pond. The pond was laid out in neat, rectangular dimensions, indicating to Sanjuro that it had been built. She stopped her vehicle to look at the creatures and the pond more closely. Each had four long, slender legs and two other limbs resembling arms. She saw one of them put an "arm" into the water, pull up a handful, and splash it on its face. Their necks were long and flexible, and their main body was not large. She guessed they would weigh around sixty kilos. Several smaller creatures wobbled about, as if they were new to walking. Offspring, Sanjuro guessed. They were covered in blue fur and had large eyes on the sides of their head. Likely prey, the theory went, since such eyes provided a wide scope of vision, the better to see a predator. Some appeared to be eating the vegetation. She caught the odor of animals en masse—a thick musky smell accompanied by dust.

Domestic animals, surely. Though whether they were raised for meat, milk, work, or some other unknown possibility, she could not say. She added it to her field notes though: the Cibolans raise animals and cultivate crops.

She started to see a few buildings here and there—sheds and huts rather than anything that looked like permanent living quarters. As yet she had not seen any Cibolans. Just as well: her vehicle would probably frighten them.

As she got closer to town, she came to another area full of what she was already calling "trees," despite her smart-assed comment to Kyo. She stopped to look around. Like the landing site, it had a small stream bed, not quite dry, with olive rocks showing through the almost-clear water. Just past the stream stood an open field.

Upon closer inspection, the field contained a large variety of plants. Interspersed with the purple groundcover—which was everywhere she'd been so far—grew tiny plants with turquoise blooms. Their leaves were needle-thin, even thinner than the slender leaves of the groundcover, and almost lilac in color. Some taller plants grew in a haphazard pattern. One had a green, bulbous fruit. Sanjuro wondered if green meant ripe in a place where foliage was red and purple. She ran a scan. The fruit wasn't toxic to humans. That didn't make it worth eating, though. She decided not to try it just yet.

# The Weave

The site seemed a good location for a campsite: scenic, visible from the road, unoccupied. Sanjuro spent several hours walking around, looking for signs that she was trespassing. She could see no buildings, no fences, no domesticated animals. If this property did belong to someone, it apparently wasn't in active use. Better to set up out here than to go any closer to the nearest inhabited area.

Sanjuro took a box out of her craft and punched in commands. The shelter quickly grew into place. The standard military gray looked out of place in this colorful field, but then, everything human was out of place here. She activated the instabuild's scan to notify her in case someone approached. And then she had nothing to do but wait.

The Cibolans showed up two days later.

# 3

When the proximity alarm beeped, Sanjuro felt a surge of excitement. *Calm down, Sanjuro,* she told herself. *Probably another animal.* She'd had two false alarms already. But the scan readout showed three distinct bodies. Each massed more than any animals she had yet seen. She went outside to look. Three creatures had just turned off the road half a kilometer away and were headed straight toward her shelter.

Sanjuro's heart rate shot up so much she could feel her pulse pounding in her carotid artery. Her hands shook from the accompanying adrenaline. She'd been waiting for this moment for two days, five years, her whole life, and now that it was approaching she couldn't think what to do first. But she had planned for it, and her instincts kicked in. She turned on her vid and data recorders, then dashed back into the shelter to make sure they were sending properly to the instabuild's backup comp so that the encounter would be recorded even if something happened to her and destroyed her implants before she could share the data. While inside she gulped a glass of water—her throat had gone dry—and quickly ran a comb over her hair. "Mustn't let the aliens see a sloppy looking human," she told her reflection. Then she rushed back outside, wanting to be visible when the Cibolans approached. She tried to calm herself by doing deep breathing exercises. It didn't work. She was too excited. Some of that was probably fear. Anything could happen here. But she preferred to put it down to excitement. She didn't want to be afraid, so she told herself she wasn't.

Sanjuro shivered slightly. According to the data they'd gathered on Cibola from the original probe and the time they'd spent in orbit, it was summer on this part of the planet. But summer here wasn't warm by human standards. She subvocalized a command to her body suit to up the temperature.

The Cibolans had seen her. They stopped abruptly. Sanjuro got the sense they were taking in the whole set up, the dull-gray shelter, the boxy landcraft, the human standing there looking completely different from anything they had ever seen before. They began moving again, slower now.

Sanjuro's mind raced even as she tried to project calm. Were the Cibolans as excited as she was? Or were they as frightened? Did they made up the same sort of "invasion by alien" stories that periodically became popular on Earth? *I hope not*, she thought, remembering how often such aliens had been defined as monsters. But probably the Cibolan civilization hadn't advanced enough to have those kinds of stories. Maybe they still created myths about gods and angels, she thought, and then scolded herself for reasoning ahead of her data. Bogdosian would have yelled at her: "Why must you persist in assuming these beings developed the same way that humans did? They are alien to us."

They certainly looked alien, the three of them. One grayish white, one a reddish color she labeled maroon, like the plants, and the third the pale gold color of sunset. *Multiracial*, she thought, and then scolded herself again. *You don't even know if they see colors like we do or have the concept of race.* Even with all her years of training, Sanjuro could not stop from analogizing from things she knew.

The Cibolans were getting closer now. Each wore a short, brightly patterned robe. Though the cut of the robes seemed similar, the patterns woven into or printed on the fabric were quite different. *Civilians*, Sanjuro thought immediately, before reminding herself once again to stop jumping to conclusions.

They did have four arms. Not a surprise, but she still found it disconcerting to look at the extra limbs. All were taller than her as well; the shortest at least two meters, the tallest a head above that. The slightly lighter gravity, she guessed. They seemed a bit thinner than humans, though all three had broad shoulders. Sanjuro stood still in front of her shelter, hands at her sides, palms turned out. A classic human gesture, showing she was unarmed, though part of her wished for the gun stashed in her shelter. She had known she must meet them with no weapons, even if they brought their own. The Cibolans halted about five meters away. Their hands were empty. They said nothing.

She could see one thing that hadn't been clear from the photos: their skin was actually covered with hair, or fur. Different lengths for each individual. Two eyes in front, looking straight at her. Placed like human eyes — predator eyes — but not appearing at all human; from what she could see they were all one color. Their faces came to a point below the eyes, and there seemed to be an opening there — perhaps a mouth. She could see neither ears nor nose, but perhaps they had those things as well, hidden under fur. They were too far away for her to smell them; she wondered if they could smell her. *Alien, but not completely unlike us,* she thought. They made no sound. Puzzling. She could stand the silence no longer. Time to try out Bogdosian's theory: act like a normal human would act meeting strangers, give the others some idea of what we were like, use ordinary words of greeting and identification, then try some math.

"Hello." Her voice sounded scratchy. Sanjuro cleared her throat and repeated the word, then pointed to herself, moving her hand slowly, nonthreateningly. "I'm Caty Sanjuro. I came from that ship up there." Here she pointed toward the sky. The Cibolans followed her hand with their eyes.

"We've come from Earth to meet you." She paused. "We come in peace." That made her feel like a parody of every first contact story she'd ever heard. She started pointing to things, naming them: "shelter, vehicle, ground, plant." And to herself again: "person." No answer. But speaking, or something, had calmed her down. Her pulse had dropped back to close to normal. The adrenaline surge had worn off. But a few images appeared in her mind: the color gold, a telescope, a row of brightly colored houses, images of Cibolans not present. Sanjuro shook her head, as if to clear it.

Using her hands, she began to clap out a numerical pattern. One clap. Two. Three. Five. Seven. Eleven. Thirteen. She waited a minute, then repeated it. No response, so she repeated it again. And then again. She thought about trying another math constant, but rejected the idea.

The Cibolans watched her for about ten minutes, and then turned and left without having made any sounds. She felt let down when they left; she had hoped for some kind of response. But she had the recording. Maybe when she went back over the interaction, frame by frame, she'd see signs she had missed while trying to communicate. That would have to wait, though. She had a raging headache.

She scrabbled through the first aid kit, looking for the pain medication. A smile formed on her face. She felt the glee and wonder of a five-year-old. *I've seen aliens*, she thought. *I'm the first person to see aliens.*

>

Sanjuro dreamed that night of a town filled with Cibolans. They came in all sizes and colors, and wandered through a marketplace, doing what appeared to be shopping for food and other necessities. The scene reminded Sanjuro of bazaars she'd seen on Earth in those countries where some of the people still lived as their ancestors had done. Brightly colored fabrics were available, produce was piled high. Some tables held what looked like tools, while others had what might be called sculptures or at least figurines. The place teemed with people and felt warm and inviting. But one thing was lacking: sound. The whole market was completely silent.

>

"Nothing new to report," Sanjuro said to Kyo over com. "They still haven't come back." The pleasure of the first meeting had worn off, but her headache had not. Sanjuro had spent the last two days reviewing every frame recorded of the meeting, trying to see something she hadn't noticed at the time. She hadn't found much. The palomino one stood more forward than the others. The leader, perhaps? Or maybe it meant nothing. All of them had followed her hands with their eyes when she gestured. But they had not responded. They had not made any signs to each other that she could see. They had stood at what she considered to be a safe distance from her and made no move that she found threatening. She wondered if that represented their culture's idea of the appropriate distance for meeting any strangers or whether they were trying to avoid getting dangerously close to something unknown.

She'd compared what she'd observed with the data she'd collated from the *Copernicus* reports and the information from *Mercator*'s initial scans of the planet. The total picture left her with more questions than answers.

"I'm thinking about going into the town," she said.

"Why don't you wait a few more days," Kyo replied. "You don't want to frighten them."

That was a good point. She sighed. "Just sitting here is as boring as sitting on the *Mercator*."

Kyo laughed. "Good science always has its down time. They know you're there. Maybe they've gone to report to high muckety-mucks and haven't gotten back yet."

Sanjuro agreed that was a logical explanation, or as logical as any. "I don't think they were scared of me," she said.

"Too primitive to know to be frightened?"

"Not unless they're completely different from Earth lifeforms. All humans are suspicious of new creatures, even new humans. And animals in the wild certainly aren't trusting."

"So maybe they think you're God."

"I don't think so. Nothing deferential in the way they acted, either."

"Well, that's certainly the kind of thing that could differ substantially," Kyo said.

"Yeah. It also could be that humans are the only lifeform in the universe that ever even thought of things like gods."

Kyo laughed again. "Well, you're just going to have to be patient. You'll probably find out most of these things soon. Unless your visitors went back to raise an army."

"You're so cheering. I'll wait another couple of days. Maybe that'll give me time to kick this headache."

"You still got that thing? Everyone else is over it."

"Must have been some weird virus, and I'm more susceptible. How's your work coming?" Sanjuro asked.

"Plant and animal life have a similar genome. And so do the bacteria. The construction is like Earth DNA, though the nucleotides have a different mix. I think we're going to be able to break it down completely in another couple of weeks. Definitely looks like life here mirrors life on Earth: everything's related."

"Be interesting if what they find out in the asteroid belt is related too."

"Don't jump so far ahead. I'm waiting for you to get me some of those domestic animals you keep talking about. Not to mention a Cibolan."

"Good science always has its down time," Sanjuro said, and punched out.

⇒

They make sounds with their mouths, Sundown sent, and felt the shocked reaction. Sundown and Iron were at Sorrel's residence along with other leaders in their region to consider the group's meeting with the lone alien. A meeting within the weave with those from other regions was planned for later in the day.

They were in the official wing of Sorrel's residence, in a large, high-ceilinged room most often used for social events. Those in attendance included the other astronomers in the region, along with leaders of the villages and the city, the head teachers from the schools, and representatives of the manufacturing guilds. The group—perhaps thirty people in all—was too small for such a large room, but too large for any other room in the building. Chairs had been arranged in one corner and an urn of tea was set out on a side table. Most of the attendees had taken a cup.

They communicate by self-generated sounds, Sundown went on.

Impossible, someone responded. Another sent a steady stream of characters from old myths: large flying animals, a huge creature who stalked the desert, tiny beings that had lives just like their own. The implication was clear: beings that made noise were just as fantastic.

They make sounds to communicate, sent the white-furred one who had gone with Sundown to meet the alien. That one was the leader of the council in Sundown's village.

The protests continued: But how can they understand each other? And why would they bother to make sounds when their images are so strong? They send out so much, and yet they make these sounds to each other? Are they blocking the things that are sent? Or not recognizing them? Like babies.

Babies. That idea again. They must be like babies.

They are adults, Sundown sent. The sending let everyone see the alien they had met, showed them its habitation.

Aliens might look very different, might even grow large to small, someone else sent.

A wave of amusement went through the room, accompanied again by images of flying animals. Impossible.

Why would anyone send children to meet us? The images died away and no one responded, an acknowledgment that it was a good question. Sundown continued: they are intelligent. Sundown showed the ship, the shuttle, the details of landing, the alien's shelter. No being without intelligence could make such things or use such things.

But they communicate like babies, Iron sent.

No. Sundown's response was firm. They do not communicate like us, but they cannot be communicating like babies. Perhaps they do not receive one another's images.

The idea shocked everyone. How could they not receive such powerful communication?

Or perhaps, sent Sorrel, they don't know they are receiving them.

The difference in ideas was subtle, and most in the room seemed puzzled. But Sundown understood what Sorrel meant.

# 4

Sanjuro was going over the record of first contact for the umpteenth time when her proximity alarm sounded. She checked the outside visual feed and saw a golden-colored Cibolan just leaving the road. It apparently had come by foot, just as the three had come on the earlier occasion. She straightened her uniform, set the temperature on her bodysuit at a higher degree—it was mid-morning, and chilly outside—made sure her recorders were on, then stepped outside to greet the Cibolan.

She was sure this was the palomino from the first meeting. After spending hours looking at the recording, she could detect small variations among the Cibolans, not only of color, but of height, limb length, face shape. The visitor stopped before it reached her, though closer than before, and waited.

"Hello," Sanjuro said. "Welcome. I'm glad to see you." She started to name herself and her things again, but suddenly stopped. The Cibolan wanted her to come somewhere. She wasn't sure how she knew—it had said nothing, made no gesture—but she was convinced of it.

"Yes, I'll come with you," she said, nodding her head in the human manner, hoping that didn't convey something strange to a Cibolan. "Let me check in first." She deliberately used speaker on her com, instead of subvocal, so that the Cibolan could hear the conversation.

The Cibolan didn't shy away, though when Sanjuro spoke the creature looked...well, startled was the only way to describe it.

She sent a general call to the astrobio camp and reached a crew member. Good. No possibility of an argument with Kyo. "Tell Major Kyo I'm going somewhere with a Cibolan. I seem to have an invitation."

"Yes, ma'am," said a doubtful voice.

The Cibolan was looking around, as if trying to figure out where the other voice came from.

"Ma'am, I can send a couple of marines to go with you."

"I don't think that's a good idea. There's only one Cibolan here. I wouldn't want to outnumber him. Her. It. My com is set on trace, and I'll check in when I can. I better go; I'm making the Cibolan nervous." She signed off. "I'm ready," she said.

The Cibolan waited for her to come alongside, then turned toward town. They walked together, a meter apart. Sanjuro wasn't frightened. She felt both relaxed and eager; kind of odd, really, when she thought about it. She wasn't usually so calm when also excited.

The Cibolan set a quick pace, like someone used to walking. The slightly lower Cibolan gravity—ten percent less than Earth's—coupled with Sanjuro's hard workouts during the trip made it easy for her to keep up, despite the other's longer legs. She looked around as they walked toward town. About a kilometer from her camp site she saw people working in the fields. Their tractors had engines that made a steady rumbling noise, not particularly loud. Sanjuro wanted to examine the tractors and figure out how they worked. Something similar to electrical power, she suspected, but how did they generate it? Or store it? Given their planet's dearth of minerals, batteries must be an expensive item, unless the *Copernicus* mineral report was inaccurate, and that seemed unlikely. To Sanjuro's regret, her companion didn't stop and speak to the others. She noticed a couple of them staring.

A herd of animals grazed peacefully in one of the fields. Six-limbed, like the ones she'd seen before, but smaller. These had multicolored fur. Sanjuro was reminded of calico cats, though these came in a variety of fur colors, some in shades of blue, green, and purple, others orange, maroon, and red, about the size of border collies. Their fur seemed longer than that on the other animals she had seen.

On the outskirts of town she saw something new: a Cibolan wearing a robe open to the waist. Through the opening, she could see a pouch, containing what must have been a baby Cibolan. She turned to verify this. Yes, a small furry head poked up from the pouch. She turned so the vid recorder would pick it up. *That must be a female Cibolan*, Sanjuro thought, then chided herself. Too easy to generalize about gender that way, to make other assumptions. She realized she had been assuming her companion was male. Human beings had spent generations trying to eliminate sex stereotyping, and yet here she was, stereotyping. She didn't have enough data to be sure Cibolans had two sexes, and knew that even if they did, that that didn't mean that all Cibolans would fit neatly into one category or the other. Humans were primarily a two-sexed species, but there were other variants, and not all of them had come about after medical advances allowed intentional alterations.

With humans, Sanjuro could almost always tell gender—not just male or female, but the ambigendered and other variations. She knew human culture, recognized the tiny signals that people gave off. So far, though, she could see no differences in the Cibolans. *You need more data*, she told herself.

They were entering the town now. The streets were filled with people. Her companion said nothing to them, and they did not speak to it. Nor did they talk among themselves. Not that they existed in a soundless vacuum. Sanjuro could hear the tromp of feet and the clatter of wheels. From inside the buildings came the sounds of work: pounding hammers, whirring machines.

Except for the lack of conversation, the Cibolans seemed to be going about their business much like people in an Earth town. Most walked, though some traveled on a contraption like a bicycle with two sets of pedals, one for feet and one for arms, leaving the upper set of arms to guide it. The wheels resembled the ones on their tractors, covered with a substance that looked like rubber. She wondered if Kyo's botanist had found any sap-producing plants. The tires didn't look inflated.

A larger vehicle had masts as well as pedals. It boasted four wheels and could carry two people as well as goods. The day was calm, and the operator used the pedals. Sanjuro suddenly visualized the same vehicle with a full set of sails, making rapid time.

Judging by the buildings in this town, soil was the major local building material, though rocks were also in evidence. The walls looked thick—insulation against the winter, Sanjuro guessed. The structures were either round or square, mostly one-story, and built to accommodate even the tallest Cibolans. Almost all were brightly colored, some because of the rocks used in their construction, but most painted in some way. Apparently all colors were acceptable for homes and businesses, for she saw oranges and lilacs along with rich browns and reds. Many were more than one color, in patterns that reminded her of abstract art. She wondered if the designs had a meaning to the Cibolans.

The Cibolans studied her covertly, much as she was examining them. Perhaps they felt it impolite to stare at a stranger, as humans might. Odd, though, that no one greeted her companion. Her mind gave her a mental image of a prisoner being taken somewhere by a guard, recalled from a holo show of her youth. No one spoke to the guard or prisoner in that picture.

That image was replaced by an image of two Cibolans walking along, calmly, companionably, but quietly. *I wonder where I got that*, Sanjuro thought.

They entered a square laid out with market stalls. Sanjuro reeled. It was the place she had dreamed about: a bustling market, full of people buying and selling and bartering goods. At one corner, before a large audience, someone played a musical instrument. The tones did not follow any scale Sanjuro knew, but the sound was not unpleasant to human ears. In the background she heard the thumps of crates, a swoosh as a large quantity of something that looked like grain was poured into a bag, clicks that came as a set of pottery objects were placed in a box for easy carrying. But no conversations.

Everywhere around her people were buying and selling: food, clothing, household goods, even things that she labeled art because they had no obvious purpose. But they did not speak to each other. Small ones ran through the marketplace, or tugged at an adult's robes. Children, undoubtedly, but they did not cry or scream, even the ones who were obviously displeased.

Sanjuro felt too flustered to take in much information. She hoped the recorder was getting it. Everywhere she looked the things she saw tracked the dream, if not exactly, than so closely that it seemed as if it had been a holo instead of a dream. What could have brought on a dream so clear in detail? She grew increasingly uncomfortable as she continued to see image after image from her dream, so she sought refuge in professional thinking. How could the Cibolans have created all this culture—commerce, craft, even art—without language? The answer to both questions came to her abruptly. She stumbled, caught herself against a table, and sat down heavily on an unattended crate.

Telepaths. They must be telepaths. What else made sense? They didn't talk, because they didn't have to talk. Obviously they were communicating. They communicated mind to mind. The dream had come from images the Cibolans had sent her.

She tried to dismiss the idea. Scientists had seldom taken telepathy seriously; it was one of those fantastical ideas people liked to play with. Experiments with it came into fashion now and again. Sanjuro had taken part in some studies of telepathic potential back when she was first out of the academy. Tested fairly high, too. But nothing ever came of the tests: no one knew what to do with the information, and those who seemed to have some potential tested just slightly better than chance would indicate.

Even if these people are telepaths, Sanjuro said to herself, what does that mean? Telepathy would be the human term, but perhaps communicating without words didn't mean what humans thought it did. She felt dizzy, and leaned forward on her arms.

A sense of peace came into her mind, and her companion—whose existence she had forgotten—touched her shoulder lightly. She jumped, and it removed its hand. Sanjuro put her fingers on her wrist and felt her pulse still racing, yet her mind kept telling her to relax, be calm, she was not in danger. The calming message must be coming from the Cibolan. Though how could it be telling her to relax if it had no human words? It must be just projecting a feeling of calmness. Her pulse was slowing now, the dizziness passing.

She thought back to the initial encounter with the Cibolans. She had felt nervous when they first showed up, but she had relaxed as she spoke to them. She had assumed she'd calmed down as she did what she had been trained to do; it was what had always happened in combat. Now she wondered if they had calmed her. Perhaps they had given her other information as well—their equivalent of saying friend and opening one's hands.

Telepaths. Powerful telepaths. Could they read her mind as well as calm it down? Well, this Cibolan knew she was scared, didn't it? She tried to think of what she should think about. The words running through her head right now must be Greek to Cibolans. Her mind immediately produced hubris, and she giggled. She thought of her campsite, what the land around there looked like. She pictured the sloping fields, the vegetation, most of it red and magenta alien to her human eye, the spring nearby, herself drinking from the spring. Water here was the same as water on Earth.

And then a new image manifested her mind: a group of Cibolan children running through the field, playing some kind of game. A children's game—the moves were the spontaneous ones of those who didn't worry about how to do something. Sanjuro could not figure out the game. Not tag, not hide and seek, not one of the multitude of games that children played in the Solar System. They made no sound. They seemed happy, bouncy, perfectly normal, but they made no sound. One of them—a smallish one, with palomino-colored fur—moved away from the others. Staring at her (how, she wondered, does a mental image stare at you), it bowed deeply.

She looked at her companion, and it made the same bow. Sanjuro knew she could not have invented that picture. The Cibolan had seen her picture of the campsite and changed it.

It could both read her mind and project images and feelings into it. No question. Sanjuro got shakily to her feet. The Cibolan offered her an arm. They began to walk around the marketplace. They stopped at a booth selling housewares. Sanjuro picked up a device, and an image came into her mind of a Cibolan using it to cut the meat out of a nut. Another was a cookpot—she could have guessed that one, though. Her escort picked up another object—an eating utensil—and she watched the way it handled it with its fingers. No opposable thumb, but opposable fingers that worked quite as well.

Another booth sold fine containers. Sanjuro thought of them as dishes—her companion sent her an image of eating from them. They seemed to be made of some natural substance, a kind of clay perhaps. Except for the handles, made to accommodate Cibolan hands, they would be easily usable by humans.

Food of all description was sold in the marketplace. As she became more relaxed, Sanjuro began to pay attention to other senses besides sight and hearing. Smell became exciting: so many organic things in one place, and all of their odors competing. The air was perfumed with a rich, sweet smell similar to fruit. Other odors seemed more yeasty. She couldn't quite find a word to describe them, for while the aroma resembled that of foods she knew, it was different enough that saying something smelled like fresh strawberries, while close, did not describe it.

Her Cibolan stopped at a booth selling something to drink. It and the vendor apparently exchanged thoughts, because it handed the vendor an object—money?—and the vendor extended a jar of something toward Sanjuro.

The analyzer that could determine the components of the drink was one of the few bits of tech that was not implanted in her body, though it was connected to her system. Sanjuro reached in her pocket for the sensor, trying to think in images of what she was doing, and placed it on top of the container. Both Cibolans watched her with an expression akin to fascination on their faces. The reading said the drink was safe for human consumption, though likely fermented. It might have a kick. The drink tasted sharp, almost as if it contained hot peppers, but it felt soothing in her throat.

She sipped on it as they walked along—apparently taking the cup that held the drink was allowed. They moved out of the marketplace and onto a street. Soon they came to a building where a group of Cibolans were constructing the wind-driven bicycles she had seen earlier. Inside a Cibolan building for the first time—the marketplace was covered, but was essentially an outdoor space—she realized that they generated solar power through panels in the roof.

Manufacturing, commerce, energy generation. Their tech might not be as advanced as that of humans, but they were not primitive. The Cibolan showing her around must have been assigned to her. Likely they had some kind of government. Probably her companion had been explaining Sanjuro's presence to everyone as they went along; the communication was just happening outside of her frame of reference. The other Cibolans must be picking up all kinds of information about her.

Sanjuro felt handicapped. All these people could look inside her head, see what was there, even put things there, but she could direct nothing back at them. She felt like the blind in the land of the seeing. She'd met a blind man once, a derelict who'd damaged his retina in a fight. Repairable damage, for those who had the money, but he had nothing and no one. A pathetic man, begging. She'd felt a funny combination of pity and contempt. She wondered how the Cibolans regarded her, if they saw her as disabled. She imagined herself leaning on a crutch. Her Cibolan friend seemed unsure of how to respond. Perhaps the image made no sense, though surely these creatures suffered broken bones. Sanjuro shook off the idea. They were different, that was all. And a lot of communication could occur, if she would make the effort to think pictorially.

What should she show them? Earth, for all that she'd spent most of her life off planet. A quick inventory of images went by—the Grand Canyon, which she'd been to once on a forty-eight-hour leave; Mt. Fuji, on which she'd done the obligatory climb during her years at the Academy; graduation at the Academy. She settled on San Francisco: a large city, typical of Earth, jam-packed with people, but one she'd always found charming. She tried to run a mental camera, walk down the street, show people, businesses, homes. She remembered the quikrail under the bay, back to Berkeley, and the university. Then the front steps of her apartment building and stairs up to her place. A kitchen, herself preparing food. Dishes. Her bedroom, neat and spare. Another version of her sat at a table and ate; lay on a bed and slept.

The Cibolan answered with images of its life: a small building, a kitchen, a bedroom, even another adult and a child. Home.

Sanjuro nodded—an instinctive thing, a way to say "I understand" without speaking. Talking made no sense in this environment. But nodding likely conveyed as little as speech. She tried visualizing her home and the Cibolans back to back, flipping between them, as a way of showing she understood they meant the same things. The Cibolan responded with the images reversed, and then, apparently trying to copy her, nodded. The stiffness of the move convinced Sanjuro that nodding was not a Cibolan gesture.

They walked around the Cibolan town, Sanjuro getting some idea of what life was like and trying to respond with pictures of the equivalent human activity. After an hour or so, they ended up back at the marketplace, Sanjuro having responded eagerly to a picture of food.

She decided to check in first. Speaking aloud into com, she tried to put images in her mind so that the Cibolan would know what she was doing. The images she got back made it clear the Cibolan was still confused. It—he—it probably couldn't quite comprehend speech, must less speech with someone who wasn't physically present.

This time she got Kyo. "About time. You okay?"

"I'm fine. Better than fine. It's all amazing. And wonderful. They aren't primitive at all, Sumi. Their tech is simpler than ours, but they engage in trade, generate power, build machines, even create art."

"Damn! Fascinating. Bring me one. I want to see their genetics."

"Patience. I'm making friends, but I don't want to frighten him—it—before we know each other better."

"Good point. You might want to figure out the gender first."

"But there's something even more important: they're telepaths."

The "what" in response was so loud that several Cibolans turned to stare.

"Or something like that. They communicate mind to mind."

"How can you tell?"

"My companion sends me images and reads pictures from my mind."

"You're sure you're not leaping to conclusions?"

"No. Damn it, you can trust me to verify as I go along. There might be other explanations, but that's the one that makes the most sense so far. I'll write up my notes as soon as I get back, send you a full report."

"I'll look forward to it. You be careful."

"Always." She cut the communication on Kyo's snort.

She and the Cibolan went through a funny exchange of pictures as they shared a meal. Sanjuro tried various ways of explaining what the analyzer did, including sending pictures of a human eating fruit off a tree, and then keeling over, followed by pictures of one using the analyzer and declining to eat. She wasn't sure the information got across, but the Cibolan didn't seem frightened by the machine.

Lunch passed the "won't kill you" test, though the analyzer was unclear as to whether the food was nutritious for humans. And it evaluated taste poorly. She tried some of everything offered but found herself unable to finish several dishes that her friend ate with gusto. One dish completely lacked taste—or rather her tastebuds didn't seem to respond to it. Another was so sour that she could swallow only one bite. But the ones that included a peppery taste—similar to that of the drink she'd had earlier—pleased her mouth.

They walked back to her campsite after the meal. This time she recognized the pictures the Cibolan sent her as communication and explanation. The oversized calico-cat-like animals were raised for their fur; the large blue ones for their milk and meat. A quick series of mental flash cards turned the plants being cultivated in the fields into their dinner-table equivalents.

Back at camp, Sanjuro tried to explain her own culture. She showed the Cibolan the recording she had made of their first encounter—nervously, knowing that a human would have objected to being recorded without being told. The Cibolan seemed fascinated rather than angry. It watched the encounter several times.

The sun moved lower in the sky, and the Cibolan got up to leave. It sent her an image: sunset, then sunrise, and, with the sun higher in the sky, a picture of a gold-colored Cibolan coming into the camp. Sanjuro replied with a picture of herself stepping out to greet the Cibolan, and they parted.

She was exhausted, but she had to pull all of her data together. After rummaging for food, she sat down at her desk, organized all the recorder and analyzer data, and dictated everything she could remember about her experiences.

Kyo called as she was trying to resort all this data into readable form. "What happened to checking in?"

"Sorry. I just wanted to get things down while they were fresh. There's so much here."

"Still convinced they're telepaths?"

"Images show up in my head that I can't otherwise account for. And the Cibolan seemed to respond accurately when I pictured things in mine."

"So you're reading its mind as well?"

"No. I think I'm only seeing something sent to me. My guess is that they can waltz in and out of minds. Though they surely must know how to keep others out."

"A society in which everybody knows everything happening in everyone else's mind is not a pretty picture," Kyo said. "So I hope you're right."

"I imagine a lot of our mental activity is incomprehensible to them. We think in our own words, which they have no way of knowing. I don't even know if they have any words at all."

"Well, maybe you can teach them to talk. If they can."

"I haven't heard any of them make a sound. But they must hear. They reacted when I made noises, and I saw and heard one play an instrument, so they have music."

"Wow."

"Anyway, my friend's coming back tomorrow."

"Well, bring him—did you decide whether it was him or her?— over here and introduce us," Kyo said.

"In good time, my dear, in good time. And I'm still not sure about gender."

"Interesting that you can't tell easily. Well, sounds like you're making friends. Of course, they could just be fattening you up for the pot."

"What?"

"Old cannibal joke."

"Don't be so pessimistic."

"Well, they're sure being damn nice to trespassers."

Sanjuro said, "Maybe they're just smart enough to figure out what we are before they start shooting."

"Nice to think so. How's your headache?"

"Gone," she said, surprised to discover it. "It's been gone for hours."

"That's good, since you're down to work. Well, ta ta."

Sanjuro shut down her system. The final touches on the report could wait until morning. For the five minutes it took her fall asleep, she wondered what had happened to her headache.

# 5

The next few days passed in similar fashion. Sanjuro learned that on Cibola, the winters reached such bitterly cold levels that people were often confined close to home. Snow, for which they built reservoirs, was treasured. The robes worn by everyone were summer attire. For her part, Sanjuro showed her companion how humans talked among themselves—though she wasn't sure that her explanation of implanted com and tech devices came across well—and explained the history of machines developed for communication over distance. She also showed images of human cities throughout the Solar System, making an effort to show that many were on separate moons and planets, though still involved with the home planet.

It bothered her that she could not truly communicate, could not control what was passed on. She required a lot of thought and planning to figure out how to convey a concept, and she wondered how her Cibolan interpreted that. Her efforts to explain humans felt awkward and clumsy, which made her focus on human technological achievement. She wanted to show that she and her people weren't backward.

She did not show war. Neither did the Cibolan. Sanjuro wanted to think that they didn't fight, that perhaps mental communication made misunderstanding less severe. But she wasn't naive enough to believe it. She guessed the Cibolan was doing what she was trying to do: editing what was shared. Sanjuro had a bad feeling that she wasn't editing all that well—stray images came into her mind constantly. She didn't know if the Cibolan could make sense of them, but she hoped it found some of the uglier ones in-comprehensible.

After a couple of days, they got around to the tricky issue of gender. Sanjuro could think of no way to show this without graphic detail. Somewhat embarrassed—she felt like a kid show-ing dirty pictures—she projected images of two naked humans, male and female. She then showed them having sex in the most conventional manner, did a few changes of seasons to show the passage of time as the woman got larger, and then showed the woman giving birth.

The Cibolan might have been embarrassed, too, though Sanjuro had not yet learned to read its body language. But it showed two Cibolans sans their robes. Even undressed they looked almost the same, with no obvious genitalia. But they joined sexually in a manner not unlike humans, though Sanjuro could not see exactly what parts of their bodies connected. Her friend apparently shied away from showing the sex act too clinically. But, indeed, one of the pair began to grow, as with human pregnancy, while the other developed a pouch. A period of time—shorter than the human cycle, Sanjuro reckoned—and the female Cibolan gave birth. The newborn, helpless as a human child, or maybe more so, was then placed in the father's pouch. He carried the child it for a period about as long as the pregnancy, nursing it from nipples inside the pouch. Eventually the child was removed from the pouch for ex-tended periods, but from what Sanjuro could tell, it was carried in that way until it outgrew the space.

She was awed by the process, so similar and yet so different. Cibolan males must feel as attached to their children as the fe-males do. She conveyed to her companion the various ways hu-mans had developed to carry infants, none as convenient as the Cibolan pouch.

The next picture in Sanjuro's mind showed her companion giving birth. Female, then. Sanjuro responded with a picture of herself in the same condition. But when the other showed herself with another adult Cibolan, and one enough smaller to be a child,

Sanjuro could only respond with a picture of herself. She wasn't sure the idea that she was capable of giving birth, but had not, had come across. But then her friend sent images of Sanjuro boarding *Mercator* and traveling through space, and Sanjuro guessed she was saying that someone with work such as that might not have children. Or at least, might not be traveling with her family. Though that might be her own cultural interpretation.

On the next day, as they parted, the Cibolan—Sanjuro had begun to think of her as Sundown, though she was unsure of whether she had created that name on her own—conveyed that she would not see her for two sunrises and sunsets. Sanjuro was both disappointed and relieved. She hadn't slept enough in days. The Cibolan day was twenty-one human hours, rather than the Earth's twenty-four, and Sanjuro had been operating on about four hours of sleep each night. She also needed more time to go over her data and wanted to discuss it in person with Kyo.

Maybe Masire could take a shuttle down. He was entitled to take a little R&R.

After spending several days with the alien, Sundown once again traveled to the main city of Golden Mountain to report to Sorrel and other regional leaders. Although Sorrel was sharing some of the information with leaders from the other regions on their planet, Golden Mountain people met privately in advance of these discussions, in a comfortable room in Sorrel's residence, one with padded chairs covered in brightly colored materials and sunlight pouring in from a skylight open for the summer.

Sundown opened the presentation by sending a picture of Sanjuro making noises into a tiny machine that produced sounds. In the picture, Sanjuro showed an image of another person while making the noises, and Sundown thought the alien was trying to say it was communicating with that person. Sundown noted that it had not yet met any other aliens and had not observed how they communicated when they were together. The machines were so tiny, Sundown reported, that it could not see them, though the alien's explanation had shown them as devices. The observation of the alien's use of the machine added weight to the speculation that they communicated by making sounds. Still, the alien receives well and sends powerful images, Sundown added. The others—several of whom had been observing the other alien encampment from a distance—noted their agreement: all these creatures sent images constantly and were difficult to block.

The images are so chaotic, Sorrel observed. If they are communication, they must be difficult to understand.

That might be our lack of understanding of the alien mind, someone else pointed out.

Sundown sent them some of the other images Sanjuro had shown: the aliens' home planet, so far distant; children; a wide variety of amazing machines, from large vehicles for travel to small items for cooking; and war. Sundown did not think Sanjuro had deliberately sent images of war. In fact, Sundown had observed that the images disappeared quickly, as if the alien was trying to turn them off. But it was not difficult to read the images of beings pointing exploding objects at each other as war, especially when many of them doing so then fell to the ground and moved no more. Exploding objects were new to them, but war was not.

Sundown made it clear that Sanjuro had not directly sent images of war. The war pictures were fragmentary, disjointed, and Sundown suspected the alien lacked control over them. The alien is not damaged or ill, and it is not a baby, Sundown sent to the others, but it appears to have little control over what it sends and what it does not.

It was difficult for the others to grasp a sane adult who lacked control.

The information that your alien is not willing to share may be the most important information of all, a healer sent. These beings kill, but it does not want us to know this. What other important things are they concealing?

We kill, Sundown sent, but I have not told the alien about our wars either. I want it to see the good in us; it may want us to see the same in their people.

Or it may be trying to hide things that are a danger to us, Sorrel sent. Pay attention to the leaked information. Find out more.

Sundown agreed, but sent one more message: I like the alien.

><

Sanjuro and Masire lay entangled on the small bed in her shelter. "It's all so fascinating, and yet so frustrating," Sanjuro said. "On the one hand, Sundown's ability to see and send pictures speeds up the communication process. We know much more about each other's species than we would ever have learned by this point if they'd had an oral language.

"But on the other hand, I can't really ask a question, or explain anything abstract. And human culture is highly abstract. I don't even know if the Cibolans have any abstract concepts or if their entire culture is rooted in concrete images."

"You'll figure it out."

"I hope so. What would help is a whole team of people doing what I'm doing. We'd make faster progress. Though perhaps the Cibolans wouldn't go for it any more than Rao would."

"Fast isn't always good," Masire said. He was slowly stroking her leg as he said it, making her take it as a double entendre. But he went on: "If you and your friend take your time in getting to know each other, by the time you get around to dangerous subjects, you may have enough trust to deal with them. The Cibolans aren't likely to approve of all of our plans, and they could have some designs on us as well."

"Ah, the voice of reason. You're probably right. I just hope Rao gives me enough time to develop that relationship before demanding that we establish a permanent base here."

"Well, you have some data that should convince even skeptics like her and Vargas to go slow. Obviously the Cibolans aren't primitives."

"But they don't have rocket ships and rayguns, either, and I can't see any of them hovering over Washington in an invincible flying saucer like the evil aliens in all the old stories. If they aren't likely to be dangerous to us, I'm not sure I can get people to listen."

Masire nodded. "It's going to be hard, no question. You need to work on your strategy."

Sanjuro made a face. "I know. I want to just barrel in there, show everybody these wonderful creatures, and let that convince them to go slow."

"Treat it as battle. You wouldn't go off half-cocked into a battle." He paused. "Sanjuro, look. I don't want to tell you your job. But don't idealize the Cibolans, okay?"

She twisted on the bed to look at him.

"I mean, you and I, we've seen humans at their worst. We know our shortcomings. I've read a lot of history, and it's rife with people stealing from weaker groups. It's also rife with reinterpretation of those weaker groups as more virtuous than their oppressors. I'm not sure that's any truer than the original idea that the winners were more virtuous.

"The Cibolans look like a pretty culture to you right now. No dark side. And maybe they really don't have one," he said, cutting off her protest. "Like you keep saying, they're not human, and they don't have to react to the world as humans. But remember: they're in charge of what you're seeing, and there are things they aren't showing you."

"Plenty I'm not showing them, too," Sanjuro said. "I'm not naive, Masire. I know there's more there."

"I know you do. But you're also excited, living out your dream. Don't let the high you get from it blind you. Not only is it bad science, but it's not really going to help with the brass."

She gave him a reluctant nod. What he said made sense, but it wasn't what she wanted to hear.

# 6

Masire stayed until Sundown arrived the next morning. He wanted to meet her, and Sanjuro wanted to show Sundown another human. If Sundown was startled by his presence, she didn't let on. Masire followed Sanjuro's instructions to come up with a basic picture. He looked shocked, and turned to Sanjuro.

"I was thinking about the first landing we made. And suddenly I could see a group of Cibolans, watching us."

"Which probably means they've been watching us all along." Sanjuro flashed back to the landing. Masire and his troops had been armed. She wondered if the Cibolans had realized what the weapons were. She tried to keep the thought abstract, but an image of the marine troop made its way into her head. Damn.

Sundown didn't respond to the weapons image. She seemed engrossed in watching the two of them talk. She sent another picture, one of Sanjuro and Masire standing together, as if a couple. Sanjuro took it as a question and nodded, wondering if Masire was getting the same picture. Apparently he was, because he smiled and nodded.

After Masire left, Sanjuro decided it was time to introduce Sundown to Kyo and the astrobiology crew. The Cibolan seemed eager. Perhaps she had consulted with others during the time away and was ready to get more information.

Sanjuro pinged Kyo.

"About time. She going to let me run an analyzer over her?"

"I don't know. We'll play it by ear. I've only showed her the type we use to evaluate unfamiliar food. Maybe she'll think we're cannibals."

"You are not making my life easier. I want a male, too."

"Weren't you counseling me about patience only a few days ago?"

"Data, Caty. I need data."

The landcraft fascinated Sundown. She sent a barrage of questioning images as they traveled to the astrobio site—images Sanjuro interpreted as requests for explanations of how various parts of the machine worked. Sanjuro managed to show the solar collector, which Sundown apparently understood, but failed miserably at explaining how it hovered off the ground and why they could go so fast. She just drove the thing; she'd never given any thought to how it worked. She sent Sundown a picture of a bunch of people working on a similar vehicle, as close as she could come to saying, "I'll find you an expert."

The astrobio site felt alien after a week steeped in Cibola. Sanjuro wondered what it looked like to Sundown. The mini-city of gray instabuild shelters contrasted sharply with the bright colors of the Cibolan town. For that matter, humans in their mostly gray work uniforms looked bland in comparison to the diversity of colors of Cibolan fur and clothing. Even the range of variation in human skin and hair color—*Mercator*'s crew included people whose ancestors came from all parts of Earth—seemed small by comparison to that of the Cibolan mix. But maybe the Cibolans saw all that color quite differently. Figuring that out was going to take a long time; a scanner couldn't tell you what someone else saw.

Showing Sundown around the astrobiology site gave Sanjuro a pang. She realized that Sundown was communicating with all of these people, just as she did with Sanjuro. Their relationship was no longer unique. A silly thing to think, and Sanjuro tried to shake it off. She knew she'd get a chance to meet other Cibolans. Besides, she'd already seen lots of the native people, even if she hadn't really communicated with them.

Sundown was fascinated by the machines at the astrobio site. Kyo demonstrated how they used a scanner to come up with a genetic analysis by running one of a small animal and showing the result on the screen. She couldn't tell if Sundown grasped what the machine was capturing, but Sanjuro thought Sundown at least understood that it gave some information about the animal. Kyo managed to ask Sundown if she was willing to be analyzed as well. She consented, and Kyo sent her genetic makeup to the screen, then contrasted hers against diagrams she had of both animals and plants. Sanjuro had spent enough time in genetics lab to see major similarities between Sundown's structure and that of the other lifeforms on the planet.

Kyo said, "These folks are definitely native. The initial spark of life could have come from somewhere else, but the Cibolans clearly evolved from the earlier life on this planet."

"Making it theirs," Sanjuro said.

"By biological ethics," Kyo said.

Unbidden images of human settlers came into Sanjuro's mind. She pushed them aside. But Sundown, who had been studying the various diagrams, turned to look at her. She sent no question, but Sanjuro felt sure she'd picked up the settlement image.

No one in the astrobio camp could explain how vehicles worked, but a tech was eager to try her hand at explaining the scanner to Sundown. Sanjuro left the Cibolan with her, though she worried about how much other data Sundown would pick up from human minds, and sat down with Kyo to go over her reports and deal with administrative matters.

"So how are things here?" Sanjuro asked as they finished up.

"Well, Chang has figured out how we can tweak a few genes in some of the plant life to make it nutritious for humans." The major sounded sarcastic.

"I gather that has a higher priority than just figuring out what the different plants are."

"Making it possible for humans to live here always has a higher priority. You know that."

"Better watch how you think about that around Sundown. She may start to figure out some of our long-term plans."

"The Cibolans will have to know about them sooner or later. At least there's room on the planet."

"Not if humans come in here the way we have most places," Sanjuro said.

Kyo sighed. "Yeah. By the way, are you sure Sundown's female?"

"She's been pregnant. Why?"

"I saw nothing on the scan about her reproductive organs. It's like she doesn't have any."

"That's odd. I've seen babies, and her image of birth seemed very similar to that of humans. So did her description of sexual behavior."

Kyo frowned. "It's just strange. I'm seeing the same thing in other animals, even in ones nursing young. I need to watch the birth process. But I haven't come across any pregnant animals, and we're beginning to think they only give birth in spring."

"Given winter here, that would make sense. But I've seen a few pregnant Cibolans. I'd guess they are like us: not tied to seasons in giving birth, even if their animals are."

"Maybe we could watch one of them have a baby," Kyo said, her eyes lighting up.

"It's too early to ask to see that," Sanjuro said.

"We need more data."

"We need to develop a good relationship before we can demand more data."

Kyo sighed. "You're probably right, but work on it, okay?"

Sanjuro grinned. "Patience, Sumi. Patience."

"I can't be patient. We're going to run out of time."

Sanjuro hoped Kyo was joking, but she sounded quite serious.

Sundown's life had settled into a routine of several days spent with the alien followed by meetings with Sorrel and advisors to discuss the findings. Sundown knew the importance of sharing the information and agreed with Sorrel that they must exercise caution before they told others what they found, but all this work meant no trips to the observatory. And no one else was willing to do it. Even Iron—who was fascinated by the alien machines—refused to spend long hours trying to communicate with them. And Iron worried about the time Sundown spent in alien company.

Others were observing the aliens, but they did so from a distance. Sundown had been included in meetings where they gave reports, but was aware that Sorrel was not sharing everything they sent. While Sorrel's leadership style appeared very open, Sundown knew that it would take in information from many different sources without sharing everything it learned.

Sorrel's child and heir had joined this meeting. Like Sundown, Sorrel's heir, Fire, was middle-aged. Fire had multicolored fur that mixed deep reds and gold and affected a regal bearing. It clearly thought its father should take a stronger stand about the aliens. They are a threat, Fire sent. These settlements they are planning—the planet cannot support so many life forms. There is not enough water, not enough shelter.

Sundown had reported the images picked up from Sanjuro about settlements. But the other observers had gleaned considerably more on this subject from observing the astrobiology site. Some of what they had discovered had not made sense until they went over it with Sundown, who was learning to work with the alien images. There seemed to be no question but that the aliens intended to settle on their planet. The idea disturbed Sundown as much as it did the others. These aliens were fascinating, but Sundown did not want to change their lives to accommodate them.

But, Fire sent, how will they react when we tell them they cannot settle here?

Sundown had no answer.

# 7

The sky was just starting to get light when Sanjuro pulled up at the astrobio site. She'd been asleep when the call had come about an emergency holoconference with the brass at 0800, *Mercator* time. The ship was operating on Earth standard time, even though the planetside operation had shifted to Cibolan. Owing to its orbit, *Mercator* would be directly overhead then, making the communication lag time minimal.

"What's this all about?"

Kyo shrugged. "No idea. But it's big. Rao called me from *Mercator*. She wouldn't have left the asteroid belt for anything less than a major crisis."

They convened in the main astrobio lab. Several techs were setting up holoconference equipment. State of the art stuff—the *Mercator* crew would look life size.

"What makes you say crisis? It might be something positive," Sanjuro said.

"Not from the tone of Rao's voice."

"Oh. Then why aren't we shuttling up to *Mercator*?"

Kyo shrugged again. "I guess they didn't want to take the time."

"They must have waited for Rao to get over from the belt. Why didn't they bring us up while she was en route?"

"You got me."

Coffee was available in the back corner of the lab. Sanjuro wandered back to grab a cup and ran into a yawning Chang.

"I wish those idiots would recognize that we're in a different system and reset their time. It's driving me nuts, going back and forth between planet time and ship time."

Sanjuro said, "Getting used to the shorter day is stressful, and since they don't have to, I can see why they don't."

"Maybe so, but they could at least remember that our time is different when they schedule meetings. When Major Kyo mentioned that in one of our holo conferences, though, the Colonel suggested we just keep Earth standard time down here."

Sanjuro laughed. "Well, she's not a biologist. I suppose rocks look the same in any light."

They joined the crowd sitting around the table. The connection went live, showing Vargas, Marley, Pham, Rao, Masire, and Gervaise sitting in a row. None of them smiled. They were in the auditorium on *Mercator*. The holo projection allowed a glimpse of *Mercator* crew seated before them. A second projector brought in the Asteroid crew, who must have been a good ten minutes behind everyone else.

Vargas stood up. His image broke up into tiny cubes for a few seconds and then settled into a projection so clear it felt like he was in the room with them. His face was drawn, and black circles shadowed his eyes. "Ladies and gentlemen, we have some new orders from the System. We're putting them out to everyone at once, so that there will be no confusion or misunderstandings.

"Our orders with respect to the *Cortez* have changed. We are now instructed to send them the same reports we are sending back to the System."

Several people in the astrobio lab said "What?" loudly. A few others cursed. A murmur of voices on holo demonstrated that those on the ship felt the same way.

"Quiet, please," Vargas said. Everyone shut up.

"I realize that some of you may disagree with this order. However, this matter is not open for discussion. We were given specific orders, and we will follow them to the letter. We have been given coordinates and will be setting up a regular A/ND exchange with the *Cortez*. Given *Cortez*'s rate of travel, those messages will take about a month to arrive now, and will go back and forth even faster as they travel out here. Are there any questions?"

No one was foolish enough to ask any. The projectors shut down, and everybody began talking at once. Kyo had to shout to restore order. "Look. Obviously this is a done deal. You heard the Admiral; we follow this to the letter. Now go get some real breakfast and get to work."

The crew was still muttering as they left the lab. Sanjuro walked alongside Kyo.

Kyo said, "You predicted this."

"Wish I'd been wrong."

"Me, too. We're going to lay the groundwork, and they're going to come in and kick us out. What'll you bet?"

"I never bet against a sure thing," Sanjuro said. "Though I suspect Rao and Vargas aren't through fighting yet. You heard how Vargas emphasized following the orders to the letter. I got the feeling he meant the letter rather than the spirit."

"Good point. But if they're still fighting, it's for military control of the Asteroid Belt. Bet you anything they sell out control of the planet."

Sanjuro made a face. "Kuso! Now you sound like me."

"Didn't mean to go that far. But you know how these compromises go."

Sanjuro sighed. She knew all too well.

# 8

A few days later Sanjuro went to town to meet Sundown's partner and child. Their home was a mud brick building, with a low stone wall setting off a small courtyard that held carefully arranged rocks and a few small plants. The outside walls of Sundown's house were magenta. The other homes in the neighborhood were similar mud-brick structures, but they varied in color—some yellow, some green, and one bright red. All of them sported courtyards, though the mix of rocks and plants differed.

The inside of Sundown's house was painted a bright yellow-orange. A large abstract tapestry took up most of one wall.

Sundown's partner—perhaps spouse would be the best word— was about the same height, but broader across the torso. His fur was steel blue in color, and Sanjuro found herself calling him Iron in her mind. Perhaps the images Sundown had sent her in introducing them had brought on that word.

The child was not yet grown, but was large enough that Sanjuro guessed he was adolescent and male, perhaps because he looked more like Iron than Sundown. The images he sent her way were more entertaining than those of his parents. He seemed fascinated by the idea that humans spoke out loud to each other. He sent fanciful pictures of humans, talking in groups. Sanjuro pictured other forms of talking for him: speeches, plays, singing. Though, of course, it was all silent.

Then he sent a picture of Sanjuro speaking. She took it as a request, and said, "Hello, it's nice to meet you."

The child jumped at the sound of her voice. He started to ask for something else, but stopped. Sanjuro assumed his parents had told him not to pester her.

Later in the day, Sanjuro and Sundown walked to the side of town away from her campsite and started up into the hills. It was colder there. Sanjuro turned the heat up on her bodysuit, though Sundown's only concession to the temperature change had been to pull on some trousers.

They walked for several hours, gradually going up, until they reached the top of the highest hill. A small building sat atop it. Sanjuro found she could see in all directions. Behind her she could just see the colorful buildings of the village over the tops of the vegetation through which they had walked. In the other direction, toward the setting sun, an amoeba-shaped lake dominated the landscape. Golden highlights sparkled in its olive-green waters, and then began to disappear as the sun sank behind the magenta hills just beyond the lake.

They watched until the light faded from the sky and the moon began to rise. Sanjuro couldn't remember the last time she'd seen a dramatic sunset. She visualized some spectacular views of Earth's sun as a way of saying thank you and showing that she also appreciated nature. Then she turned to head down the hill, assuming they should be getting back. Dark would arrive long before they returned. But Sundown hadn't brought her up for the view. Instead, the alien led her into the building.

Inside, Sanjuro saw two telescopes. One was enormous, as big as one she'd visited once while in grad school out in the small bit of remaining desert in Southern California, though not as big as ones she'd heard about, located in more remote parts of Earth and on the outlying moons and planets of the System. The other was smaller and older, but still a professional tool.

Her friend sat on the stool in front of the smaller one and adjusted knobs, then gave way to Sanjuro. The image she saw was blurry. Sundown showed her how to fix it. The controls had clearly been designed with four hands in mind, though, and setting the focus for her eyes took some time. By the time they finished, the sky had darkened considerably, revealing vast quantities of stars. As she stared, awed at the sight as she had always been in front of telescopes, something moved across the sky. After a moment, she realized it was *Mercator* in orbit.

She put the picture of *Mercator*'s movement in her mind. Sundown seemed excited, and replaced her at the scope. Her fingers quickly readjusted focus, and she sent Sanjuro a picture of what she saw. Sanjuro visualized a sequence of images: the light moving across the sky, gradually growing until it looked like a spaceship, then a door opening in its side and a view of the people within, herself included. She had tried before to show the ship, but this time her effort was more successful.

Sundown sent her pictures of Sanjuro in the ship, and Sanjuro on the planet, and Sanjuro showed her the shuttle flight. Then Sanjuro, growing more ambitious in her efforts to communicate, showed the ship on Earth. Dramatic license, she told herself, not feeling up to explaining space stations. People got on, the ship went into the sky. And then Sanjuro tried to convey the passage of time by showing a series of seasons—winter, spring, summer, fall—and then repeating the sequence. Though she hadn't been on Cibola long enough to see their actual seasons, the planet's orbit and rotation had been precisely calculated, and she knew it went through a pattern of seasonal changes over what humans would label a year. She could think of no better way to convey the passage of time, if not the actual distance. Given that Sundown was an astronomer, it was reasonable to assume that the Cibolans had figured out light years and other basics of astrophysics, but Sanjuro could think of no way to explain that in images.

Sundown sat, as if taking this all in. Sanjuro had figured out that sometimes Sundown was communicating with others when she did not respond immediately. She knew Cibolans didn't have to be in close proximity to communicate—Sundown had shown herself sending a message back to Iron as a parallel to one of Sanjuro's com messages to Kyo. And then Sundown, too, conveyed the passage of time and ended with a picture of herself as a child, an image with which Sanjuro had grown familiar, sitting in this very building, on the lap of an adult Cibolan, peering into the older telescope and seeing a light streaking across the sky. But when she let it grow to look like the pictures Sanjuro had shown her of *Mercator* and then showed the opened door, there were no people in it.

They saw *Copernicus*, Sanjuro thought. She responded with an image of *Copernicus*, and showed her the inside, all machines. And then showed *Copernicus* on Earth.

Sundown nodded—she'd gotten better at the nod. And Sanjuro thought she had begun to understand that humans used machines to gather and transmit information. She showed the launch of *Copernicus*, flashed through a rapid sequence of seasons changing—surely the Cibolans had some better way of showing passage of time—showed it in the sky over Cibola, tried to convey the image of it taking pictures, and then showed Earth again and people looking at pictures of Cibola. Finally, she showed herself getting on *Mercator* and its launch.

Sundown responded with images of all the people in the landing party, and then showed Vargas and the others leaving.

Sanjuro adjusted the telescope until it focused on the asteroid belt and showed it to Sundown. She tried to put everything she knew about asteroids into pictures. She showed the geologists on hunks of rock, taking samples and using devices similar to those used by the astrobio team to analyze the samples

The images Sundown sent seemed confused, so Sanjuro visualized metals she had seen on Cibola and showed Cibolans digging them from the ground. In reply, Sundown sent an image of a small coal-fired forge, placed on an asteroid. Sanjuro nodded. The process was different, but the principle was the same.

They slept that night in the telescope hut, on mats left there for the purpose. On the way back to her camp the next day, after leaving Sundown in town, Sanjuro let her mind wander. Sundown had developed a good understanding of why the humans had come. But Sanjuro didn't know what the Cibolans thought about the human presence. The Cibolans had treated her well, and she and Sundown had developed something that could only be described as friendship, yet she knew she wasn't getting all the information she needed.

Sundown wasn't telling her anything about the Cibolan reaction to humans. Sanjuro had tried to ask, but it was a difficult thing to phrase in pictures, and Sundown hadn't seemed to understand what she was saying—or had pretended not to.

Sanjuro knew the Cibolans were picking up all kinds of information out of her mind and out of those of all the others on planet— perhaps even those on *Mercator*. She wasn't sure they could reach that far, but from the discussions with Sundown about *Copernicus* she was beginning to suspect that they had some method of doing it. Those images had to be a chaotic jumble, perhaps impossible to comprehend, but Sundown hadn't asked her anything about them. Sanjuro couldn't help but worry about what they might be concluding based on that information.

She also wondered what information about Cibolan culture Sundown was withholding. Sanjuro had gleaned some understanding of communication, and of small-town life, but she didn't know much more than that. There was a whole planet here; likely the other societies differed from Sundown's. The society Sanjuro had been shown seemed very peaceful, and she wanted to assume that telepathy led to a society with little conflict. But it wasn't reasonable to make that kind of judgment based on small-town life. An alien visiting the university compound on Luna might assume humans were cooperative folks, too, since academic conflicts were not obvious to the untrained eye and violence rarely occurred. They wouldn't see the poverty that still existed on Earth, the exploitation of the workers in the Asteroid Belt, the local wars, the trade conflicts conducted in civilized language.

Masire had been right to remind her not to idealize the Cibolans. She didn't want to think Sundown was withholding anything horrible, but hope was not an appropriate standard for learning about a new culture.

# The Weave

Sundown had spent enough time watching Sanjuro use machines for everything from travel to communication to analysis of component parts to have some understanding of how the ship with no life forms must have operated, but it was difficult to find a way to explain it to others. The night before the next meeting with Sorrel, Sundown practiced on Iron: a ship, full of machines, first orbiting the planet, then traveling to the other planets and the Asteroid Belt, taking pictures, analyzing contents.

Iron replied with an impression of the vast distance between the planet and that ship. How could it see so much?

Sundown didn't know the answer to how, but Sanjuro had shown her some of the pictures the ship had taken. Sundown showed Iron a picture of the street in front of Sorrel's home. From the ship with no minds, Sundown sent. Iron waved all four hands in disbelief, but accepted that the picture was real.

When Sundown showed pictures of the ore in the asteroids, Iron began to get excited. These were recent pictures from the geology team, taken at close range. Anyone who had ever looked at a mineral outcropping—and Iron had seen many—would recognize what they represented.

Where, Iron demanded.

Sundown showed it the asteroids rollicking along in their orbits.

Again Iron waved all four hands.

Sundown showed Iron more pictures from the geologists: their operation center on one large asteroid, their refining apparatus orbiting in sync with the rocks, their extraction operation. Sundown sent images of rock after rock, letting Iron know that all contained such wealth.

This time Iron's hands were still, but its mind formed an image of a simple mine on the planet, one used to extract what bits of iron ore they could find. More than this, Iron asked.

Much more, Sundown sent.

The asteroids belong to us, not to long travelers, Iron sent. These rocks are ours.

We cannot get to the asteroids, Sundown sent back. We do not know how to build a ship that will travel that far. And until the aliens came, we did not know the riches available in that region. They found them. On their planet, things found on unused land belonged to the finder. Under that principle it was hard to argue that the aliens had no rights. Sundown reminded Iron of this.

Iron waved it away. Those minerals, that iron, they belong to us.

We cannot get it without them, Sundown sent back.

But we cannot let them take it. We need it.

Sundown sat quietly, digesting this and then sent: If we can find a way to work together with the aliens...

And then it was Iron who sat quietly, thinking.

# 9

The big conference room on *Mercator* was packed. Rao and her senior people had come in from the asteroids. Sanjuro sat next to Kyo and wondered whether she should have linked in from the astrobio site on planet or even from her own camp instead of coming up to the ship. Maybe she would have found it easier to deal with Rao if she'd been looking at her on a tiny holoscreen. But though the time delay was only a minute or so, it would have been difficult for her to do anything but a canned presentation from her camp. Besides, all the other scientists planetside had shuttled up.

Rao called the meeting together. Vargas, Marley, and the rest of the senior Space Corps crew were sitting in, but the meeting was officially a Sci/Tech show and Rao's baby.

"I'm sure everyone has been reading each other's reports," Rao said, in the tone of a teacher who is convinced no one did the homework. "So your summaries should be concise, just enough to give us the high points. Major Case."

"Well, boys and girls..."

No one missed Rao's wince.

"The good news is, *Copernicus* was right. There's plenty of Helium-3 in the asteroid regolith, enough to set up regular travel between here and the System and provide fusion power both here and there. And enough to get us started on our way farther out into the universe."

People clapped. Rao didn't appear to like that either.

"And that's just in the asteroid belt itself. From what Admiral Vargas tells me, it looks like we've got substantial amounts of Helium-3 on most of the moons in the Doradoan System."

Vargas gave what was probably intended to be a modest smile.

Sanjuro sent Kyo a message. "What does Vargas have to do with it?"

"He brought back the big shuttle as soon as they got the station up and operating in the belt and sent a Space Corps crew out to do a more detailed read on what's on the other planets."

"I thought the big shuttle was staying out in the asteroid belt in case they needed a quick exit at some point."

"So did Rao."

Sanjuro look at Kyo and raised her eyebrows.

"Vargas wants to make sure Space Corps gets some exploring credit," Kyo sent back. "And the pilots are bored—you know pilots. The smaller shuttles can't run a planet scan, so they needed the big one."

Case was explaining about the high concentration of platinums in the asteroids as well. "We can finance other operations out here on the sale of the rhenium alone."

Sanjuro got a ping. Kyo had sent, "Do you suppose the companies behind the *Cortez* already have a deal for the rhenium?"

She sent back, "Maybe. If Rao's told *Cortez* all the fine points. Odds are she's keeping something back. They're probably cutting Helium deals, too. Lots of money to be made in Helium-3."

Kyo wrinkled her nose.

Case had turned the platform over to the senior geologist, who was giving some details of the geological history. His studies suggested the belt was the remains of a onetime planet struck by a major meteor. In addition to the platinums and other things valuable enough to ship back to the System, the asteroids contained high concentrations of iron and other more basic minerals, things that would be useful for developing a local economy.

Another ping. "I bet some company is going to make a fortune selling iron to Cibolans," Kyo had sent.

This time it was Sanjuro who made a face.

The gist of the report was to confirm the *Copernicus* data: valuable elements existed here in such quantities as to outweigh the expense of bringing miners and other techs—robotic and human—up here from the System. Given enough time, the proceeds would pay the cost of establishing a permanent presence here and even fund the process of future exploration from this point.

Rao turned to Kyo. "So, Major, what do your studies show about the future of human settlements on Cibola?"

"The planet is habitable by humans and, outside of the shorter day, will be comfortable for us without any significant bioforming. The native plants, both wild and cultivated, are generally edible by humans, though few, if any, provide appropriate nutrition. However, Lt. Chang thinks we can modify some of them to work for us. Some of our own plant and animal life will likely thrive here as well, if we can provide sufficient water. And we're working on a number of experiments with the microbial life. At a minimum, we'll be able to get some energy sources out of them."

"Excellent," said Rao, about to go on.

"However," Kyo said, determined to get this point in. "Cibola is a relatively fragile ecosystem. The annual rainfall is much less per square meter than Earth's, and it falls in a spotty pattern, roughly corresponding to the Cibolan settlements. The planet won't support a large human population in addition to the Cibolans without some alterations."

"But that's a much simpler type of bioforming, isn't it, Major? Much like what we've done on Earth in the Sahara and the Arctic. We can do it in a few years, unlike the decades it would take on a less hospitable planet."

Kyo admitted that was true. "One other point I'd like to make, ma'am, if I could."

Rao sighed, but nodded.

"We've made one very important finding from a biological point of view: all of the life on Cibola—or at least, all of the life we've run into so far—has a similar genome. Their DNA includes different nucleotides, but it forms a similar structure to human. Even the simplest plant matches ninety percent of the genome of the sapient life forms."

"Thank you, Major. I'm sure the biologists back in the System will find your study fascinating. Captain Sanjuro, can we have a brief report on the dominant life form?" She emphasized the word "brief."

Sanjuro took a deep breath. "Thank you, ma'am. The most interesting fact about the Cibolans is their apparently telepathic means of communication. I say "apparently telepathic" because while I have enough data to document that they send information from mind to mind, I don't yet understand how this process works. Biological scans of the Cibolans haven't provided us with much help on this point.

"I have been able to establish communication by means of forming pictures in my head and receiving pictures back from the Cibolans. This, of course, limits us to exchanges of information that can be done through visualization."

"They really don't speak at all?" The interruption was from Captain Marley.

Rao glared at him.

"Not that I've seen, sir. Biological scans show the presence of vestigial vocal cords, so I believe they might have had speech capability at some point in their evolution. They clearly hear."

"Thank you, Captain Sanjuro," Rao said in an icy voice. "I suggest those who want more data read Sanjuro's extensive reports. Or speak with her privately. We have more work to do.

"Admiral," she went on, "I'd like to suggest that we have enough information to begin to move forward toward establishing a more permanent presence in this System. I imagine that about another month's worth of data gathering will tell us where to locate the initial human colony on the planet. Given how little trouble the astrobio team has faced in conducting their studies, we can report officially that the Doradoan System is safe for human settlement. The SSU should start recruiting miners. The sooner they get started, the sooner we can have a real operation up here. We don't have anything like enough robot potential to do more than scratch the surface of the mining operation; we also need human miners and robotics engineers. And of course"—she looked directly at Sanjuro—"the *Cortez* will be arriving all too soon. We'll need some place to put those people."

It didn't take telepathy for Sanjuro to hear Rao think "and not in my asteroid belt." Or to recognize that Rao still thought she'd had something to do with the *Cortez*.

"Let's finish the next month of data gathering before we send off the official report," Vargas said. "But we'll send an optimistic preliminary."

Rao's frown deepened, but she said, "That will be fine, sir. Is there anything else?" Her voice made it clear there wasn't supposed to be.

"Ma'am," said Sanjuro. Kyo kicked her shin, but she ignored her. "A month isn't going to give me enough time to find out everything we need to know about the Cibolans before we establish a settlement." She rushed on before Rao could cut her off. "While the telepathic process makes communication possible, it's still slow going. We'll know more in another month, true, but I doubt that even then we'll be able to communicate well enough to get Cibolan permission for a human settlement."

The edges of Rao's mouth turned up. "Captain, have you discovered a major source of weaponry down there that *Copernicus* missed?"

"No, ma'am."

"Or any other way they can stop us from doing as we please?"

"No ma'am, but that doesn't mean we aren't obligated to negotiate with them."

Kyo kicked her again, harder.

"And why is that, Captain?" No way to miss the amused tone in her voice.

"It's their planet. That's part of the significance of the biological findings. The Cibolans evolved there, from the lower life forms.

We have the obligation to respect that; we would certainly expect the same of any aliens who landed on Earth."

Rao laughed outright. "Where do you get your ideas, Captain? Fantasy stories about intergalactic compacts? I agree we should try to avoid wiping the creatures out, but the planet is far from full. There's plenty of room for us both. We'll even give them the advantage of increasing their rainfall and expanding their usable land area by reducing the glaciers. They certainly can't exploit the wealth of the asteroid belt. Don't your reports show that the most advanced tech they have is a solar-powered tractor?"

The sarcasm made Sanjuro furious. She said, "Commander Gervaise, isn't there a legal finding that if an intelligent life form is genetically related to the rest of life on a planet, it can be assumed that it has rights to that planet?"

Gervaise, who was sitting between Vargas and Marley, frowned. "The legal precedent is pretty tenuous, Captain. It's included in a proposed statement of principles for exploration, but the SSU has never officially adopted the statement. These are the first aliens we've actually dealt with."

"But there's a strong ethical argument for it, correct?"

"Of course, but that's all very theoretical."

Rao said, "If you're quite finished, Captain Sanjuro…"

Sanjuro felt Kyo dig the heel of a shoe into her toes, but didn't let herself wince. She stood up, yanked her foot out from under Kyo's heel, and turned to Vargas. "Sir, please give me more time to improve the lines of communication, so that we can negotiate properly with these people."

Kyo said, in a no-nonsense command voice, "Sanjuro, sit down and shut up."

If anyone else had said it, Sanjuro would have ignored it. But from Kyo it was a wake-up call. She sank into her chair, looked at Kyo, and knew she had to apologize as well. "I'm sorry, Colonel, Admiral. I…I'm just very focused on my work."

Rao glared at her, but Vargas said, "We understand, Captain. All of us are inclined to find our own work more important than anything else. But we must keep in mind the overall mission." He smiled at her. "And we're relying on you, Captain, to develop a good working relationship with these Cibolans, so that our settlements will go smoothly."

Rao said, "If there's nothing more?" in a voice that left no doubt that there had better not be. "Then this meeting is adjourned."

Kyo grabbed her arm. Sanjuro didn't want to meet the Major's eyes—she'd never seen her so angry before. "Bakatare! You fucking…" Kyo's com went off. She glanced at it briefly, and said, "Wait for me in my quarters, Sanjuro."

She said, "Yes, ma'am," without a trace of sarcasm and went.

About half an hour passed before Kyo got there, which was time enough for Sanjuro to think back over everything she'd said and come to the conclusion that idiot was indeed the correct word. She leaped to her feet when Kyo walked in.

"Sit down, Caty," Kyo said in a tired voice. "I'm not pulling rank on you anymore."

She sat on the edge of her chair and watched Kyo slump down on her bunk. Their knees almost touched; Kyo's *Mercator* quarters were bigger than hers, but only marginally. "I'm sorry. I just lost it."

Kyo waved a hand.

The expression on her face was hard to read, but it looked more sad than angry. *I must really be in trouble,* Sanjuro thought. She said, "Go ahead and chew me out."

"Not necessary. You already know how stupid that was. Lecturing Lakshmi Rao on ethics! Not to mention how nasty it was to drag Gervaise into the fight with no warning."

She winced. "It was a sudden flash. I thought maybe if she told them it was illegal, they'd listen."

"But it's not illegal. Surely you didn't think she'd make up law, did you?"

Sanjuro looked at the floor. "We've talked about this stuff. I know she agrees with me about the ethics. Oh, hell, I wasn't really thinking."

"Even if she agrees with you, she's stuck with the law as it is, not the law as she'd like it to be."

"I know. They just took me by surprise. As cynical as I've sounded, I had no idea they'd move this fast. I thought I'd have more time to build up a relationship with the Cibolans so we could negotiate this sort of stuff properly."

Kyo sighed. "The *Cortez* situation is putting pressure on them. Vargas is constantly back and forth with the System about how the corporations are going to fit in. Rao feels about the asteroid operation like you feel about Cibola—she'll sell out everything to protect her empire. I doubt she can pull it off—after all, most of what the companies want can be found out there—but she's going to do everything she can."

"Well, hell, the asteroids really belong to the Cibolans, too."

Kyo threw up her hands. "Don't you get it, Sanjuro? It doesn't matter. They don't control them. Would you quit thinking about the theoretical issues and address reality? The *Cortez* expedition changes things. We don't have time to spend meeting the locals; the corporations are going to come in and run over us all sooner rather than later. Rao and Vargas have decided on a strategy of giving them crumbs, in the hope of buying time."

"And we're the crumbs."

"Afraid so."

"You're telling me that Vargas and Rao aren't going to listen no matter what I say."

"I'm telling you that they aren't the real enemy. Have you looked at all the corporations behind the *Cortez*? They aren't just energy firms, mining companies, biotechs. Kuso, some of them are even planning theme parks on Cibola."

"Theme parks!" Sanjuro immediately imagined Cibolans in colorful "ethnic" costumes, waiting on humans.

"Don't scream at me. It isn't my idea, and anyway it won't happen until there's enough human population out here to take advantage of them. But that should give you some idea of what we're up against."

Sanjuro ran her fingers through her hair. "We're just here to make sure the place is safe for humans." Her voice was bitter.

"Did you really think they'd sent us so you could meet aliens? Or even so Rao could explore a bunch of rocks?"

"No. I just didn't want to believe we'd waltz in and take the planet over."

"No," Kyo said softly. "Neither did I. It's their planet, and it's not right. But you can't stop it by calling Rao names."

"I've got to apologize, don't I?"

"Yes. Formally, in writing, and with sincerity."

Sanjuro made a face at her.

"With sincerity," she repeated.

"Yes, ma'am."

"I'd like to see a draft by 1700 hours."

"Yes, ma'am."

"And can the 'yes, ma'ams.' You know I hate that."

"Sorry. I do it automatically when you act like my commanding officer."

Kyo grinned. "Just because I don't do it all the time doesn't mean I don't know how."

"I really am sorry, Sumi."

"Get out of here, Caty. Go get the letter written and I'll smooth things over with Rao."

⤜

Sundown was thinking about the last day she had spent with Sanjuro, before the alien had shuttled up to the ship. They had traveled over the astrobiology site, where one of the support techs had explained the inner workings of the landcraft. Sundown hadn't understood all the concepts, but had kept notes of them to share later with Iron, who might.

Then Sundown had sat with Kyo and several of the researchers, explaining the uses of various plants and answering questions about the wildlife on Cibola. Some of the questions were about flying creatures, a confusing concept. There were no flying animals on the planet. Flying bugs, yes, but no animals. Sundown caught images from the others of a collection of creatures flying in a formation, of others in a large plant with bushy leaves singing loudly, of a single animal—beaked, with strange feathery fur—standing on a fence. Obviously Earth had such animals, but Sundown found the whole idea puzzling. How could animals fly?

For that matter, how could people fly, even in their machines? No one at the site had been able to explain how their spaceship worked, or even how to operate the shuttles that they used to get back and forth to their large ship. Sundown could tell that the machines were very heavy—too heavy to float on a wind, too heavy not to be bound by gravity. The images Sanjuro sent of engines implied that power and speed made up for the weight, but while Sundown was prepared to believe it, that belief was based on trust, not understanding.

While at the site, Sundown had picked up images of planned human settlements on the planet, though none of that information had been given to her directly. The humans gave off an evasive air. The settlements were something they could not help thinking about all the time but that they did not want to share.

Even Sanjuro refused to answer when Sundown asked her direct questions on their way back. Sundown picked up images suggesting conflict between Sanjuro and some of the other aliens, but Sanjuro didn't want to explain those images either.

Maybe Sundown wouldn't have understood the explanations. But the humans were uncomfortable about something, and settlements had something to do with it. Something was about to shift.

# 10

"She just pissed me off," Sanjuro said.

Masire stroked her hip. "I know."

They were lounging on the bunk in his quarters, sipping wine. The lights were turned low, and Masire—whose taste was nothing if not eclectic—had selected Bach's cello suites to set the mood. Sanjuro put her hand on his and gave him a wan smile. She was still too keyed-up from the day's fiasco to relax and enjoy a rare romantic evening. "I spent over five years keeping my mouth shut when she got nasty, and then, when it really mattered, I let her get to me."

Masire shifted around so he could massage her neck. She gave a small moan as his fingers began to work out the knots. "Well, this time it wasn't just you under attack. You were trying to protect the Cibolans. That's why you went off."

"You're probably right. Oh, that feels so good." She set her wine glass down and gave herself over to the massage. "Still, logical or not, it really fucked up my credibility. Now everybody sees me as a loose cannon."

"True. You're going to have to work to repair that, if you want to have any influence."

"I'm not sure I can fix it." She wriggled loose from his hands and turned to face him. "Everybody seems to think I'm nuts. Even the astrobio team. I mean, they're annoyed because they wanted more time just to explore, but they don't seem to have any problem with setting up human settlements and bioforming in the long term. Chang kept arguing with me about it at dinner. He said, 'Look at them. They're surviving on primitive agriculture, at the mercy of the weather. And more than half the planet isn't even inhabited because it's too cold.' And he just shrugged when I said we should ask first."

Masire sighed. "He has a point, Caty. Not that you don't," he added as she scowled at him. "But it isn't like we mean them harm. You've seen the value bioforming can bring. Look at how Australia has blossomed."

"Look at how few indigenous Australians are left."

"That wasn't the bioforming; that came much earlier."

"Exactly," Sanjuro said. "It was set in place by explorers who thought they had the right to make decisions because they had superior tech."

Masire winced. "Okay, good point. But we aren't those people, Sanjuro."

"Aren't we? Oh, sure, we don't plan to kill off the Cibolans. I even gather from the lab work that so far we don't seem to be bringing them any nasty germs—human viruses can't survive in Cibolans; our genome is too different. Though that seems rather optimistic to me—you know how viruses evolve. I agree we're not evil, but I don't think we're taking into consideration the law of unintended consequences."

Masire took her hands. "You don't have to convince me. I agree with you. But there may not be a lot we can do to stop things. If it wasn't for the *Cortez*, we would have had a lot more time."

"Rao would still be pushing to get miners up here."

"Yeah, but that would be a small thing. The *Cortez* is the problem, and you know damn well Rao's not responsible for that."

"You're right," Sanjuro said. Masire pulled her close again. Being connected to him felt good, but the events of the day were still digging at her. "It was so stupid of me to blow my credibility like that. I didn't have much with her to begin with, and now I have none. If I come back to them and say 'we've got to negotiate with the Cibolans or something's going to happen,' they aren't going to buy it."

Masire sighed. He let her pull away, though he didn't let go of her. "You know something that's not in your report?"

"No. Didn't you hear Rao? My reports are extensive."

He grinned.

"It's just a gut feeling. There's more going on among the Cibolans than I can put my finger on. And it's all just out of my reach. I think the idea of a human settlement is going to make them angry, especially if they have any idea of how extensive we want to make it."

"They don't seem to mind the astrobio setup."

"It's small. And they're as interested in us as we are in them. They want something from us, too, I'm sure of it."

"You haven't told them about the settlement plans, have you?"

"Not on purpose. But I don't think I have to. I can't block my thoughts, so they are likely be getting parts of it from my brain. Anyway, I'm not their only source of information. They must be reading the astrobio crew and all of your marines planetside."

"Nobody's reported seeing them."

"It's their planet; they know how to stay out of sight. Plus, they can do this stuff from a pretty fair distance. I'm not sure how far yet, but far." She hesitated a minute. "I think that's what caused the headaches when we were landing; I think they were trying to communicate with us. Once they figured out we couldn't 'hear' them, they stopped sending. But I'll bet anything they're still paying attention."

"That wasn't in your 'extensive' report."

"I've got enough problems without saying something that is obvious speculation. I haven't even tried it on Kyo yet. It won't make any difference if it's true. We can't stop people from thinking, and they're going to think in scraps of pictures from time to time. People do. We're not just verbal. Some of those pictures are going to make sense to the Cibolans, especially with what Sundown's getting from me."

"Even if they figure it out, what difference will it make? You and I may not like it, but Rao's right: they can't stop us."

"Are you sure about that, Masire?"

"You think they can? Come on, Sanjuro. You know combat. If it comes down to war—and it won't—it'll be a slaughter. They've got nothing."

"Yeah? I wouldn't call the ability to walk in and out of other people's minds nothing."

He thought about that a minute. "Okay. Neither would I. But I can't see how they can use it against us."

"Me either. I just have a bad feeling." Masire pulled her close again. Like Kyo, he believed there was no way to stop this process. The fact that they were probably right didn't make her feel any better. Even as her body connected with Masire's, a small part of her mind felt bitterly alone.

Masire dropped off soon after they finished making love. She usually did that, too. But tonight her worries about the expedition kept her awake. She tried snuggling closer to him. But she still lay there, wide awake, for the better part of an hour.

The next thing she felt was someone shaking her.

"Wake up, Sanjuro." Masire had a hand on her shoulder.

"What?" she said sleepily, trying to figure out where she was and what was going on.

"You were having a nightmare. Or something. Crying out in your sleep, anyway."

She sat up, shook her head, and tried to remember the dream. A large crowd of people were standing in the middle of some sort of city. A loud sound, like thunder, no, like gunfire. "Oh, kuso," she said.

"What is it?"

"You ever dream about the heat of battle?"

He made a face. "Yeah, I know those dreams. Bad one?"

"Ceres."

"Oh." Masire got up, rummaged around for the wine, and brought her a glass.

She gulped down about half of it. "Thanks for waking me up. I could do without that dream."

"What happened on Ceres, Sanjuro?"

"You know what happened on Ceres. It was a stupid war, a bad war, fought for economic reasons against people who didn't have a chance. The situation should have been handled some other way. A lot of people died there unnecessarily. Including my father."

"Is that all?"

"Kuso, Masire, isn't that enough?"

"It doesn't tell me why you left the Corps."

"I already told you that, years ago. They wouldn't let me study xenology. And I'd had it with combat."

"Yeah, but I don't buy it. You were the fair-haired child. They made you a captain, bumped you up the promotion list."

"Combat time counts double. You know that."

"About the only medal they didn't give you was the one your mother got. And you're Becca Sanjuro's daughter. I think they'd have let you go for the degree, if you'd pressed it."

"You've been looking me up."

"It's official record. Why shouldn't I?"

She shrugged.

"You going to tell me what really happened?"

She stared at him for a minute. Funny that no matter how long you were in a relationship with another person, there were always moments when you realized that there were things you still hadn't shared about yourself. She realized she was wondering if she could trust him with this—after five years, she was still wondering if she could afford to be honest. Get a grip, Sanjuro, she told herself. This is Masire, not some one-night stand. She got up and poured the rest of the wine into her glass for fortification. "After we broke the back of the resistance, there was still a lot of mopping up to do. And there were riots—like I said, most of the folks didn't have much to lose.

"We were sent out to put down one of those riots. It was in downtown Demeter, the capital of Ceres, and over food. Army MPs were supposed to be handling this kind of stuff, but the company assigned to it was in over their heads. Our standing orders were to respond to the level of violence we met: weapons on disable for those with rocks; lethal force if they carried weapons.

"Things had already deteriorated badly by the time we got there. Smoke everywhere from gas and homemade smoke bombs. We had to rely on scan to see what we were up against. And scan told us people were shooting at us. We heard shots, saw burst of fire on scan, responded in kind. You know: full throttle. I gave the order.

"And then one of my sergeants screamed at us to stop firing. As I tried to get to his position, I stumbled over something. A dead kid, with a rock in his hand. We stopped firing. All we heard was screaming. That's when we realized they weren't armed."

"Scan malfunction? Or misreading?"

"Neither. Somebody hacked the system and our com."

"So who set it up?"

"I have some guesses, but I don't know. Media coverage was still tightly controlled out of Ceres, so it got no press. The massacre broke the back of what was left of the rebellion. I suspect one of the big corporations that control the Belt interests planned it. But I don't think they could have pulled it off without some kind of cooperation from mil intel."

"Pretty hard to take, I guess. But not your fault."

"No, I was just the patsy. But I should have seen it. Something was wrong. I could feel it. The sound of gunfire threw me; I didn't want to kill the people out there, but I wasn't going to just let my people get shot. Whoever set it up relied on that. They knew most of the soldiers they had on Ceres were sick of fighting these people. But they wanted to drive the rebellion into the ground, so they tricked us."

"So you quit."

"I tried to get the incident investigated. I even sent a message to the commandant. But he just sent it back to the colonel in charge, who told me the only thing an investigation would produce would be a scapegoat. They assured me it wasn't really my fault and bumped me to captain."

Masire said, "The colonel was probably right. Investigations into incidents like that almost never come up with the real truth."

"Yeah. Sometimes I believe that."

"How come you resigned, instead of pushing them to send you to school?"

"I just wanted out. To get as far away as I could. Bogdosian got me a fellowship. She believed me when I said the military wouldn't pay for it."

They sat there quietly a while. Sanjuro finished her wine. Masire said, "Man, am I glad I missed Ceres."

"I don't ever want to fight anybody like that again," Sanjuro said. "I don't ever want to shoot anyone who can't shoot back."

"No," Masire said. "I can see why you wouldn't." He paused. "I've got one more question."

She made a face at him.

"How come you still wear a marine uniform, after all that?"

"Because I'm the kid of Becca Sanjuro and Jake Horner. Because even with baka officers like the one that got Jake killed, the marines are still the best forces out there." She swallowed the rest of her wine. "Because I want to believe that whoever set us up, it wasn't a marine."

He held her until she fell asleep. But it took him a long time to join her.

>≡

Sanjuro went back to her own quarters when Masire went back on duty. She had a few hours to kill before taking the shuttle planetside, and she wanted to spend the time reviewing her data.

A message pinged just as she shut her door. It turned out to be a forward of a message from the *Cortez*, odd because usually the personal messages that came from Earth or the *Cortez* were sent out weekly, right after they arrived. She'd had hers yesterday.

The message was from Derek. "Caty: I hear the powers that be are ignoring what you've learned about the Cibolans. I told you they only wanted you for window dressing. I'm sure you've got stuff that's not in the official reports. Send me what you've got. I can bring some System clout to bear." Below the message were some instructions for delivery—a way of sending to the *Cortez* that would fool the official checkpoint, which implied that it was secret from that ship's command as well.

For a brief moment she felt tempted. Maybe Derek Li hadn't sold out to the corporate interests. Maybe if she fed him stuff—the speculations that weren't going into her official reports—he'd bring Bogdosian into the picture and they'd get orders to deal with the Cibolans that even Vargas couldn't ignore. But common sense prevailed. Li liked to parade his integrity, but he was too ambitious to be that pure. He didn't want her material to help her or the Cibolans; he wanted something to give himself an edge. Regardless of what humans did with Cibola, any xenologists who studied the Cibolans were assured academic success. The message might even be some kind of trap, to see if she did have some kind of clandestine dealings with the *Cortez*. She wondered how it had been sent and if it had been programmed to wait to ping until she was alone.

She thought about just setting it aside, like she had the earlier message. But the idea that it could be a trap made her nervous. So she went to Gervaise. The legal officer didn't look thrilled to see her, but the message got her attention.

"We've been working on the assumption that there's a mole on board and that they have a collaborator back in the System who sends things to and from the *Cortez*. Maybe if they're getting this brazen, they'll make a mistake."

"Why would they risk it, now that we're cooperating with the *Cortez*?"

Gervaise made a face. "I suppose they're assuming that we're not sending everything we know. Your message from Li implies that. And we've found traces of unofficial communications with the *Cortez*. We just haven't been able to trace the sender. This has to have been via ETQ, given its reference to what happened at the meeting. Maybe we can try to trap them by planting something for delivery. Thanks for letting me know."

"If I thought I could trust those people, I'd have been tempted to respond," Sanjuro said, then wondered whether it was politic to admit something like that to Gervaise. "But somehow I don't think a bunch of major corps put together a multi-trillion dollar expedition just to make us negotiate with Cibolans, even if Bogdosian did have something to do with it. They have their own agenda."

"True enough." Gervaise looked away. "I'm sorry I couldn't back you up better yesterday."

"I'm sorry I put you on the spot."

"You're right, of course. Ethically. But there's no law on how to deal with alien species. A lot of people back in the System are spending their time making suggestions, but I don't think any deliberative body is going to adopt anything until they see what we actually end up with up here."

"All the more reason to follow general ethics."

"I know. I'm trying to get that point across. But I have to be careful or I'll lose my influence with Vargas."

"And throwing in with me wouldn't exactly give you credibility."

"No. I can't afford it."

"It wasn't good strategy to drag you into it. Next time I want your help I'll ask you in private."

"And I'll try to be more useful—behind the scenes."

They shook on it, friends again. Sanjuro realized that Gervaise might be deluding herself into thinking she was having some influence, without really pressing the point with Vargas. Admirals didn't like to be argued with. And ambitious young officers didn't like to cross admirals.

She sent Li a reply through the official A/ND system: "No need to contact me on the sly. Everything you need to know is in my reports. Hope you're having fun with the theme park companies." That would make him angry: Li hated theme parks even more than she did.

# 11

Sundown was sitting outside the telescope hut under a clear, dark sky that was perfect for telescope use, thinking about the alien invasion story all Cibolans learned in childhood. Ancient history, now, but the images had been passed down through the ages. Sundown could almost feel what that time was like.

*Many generations ago, long before our grandparents were first in their pouches, a new object appeared in the sky. Even in those ancient days, we watched the skies. Unlike the stars and planets we knew, this object grew larger and larger.*

*At first the watchers thought the object a meteorite, for those had come before. Some scholars believe that most of our iron comes from rocks that crashed into our planet thousands of generations back. But this object frequently changed speed and otherwise seemed to differ from meteorites. The watchers continued to observe and began to do calculations. They discovered the object was aiming directly for us.*

*Since we knew we could not stop it, we planned for its eventual landing. Those in the direct path would be evacuated. We dug underground shelters, for such a large object could cause storms if it struck. Then we waited.*

*As the object approached, we heard a new mind within the weave. At first we thought the object alive, a huge being that traveled through space. That amazed and frightened us, for we could barely conceive of such a thing. But as it got closer, we could distinguish several minds, though all seemed to think about the same things. This surprised us, because each of us thinks very differently, even though we come together in the weave.*

# The Weave

*We argued, as we do. Was it a being with many different minds? No creature we know is like that. Was it a ship carrying many beings that traveled through space? We build ships that travel on water and other vehicles that move on land, but we had never heard of ships in space. We tried to send messages to this creature or creatures, but they could not hear our minds.*

*The ship—that was our best guess—came close to our planet and then began to orbit us as we orbit the sun.*

*Once we realized they could not hear our minds, we devoted our time to understanding theirs, to see what they wanted. The images that came to us were disturbing. Most of their thoughts were of destruction.*

*Their minds filled with images of elaborate cities, inhabited by beings we could not even begin to imagine. Invariably the beings on the ship caused explosions in these cities, reducing them to dust. We saw them fighting other creatures, some that looked like them, some that looked very different. Sometimes they pointed objects at these others and made them explode; sometimes they tore them apart, piece by piece. On occasion they thought of food or of sex, though their images of sex were almost as violent as those of war.*

*They were large creatures, all colored the same reddish-brown. Their faces were smooth, with a clear space for their eyes. Where we have hands and feet, they had claws. They were further handicapped: they had only two arms.*

*Seeing the explosions in their minds, we continued to dig shelters. We knew, and know, nothing of explosions, neither how to create them nor how to defend against them, so we concentrated on learning to control their minds.*

*We entered their minds easily—the creatures knew nothing of blocking—but because their thinking was so limited, it took us some time to figure out what to do once we entered. Our initial success was in turning one of them against another, for they harbored suspicions of each other.*

*Just in time, as it happened, because without warning they caused great explosions in one of our cities. Deferring our mourning, we sent people everywhere to the shelters. Three more cities were hit by explosions. By then every adult was working together to affect the creatures, and we caused them all to turn on each other. The images of these creatures firing explosive weapons at each other and ripping off limbs, even heads, scarred our minds, for we had to watch, to continue to spread the chaos among them.*

*The fighting caused them to lose control of their ship, and it fell from the sky. It took a long time to fall. Thankfully, it crashed in an uninhabited place, a freezing desert where no one can comfortably live.*

*But there were still a few minds alive in the wreckage. An army of us went to find it. We could see them gathering their explosive weapons before we arrived, and so we sent pain into their minds. None still lived by the time we got there.*

*They were grayish in color, not the red we had seen. The red was a suit they wore over their skins. They were grayish and wrinkled and not especially large outside of their suits. They had eyes and large ears, and mouths full of sharp teeth. Their bodies decayed as ours do in death. We buried them in the ground.*

*The ship was constructed of a metal that doesn't exist on our world. We took what we could make use of; the rest has been covered by the sands of the desert. No one knows the place for sure, now.*

*Perhaps that was all of their people, for they have never come again.*

Perhaps things can be different this time, Sundown thought. These new aliens, though greedy, are not the same as the ancient invaders. They do not kill just to kill. And I trust Caty Sanjuro.

There were things Sundown would like to tell Sanjuro, things it had been forbidden to say. Sundown was thinking about saying them anyway.

⋙

Sanjuro tried to put aside her misgivings about the mission so she could concentrate on understanding Cibolan culture. She needed to know what the Cibolans were learning about human culture and how they were interpreting that.

She and Sundown traveled in her landcraft to the nearest city, which was much larger than the town where Sundown lived. Sanjuro gathered it was a seat of government, complete with official buildings and functionaries. Sanjuro saw some in person—they looked much the same as other Cibolans, though their robes were made of more elaborate materials. She had the impression that some of the posts were hereditary. Perhaps they were most accurately described as nobles rather than as mayors or presidents.

The city did not seem large by human standards, and the buildings were painted in the same colors as those in Sundown's town and likewise constructed mostly from mud bricks. But they were often larger, some even two or three stories tall. The streets were wider as well and carried more traffic. While there was a marketplace—much larger and grander than the one she knew—there were also shops open on a regular basis. In the city, Sanjuro concluded, Cibolans had developed a more detailed division of labor than in Sundown's town.

Sundown showed her the industrial district. They toured a factory making glass for solar panels and other uses. An enormous coal-fired furnace melted the sand and other ingredients into a soup that poured into a form and cooled, becoming sheets of glass. In other parts of the building, workers cut and framed the glass. Sanjuro watched, amazed, as they used three hands to hold the sheet steady while they cut with the fourth. The furnace, she learned, was shared with the factory next door, which made steel. It was set in the shared wall of the two manufacturers, so that they could make maximum use of it. One or the other side was always working.

In response to a query about where the coal came from, Sundown visualized a mine located in a hilly area within their region. The miners were using picks and hammers. Their geologists thought there might be more at lower levels, but they lacked the equipment to mine it safely.

We are fortunate to have coal near the surface in Golden Mountain, Sundown sent. Not all regions have so much.

They stayed overnight, and Sundown took her to a performance at an outdoor theatre. To Sanjuro it looked like dance done in silence. Evidently, though, the performers were also sending information that the Cibolans could receive. Sanjuro picked up pieces, but it made little sense to her and indeed brought back her headache, reminding her that she could only see what a Cibolan sent to her and then apparently only if they sent it directly.

Sundown's attempts to explain the performance didn't help, but Sanjuro enjoyed watching the movement, which involved a lot of physical interaction. The Cibolans were certainly not averse to touching; in fact, they frequently touched each other in a friendly manner.

They went afterwards to a small cafe. Sundown had apparently taken note of the things Sanjuro liked and did not, for she thoughtfully ordered Sanjuro's favorites. They polished the meal off with the spicy drink Sanjuro had learned to love, though it didn't seem to make her high, as it did the Cibolans. As they lingered over the drink, a musician took the stage, playing a stringed instrument. Here was something else where four hands made a difference—the instrument had a double fretboard and extended down into two resonating chambers. One was relatively small—and made higher-pitched sounds—the other quite large and much lower in range. The harmonics were melancholy, and Sundown relayed images to her from the performers. Most of the pictures made her think of someone mourning the loss of another. She managed to ask Sundown about it and discovered it was indeed a story. Sundown sent her a direct image of two Cibolans staring at each other until one collapsed, and then the spouse of the dead one mourning the loss.

It looked like a duel, without weapons. Sanjuro tried an image out of history: two people with swords, fighting, until one is killed. And then a lover mourning the loss, for that was certainly true in human culture as well as Cibolan. She then did the passing seasons in reverse, their method for showing the past, to demonstrate that such duels were not current human activity. A bit dishonest, perhaps, since humans still managed to kill each other with regularity, but a way of asking if the Cibolan story was historical.

It seemed she had waded into difficult waters, for Sundown did not answer right away. Another person performed, this one on a wind instrument, and Sanjuro did not push during the performance. Afterwards, Sundown sent her an image of the park they had seen in the city earlier, near the main hall. Exactly as they had seen it, down to some of the people in the park—as a way of saying today, Sanjuro thought. Two Cibolans faced each other, and one eventually fell.

Sanjuro used the picture and sent images of people coming in and taking charge of the winner. Sundown painted them back out. She showed the winner later, before a panel of judges, and then walking free.

Legal, though apparently it must be done by the rules.

*So they kill,* Sanjuro thought. *As do we.* It was a sobering thought.

Sanjuro listened to the other musician, finding the sound pleasing to her ears. The scale and harmonics were not the same as any human ones she knew—and humans had developed many different ones—but they did not jar the human ear. This realization gave her an idea. She sent Sundown an image of herself on the stage, singing. She used the instruments to imply the making of music, and then showed her doing things with her voice.

Sundown was enthralled with the idea. She checked with the person supervising the performances and then told Sanjuro to take the stage. Sundown sent out pictures introducing her. Sanjuro, as usual missing most of a general broadcast, caught some of it. She gathered that the audience had been told to watch her mind for images.

Sanjuro's musical background was not extensive, but she'd spent time in school choirs and had been involved in a singing group on the *Mercator*. She decided to sing an old English ballad, a sad song about parted lovers, because she knew it would form pictures in her head. Her voice started out uncertain, but grew in strength as she went along.

The audience was mesmerized. They stared at her as she made the sounds—sounds which they apparently found beautiful—by herself, with no instrument. When she sat back down, Sundown patted her on the back and helped her make sense of some of the audience response.

On the way back to the room they had for the night, Sanjuro thought of bringing the *Mercator* choir down for a concert. It might be a way of bridging some of the gaps, of demonstrating that they must take the Cibolans seriously. She was excited by the prospect, though her head still hurt from all the images thrown at it.

Sanjuro remembered as they got to the room that she had a medkit in the landcraft. Her head ached enough to make her consider going after it, though it was parked at the edge of the city. But when she explained—cumbersomely—her headache to Sundown, her friend shook her head, a new skill she was developing. Having Sanjuro lie down, she sat next to her. Sanjuro could almost feel something entering her head, though mostly she felt the headache dissipate. She fell asleep before Sundown had finished.

# 12

During their return from the city, Sanjuro made another attempt to explain how shuttles and spacecraft worked. She didn't understand the mechanical side of flying machines any better than she did that of landcraft, so she didn't do a very good job of showing the particulars of the engines. Most Cibolan machinery was mechanical in nature, easy enough for even the non-tech mind to comprehend. Sundown obviously understood the basic workings of most Cibolan tech.

Human tech had once been that simple, or so Sanjuro had learned in history. But most of it now consisted of intricately complex machines—some highly intelligent—that most of those who used them could not construct. Sanjuro could show Sundown how she spoke over com, but she couldn't explain how com worked. But then she had difficulty explaining how her voice worked. She consulted the Mercator-net encyclopedia (another activity fascinating to Sundown) and used holos to show how vocal sounds were made. In the end, she showed a newborn baby crying, the only way she could think of to explain that it was instinctive.

The Cibolan equivalent of getting on the net and looking something up was apparently consulting others who might know. As near as Sanjuro could tell, some members of the community specialized in remembering things. They taught the children as well, though the lessons did not seem as formal as those taught to human children.

When Sanjuro pressed Sundown to take another trip and Sundown declined, she considered taking one on her own. But something told her she needed Sundown's protection in this world.

Time seemed to speed up. She felt the pressure to find out as much as she could, to come up with some kind of lever that would convince Rao and Vargas that they needed to work with the Cibolans rather than roll over them, *Cortez* or no *Cortez*.

"I just don't get it," she complained to Kyo. "How can they not understand that it's wrong to just take things. That's elementary school ethics."

"Yeah, but once you grow up you learn that life isn't fair. Hell, look at human history. Even those explorers who did negotiate with Earth's native cultures didn't exactly trade fairly. What did those people pay for Manhattan: twenty-three dollars and some beads? Even then it was worth more than that. You've got to forget fairness. It's a losing argument."

⋗

Sanjuro and Sundown sat inside the shelter at Sanjuro's camp. The sun had just set, but Sundown made no move to leave. They had spent most of the afternoon going over human tech, using Sanjuro's Mercator-net connection to bring up images of things that Sanjuro couldn't explain on her own. Now they sipped native tea. The mix of leaves they'd used to brew it smelled like damp moss, but it tasted almost like cloves. Sanjuro had developed a taste for much of the Cibolan food, in part at least because it was grown rather than constructed from its basic elements. Humans couldn't get much of their nutritional needs from Cibolan food—and there was plenty of it that just tasted too wrong to eat—but some of it was both tasty and satisfying. Eating food that had been grown in earth just felt better. Ridiculous, for someone who'd spent most of her life in an artificial environment eating reconstituted food. Like being convinced you could tell the difference between Earth air and bioformed. Of course it wasn't different—if you broke down the chemical composition it was exactly the same—only it was.

Sundown wasn't sending, and Sanjuro was mostly thinking in words. She was, in fact, trying not to think about the deadline and the fact that crews would soon start building a basic settlement, though she couldn't keep the occasional theme park image from flitting through her brain. She felt depleted, depressed. Telling Sundown directly about the human plans would be violating orders—she was supposed to "make friends," not give out information. But not telling Sundown was a betrayal of the trust they had developed. And without that trust, she might not have access to Cibolans once the human settlement started.

She assumed they had some idea about the settlements. She always had the feeling that more was going on with the Cibolans than she could read. "I wish I were a telepath," she said out loud, startling Sundown, who had been lost in her own mind.

Sundown sent her one of the few symbolic images Sanjuro understood, a blank picture that she had learned meant "what are you thinking?" She tried to put her frustration into pictures: Sundown sending pictures, and Sanjuro seeing; Sanjuro forming pictures and Sundown reading. All one way, all generated by Sundown. She sent an image of herself on crutches, amid a mass of Cibolans, all walking. Crippled, she tried to say. Mindblind.

Sundown didn't respond at once. Sanjuro tried again, making the pictures slightly different. But Sundown held up two hands, a variation on the one-handed stop gesture Sanjuro habitually made when overloaded.

When Sundown finally replied, she used the image of Sanjuro on crutches. But in the image Sanjuro dropped the crutches and was whole among the Cibolans. It was followed by an image of Sanjuro sending, and Sundown receiving.

Sanjuro stared at her, uncomprehending.

Sundown repeated the sequence.

And this time Sanjuro had to take it in. Sundown was telling her she was telepathic. She saw another image: Sanjuro walking down the street, broadcasting to everyone.

And then a second one, of Sanjuro receiving from everyone, until she bent double and fell over.

She got it, then: they had been shielding her from overload. That was why Sundown had been careful where she had taken Sanjuro, why their one trip to the large city had been planned, and brief, with Sundown always at her side, blocking as much as she could. It wasn't the ability to send and receive that she lacked; it was the ability to manage the information, something Cibolans begin learning in infancy.

The possibilities! If she could learn to manage it. She wanted to ask that, but was suddenly too nervous. Just me, or all humans, she asked instead.

Sundown sent her an image of *Mercator* nearing the planet and Cibolans holding their heads. At least those on *Mercator*, it was clear. Or most of them.

Sanjuro couldn't quite think of a way to ask why she hadn't been told this before. Puzzling images ran through her mind and she felt a cold stab of fear. She looked at Sundown, and the feeling deepened. Then Sundown sent images of fighter planes bombing cities, marines shooting weapons. To her horror, Sanjuro saw herself giving orders to fire on civilians on Ceres, an image straight from her nightmares.

Sanjuro leaned forward on her knees, hands on top of her head. For a moment she thought she might be sick. All those things she had wanted to keep from Sundown, to share at some future point when they understood each other better had been there for the taking. And Sanjuro couldn't even argue that the people of the *Mercator* expedition were different. They wore the same uniforms as those marines and soldiers.

Sundown touched her, gently, and Sanjuro looked up. She received a series of images, of a large group of Cibolans moving toward one of the cities, of the leader of the group, of the ruler of the city planning a defense, of the attackers demanding surrender. Cibolans on both sides began to fall, though no one fired a weapon or struck another with a hand. They just fell.

Sundown let the story drop, without showing who had won that war.

*We both kill,* Sanjuro thought. *We both fight wars.* Likely the Cibolan wars were fought for reasons both petty and grand. She was pathetically grateful to Sundown for telling her this, for refusing to assume the moral high ground.

Sundown sent other pictures, then, of more ships, more humans, of buildings on Cibola.

A question, of sorts, though Sanjuro thought Sundown knew the answer. She nodded, expanded on the image, showing the kind of settlements humans had in mind, the eventual changes in the polar regions.

Sundown showed her a large group of Cibolans, blocking the way to such construction.

"Can you do it?" Sanjuro whispered, trying to find a picture that asked the question. She felt a sharp pain in her head, and began to crumple. The pain went. She looked at Sundown and felt something else, a compulsion. With her mind protesting all the way, her hand picked up the cup from which she had been drinking tea, a pottery cup of classic nanotech but just as brittle as a real one, and dashed it against the floor of the shelter where it shattered. Sanjuro looked at her hands and knew that those same hands could have been forced to seize a knife and press it into her own heart. She knew Sundown's people had observed the humans on *Mercator*, even before it reached orbit. She remembered the headache she had suffered before they reached the planet. They could attack *Mercator* in orbit, of that she felt certain.

*They will kill us if we go too far,* Sanjuro thought. *And they can.* Knowing this gave her a strange sense of relief. She had been put back into her old job, as a marine: to protect her own, who were no match for the Cibolans.

She formed the question: Can I learn?

Sundown did not answer for several minutes before the image came of Sanjuro, hand across mouth, walking among her colleagues.

And now it was Sanjuro who sat without answering. Minutes earlier she had felt the familiar comfort of protecting her own, and now she was being asked to keep secrets from them. Skill with telepathy was a valid thing to trade. She sent a picture, clear that she was really sending: a Cibolan teaching a human to control the mind; a human teaching a Cibolan to fly a shuttle.

Sundown added in other images: building machines, mining, the myriad tasks done on comps. Sanjuro nodded.

Sundown again sat silent, this time for many minutes. Sanjuro got up and looked for the cup. It had broken into a dozen or more pieces, and she carefully picked them up, one by one, getting down on her hands and knees and finding the shards that had rolled under the chairs. She laid the pieces in a pile on the table and stared at them for a long time.

When Sundown finally began to send to Sanjuro again, she had much to say. It took a long time, most of the night. By the end, Sanjuro understood that there were factions among the Cibolans who would not approve of teaching Sanjuro to use telepathy. Sundown's faction wanted peace and trade with the humans. They could see the risks, but also the rewards. They had concluded that humans were no more evil—or good—than they themselves. The machines humans had would make their lives easier. And some of them—Sundown especially—wanted to see the stars. They had decided to trust Sanjuro, to show her what she could have, hoping that she could convince her people to take training in those skills—and, not incidentally, their own personal survival—as trade for human tech. She could speak or not, as she found prudent.

The next morning, Sanjuro packed up a small kit of necessities and left with Sundown. She was going to learn the basics of telepathic control. By the time she returned, she hoped, she would have figured out how to bridge the gaps between the two species, and negotiate a relationship in the interest of both groups. She was as excited as a small child on the first day of school, and as scared as she had ever been in battle.

# 13

Many of those meeting with Sundown and Sorrel were angry. The aliens are killers, they sent, using images of explosions, bombing raids, and battles. They kill each other and they kill other beings. Sundown considered trying to explain that they had only killed each other—Sanjuro had said some of the beings who looked very different were, in fact, the same as her people. But it probably wouldn't make any difference. The images showed that the aliens were capable of mass killings, and Sanjuro had acknowledged the truth of it.

We kill, Sundown sent. But killing is not all we do. Killing is not the only thing these aliens do.

They want our planet. They are dangerous. You encourage them by teaching this alien to communicate. That was sent by Fire, who disagreed with its father on dealing with humans.

I open the door between us and the aliens by teaching this one to communicate, Sundown sent, adding images of the iron and spent comets in the asteroid belt. If we can communicate with them, we can work with them to mutual advantage.

Can they learn to communicate? Sorrel sent.

My alien can. Sundown provided example after example of Sanjuro's progress in learning to block unwanted conversations, to send to just one person, to deal with complicated issues. This one is very smart and eager to learn, and it says the others on their expedition are also very smart. We all know how much ability they have.

Everyone agreed with that. The mental bombardment when the alien ship arrived was still fresh in their minds.

Communication prevents killing, someone sent.

Most of the time, another added.

But these are aliens. They make all this noise to each other—a form of communication, according to Sundown—and still act with violence. Will they change?

Sundown sent images of all the aliens lying dead. Do we want this?

Fire sent an image from history of the invasion so long ago. Better them than us.

And Sundown responded with images of their people and the aliens together, working, eating, listening to music. With communication, we have choices.

No one has attacked us, Sorrel sent. We can always fight, if we must. We are prepared. Let us continue communication.

Sanjuro pulled Masire to her. Their mouths met in a deep, long kiss that raised the intensity level. She felt an overwhelming desire to merge her body into his. And her mind. The awareness of other people's thoughts delighted and frightened her at the same time. She tried to avoid eavesdropping on things that were none of her business, but the urge was difficult to resist.

Especially in bed. Damn, she wished Masire knew about his telepathy as well. But even now, even at a moment of passion, she knew she could not tell him. Or show him. She suspected he would resent her peeking into his mind, too. Humans had a well-developed sense of privacy. But as she gave herself over to the kiss, letting her hands stroke down his well-muscled back, she found she could not stop herself from looking inside.

What she got from him was an overpowering feeling of urgency, a drive as strong as her own to merge the two of them together. Wanting him even more, she put her hands together behind his back and pulled him to her until there was no space at all between them. She could barely breathe, and didn't care. Nor did he. When he entered her, she felt the surge in his brain. That drove her own

196

passion. She stayed in his mind all the way to orgasm and felt him almost explode.

Afterwards, as they lay there entangled, Sanjuro's self-discipline returned, and she pulled out of Masire's head. Completely relaxed for the first time in weeks, she realized that for a few minutes she had been completely caught up in the moment. Sex alone could do that, but being completely aware of Masire as well as of herself took it to a higher level.

Her worries and concerns crept back in. How was she going to convince Vargas that they could not go forward with their plans for the settlement without coming to some agreement with the Cibolans? The Cibolans could stop them; the only question was whether they would stop them without killing people. She didn't think they would. The time she had spent among them had shown her that in one key way they differed very little from humans: they disagreed passionately, even violently, about the best way to do things. Telepathic contact improved communication, but it had not made the Cibolans more harmonious than humans.

Conventional wisdom held that most human conflict grew from misunderstanding. Watching the Cibolans had shown her just how flawed that idea was. Even when communication was crystal clear, the Cibolans could still disagree on the best solution. And they frequently disagreed on the true cause of a problem, which also affected possible resolutions.

She'd given up any hope of convincing Rao how dangerous the Cibolans were. And Vargas was no better. He had decided official negotiations weren't necessary, in part due to the friendly relationships she had developed. As the crew began developing settlements, Sanjuro was supposed to prevent any trouble by explaining to her friends how good human activity would be for the Cibolans. He had put down her opposition as a misguided attempt to protect the Cibolans. And he wasn't completely wrong: she had wanted to protect the Cibolans, before she had figured out they could protect themselves. Worrying about how to do it without betraying her own people had given her nightmares.

Now, though, it was humans she was trying to protect, humans and a rewarding potential relationship with the Cibolans. But her earlier argument for negotiations made it likely that Vargas wouldn't believe her, would think this was something she had dreamed up to try to change things. She needed to try, though. The Cibolans were going to stop anything they didn't like. Several weeks of learning telepathy had convinced her of that.

Sundown had started her lessons out at the telescope hut, a good place for privacy. Up there, away from the others, Sanjuro wouldn't be likely to stray into the mind of someone who might not approve of her learning the skills before she learned to control the process. Sanjuro had run Sundown ragged, trying to glean every last ounce of information out of her.

Much of the ability to manage telepathic communication turned on being relaxed, rather than tense—a difficult state to attain when one desires the end object too greatly. It wasn't unlike learning to manage weightlessness. You had to let go, to stop clinging to what you thought was happening. In weightlessness you had to accept that you wouldn't fall and crash if you weren't hanging on to something. In telepathy, you accepted that thoughts were out there, for the reading. And that others could see into your head. Before you could learn anything else, you had to just let that happen, let the thoughts in, let them out.

Sanjuro had been doing that for weeks, though she hadn't realized it. In some ways, she had mirrored the learning of a baby Cibolan. Babies broadcast all their thoughts; children didn't start learning to block until they were several years old. Parents, of course, had to block some thoughts, especially negative emotional ones, from their children—just as Sundown had been doing with her.

Sundown had found it necessary to create a barrier to block the thoughts of others. Cibolan society was, on the whole, highly social, and people communicated back and forth all the time. Because they were naturally curious about Sanjuro, they had been constantly querying. During her training, Sundown let the barrier down a little at a time, showing Sanjuro the natural cacophony of Cibolan society. As she began to tap into the weave, to accept the communication without trying to block it using tension that would inevitably lead to a headache, Sanjuro realized how much power Sundown must possess, to have protected her from so much input.

Sundown found teaching Sanjuro a challenge. The Cibolan tried to explain the difficulty by sending her the image of drawing a detailed picture, and then sending a small portion of that picture rendered in even greater detail, and then doing the same thing again and again, until it had been reduced to drawing one small line. She had never taught an adult how to use her skills before. Teaching Sanjuro required her to figure out how she did things she had always done without thinking.

For several days, Sanjuro suffered from raging headaches. But gradually she began to block thoughts without doing the mental equivalent of tensing her shoulders and neck, and the pain subsided. Her first attempts at knowingly sending messages were equally clumsy: she broadcast to everyone within range. But over time she learned to focus a message to one person, or to several, depending on circumstance. And marveled to realize that two Cibolans could carry on a completely private conversation in a crowded room. Almost private— unwanted eavesdropping happened, though it was considered ill-mannered. The process was something like using subvocal on com, except that the Cibolans didn't have implants in their eyes, ears, and throats.

Learning to use her own powers showed Sanjuro just how much the Cibolans had learned about humans. They hadn't been able to make sense of it all, of course: humans thought verbally as well as graphically and the words made no sense to the Cibolans. But they had accumulated a great deal of data, far more than humans knew about Cibolans. *With all our tech and scans,* she thought, *we missed the most important thing about these people. And the most dangerous.* Human didn't know to look for it, because they couldn't see it in themselves. The Cibolans had looked for it, of course; they expected it. But they were also aware of human tech, even if it didn't make a lot of sense to them. They were smart enough to realize that any people who could build machines that flew across the galaxy had ones that did other things, both good and bad.

Human information about the Cibolans was carefully documented, organized into neat files, but incomplete. Cibolan understanding of humans consisted of millions of images held in many different minds, a hodge-podge of information, non-linear, but much more accurate.

Sundown let Sanjuro eavesdrop on some of the Cibolan discussions of what to do about the humans. As she followed the debate about whether to just drive humans off, or try to work with them, one fact hit her like a blow to the stomach: "They don't trust us," she whispered aloud, to Sundown's confusion.

They were right not to trust. Human intentions toward the Cibolans were not benign. The human race had matured over time. They had no intention of enslaving the Cibolans, or of killing them off. Compared with the conquistadores who had sought the original Cibola, humans were civilized. *But we still think we're entitled to anything we can take,* Sanjuro thought. She found herself wondering if that was an inherent attitude in an exploring species, a holdover from being predators.

The Cibolan willingness to do whatever was necessary to protect themselves was probably inherent as well. Humans had the same instinct. Would the Cibolans also try to take, were the situations reversed? Possibly. She had been given enough stories by Sundown to know that Cibolan history hadn't been more peaceful than human. More than one ruler had tried to cement power by controlling the minds of others. A pyramid effect: the king controlled the minds of those closest to him, who then controlled those of their subordinates, and so on. They created a wall that was virtually impregnable.

Those kingdoms hadn't survived. Like their human counterparts—governments based on fear—they eventually imploded. Control requires constant attention. The bits of history that Sanjuro gleaned from Sundown told of Cibolans who banded together to topple oppressive regimes. Individual heroes didn't stand out in those tales; cooperation became the watchword taught to children. These days, only two of the seven countries on Cibola were actually run by their royal families; the others all used some hybrid of participatory democracy. These varied sharply, from one country that approached true anarchy to one that delegated authority to a group of officials chosen at regular intervals.

The ruler of Golden Mountain, the territory in which Sundown lived—Sorrel, as Sanjuro had taken to calling him—was the fifteenth in an hereditary line. But he functioned more as the first among equals; he couldn't enforce a ruling that was opposed by a significant majority of his people. Decision-making here operated in what Sanjuro thought of as a telepathic town meeting. He had gone way out on a limb by leading the peace and negotiation faction, which was partly international—he was working with the governments of two other countries and leading citizens from a couple of the others. But he barely had a majority of his own people. Significant differences existed within his country on the subject, and his heir favored driving the humans out; he could lose his throne over it. Revolution was not unknown even in countries without harsh rule.

# 14

Sundown took Sanjuro to meet with the ruler a few days before she was scheduled to go up to *Mercator* for a shipwide meeting—one Sanjuro suspected would officially order the development of settlements on Cibola. Sorrel lived in—and ruled from—a massive structure at the heart of the great city. As with most buildings on Cibola, it was built of a combination of mud bricks and stone, with thick walls to insulate occupants from the winter snow and wind. A massive stone fence, at least four meters high, stood before it; each stone in the fence had been selected for its color, size, and beauty. At the center of the fence, a great archway opened to the palace, which, open to all comers, lacked a gate. A large garden of carefully arranged boulders and stones enclosing plants, some with summer blossoms still bright, lay beyond the arch. Water trickled from a fountain and ran among the rocks, and Sanjuro saw that it was a closed, circulating system. The Cibolans did not waste water for decoration.

They entered through a high-ceilinged foyer, but Sanjuro noticed that the other rooms were of a more practical height, sparsely furnished with necessary tables, chairs, and cabinets, every piece hand-crafted by a master. Abstract tapestries lined the walls—beautiful and practical at once, since they were made of a heavy material and added insulation.

A dark red in color, Sorrel stood taller than Sundown. Sanjuro was startled to see that the fur around his eyes was turning gray. Apparently Cibolans, like humans, grayed with age. He greeted her with warmth and curiosity. While the initial images he sent were formal ones of greeting—to which Sanjuro sent the replies that Sundown had taught her—he quickly moved on to pictures that posed questions about humans and their place in the universe. Sanjuro found herself trying to visualize Earth as a part of the Solar System as well as providing some scenes of what the planet itself was like. In response to further visual questions, she did her best to explain the automatic workings of *Copernicus*, the settlements in the System's asteroid belt, and what life was like on *Mercator*.

This was, she realized, Sorrel's first direct contact with a human, and it was obvious that he was as fascinated by meeting someone from another intelligent species as she had been. No wonder Sundown thought so highly of him. Sanjuro did her best to answer his questions as fully as she could.

Eventually, the discussion turned to the purposes of the human expedition. Sanjuro initially replied by visualizing the history of human exploration, going back to the initial movement out of Africa and eventually showing settlements on Luna, Mars, and Titan. Sorrel followed these images patiently, but kept bringing her back to why *Mercator* had come to Cibola. And then he sent a picture of humans setting up permanent settlements on the planet.

Sanjuro struggled to send him a blank image while she frantically tried to figure out how to respond. Her orders said she should tell him nothing about settlements, but she did not think he would have asked the question had he not been told about the plans by those observing the humans. She didn't want to lie to him; that would destroy the rapport they were building, especially if he knew it was a lie. Saying she didn't know was likely just as bad. In the end, she decided to give him the truth: she showed human settlements in unoccupied land. He responded that this was unacceptable. She told him she would convey that to her superiors, doing her best to make it clear that she did not make the final decision.

She explained some of the technological things that humans could offer as exchange for settlements, though she cautioned Sorrel that her superiors had not yet agreed to such programs. He responded enthusiastically to the idea of learning about the machines they used for travel and the ones that made farming easier. But her descriptions of the bioforming process did not meet with success. The idea that the humans would change the way the planet—his planet—worked troubled him, even as she explained that it could improve their agriculture and solve their drought issues. Back when the effort was made on Earth to bioform the deserts and the vast northern snow fields, many people had reacted much as Sorrel did. Bioforming of other planets, of moons and asteroids, was fine, but humans did not want their own world changed. For Sorrel, perhaps, the jump from what was—in human terms—nineteenth-century tech to twenty-fifth was just too great.

Sorrel was more receptive to her description of asteroid mining. Mining was a concept he could understand. And he knew his people could not do it without humans: they could not build the ships to get there, could not come up with mining equipment, could not even use some of the minerals without human aid.

Sorrel would continue to work for a negotiated settlement with the humans. He wanted the tech, wanted the asteroid wealth. He saw a cooperative exchange as a boon for his people. And he was willing to trade: bases on Cibola, maybe even small settlements, and telepathic training in return for tech and access to the asteroids. But no large settlements. And no bioforming. Sanjuro left with the clear understanding that if she could not convince her people to negotiate, Sorrel would stand in defense of his own. We will not become your slaves, he told her. Everything you offer is not worth that.

All I have to do, Sanjuro told herself, is convince humans they can't win here. She laughed at herself, a little bitterly. Right. Convince humans that a power they can't see and measure can beat them.

She and Sundown left Sorrel's quarters and walked toward the inn where they had stayed on their previous visit to the city. Sanjuro was lost in her own thoughts, trying to figure out a strategy for convincing her people they must work with the Cibolans, when she saw two Cibolans approaching. Her soldier's instinct put her on alert even before Sundown sent her a message that felt like a scream in her head.

Sanjuro made her mind a solid wall; she knew she had not yet learned enough to do more than block an attack. She doubted she could keep the attacker out for long. She cut her eyes toward Sundown—not daring to open even a tendril of her mind to check on her friend—and realized that the Cibolan was locked in combat as well. Possibly Sundown could take both of the attackers. Sundown's power had impressed her, but she did not know how it rated on a relative scale.

Sanjuro wasn't used to letting someone else fight her battles. She felt the pressure in her mind, knew her block would not hold for much longer, and dove suddenly into a forward roll straight at the Cibolan attacking Sundown, rather than at the one attacking her. As her feet came over, her heels struck him in the stomach, knocking him to the ground. She came to her feet, dropped on top of his stomach, and pinned his arms to the ground. He lay there, gaping at her, clearly unsure of what to do next. The other's attack penetrated her block. She felt searing pain, and then everything went black.

When she came to, she found herself lying on the ground, Sundown sitting next to her. Her head throbbed painfully, but she didn't think she had suffered any permanent damage. She could feel relief from Sundown as she returned to full consciousness and took in the situation. The Cibolan she'd rolled into was standing nearby, looking a little dazed. Two others stood with him; Sanjuro gathered they were something like police officers. They had put him in mental lock of some kind. The one who had attacked her lay on the ground. Someone was attending him as well, but Sanjuro knew he was dead. She sent a question to Sundown and met a feeling she recognized: the bitter knowledge that one has killed mixed in with the relief that one has survived.

Sanjuro reached out and took Sundown's nearest hand, squeezed it.

It took time to sort the situation. Sanjuro assumed she had broken some sort of law by physically attacking the Cibolan. Though she had seen friendly contact among Cibolans, she had never seen anything resembling a physical fight. But apparently her act was so unprecedented that neither social nor political rules governed it. Her move was applauded as a practical solution for someone who could not fight off a mental attack. Killing in self-defense, or in defense of others, carried no legal penalty as near as Sanjuro could determine. She, Sundown, and the surviving attacker were questioned by the officials; "questioning" consisted of letting the authorities read the incident as remembered by each person.

Eventually, Sanjuro and Sundown were allowed to leave; the attacker was held. Worried about damage to Sanjuro's mind, Sundown took her to a healer, where Sanjuro spent half an hour lying on a pallet while the healer moved around in her mind and cured her headache. Sanjuro caught glimpses of a conversation between Sundown and the healer, who seemed to be surprised by what she found in Sanjuro's head. When the healer explained what she had done, Sanjuro understood nothing. Another thing to explore with Sundown, when she had more time.

They ordered strong drinks when they returned to the inn. Humans and Cibolans apparently reacted similarly to mortal stress: with a desire to get drunk. The Cibolan equivalent of alcohol wouldn't make a human drunk, though, so Sanjuro longed for the wine she had back at her campsite. As they sat in the comfort of their room, Sundown asked Sanjuro why she had not gone after the Cibolan attacking her instead of the one fighting Sundown.

Sanjuro shrugged. The concept of instinct was hard to get across. Sanjuro managed to convey that she didn't think a physical attack on a person attacking her mind would do much to stop him from hurting her. But if she attacked the one focused on Sundown, it would break his concentration enough to give Sundown an edge. As indeed it had. Sundown had managed to knock the man out in the moment after Sanjuro pinned him, which had allowed her to turn full attention to Sanjuro's attacker. Thinking about that made Sundown gulp down more of the liquor and close off her mind. Sanjuro wanted to ask Sundown if that was the first time she had killed, but it seemed too personal a question, even after what they had been through. Clearly, though, Sundown both knew how to fight and did not take killing lightly.

As she had earlier, Sanjuro reached over, took one of Sundown's hands, and squeezed it. After that, the conversation turned to nothing of great importance.

But the bond between them was now forged in blood. They had become much more than friends.

# 15

Sanjuro shuttled up to *Mercator* with the rest of the Astrobio crew the day before a major shipwide meeting. Like everyone else planetside, she felt the need for a short break. A couple of dances and several private parties were planned, though the main item on Sanjuro's social agenda was an evening with Masire. They saw so little of each other these days. Of course, as soon as they got together, they began discussing the issues likely to come up in the meeting.

Sanjuro told Masire about the meeting with Sorrel and her conviction that the Cibolans would fight if the humans went forward with settlements. "I don't blame them for resisting," he said. "And you know I agree with you that it is ridiculous not to work with them. But you're going to have difficulty convincing Vargas that he has to take the time to do that. He thinks your friendship with them will be enough to manage them."

"Can't he comprehend that I'm friends with only a few Cibolans, and even they are opposed to settlements?"

"Well, he does assume they all think the same way. Besides, it makes his task easier if he just decides his plan is going to work; he's getting a lot of pressure from back in the System to get things ready for the *Cortez*. So he doesn't want to hear your objections."

"Would he rather see us all die here?"

"See, Sanjuro. That's your problem. That's why he won't listen: you keep exaggerating the situation. I'm sure they can fight, but you know what kind of weapons we have. From what you're telling me, they have no power over our tech. They won't even know what we're doing."

"You can't push buttons if you're unconscious. Or screaming in pain."

"I'm sure they can inflict some damage, but they won't be able to protect themselves from our bombs. We don't have to get close to do damage, though I hope it won't come to that. With luck, the worst that will happen is that we drop a couple of bombs in an unoccupied area to scare them."

"You're awfully calm about this. After all, it's your people who will do the dying if Vargas makes the wrong call."

He flinched.

They had let the subject drop. Neither had wanted to push the discussion to the inevitable fight. They shifted the conversation to ship's gossip and other innocuous subjects, and gradually moved on to making love. Masire fell asleep immediately afterwards, but Sanjuro had too much on her mind. If she couldn't convince Masire that the Cibolans could defeat them, she despaired of getting Vargas to even listen. Masire would follow orders. He'd had the good fortune to do most of his fighting in just wars. He knew evil things could happen—would happen—but he dismissed that as the price of being a soldier. And, of course, he didn't think things would get all that bad. He thought that, if it came to a fight, the humans would quickly demonstrate their superiority and the Cibolans would acquiesce.

Sanjuro almost wished that were true. She did not want to see war here. But the idea of the Cibolans as "happy natives" in a human-run world bothered her as much as the horrors of battle. Even if Cibolan cooperation would avoid bloodshed, she couldn't support it.

She propped herself up on her elbow and stared at the sleeping Masire. He almost looked like a little boy lying there; sleep had washed the tension away from his face. They were good friends, they liked to sleep together, there was no one else that they wanted to spend that kind of personal time with. But she had been careful not to let it go beyond that. The incident over the *Cortez* had shown her that the relationship could interfere with her work. She wanted to be able to walk away if she had to. Maybe if she could show him telepathy—in bed as well as out—she might be able to take the relationship deeper. But she couldn't trust that he would keep the secrets she needed to keep. She thought he loved her, but no relationship was worth risking so much damage to her work.

Montoya should have warned him about me instead of the other way around, she thought to herself.

>-

She spent the next morning trying to arrange a private session with Vargas before the meeting. But the Admiral's assistant had been given firm orders to keep people away from him, and she couldn't find a way in. She sent him a com message but received no reply.

Kyo caught up with her about half an hour before the meeting. "We need to talk. In private."

She shrugged her shoulders, and followed Kyo back to quarters.

"Going forward with the settlements is a done deal," Kyo said. "The bioengineers have told Vargas that the deadline is tight now for making the place human-friendly by the time the *Cortez* shows up. Plus once we give the go ahead the System will be shipping us all kinds of mining crews, engineers, support staff. The latest word is that they've made yet another improvement in the A/ND; travel is getting close to a third of the time it took us. We're going to have a lot of company in a couple of years, and we'll need some place to put them." Kyo took a deep breath and stared at Sanjuro. "I didn't expect to get all that out without an interruption. Are you okay? You look like shit."

"I couldn't sleep."

"Caty, I know you think it's wrong. I think it's wrong, too. No reason not to do business with the Cibolans. But Vargas is in a hurry. The System is leaning on him, and he doesn't want to look bad. If the *Cortez* gets here and finds a mess, he's going to get the blame."

"They won't let us do it."

Kyo looked confused.

"The Cibolans. They're going to stop us. The only question is how many people are going to die before we come around."

"You don't know that."

"Yes, I do. And so should you, if you've been paying any attention at all."

"Caty, I know you want to protect the Cibolans, but —"

"God damn it. I'm not talking about protecting Cibolans. I'm talking about protecting us."

"Don't yell at me. I know you don't really mean that."

"The hell I don't. They kill with their minds, and we don't have any protection from that."

"And we've got firepower they can't even imagine."

Sanjuro stared at her. "Kuso. Do you want to bomb these people?"

Kyo flushed. "Of course not. I'm just not buying your merde about how weak we are next to them. And you're not listening to me. Vargas is between a rock and a hard place. He's not going to let the Cibolans stop him."

"Since when did you become someone who cared what the commanding officer thought? The Sumi Kyo I used to know would have mocked Vargas's situation."

"Have you completely forgotten about the chain of command? You, who were always so by the book?"

They stood there, breathing hard, as if they'd been fighting physically instead of arguing. They'd never fought like this before, even under the stress of finals at the Academy.

Sanjuro willed herself to calm down. "Sumi, I'm not trying to just come up with something to protect the Cibolans. I really am frightened of what they will do if we push the settlements."

But Kyo was still angry. "Are you going to behave yourself in the meeting, Sanjuro?"

"I'm not going to lose my cool. But I'm going on the record with what I know."

"Caty. Goddamn it. They don't want to hear it."

She gave her a sad smile. "But it's still my duty to tell them. And I always do my duty. Ma'am."

"Caty."

"If they want to throw me in the brig afterwards, let them. Whatever. Just let me say my piece, Sumi."

"I'll let you hang yourself, Sanjuro. But I won't go down with you." She stalked off.

Sanjuro stared after her. She'd felt guilty because she hadn't told Kyo about her telepathy training. But the fight made her glad she hadn't. If Kyo was citing the chain of command, there was no way she would keep Sanjuro's efforts to master telepathic communication secret.

Kyo avoided sitting by her at the meeting. Vargas was presiding. Rao had shuttled in from the belt. Assisted by Case and a few other senior people, she told them that the initial work and survey in the asteroids had produced very positive results. They had found at least twice as much Helium-3 as expected, and the store of platinums was much larger than found in the comparable belt in the Solar System.

Entirely new industries could be developed out here, not just a mining operation. Sanjuro realized she had not been paying enough attention. There was enough wealth in the Doradoan System to build a major economy. No wonder Vargas and Rao were so committed: this was what they'd been sent to find. And no wonder they wanted the planet: a billion or more humans could live there. The *Cortez* expedition might well end up controlling all these operations, but the *Mercator* crew would at least have the satisfaction of having discovered it. Besides, one of the industries would be further exploration of space, which would include a major military component.

Kyo reported on the compatibility of the planet with human life, and then deferred to the bioengineers, who presented charts and timetables.

Sanjuro wondered how to get her own report in. She was pretty sure that Vargas wasn't going to call on her, and Rao certainly wouldn't include her among the list of reports, not after the last meeting. But Kyo surprised her by saying, after the chief bioengineer finished his statement, "Captain Sanjuro has information about the intelligent life on the planet that we need to take into consideration."

Kyo gave her a rueful look as she stood up. Perhaps, in the end, she trusted Sanjuro's instincts. Or had decided she valued friendship above career. Or just possibly her anger at her family's involvement in the *Cortez* had overridden her own misgivings.

Sanjuro spoke quickly before anyone could cut her off. "Thank you, Major. I'll be brief, sir"—that was aimed at Vargas. "I met this week with Sorrel, the ruler of the Cibolan country in which we have our camps. We are fortunate to be in his country, because he is leading the peace faction: he wants to trade with us. Several of the other rulers, and a good percentage of the population, would prefer just to drive us off."

Vargas cut in. "I trust you made him no promises, Captain."

"No, sir. I told him I would have to consult with my superiors."

"Good. Please tell him we intend him no harm, but we will put our settlements where we please, and we will begin our bioforming. His people will reap a benefit from that, and they should settle for that. Your job is to make that clear to them."

Sanjuro looked at Ari Gervaise, sitting at the dais next to Vargas. The legal officer gave a tiny shrug.

Sanjuro was supposed to sit down. She didn't. "Admiral, they aren't going to let us do it. And they can stop us."

He laughed. "Captain, they lack even the primitive weaponry our people developed a thousand years ago."

"Sir, they have mental powers that we are only beginning to comprehend. Make no mistake about it: they can stop us, and they will. And we have other choices. We can negotiate for settlements, at least until we can bioform one of the empty planets. They will trade settlement space for tech and some of the asteroid wealth. We won't make humanity as rich as we might have hoped, but given what the geo crew has found, there should be more than enough to go around."

Vargas said, "Captain, your eagerness to share wealth with people who had no hand in finding or developing it is misguided. I understand that you fought on Ceres, and like many of the soldiers there you suffer from some post-traumatic stress. We all know that war was unpleasant."

Sanjuro hoped the shock of hearing those words wasn't showing on her face. Only Kyo and Masire knew the details of her experience on Ceres.

"But you should not let old emotions affect your professional judgment. I believe we have heard enough." Vargas made a signal, and someone knocked her sound system offline.

"Sir," she said in her best battlefield voice, the one honed for all those situations where tech could fail. She knew everyone in the room could hear her. "Please note my objection to your course of action for the record. While no doubt it comforts you to believe that I am trying to protect the Cibolans out of some mental disorder, you would do well to remember two things. I am trained to study alien cultures, and I am also trained to evaluate military situations. When I tell you that the Cibolans can stop us, I am speaking based on that experience, not misguided sympathy."

"Captain, you are out of order."

"Yes, sir." She sat down. There was nothing else she could say, anyway.

The meeting didn't continue for much longer. Vargas gave the orders that would start settlement construction. He ended with a ceremonial transmittal of their report back to the System. Settlers would be underway within six months. The look Rao gave Sanjuro as she left told her she was in for more trouble. But she had stopped caring. Right now she wanted to confront Kyo and Masire.

Kyo was waiting for her in the Sci/Tech lab. She put her hands up as Sanjuro came toward her. "Peace, Caty. I didn't tell him."

"Why should I believe that? You weren't going to let me report, and then suddenly you did. Looks to me like you set me up."

"Did it ever occur to you that, once I got over being mad about what a stiff-necked bakatare you are, I realized that Vargas should hear what you have to say. I still think you might be over-rating the Cibolans, but I don't think you're delusional. Or suffering from PTSD."

Sanjuro took a deep breath. She didn't think Kyo would lie to her, not about something like that. If she'd told Vargas, she'd say so.

"Maybe there's something in your official record that you don't know about," Kyo said.

Sanjuro shook her head. "No. Somebody else told him."

Kyo gave her a puzzled look.

"Did you see where Masire went?"

"Toward his quarters. But surely you don't think he would say something."

"If it's not you—and I believe you that it's not—it's got to be him."

She ran into Montoya as she approached the Marine quarters. The sergeant had apparently been pulled up from the planet, even though no enlisted had been included in the meeting.

"Is it true," Montoya asked her, "that you don't think we can take these furry people?"

Rumor traveled fast. Vargas would be pissed if he knew how fast. "Yeah."

"No offense, Captain. I'm sure you have your reasons. But you know how we can fight, know what kind of weapons we have at our disposal."

"They don't need weapons to stop us."

"You think that telepathy stuff is that strong?"

"I know it is. You going to run security for the building crew?" Sanjuro asked.

Montoya nodded. "Going to put a troop of ten down there."

Sanjuro sighed. Ten would be a joke, but more wouldn't really help. "Be careful." It sounded weak to her.

"Always am," Montoya said.

Sanjuro heard her own arrogant self-confidence there. She didn't like it. Kuso! Now she was going to worry about Montoya, too. But she couldn't look a marine sergeant in the face and tell her that. "I need to see the Colonel. Is he in his quarters?"

"Yes, ma'am. He said he wasn't to be disturbed, but I don't suppose he meant you."

"Actually, he probably did, but I'm going to disturb him anyway."

Montoya looked puzzled as Sanjuro walked past her. The door was shut. She pushed the signal. When Masire didn't respond immediately, she pushed it again.

He opened the door. "Come in, Sanjuro," he said. "I don't know why I thought I could avoid this."

He shut the door behind her, indicated a chair.

She didn't bother to sit. "You told Vargas about what happened to me on Ceres. There's no way he could have known otherwise. That's not in any official record anywhere."

He cut her off. "Yes, I did. You don't have to make a case. I wasn't planning to deny it."

"I told you that in confidence—as a friend. As your goddamned lover."

"I know."

"And you took it to him." She had difficulty controlling her voice.

"He asked for an evaluation of you. What did you expect? That I wouldn't do my job?"

"That you wouldn't betray my confidence."

"Damn it, Sanjuro. I didn't like doing that, but once I knew about what had happened to you on Ceres, I had to take it into consideration. The safety of this ship is my responsibility. You know that. You're professional enough to know that sometimes you have to hurt your friends to do your job."

"Yeah. Like sending Montoya and her troop down to get killed defending the settlement."

"Come on. You know Montoya can handle an assignment like that."

"Yeah? She's going to have trouble handling it when she's passed out from an attack direct to her brain and while several of her soldiers are turning their guns on each other instead of Cibolans. I understand why Vargas doesn't want to believe me, Masire. But you're not invested in his dreams. Why aren't you listening to me?"

He sighed deeply. "Because I think your judgment's skewed on this one, Sanjuro."

"You think I'm lying to protect the Cibolans?"

"No. Not exactly. More that you've convinced yourself that they can stop us as a way of making us do what you consider to be the right thing."

"Not dishonest. Just deluded."

"I may not have been on Ceres, Sanjuro, but I know what something like that can do, even to the best soldiers. And you knew it too. I know that's part of the reason you got out; you didn't trust yourself to ever give orders again."

"Armchair psychology. Surely a man with your intelligence can do a better analysis than that."

He ignored the remark. "I had to tell Vargas. I'm sorry, Sanjuro. I had to do my job."

She turned to go.

"I don't expect you to forgive me. But, just for the record: I love you."

She looked back at him, her hand on the door. "Love without respect isn't enough."

He flinched as if she had slapped him.

She closed the door behind her.

She found some of the astrobio crew in the shuttle area, preparing to go back down to the planet. There was room for one more.

>➤

The Cibolans had not missed the alien discussions. The weave was active planet-wide. Those who had been paying the most attention to the aliens reported to the others: the aliens want to take our land and build homes for their people, not just for the few who are here now, but for the many more who are coming. For now they want our unused land, but in the future, who knows how much more they will take. See the images they have of home; see how many of them there are.

Others chimed in: they not only want to build on our land, but to change it to be more like theirs. More rain, warmer weather. They would create a paradise. For us as well as them, they say. But they do not ask if we want these things.

They must be stopped. A groundswell of agreement: they must be stopped.

As the fervor died down, the subject turned to tactics. The most fervent argued for destruction of them all, but more moderate voices urged restraint. Destroy their attempts at settlements. Damage their work down here. Make them see reason.

The moderate voices carried the day. Many on Cibola could see the possibilities of human tech: improved farming, fast travel, perhaps even some changes to the climate. The wealth of the asteroids beckoned as well; all on this metal-poor planet could see the benefit of more metals and most of them recognized that they needed the aliens to get those metals. Only the most xenophobic were willing to sacrifice that possibility.

But none were willing to sacrifice their independence.

# CONFLICT

# 1

Sanjuro knew Rao wanted to talk with her before she left *Mercator*, but she turned her com off to avoid knowing the messages were there, even shutting down the emergency override despite the fact that doing so was prohibited. If the messages didn't register as read, she could at least argue that she hadn't disobeyed a direct order.

When she arrived at her campsite, the only thing she could think of to do was go to Sundown and try to keep a dialogue going. She rummaged around the cabin, packing up a few essentials. She was just about to leave when a landcraft pulled up. Kyo stepped out. "Rao was looking for you."

"I'm not hard to find."

"But you're not still on *Mercator*. And that's where she was looking, until she went back to the belt."

"I didn't get the message."

"You know the penalties for disobeying an order, Sanjuro?"

"Of course I do. But I didn't disobey it intentionally."

"No power on your com?" Kyo said it sarcastically, since the implanted system constantly recharged itself from human energy. "Or did you switch your override off by mistake?"

Sanjuro was still holding the various belongings she had collected. She set them down. "I was afraid she wouldn't let me come back down. The only thing I could think of was to make sure I didn't get an order. So I did."

"You're probably right she wouldn't let you come back down. She thinks you've been giving the Cibolans way too much information about us. I'd say she's within a hair's breath of calling it treason." Kyo's voice was flat, her face unreadable. "If I were you, I'd get on com and grovel. You've got more than your work and your career on the line here."

"That an order? Ma'am?"

"Would you obey it if it was?"

Sanjuro sighed. "I can't let her keep me from the Cibolans. Not now. There's too much at stake. Maybe I can help keep things from escalating on their side. I've got to try."

"You go out there, and Rao is going to move from hinting at treason to saying it openly. Damn it, Caty. You obviously told them about the settlements. And probably everything else."

"I didn't tell them anything they didn't already know. I had to deal straight with them, or they'd have dismissed me as a liar."

"What makes you so sure they already knew?"

"Goddamn it." She smacked the side of the landcraft with the flat of her hand.

Kyo jumped.

"They can read our minds. Hasn't anyone been listening to me? They aren't just reading *my* mind; they're dipping into *everyone's*. They've pulled info from everyone on planet in detail—they have way more data on us than we have on them. And if they combine enough of their folks together, they can even read the people on *Mercator*. They know every fucking thing we're doing."

"But they can't possibly understand our language."

"They don't have to. People don't just think in words, Sumi. We think in images, too. Here, I'll give you an example. Remember that dinner at the academy, the first one?"

"What? Oh, shit. I get it. When I think about that, the first thing I get is a picture of you with your service ribbons on. And some asshole sophomore jacking you up. All image—no words. But that's such a hodge-podge of stuff, Caty. How do they make sense of it?"

"Well, they have experience with it. They do mentally what we do by computer: not as efficiently, perhaps, but they can sort data. Plus they have a hell of a lot of folks working on it. We're a threat to them; dealing with us is their first priority right now."

"It makes sense, but it's not going to save your ass."

"If I don't do what I can to keep the lines of communication open with the Cibolans, we're all going to die here, and it won't matter anyway."

"I know you think they're dangerous to us, but so far—"

"So far the peace faction's been holding the war faction in check. But we just took the step that's going to change that. We just sent a crew down to start a settlement and begin bioforming. That crew's setting up as we speak. And I guarantee you there are some Cibolans nearby, paying attention to everything they're doing and figuring it out."

Kyo held up her hands to stop the flow of words. "Caty—"

"They can stop us, Sumi. They can't fight our machines, our weapons. But they can fight us. And we don't have anything that can stop them. Now I've got two choices: I can sit up on *Mercator* and try to get someone to listen to me. Or I can go to the Cibolans, and try to get them to believe we're not as bad as we look. So far I've been having better luck with the Cibolans than my own people."

"Caty. Please. I know you think what we're doing here is wrong-headed. So do I. But getting into serious trouble isn't going to solve anything."

"Sumi, Sumi," she said sadly, rubbing her eyes. "I keep telling you, I'm not trying to protect the Cibolans from us. I'm trying to protect us from them."

"You really believe that, don't you?"

"What did you think I was doing, trying to scare you? Yes. I think they can kill us all, any time they want to."

"What if you're wrong?"

"Then Rao can bring me up on all the charges she can think of."

Kyo covered her face with her hands.

Sanjuro said, "You know, my daddy told me a story about my mother that didn't make it into the official Marine records. Seems that when she put together that transport and got all those people off Europa ahead of the attack that damn near destroyed the whole moon, she was disobeying a direct order. The strategy AI had predicted no attack in that vicinity, even though the air troops protecting the port had caught signals. Becca was a lot more inclined to trust some veteran Space Corps pilots than fettered AI, but her commanding officer wasn't. She set up the evacuation, and history proved her right. Given that she wasn't able to save everybody, she might have preferred being wrong and ending up with the court martial instead of the posthumous medal."

"It really doesn't matter what I say, does it?"

"No. Unless you're planning to try to stop me physically."

"I couldn't take you without a weapon, and I'm not that melodramatic anyway." Kyo stared at her. "You're in luck. Rao was in such a hurry to get back to the Belt that she told me to talk to you."

"And?"

"So I've talked to you. Be careful out there, Sanjuro."

"Always am."

"Right." Kyo turned to go, then looked back toward her. "And turn your baka com back on. We might need you."

Sanjuro said, "On," letting Kyo hear it. The Major made a face, then got into her landcraft and left without waving goodbye. Sanjuro watched her disappear into the distance. It was only when she'd started for the Cibolan town that she realized Kyo hadn't ordered her not to go.

Maybe she should have told Kyo about her telepathy studies. She started to call her up on com, then changed her mind. Kyo had gone way past her comfort level in letting Sanjuro go. She would have to let Vargas and Rao know about human telepathy if she knew. But she was going to be very pissed when she found out that Sanjuro had been keeping secrets.

# 2

Since the aliens had begun their development projects in Golden Mountain, people from that region were taking the lead in the resistance. Sorrel kept as close a rein on the affairs as possible; it hoped that the aliens could be frightened into backing off and negotiating properly without blood being shed. But Sorrel knew it would be difficult to stop Fire and some of the others from taking stronger measures. It hoped the aliens would realize the danger and back off.

The alien Sanjuro was staying with Sundown. Several advisors had suggested that they ask for its help, but Sundown had firmly rejected that idea. The aliens are its people, Sundown had sent. Sanjuro cannot betray them, even if they are wrong. Fire had suggested expelling Sanjuro from the planet, but that idea did not garner strong support. We will need to communicate with the other aliens through that one, Sorrel sent. Better that it continue to study with Sundown.

A crew was dispatched to the alien encampment, with instructions to read the human minds and develop ways to sabotage their building program. Sorrel ended the meeting with an exhortation to be creative, but gentle, in their actions. From the tone in the weave, though, the leader knew violent responses would occur. The war images coming from the aliens would inevitably set off reactions.

⤞

"It's jinxed," Montoya said. "The whole project. Jinxed." She sat in her cabin, reporting to Masire via holo.

"Jinxed how?" Masire rubbed his head and wriggled his shoulders.

Montoya thought he looked tired. "Things just keep going wrong. First day, all the instabuild cabins came down in the middle of the night. Turns out somebody had set the close-up timer on them, like you do in mobile operations. Only, of course, this one isn't mobile. The guy who must have done it denies it, though."

"And then the bioengineers set out the first line of trees, the ones they nurtured on the ship all the way out from the System. Two days later, they're all dead. They run a scan, find arsenic in their roots. No one even knows where it came from. Apparently got mixed in with the fertilizer."

"Any more things like that?"

"Dozens, sir. It's all in my written report. Half of 'em look like some dumb mistake, the other half like sabotage."

"Any Cibolans around?"

"Haven't seen a one. We thought of that. But some of this stuff they wouldn't know how to do. Would they?"

"I don't know," Masire said. "Maybe I'd better come down and take a look."

"It's not too far from here to Captain Sanjuro's camp," Montoya said. "By landcraft, anyway."

"I won't have time for that," Masire said. "I'll shuttle down in a couple of hours. Have someone set me up a cabin."

"Yes, sir," Montoya said, spit and polish to match his curt tone.

The settlement was officially a Space Corps job, since their engineering techs were in charge of set up. But the bioforming crew came under Sci/Tech. Both of them would be touchy about a Marine-run investigation, Masire thought. So he'd brought Gervaise planetside as well. Now the two of them sat in the main headquarters with Sumi Kyo and Space Corps Lt. K.C. Wu, going over incident reports.

Masire finished reading. "Looks like we've got a baka mess on our hands."

The other three did not argue with him.

"Do you think it's Cibolan sabotage?"

Wu shrugged. "It's something. Even incompetents couldn't screw up this bad. And my crew isn't incompetent. I hope it's Cibolan, because the alternative is too unpleasant to think about."

Kyo said, "What K.C. here doesn't want to say is that everything looks like it was done by one of us. And we haven't seen any damn Cibolans."

Wu looked grim. Masire sighed.

"But," Kyo said, "if Sanjuro's right about the Cibolan ability at mind control, it would look like that."

"Is that really a possibility?" Gervaise asked.

"Makes more sense than some of my people doing it on purpose," Wu said. "Hell, this crew's only been planetside for a few days; they haven't had time to go native."

Everyone nodded.

Wu cleared his throat. "I hate to say this, but has it occurred to anyone else that Sanjuro might be behind the sabotage?"

Masire slumped in his seat. He'd been thinking the same thing, but he hadn't wanted to say it.

Gervaise rubbed her face.

Kyo said, "No way in hell."

Wu looked uncomfortable. "I know all of you are friends with Sanjuro, but we at least ought to think about it."

"She wouldn't do it like this. It's not her style." Kyo spoke in the voice of an officer who expected no argument.

But these people were her peers, not her staff. They argued. Ari Gervaise said, "Are you really that sure about it, Kyo? I know you wouldn't want to think Sanjuro would do something like this, but you know how upset she is about the settlements."

"And even if she's not doing it herself, she could be telling the Cibolans how to do it," Wu said.

Gervaise nodded. "That's a good point."

Masire bit his lip. He should say something, but he wasn't sure what.

Kyo shook her head. "Look, if Sanjuro was helping the Cibolans stop us, she'd have a bunch of them sitting over there where we're trying to plant trees singing 'We Shall Not Be Moved.' She fights out in the open."

Masire said, "Well, we ought to get her evaluation of the situation, anyway. Can we get her over here?"

Kyo said, "I doubt it. She's deep in country, studying Cibolans. I can beep her com, but I don't guarantee an answer, certainly not an immediate one."

Both Wu and Gervaise looked at Masire as if they were surprised he hadn't already known she wasn't nearby. And Kyo raised her eyebrows. Damn. Whatever he said would probably make him look worse.

"Oh, I hadn't realized she'd gone in-country. I thought she was planning to stay at her campsite," Masire said. Pathetic, he thought.

Kyo said, "Unfortunately, no. It would be nice to have her here, but I can tell you what she'd say. She'd say, 'Of course the Cibolans are doing it, you bakatares.' Though I suppose if she were here she might have some suggestions for ways to prove that. Or even how to stop it."

"Does she know about the trouble?" Gervaise asked.

"I sent her a message, and got an acknowledgment. So I hope she's trying to calm the Cibolans down, if they're really the problem."

They talked it over awhile longer. Masire decided to beef up the security crew to twenty. Wu said he'd have everyone do things in pairs; that would help spot mistakes or prevent sabotage. Gervaise said she'd have intelligence run an analysis on all the incidents, see if they could find any unusual patterns. And Kyo promised to talk to Sanjuro.

The meeting broke up, but Masire took Kyo aside. "How did Sanjuro get permission to go back in-country? I got the idea Rao wanted to pull her off planet, and I figured you had worked out some kind of compromise that kept her on a short leash."

"She didn't get Rao's permission," Kyo said, and explained what had occurred.

Masire shook his head. "What the hell can she be thinking?"

"That she's right. She can be damn pig-headed when she thinks she's right."

"Didn't you try to stop her?"

"Yeah, but she invoked the memory of Becca Sanjuro. Been my experience that it's a waste of time arguing with marines when they invoke St. Becca."

Masire didn't grin. He rubbed his arms as if he'd suddenly gotten cold. "Is she right?"

"I don't know. Even if you believe that the Cibolans are telepaths—and I do, although I don't think Vargas or Rao has ever taken the idea seriously—it's hard to buy that they have the kind of power Sanjuro claims. But she's spent a lot of time with them. I can't kick any holes in her theories. And I've tried." She gave Masire a look. "I thought she might have told you what her plans were."

Masire looked away. "We're on shaky ground right now."

Kyo said, "She's a complicated person."

Masire shook his head. "It's not her fault." He wanted to say more, but old habit held him back.

Kyo didn't press him. "If I have to take sides, I'd say Sanjuro is right. Her theory about the mental power of the Cibolans is the only explanation that answers all our questions."

Masire said, carefully, "Are you really sure Wu's theory is wrong?"

Kyo looked startled. "You've been sleeping with Caty Sanjuro for five years, and you don't know her any better than that? I figured you didn't say anything earlier because it's hard for you to defend her when you're in charge of the investigation. I didn't think you actually bought into any of that merde."

"But if she's really worried that we might massacre the Cibolans—"

"She'll stand in front of them and make us go through her first. You don't believe that post-traumatic stress nonsense that Vargas gave out, do you?"

"She's carrying a lot of guilt over Ceres."

Kyo gave him a look. "I don't buy it. And anyway, what she says makes sense from a scientific point of view. It's just improbable. So are lots of discoveries, at first. Look at that crazy baka Nguyen and her exotic matter theories. Nuts, like her. But they work." She patted Masire on the shoulder. "You want to worry about the woman, worry about the trouble she's gotten herself into, not some cock-eyed idea that she's a saboteur."

# 3

Sanjuro sensed tension between Iron and Sundown, even though they blocked their arguments from her. Kyo had told her about the problems at the settlement site, and Sanjuro was sure Cibolans were behind it. She didn't think Sundown had anything to do with attacking the sites, but Iron might be involved.

Sundown and Sanjuro went up to the observatory, practicing communication skills as they walked. Sanjuro surprised several of the people they met by greeting them individually. As they climbed the hill, Sundown taught her about the plants and small animals they passed.

Only when they had settled in at the observatory did Sanjuro broach the subject of the stress between Sundown and Iron. Is it because of us, she sent, adding an image of humans en masse.

We have different opinions about your people, Sundown sent. She added no details, but sent a second message: Iron is pregnant, and that is always a difficult time.

Sanjuro blinked. She could have sworn Sundown had said Iron was pregnant. But how could that be possible? Iron was male. She responded with a query, showing Iron with the growing belly of pregnancy—an image that was the same in both humans and Cibolans. Sanjuro had met several pregnant Cibolans as well as several nursing fathers and had been using the clues she got from those meetings to determine gender. She hadn't found any other obvious differences between the Cibolan sexes, though she had been classifying people as male or female as best she could.

Sundown replied with the same sending. *Iron is pregnant. We wanted another child, and I want to nurture this little one.* Sundown showed Sanjuro the pouch beginning to form.

*Both of you can get pregnant?*

*All of us can get pregnant or nurse children,* Sundown sent. *Is it not the same with you?*

Sanjuro was stunned. Months on the planet, all that time with Sundown in telepathic communication, and she had still missed the basic fact that Cibolans were not two-sexed. They must be more like ambigendered humans. But the ambigendered had altered their genetic structure to give themselves the genitalia and reproductive system of both sexes. Genetic modification had made the process heritable, but the original ambis had gone through complicated medical procedures. Had the Cibolans genetically modified themselves using their telepathic powers?

But Sundown had said everyone could do it. That sounded like it was their inherent natural process. They were alien. And Kyo had said the astrobiologists were having difficulty sorting animals by sex. Maybe the animals were the same way. Maybe this was just the way Cibolans were. How amazing! And then she realized that Sundown had assumed humans to be the same as Cibolans. *No, we are not like that,* Sanjuro sent. She sent first a picture of herself pregnant and then one of Masire with negatives—she was getting good at the images for concepts not considered visual in human culture. *I have no children, but I could have them. Masire could not, but he could father them. It takes both a woman and a man to make a child.*

As Sanjuro explained, she marveled at what she was leaving out. This was human reproduction from before the twentieth century. Medical technology had changed it dramatically. Ambis could both sire children and give birth. Same sex couples often merged ova or sperm to reproduce. She herself had been conceived in vitro years after her mother's death and nurtured to birth in an artificial womb, making her a person who shouldn't have been stuck in outdated thinking about reproduction.

But she had been, partly because of the technological level of the Cibolans. Bogdosian had been right in her constant exhortations to remember that intelligent life could come in many different packages. The Cibolans had seemed so similar to humans, especially once Sanjuro had begun to learn to control her telepathy. And yet here was something basic and very different.

Has it always been true that all of you can give birth and sire children, Sanjuro sent? It took several tries to phrase the question, because it made no sense to Sundown at first. Eventually, Sundown replied yes, of course, we have always reproduced this way.

The two of them did then what they should have done the first time they discussed reproduction: provided detailed images of both humans and Cibolans. Sanjuro showed Sundown the genital reproductive organs of women and the contrasting ones of men. Sundown was fascinated. You are like this all the time? But it is not obvious when you are wearing clothes.

Sundown showed her Cibolans in daily life, and then the variations on genitalia that could develop. The aroused Cibolans had genitals similar to vaginas and penises—they did, in fact, connect together much as humans did. But couples frequently reversed roles when having sex for fun. Only when they became serious about having a child would they made a decision about who would mother and who would father.

Sanjuro had known Cibolan conception required mental and physiological consent from both parties, but now that she understood how it really worked, she realized that reproduction wasn't the slapdash system that it was in humans. No unintended pregnancies for Cibolans. No accidents.

I still see you as like me, Sundown sent. You, Masire, Kyo—all seem the same to me.

And I see you as like me, Sanjuro replied. But I can't change as you can.

They said it in good humor. Sundown appeared unconcerned. She—it—did not seem to consider the differences in reproduction systems to be significant. But for Sanjuro, the difference felt vast. Humans had built whole cultures on these differences, and even though much of recent history had ended the limitations imposed by those cultures, had given men and women equal footing in the world, had opened the door for recognition of other genders, born and made, still, when a new baby was born, human beings asked whether it was a boy or a girl. The knowledge of that difference might not have been the biological imperative that a few still wanted to believe in, but Sanjuro's reaction to Sundown's explanation told her that the cultural belief in the difference remained.

Sanjuro was disturbed by her failure to see something so basic about the Cibolans. Perhaps she was no more clear-headed about meeting aliens than Vargas and the rest. And that brought her mind back to their current situation, humans demanding one thing, Cibolans another. That, at least, was not due to reproductive differences, but to the differences in their positions. Had the roles been reversed, the humans would have resisted any effort to change their lives, too. Sanjuro wondered if the Cibolans would have been as aggressive as humans had they been the invaders.

>~

The group of Cibolans watching the alien settlement was disappointed to observe that they were once again setting out new plants and putting up buildings.

Poisoning plants is not enough, someone sent. They just plant more. They must have infinite supplies of alien plants. Perhaps they grow them on that ship up in the sky.

The buildings grow back, too, no matter how many mistakes we encourage, another sent.

These soft methods are not enough, sent a third. We must do something more damaging if we want them to react.

Sorrel would be displeased.

Sorrel is old. And Fire would back us.

They entered the closed weave of those committed to sabotaging the aliens, looking for new ideas. And permission.

>~

A week later Masire found himself planetside again, in Tish Montoya's cabin, trying to get a clear explanation out of her. Masire sat on the only chair; Montoya stood at rigid attention in front of him. Told to relax, she moved into an equally rigid parade rest. "Okay, Sergeant," Masire said, "tell me what happened."

"I shot Lt. Yung, sir."

"But why?"

A spasm passed across her face. "I don't know why, sir. I just know that I did it."

"You've got no explanation at all?"

"No, sir." Her jaw rigid.

"There wasn't something unusual going on in your mind, for example?" He watched the same look go across her face.

"It wouldn't make any difference. I still shot him."

Masire rubbed his left eyebrow and sighed. "Sit down, Tish," using her first name on purpose because he never used it. His voice was quiet.

She looked at him, then perched uneasily on the edge of her cot.

"You got anything to drink in here?"

She gaped at him, then said, "There's some wine in the storage bin, sir. Homemade stuff. The astrobio crew make it."

"It'll do." He filled a couple of disposable cups with the wine— barracks style entertaining. Masire poured a glass of wine, handed it to her, and then poured another for himself before sitting back down. Montoya held the glass with the same rigidity with which she'd been standing.

"Take a drink of that, and then take a deep breath and forget I'm your commanding officer. And tell me what the fuck happened out there."

She took the drink, but the breath didn't sound all that deep. "Colonel, I don't really know what happened. Anything I can say is going to sound weird, like some kind of insane excuse, and I don't want to make excuses. I don't understand why I shot the Lieutenant, but I did it and I don't want to sound like I'm trying to avoid responsibility for it."

Masire sighed. "Tish, no one would ever accuse you of ducking responsibility for something. But it's also inconceivable that you shot a man for no reason. So either Yung did something that made you think you had no other choice, or something else was going on in your mind."

Montoya took a breath again, this time a really deep one, from down in her diaphragm. "It was right after the new buildings blew up. We were sifting through the damage, trying to find some sort of clue to what happened. Yung called me off, along with three more troopers. All the senior people here. He had an idea he'd seen something in the woods, and he wanted us to follow him in there."

Masire nodded.

"It was just after dark, getting cold. And you know our suits keep failing down here; we've had to hustle someone back to shelter more than once because all of sudden he had no heat. Plus the night vision glasses keep blowing out at odd times. They aren't recharging right, for some reason. So it didn't make any sense, you know, chasing odd ideas through the woods in the dark. Not to mention drawing off the senior enlisted right after a crisis. But Yung insisted, and I couldn't see any way to talk him out of it." She gave Masire a look.

He understood. Like most good sergeants, Montoya saw it as her job to try to keep officers from making stupid mistakes. But sometimes there was no way to do that.

"So we followed him. Got deep into the woods, and all of a sudden, the Lieutenant just went crazy. Started dancing around, tearing off his suit, making odd noises. Two of the others tried to grab him, stop him before he hurt himself, and he just stuck his arms out straight at them and they fell down, stunned. That left Hwan and myself. I'm not sure what came over Hwan, but she suddenly started running deeper into the forest.

"And Yung was coming at me, laughing like a nut case, still kind of dancing around."

She gulped down the last of the wine. "And all of a sudden, I felt like I was a million miles away, just watching what was going on. I saw myself pick up my weapon, watched as I set the coordinates, knew I was setting them to kill. I kept shouting in my head 'but that's the Lieutenant,' but it was like those dreams you have sometimes when you want to scream and can't. I just watched myself point the gun and fire."

He poured the rest of the wine into her glass. She swallowed it all.

"And then I was normal again, and trying to get a pulse. But he'd ripped off most of his suit, and I'd shot him clean through the heart."

"Sounds like it might have been self-defense," Masire said.

"He was acting nuts and that might be a nice excuse, but he wasn't pointing a weapon at me. I could take Lt. Yung anytime I wanted to." She wasn't bragging; just stating a fact.

"But he'd already knocked the others aside."

"Colonel, you want to make excuses for me, go ahead. But I don't think I was scared of him. If you want my opinion, I'd say I wasn't in control of my own hands. But that's completely nuts."

"Not if Sanjuro's right about the Cibolans," Masire said, half to himself. He was about to say something more when they heard a sound like a tremendous clap of thunder. The ground shook under their feet. They stepped outside to find the main astrobio lab in flames. People were racing around, trying to find a way to put the fire out. As Masire and Montoya stared, a figure walked out of the lab and began to roll on the ground.

Montoya didn't hesitate. She leapt toward the figure and rolled on top of it, trying to smother some of the fire. Masire ran back into the shelter, grabbed a blanket off the cot, and raced over to throw it on them both.

The flames went out. Montoya climbed shakily to her feet. Masire could see some burns on her suit and wondered if they'd gone through. The person on the ground was still trying to roll, and giggling. Masire stared down at the badly burned face and realized this was Corporal Hwan. He screamed "Medic," but someone was already running over with a portable kit. He watched as they shot her full of painkillers and coated her body in a foam that hardened on the outside.

Masire walked over to Kyo, who was directing the firefighters. "As soon as we get this out, Major, get all your people together. We're taking everyone back up to *Mercator* until we figure out what's going on."

"Yes, sir," said Kyo fervently.

"And get hold of Sanjuro. I want her up there, too."

Kyo looked at him.

"She's the only person with a goddamned explanation of what's going on down here. We're going to need her."

"I'll tell her that."

⤜

The sabotage group, Iron among them, watched the aliens crowd into their ships and leave the planet. They're gone, someone sent. We forced them away. They're leaving. Others agreed. Let us celebrate. We have won.

We should wait to celebrate until we see if their large ship leaves our sky, a more cautious person replied. Perhaps they have only left to regroup. They might come again, might try something new. Remember, these people kill.

We have killed, Iron sent. Iron was angry about the aliens, but had not liked the deaths caused by the saboteurs. It had refused to participate in those activities, but knowledge of what had happened weighed heavy in its mind.

But the aliens have left, the first person sent. Even the one who was studying with Iron's spouse has gone. Now they know they must fear us. Maybe they will leave forever.

Or maybe they will just get angrier and do something terrible to us, Iron sent.

Sundown's friend will help us, the first one sent. It will convince them to leave.

They do not pay heed to Sundown's friend, Iron sent, anger showing. It cares—Sundown is right to be its friend—but it has no power to stop anything.

Iron did not join the others when they went back to celebrate.

# 4

Sanjuro, Kyo, and a few other stragglers caught the last shuttle off the planet. During the flight, the shuttle's main com screen displayed a mission-wide broadcast. Vargas looked haggard. "Ladies and Gentlemen, as you know, we have had some very unpleasant incidents on the planet, as well as some unusual occurrences here on the ship. I am conducting a court of inquiry to get to the bottom of the problem.

"Meanwhile, I have just received notification from the System. They are putting together the first follow-up team: enough mining engineers and technicians to run a full-scale operation in the asteroid belt, along with a core group of settlers to establish the beginnings of an industrial sector. With a regular Space Corps crew, and some marine reinforcements, the total group will come to about a thousand people. Since the engineers have been working on improvements to the A/ND, the trip is down to less than two years. The first group ought to be leaving in about three months. We're going to need some place to put them.

"So finding out the source of our problem is more than an intellectual exercise. The development of this sector of space depends on it. I am sure I will have the complete cooperation of each and every one of you as we resolve this problem."

When the screen went dark, Sanjuro said to Kyo, "Five will get you ten he hasn't told the System about the problems."

"I won't take that one. It's dead certain he didn't tell them. He wants to fix it first."

"He's going to have to talk with the Cibolans to fix it. And they're not feeling very friendly."

Kyo sighed and looked away.

Sanjuro ignored her body language. "Is Rao coming in for the inquiry?"

Kyo shook her head. "She doesn't want to leave the belt. But she's going to follow it by holo. The delay will keep her from participating, but she'll certainly have something to say to Vargas after you testify. She's leveled some serious charges against you, Caty."

"To be expected. Think anybody will listen to me?"

"You'd better produce something pretty damn solid tying the destruction of the settlement to the Cibolans."

"I guess my word's not enough."

"Easier to blame the crew members who actually did things than to believe some complicated telepathic theory. Or to blame you."

"Me?"

"It fits in with Vargas's PTSD line. More than one person has suggested it."

"Kuso. Though I guess I should have thought of that." Sanjuro got quiet.

Kyo unhooked her seatbelt, stood up, and stretched.

Sanjuro wriggled around in her own seat, trying to get comfortable. "You believe me, don't you, Sumi?"

"Yes, I do. Because otherwise I have to believe in an undetectable psychosis that hits random individuals. A telepathic attack makes a hell of a lot more sense than that. And I don't think you'd attack your own people."

"Thanks."

"Of course, I've actually spent time with Cibolans. Outside of my team, no one else has. And believing you means Vargas has to do things differently. We might not be able to house all those people the System wants to send. A thousand's just the tip of the iceberg, after all. Vargas isn't going to want to deal with that."

"He's going to have to."

Kyo brought her right arm straight across her chest and used her left to pull it close, then switched arms. She rotated her neck a couple of times, and then sat back down and looked straight at

Sanjuro. "Look, you're really not considering his situation. The System is putting all kinds of pressure on him. And it's contradictory pressure. His superiors in Combined Forces are telling him he must cooperate with the *Cortez*, but they're giving him a 'wink, wink' when they say cooperate. The civilian side of the SSU is telling him to get the whole place ready to turn over to the corporations. He's trying to walk a careful line, work with the *Cortez*, but keep enough back so that he can put up the fight his superiors demand.

"And Rao's making it harder. She's damned determined not to give up her asteroids, and the professional Sci/Tech crew will back her up. He's up to his ass in alligators, and you're just a damn mosquito. He figures if he listens to you, he's going to get eaten alive."

"If he doesn't listen to me, no one is getting anything out here." Kyo just shook her head.

Sanjuro wondered whether now would be a good time to tell Kyo about her telepathy. The Major had gone out on a limb for her more than once, even after their fight. And she'd had personal experience with Cibolan attacks. Maybe if she understood human capacity for telepathy, she'd believe that the Cibolans posed a serious risk. Sanjuro also wanted to tell Kyo what she had discovered about Cibolan gender. But the timing seemed wrong. Kyo would be furious at Sanjuro for not having told her earlier, but would probably also dismiss both facts as things that wouldn't change the current situation. Her arguments about the pressures on Vargas indicated that she didn't think anything Sanjuro said would affect him.

Kyo's com beeped as they docked on *Mercator*. "Damn. They want me now. I was hoping to have time to clean up."

"Thanks for waiting for me back on Cibola."

"I wanted to be damn sure you made it. I hope you have some answers. If you don't, I think some very good people are going to be hung out to dry. Starting with you."

"I've got answers. If they'll listen." Her voice was grim.

"Well, don't forget to bring the smoking gun."

"Back me up in there, Sumi."

"If I can." Kyo started for the door, then stopped. "You might want a lawyer, Caty."

She laughed. "In my experience lawyers are basically useful for muddying waters when the facts will hurt you. What do you want, Sumi? For me to protect myself or for me to produce some hard, cold facts?"

"Both."

"I don't think we get both. You can't attack without leaving yourself open."

Kyo didn't laugh, though she'd probably heard that adage as often as Sanjuro had.

⋗

Montoya's lawyer was trying to convince her to present the facts as self-defense. "You get into all that mental stuff, you just make it too complicated for them, Sergeant. The simplest answer is the best one: Yung went off his rocker, hurt the others—medical will verify that they're both still in comas—and you had to defend yourself."

"If that's all there is, then I screwed up. I should have been able to take him out without a gun."

"He was nuts, Sergeant."

*So was I,* Montoya thought to herself.

⋗

Lt. Wu was getting impatient. "Commander, with all due respect, you keep hinting at some kind of sabotage by crew members. And it just doesn't make sense."

"Why not? The physical evidence points to a crew member in every case," Gervaise said.

"Yes, ma'am. But if you look at each incident, you'll see that we've got more than sixty crew members who must have done something. That's close to half the people who've been planetside. If we've got a conspiracy going on, it's one hell of a lot bigger than anything I ever heard of."

"So you think the Cibolans are behind the sabotage?"

"Yes, ma'am."

242

"And do you have any proof of this?"

"Ma'am, it's the only logical—"

"Any proof, Lieutenant?"

"No, ma'am."

"Thank you, Lieutenant."

⇒

"Major Kyo, if you blame all the sabotage on the Cibolans, please explain something to me: Why didn't these problems manifest themselves when we first put the astrobio crew down on the planet?"

"Well, Commander, the only answer I have is speculative. I assume that they didn't consider us a threat when we initially began surveying the planet. Our efforts to build a more permanent settlement are what upset them."

Gervaise sighed. "I was hoping for something other than speculation, Major."

"I'm sorry. I don't really have anything else. Nothing I've found in a detailed examination of the planet would explain a sudden fit of madness running through a large number of crew members, all of whom passed psychological testing for this trip. And the Cibolans do communicate telepathically. A telepathic attack makes more sense than a virus or bacterium that leaves no traces in its victims."

Vargas said, "Well, at least the speculation by everyone who has been on the planet is consistent. But what makes you so convinced the Cibolans are telepathic?"

"I've communicated with them by thinking, sir. The ones I've met have sent me messages and responded logically to what I've thought."

"But you have no physical evidence of this from your scans of their brains, your analysis of their genetic material?"

"No, sir. But we've got a long way to go in analyzing everything in the Cibolan brain. They're appreciably different from human brains, and there are still parts of our own brains we don't quite comprehend."

"So no proof?"

"No, sir."

# 5

The hearing was being held in the small conference room. Vargas sat at the head of the table, with Gervaise next to him, and the other senior officers around the table. Both Kyo and Masire were there, even though both had given testimony earlier. A holo feed was going out to the asteroids. The lag time on that was about ten minutes.

Sanjuro came in, saluted, and waited. She wondered who made up the official board here.

Gervaise said, "Sit down, Captain. These proceedings are informal. We're just trying to determine some facts. Though of course you are entitled to counsel, if you feel the need."

"I'm fine on my own, ma'am."

"You're sure?"

Sanjuro thought she detected some personal concern in Gervaise's voice. Or maybe it was just lawyer talk. "Yes, ma'am."

"Okay. Now, I gather you've seen the evidence of the sabotage at the settlement site."

"Yes, ma'am."

"It seems to point to crew members, but to large numbers of them. And all of them deny they intentionally did any of these things. All of the evidence indicates they are telling the truth, and also that they do not have any psychological disorders. So we're faced with a mystery: What caused these normally reliable people to damage things, even to assault each other and kill?

"Now you have said repeatedly that the Cibolans have the telepathic capacity to fight us. Are incidents such as we have had consistent with that power?"

"Yes, ma'am. Entirely. Forcing another person to do something damaging to himself is one method of fighting among the Cibolans."

"But not the only one?"

"No, ma'am. They also attack the mind directly. It's not unlike a physical fight; an attack can be blocked, though the defender must keep some ability to attack while blocking."

"You've seen examples of this?"

"Yes, ma'am." She remembered the attack on her and Sundown all too vividly. "It's much more dangerous than most of the sabotage we've had so far. A direct attack often kills, and if it doesn't, it can leave the victim so mentally damaged that he cannot be healed."

"But we've had people killed."

"Yes. Using the indirect attack works well on us. Unlike most Cibolans, we don't have any conception of how to resist it. What I'm trying to say, ma'am, is that they're not using their whole arsenal on us."

"Why not?"

"Because they'd rather trade with us than fight us. We have things they can use—access to the asteroid wealth, technology. They're willing to give us some space for settlements in return for a share of the minerals in the belt and some tech. Or rather, some of them are. The Cibolans don't speak with one voice." Sanjuro figured Gervaise was actually interested in gathering facts, but she was surprised that Vargas was listening to all this.

Vargas said, "And how did the Cibolans find out about the settlements? Did you tell them about our plans, and about how our systems work?"

Obviously, he hadn't really been listening. Sanjuro said, "We all did, sir. Every one of us has given the Cibolans information every time we've thought about what we do."

He waved his hands. "Yes, yes, you've said that many times. But did you tell them directly?"

"I told them directly that we planned settlements on the planet and mining in the asteroids. I told you that before. They asked directly, and I answered honestly, because I thought they already knew the answer and would no longer trust me if I lied. I did not tell them how to blow up buildings or cause one soldier to shoot another. I would never do that. But no one had to tell them; they could figure it out. Images of how to do those things run through our minds all the time. When you think about firing your weapon you mostly do so in images. Easy enough for a Cibolan to take in those images, file them away for future reference, and later use mental power to force you to turn that weapon on someone." Sanjuro gave an inward sigh. It sounded as if Vargas had decided to accept that the Cibolans caused the sabotage, but also that he was going to blame it on her. That would give him an out if it all went south.

"Well, Captain, exactly how the Cibolans learned of our weak points will have to be determined. We will have a further inquiry into it." He gave her a firm look.

Gervaise looked worried. *Perhaps I ought to get some legal counsel at that,* Sanjuro thought.

"But first we have to deal with the matter at hand. The Cibolans have attacked our base, killed and injured our people. We cannot allow them to get away with these attacks. They must be shown that we will not be trifled with."

Sanjuro stared at him. Out of the corner of her eye she could see that Kyo's face also registered disbelief. Gervaise was shaking her head. Masire kept his face professionally blank, but she listened with her mind, and heard him think, "Kuso."

Vargas turned toward Marley. "Captain, I want a squadron of the best pilots you've got. Colonel Masire, get your people ready to hit the ground. We're going to show these people a thing or two about the human race."

In Vargas's mind Sanjuro read the cold anger: how dare these people stop our plans. But her own anger was rising, and it felt red hot. She stood up, kicking back her chair as she did so. "Admiral—"

Vargas cut her off. "Captain, I assure you we will get back to these questions. I will want to know a great deal more about what you told the Cibolans. But for now, we will solve the immediate problem. You are dismissed."

"No, sir. You will hear me out now." She opened her mind, linked to every mind there. Gervaise was running through legal options. Masire was still shaken. Sanjuro felt Kyo start to say something. "No, Sumi, not this time." She walked around to the head of the table.

Vargas started to call for a guard, but she stopped him in midthought. He shook his head, as if he couldn't figure out what had happened.

"I'm not a threat to you, Admiral. You won't need those people. But you do have to listen. If you go forward with this attack on the Cibolans, we will lose. They can stop us. You send a bunch of pilots out on a bombing run, and they may drop a few bombs. But sooner or later, the Cibolans are going to figure out what they're doing. They'll assign a group of people to each ship. And then your pilots are going to shoot at each other. Or blow themselves up.

"You send in a troop of marines, hell, that will be a piece of cake for the Cibolans. They'll just go right in and switch those marines off. It'll be a massacre. When everything's said and done, the Cibolans will have suffered some damage. But we'll be dead. And all hope of developing something in this sector will die with us.

"The Cibolans can defeat us all as easily as I just made all of you be quiet and listen." Sanjuro could tell the truth was starting to dawn on Kyo. "I didn't mean to be so melodramatic about it. But you weren't going to listen unless I stopped you from throwing me out. As some of you are beginning to guess, I'm a telepath. So is everyone in this room. The whole human race has extensive telepathic ability; we broadcast so much that the Cibolans spend most of the time shutting us out. But right now, I'm the only human who knows how to manage the skill.

"And I'm just a beginner. I've been learning to use telepathy for the last month, and I barely know what I'm doing. I got attacked head on by a Cibolan recently, and only survived because someone else protected me. Yet I know what everyone in here is thinking, and right now I'm blocking several of you from grabbing hold of me. Do you understand? All of you together can't handle me, and I don't have even a quarter of the ability of the average adult Cibolan. Our very capacity for telepathy makes us that much more vulnerable. We're incredibly easy for the Cibolans to read. A completely mind-blind race would have more natural resistance."

The com attached to the holo sputtered to life. Rao was saying something about Sanjuro's actions in giving information to the Cibolans—addressing something she'd said when she first came into the room. Everybody turned to look at the holocam. Marley was sitting next to the holo controls. Sanjuro made him punch the button that killed the connection. He stared at her, half frightened, half fascinated.

"Admiral, I know you want revenge on the Cibolans at this point. We have suffered casualties. But things could be much worse. The door is still open to negotiations. We can still get much of what we want." She knew he wasn't listening. Even as he was held in place by her mental force, he was denying that the Cibolans could have this much power. The only way she would be able to stop him would be to completely control him.

And even if she were willing to do that—and she wasn't—she couldn't do it once he was out of range. She hadn't learned how to permanently affect someone's mind. She wasn't even sure the Cibolans were going to show her that. They used it only sparingly, in the case of serious criminals. Their history contained ugly examples of times when people had gone too far with it.

She couldn't stop everyone on *Mercator* at once, either. Sanjuro had pretty much reached her limit with the group in the room. Most of them weren't really trying to stop her. A concerted effort would overpower her. She tried to think of something else she could do—maybe make Vargas jump around like an idiot. But she didn't think it would work. It would humiliate him, but not change his mind.

Sanjuro shook her head. "I don't understand you, Admiral. Even though you can see what the power is like, you're still not willing to listen."

Vargas said, through clenched teeth, "I will not be bullied."

"I'm not trying to bully you, sir. I'm trying to save the mission. But I can see I'm wasting my time. I hope you'll reconsider, once you calm down. I'm listening to the others in this room, and I can guarantee you there's a lot of doubt about your plan. Maybe they'll be able to talk you out of it. But I'm not going to be able to do it. So I'm going back down to the planet to try to keep the Cibolans from killing us all."

"I order you to stay up here and help us fight this war," Vargas said.

"No, sir."

"That's an order."

"And I'm disobeying it. I can do a better job of protecting us down there. At least some of the Cibolans pay attention to me, even when your every action contradicts what I say."

"If you go back down there, you're a traitor."

"You still don't get it, do you, sir. I'm not going to fight for the Cibolans. I'm going to try to protect you from them."

"Sanjuro—"

"If we both live through this, Admiral, I'll answer any charges you want to bring."

She sensed Gervaise's mind running through legal precedent for refusing to follow unlawful orders and gave her a smile. Kyo was close to tears. Her thoughts were an interesting muddle: on the one hand she was thinking damn it, Sanjuro, you should have told me about the telepathy and, on the other, that's my girl.

Masire started to get up. She froze him in mid-move.

But his intent wasn't to stop her. She could read his anguished thoughts. "Please, Sanjuro. Don't walk out. This is treason. You can't go to the Cibolans, not now."

His concern was for her; it wasn't hard to tell that he had grave reservations about attacking the Cibolans. His thoughts reminded her that nothing was black and white here. Walking out that door, would be treason, no matter what precedents Gervaise came up with. She was refusing to fight. She knew what that meant. And she was lying to herself when she said she wasn't also considering the Cibolans. Her loyalties were divided.

She sent Masire a message: "I'm sorry. I don't want to do this, but I can't think of anything else to do." Then she turned back toward the Admiral.

"Sir, I don't want to see anyone die, not our people, not Cibolans. We have other choices." She was almost begging, but all she could read from Vargas was a brick wall. "Obviously, I'm not a marine anymore. I'm not sure what I am exactly, but I'm not a marine." She reached up to her collar and unpinned the captain's bars, then turned and handed them to Masire. She could see tears in his eyes, felt them in her own.

"Consider this a resignation. I know it's contrary to regulations; it's just a gesture. I'm going back down to Cibola as a free agent, to do whatever I can to pick up the pieces of this expedition. I give you my word, Admiral. I will not tell the Cibolans what you are going to do, or how to stop you. Though I won't help you fight them, I won't help them fight you, either."

She walked out.

By the time she'd gotten ten meters away from the room she knew she'd lost her hold on the people in the conference room. They'd be punching com buttons, giving orders. But she could get past most people one on one, as long as it didn't occur to the commanders to send a large number of people to take her en masse.

Sanjuro let her mind relax and read the space around her. People coming up from a corridor on her left, so took the corridor on her right. Shuttle bays were three decks down, the fighters a deck below that. A fighter would be best; they were faster. Better to take the stairs instead of the lift. The lift could be jammed. It didn't matter which stairs she took; the fighter bay took up the whole deck. She could sense the presence of people in groups of two or three as she raced down the steps. She managed to confuse them several times when they got too close.

When she reached the fighter deck, three marines blocked her way. She made them shoulder their weapons and sent one to run the controls while she took the fighter out and got a second to jam the door controls to prevent any other pilots from getting to the fighters quickly. She had the fighter out of the bay and en route to the planet by the time her control of them broke.

A shuttle followed a few minutes behind her. The fighter was faster, being small and built for maneuverability and speed. She had a good head start, and the shuttle couldn't catch her. Her training on the trip out had stood her in good stead.

Only after she'd passed beyond *Mercator*'s weapons' range did it occur to her that they could have shot her down. Her hands were suddenly shaking at the controls. She was, by military standards, a deserter and perhaps even a traitor.

As she approached the planet, she disconnected the fighter's com equipment to prevent *Mercator* from finding it and told her personal com system to self-destruct. She landed near the hill where Sundown's telescope stood. Sanjuro knew the moment she stepped out of the ship that Sundown was in the telescope hut, and things were no better on the planet than they were on *Mercator*.

The alien ship was still circling the planet, so close that it was visible with the naked eye. The planetwide weave had come together to try to figure out what the aliens would do. Some of the sendings they received from the ship were disturbing—anger, hostility, images of small ships flying close to the planet and buildings exploding in their city. Others were more nuanced—sadness, regret, images of pleasant times on the planet.

Their images are violent. Perhaps we should destroy them now, before they decide to attack us, one person sent. Many agreed.

No! The signals from them are mixed, another sent. We do not want to become mad killers, destroying all who come. We should not fight unless we have no other choice. This argument also attracted support.

Killing in self-defense is not madness; it is necessary.

It cannot be self-defense unless one is attacked. Attacking because one expects an attack has never been our way.

There was more support for waiting than for attacking immediately, though the images of explosions had everyone concerned.

Iron sat with Sorrel, following the discussion. Sorrel looked exhausted. The crisis was taking its toll on all of them. Iron was tired as well; pregnancy coupled with stress was hard to manage.

Sundown's alien friend is back on the planet, Iron told Sorrel.

I do not feel it in the weave, Sorrel sent in return.

No. The alien is blocking contact. But it is not happy. It does not want to be with its people and it does not want to be with us. Sundown has taken it to the observatory. I tried to ask questions of it, but Sundown prevented me.

This is not good news, sent Sorrel. That alien is curious, always wanting to communicate with others.

Iron agreed. I fear it means the aliens will attack us. We should not have killed their people.

We might have come to war even without that, Sorrel said. Only Sundown's friend listened to us, and it is clear that it has little influence with its people.

# 6

Vargas's com beeped. "Yes?"

"The shuttle couldn't catch Sanjuro, sir. And we've lost the signal. She could have put down anywhere on the planet."

"Keep scanning. I want her back up here."

"Yes, sir."

Vargas turned to Masire, Gervaise, and Marley. "You know, there was a strong debate about whether we should include a xenologist on this trip, even after the presence of intelligent life was detected. I thought it would be a good thing, but it turns out the opponents were right: anthropology types often go native, and xenologists seem to be more like anthropologists than like astrobiologists. Surprising, really, with Sanjuro's background. I wouldn't have expected it, but I guess the Ceres experience crippled a lot of otherwise good officers."

Masire shifted uncomfortably, but said nothing. If he came to Sanjuro's defense now, it would look suspect. But her show of telepathy had left him badly shaken. He should have trusted her. He probably would have trusted her, had they not been sleeping together.

Marley said, "Admiral, Sanjuro may have gone native, but her display of telepathic power was pretty impressive. I think you should consider whether she might be right about the Cibolans."

Vargas glared at him. "Don't tell me you were taken in by her parlor tricks?"

Marley met the Admiral's gaze. "She controlled a whole roomful of us, sir. And then took a fighter and got off the ship like someone taking an afternoon stroll in the park. I'd call that more than a parlor trick."

"It doesn't mean the Cibolans can affect what we do on *Mercator*. Or anything our fighters do. I'll grant there may be some problems for the ground troops." He glanced toward Masire.

"Something affected my people down at the settlement site," Masire said.

Vargas nodded. "We have to accept that some of this power is real. But I refuse to believe these primitive people are as all-powerful as Sanjuro wants to make out."

Marley said, "It wouldn't do any harm to go slow, try to check out her findings. If she's right—"

"She's not right, Captain." It was a statement that brooked no argument.

Marley said, "Yes, sir," but his eyes made it clear that he still disagreed.

Masire was impressed. Marley didn't have anything to gain by arguing with Vargas; in fact, he had a hell of a lot to lose. Yet there he was, making it clear what he thought.

While I'm sitting here, swallowing my words, Masire said to himself, because I don't want those knowing looks I'll get if I argue Sanjuro's case.

Vargas said, "I want two squadrons of fighters out there, Captain. We'll attack this whole region of Cibola: the smaller towns and the large city. The saboteurs most likely came from around there, and not from the other regions."

"What do we aim for, Admiral? The maps we've created with our scans and from Sanjuro's reports don't show anything resembling a military target."

Masire would have sworn he heard a sarcastic tone in Marley's question.

Vargas said gruffly, "We don't have any choice, Captain. We're fighting some kind of guerilla action here. Target the official buildings—they do have a few of those, don't they? And some of their factories. Try to avoid private homes."

Gervaise had been quiet, but now she said, "Admiral, you're talking about attacking civilians here. That's a dangerous precedent."

Vargas glared at her. "Study your history, Commander. We're dealing with terrorists here. You can't fight terrorists like soldiers. They don't declare themselves."

"History indicates that bombing civilians just leads to more terrorist attacks, sir."

"That's human history," Vargas said. "We're dealing with something else entirely. With some careful bombing we should be able to frighten them into submission."

"Admiral—"

"Commander, I don't need your ethical qualms. If you think there are legal issues, go research them. But I expect you to back me up on this."

"Yes, sir." It was the only possible answer. Gervaise walked out of the room. Masire wished he could read her mind.

Vargas turned to Marley. "Captain?"

Marley closed his eyes briefly, and then nodded. "I'll assemble the pilots in the large conference room for a briefing," he said.

"Colonel, once the bombing opens things up, your troops will go in on the ground to secure the area. I want the leader of this region taken alive. And Sanjuro, if you can find her."

Masire didn't trust his voice. He nodded.

"Let's get to it, gentlemen."

Marley sighed as the door shut behind Vargas. "What I wouldn't give for a few more good AI fighters right now. We've only got about ten."

"It's amazing we have that many, given the problems during the Mars rebellion, when hackers made System AI pilots fire on their own ships," Masire said.

"I was there; I remember. And until today I'd have made the same call. Nobody's ever figured out how to construct non-hackable AI. Makes them unreliable war machines—if you're fighting someone who knows how to hack. But we're fighting someone who can hack human brains and doesn't have a clue about artificial ones. Still, got to be safer in the air than on the ground. I don't envy you your job. You going to send your sergeant back down there, the one that shot Yung?"

"I don't know. She shouldn't have to deal with more of that kind of fighting, but she's going to resist being left behind. She's convinced Yung's death was her fault, no matter what anybody says. And, frankly, I need her, even if she's not a hundred percent. I'm down an officer as it is, and I'll need to leave somebody on board, along with a few troopers, in case we get wiped out and *Mercator* gets the hell out of here. With just two officers on the ground, I'm going to need all my sergeants."

"You're going down there?"

"It's my job."

"Punishing yourself because you gave Vargas ammunition against Sanjuro?"

"That's not why I'm going. I'd be going in any case." But he didn't deny the guilt feelings.

Marley said, "Maybe you don't believe her?"

Masire said softly, "No, I believe her. I always believed her. Just not enough. She felt so passionately that what Vargas wanted to do on Cibola was wrong. I thought she was, well, not lying so much as exaggerating what she'd found."

"But her little demo convinced you otherwise?"

"Yeah. Scary, wasn't it?"

Marley nodded.

"Plus she said something in that last meeting that's haunted me ever since, about being trained to evaluate both alien cultures and military situations. She was, you know. So why haven't we been listening?"

"Some of us have been. But Vargas is under major pressure from the System, Rao isn't interested in anything but exploiting the asteroid belt, and you've been afraid your opinion was colored by being in love."

"You're blunt. What brought this on?"

"I think Sanjuro's right. And if she is, there's a good chance we're all going to die here. And a lot of the reasons we came out here will die with us. But maybe, somewhere in the midst of all this chaos, someone will find a way to turn things around. It might be you, down there on the ground. I hope you'll do it."

"And yet you're going to follow orders."

"I can't accomplish anything by disobeying. The pilots will still go out. If I'm here, maybe I'll get a chance to change things. At least I can try to keep this ship safe."

Masire nodded. He stood up. Time to go to work.

Marley said, "Do you think she's right, that we're telepathic, too?"

Masire shrugged. "Maybe. She certainly was doing something to us. Kind of hard to get my mind around the idea, actually."

"I always wondered what it would be like to read minds," Marley said.

# 7

Sanjuro thought the telescope hut might get bombed. Certainly her reports had been incorporated into the scan details they had on the planet, and they gave a location for it. The Cibolans lacked obvious targets: no government buildings or military bases, and only a few large factories. That left symbolic features.

Sanjuro wasn't just worried about their safety; she couldn't stand the idea that the telescopes might be destroyed. She thought of Sundown up here, watching the sky for so many years. Preventing the destruction of property wasn't really a violation of her promise to interfere, she told herself.

She explained to Sundown that they should move what they could of the scopes. They dismantled them and loaded the important components into the flyer, then flew back into an unpopulated area interlaced with caves. It took several trips. Sanjuro blocked out the weave and concentrated on what she was doing, only opening her mind to Sundown. But she could tell Sundown was actively doing things within the weave.

The caves were in a rocky region that looked as if it had been formed by a retreating glacier. A geologist would be an asset on the planet, Sanjuro thought. Too bad they didn't include any in Kyo's group. Funny how her mind kept observing things.

Sundown chose a shallow cave with a large opening for their base of operations. The cave was dry but colder than outside. Sanjuro turned up the heat on her bodysuit. The fighter contained an emergency rations kit, and they'd grabbed the mats from the telescope hut—enough supplies to keep them for a while. They settled in.

# The Weave

Kali Parabhada was a friend of Lt. Yung's. "No one should die like that," she told one of the other pilots. "Made to act crazy and then shot by your own people. It's cruel."

So when she and nineteen other Space Corps pilots took off at dawn two days after the Admiral decided to go to war, she didn't object to bombing the Cibolans. "They shouldn't have sabotaged our operations," she said.

Her primary target was the ruler's home in the main city. Her first run went without a hitch, no response by the Cibolans, bombs dead on. She circled back for her second run.

Goran Yurinko was supposed to take out the manufacturing shops in the village nearest the astrobio site. He didn't like the target.

"Why those people? We don't have any reason to think they sabotaged our project." He made the complaint to a friend in operations; he wasn't dumb enough to say anything to Marley.

His friend shrugged. "I guess we have to make an example of somebody."

"It's not right. I've met some of the Cibolans. They don't seem like bad sorts. If some of them are killing our people, I bet it's not official. Probably just some crazies, like those anarchists on Ceres."

Yurinko—who had graduated at the top of his flight school class—bombed an empty field.

He circled around, trying to spot another harmless target. As he started his second run, he saw the fighter in front of him—Parabhada—start a kamikaze dive toward the ground.

Yurinko screamed into com: "Kali, pull up, damn you, pull up." He got no answer. He followed her, but knew his efforts were futile even before her fighter hit the ground and exploded into flames.

He knocked the fire out with foam spray from the air, then set his fighter down beside Parabhada's to see if he could do anything, though he knew she couldn't have lived through the crash. An overwhelming despair came over him as he touched the ground.

He turned off the engines, disconnected his com, and just sat there, watching the other fighter burn.

➤

Iron was sitting over breakfast at a lodging house in the capital city. Sundown was off with the alien, but their child had accompanied Iron. Sorrel wanted Iron and several other leaders to stay close by.

The weave was very active. Large numbers of people were monitoring the aliens on the ship in orbit, trying to figure out what they might do. Everyone took turns with that responsibility so that the aliens were under constant surveillance. As Iron took a last sip of morning tea, an alert began to pulse in the weave. Image after image came of aliens getting into small vessels and flying toward the planet.

An attack; Iron was sure. The images in alien minds regularly showed flying vehicles passing over cities and causing explosions. Danger, danger, Iron sent into the weave. These machines bring death. We must stop them.

Iron wanted to take the child somewhere safe, but what was safe from flying machines that rained down death and destruction? They remained in the lodging as Iron joined together with thousands of others to affect the minds of those flying the small ships. It was difficult, because while they could influence the pilots, they did not know what actions would keep them safe and what might bring down more destruction.

Iron assisted in putting one fighter on the ground and keeping it there. But then there was a thunderous sound—so loud as to leave Iron's ears ringing for hours afterwards. Those nearby in the weave reacted with shocked silence. And then the images began to pour in. Sorrel's house was in flames.

Iron and the child joined the firefighters at Sorrel's house. Those farther away redoubled their efforts to stop the pilots. Iron searched for Sorrel in the weave while helping with the hose, but Sorrel did not respond.

Marley beeped Vargas. "Admiral, we've got big problems. Fifteen of our fighters have been put out of commission; twelve of those pilots are dead. We've managed to hit near only seven of the intended targets. And at least one of the fighters still operational is firing on a couple of the other fighters."

"Send out another crew, Captain."

"Sir, with all due respect, we're losing people right and left without accomplishing much of anything."

"I know it's hard to lose people, Adam," Vargas said in a quiet voice. "But we must make these people understand."

Marley sighed, and hit com.

Masire watched the progress of the air battle from the shuttle bay, where he was about to brief his troops before taking them down. He shuddered as one fighter shot another out of the sky. Montoya flinched. He didn't like taking her back down, but he wasn't sure what else to do with her. The inquiry had cleared her, for now, as it had cleared everyone else except Sanjuro. And she wanted to fight, to get back at whatever had forced her to kill her own.

"Let's start with one brutal truth, ladies and gentlemen," Masire said. "We don't know what we're fighting down there. We aren't going to meet any people with guns, and we aren't going to know who to shoot. This isn't a conventional battle. Our job is to get into the city, and take the ruler prisoner. You have details on what he looks like and where to find him. You also have info on his advisors and associates. We'll take them if we find them. Set your weapons for disable, and leave them there."

"Will that work on the Cibolans, sir?" someone asked.

"I don't know," Masire said. "But I hope it will. And at least if you're not using deadly force, you won't kill each other."

The trooper cut his eyes toward Montoya and nodded.

"One more thing: if you come across Captain Sanjuro, take her into custody as well."

A couple of people gasped, and a few more muttered.

"That's an order," he said, giving them his coldest "no questions" look. Then he softened. "I don't like it any better than you do, but better us than someone else."

That worked.

A couple of Space Corps pilots walked in: "Sir, we're supposed to shuttle you down."

"Thank you, but we won't need you. We're going down on autopilot."

"Sir," one of the pilots said, "they use weak AI on those autopilots. It's slow, and doesn't react well in a combat situation."

"I know, Ensign. But I don't think it's as vulnerable to the Cibolans as you are."

One of them looked relieved, the other disappointed. They were the most junior of the flight crew.

"You'll probably get your chance," Masire said, "the way things are going."

The marines boarded the two shuttles, Masire on one, his remaining Lieutenant on the other. Each set the autopilot, then strapped in. The shuttles took off, lumbering out of the hatch.

Seventy troopers. What the hell were they going to be able to do down there?

⊱

Yurinko stared passively at his scan, watching as half of the second group of fighters crashed almost immediately. Two of them hit buildings, setting them on fire. He speculated as to whether the pilots had deliberately crashed into the buildings or simply hadn't been able to pull up in time. He wanted to cry, for the pilots, for the Cibolans, for something. But whatever had shut down his mind wouldn't even let him do that.

Three of the remaining flyers began firing at each other, all eventually going down. The remaining ships landed in an unoccupied, desert region. Yurinko could probably have raised them on his com. He wanted to, but he couldn't make himself move.

# The Weave

Sanjuro cautiously tapped into the weave. She monitored only—the first skill she'd learned. The chaos present in planetwide Cibolan communication almost knocked her over. So many contradictory things were going on. Machines flew through the air and rained down fire—that was the way the pictures ran. But some of the machines attacked each other, or dove into the ground. Sanjuro could feel the people attacking the pilots, saw them pushing on the pilots' minds, watched the pilots lose control.

And yet here was another group of minds, also focused on the pilots, but this one getting them to land their fighters. The pilots seemed incapable of moving. Obviously that group included some of the peace faction, which still hoped to find a non-violent solution.

She saw Iron, Sundown's spouse, carrying a body from a wrecked building. Sorrel, she realized. Iron's pain and anger threatened to overwhelm her; it hit her mind like a scream from the pit of a soul.

Sanjuro felt great sorrow from Sundown about the loss of Sorrel, but no anger, or at least, none directed at her. Sundown lent support to the peace faction, trying to ground the fighters without killing anyone. But the peace faction represented only a small fraction among the minds. Most of Cibola wanted to kill now. Sanjuro couldn't blame them.

Several places in the city were burning, and the fires were spreading. Groups of Cibolans were out fighting the fires. Hoses were tapped into the nearest rain collection storage tanks, and wind-run engines were powering pumps to get water on the fires.

Sanjuro found it natural that firefighting was the most technically advanced activity on Cibola. Limited rainfall led to greater risk of fire. Her mouth twisted in a wry grin; she was observing again. She also saw that the water they were pumping wasn't going to put out all the fires. She knew it because the firefighters knew it.

Sanjuro scanned for the human minds out there, the pilots still alive, sitting out in some godforsaken place, some of them hundreds of kilometers away. Masire and his troops just landing on the planet. She felt Masire brace himself as the shuttle landed. Watching the troops split up into several squads, she realized that she could see this so clearly from so far away because so many others were watching it, too. Even a Cibolan couldn't read people from that distance without amplification from others who were closer.

Masire and his people were in danger. She drew Sundown's attention: help me tell him to get out of here, she begged her friend. Sundown brought in several others among the peace faction, and they boosted Sanjuro's mind until she felt as if she were standing next to Masire.

She sent him words. "Get out of here, Masire. You're going to die down here, you and your people. Go back up to *Mercator*."

"I can't," she felt him say. "It's my duty."

Sanjuro couldn't tell if he knew she was speaking to him, or if he thought he was talking to himself. She tried once more, but Masire and his people pushed on toward the city.

Already they were under attack. Sanjuro watched in horror as two of the troopers began to fire on each other. But then someone helped up the one who had fallen. They weren't using lethal force. An imperfect solution, but it might help keep them alive.

Sundown watched the bombing through the weave. The images were horrific: flying objects dropping things that exploded into flames. Homes were burning, people were running in the streets, bodies lay in awkward positions. Pain, incredible pain, began to rise in the weave, pain so strong it overpowered the sufferers' ability to block. No one would deliberately send their pain to others; they were just so badly hurt that they had no choice. Healers were doing what they could from afar, but many injuries were too severe for distance healing. Others were scrambling to get to the injured, to heal if they could and release the ones they could not help. But the healers were at risk from the falling fires as well, and some fell even as they tried to give aid.

None of this was new to Sundown, even though nothing like this had ever happened here before. Natural disasters had occurred: the planet had been buffeted by fires, great windstorms, cold so deep that it damaged heating systems, even once a flood. But only in ancient history had something similar occurred, and only the facts about that remained, not the emotional feelings. So why did Sundown find this assault so familiar?

The answer was clear: from the alien minds. Sundown had seen violence like this in the minds of Sanjuro and the others. This is their kind of war, this is how they fight. Sundown looked at Sanjuro and for a few moments could feel nothing but hate.

But the feeling passed. Sundown knew Sanjuro opposed this attack, knew still that this evil was not the only thing the aliens brought with them. That knowledge provided some relief even as Sundown searched the weave for traces of Iron and their child. I should have brought them with us, Sundown thought. But Iron would not have come, and Sundown knew the child wanted to be with Iron right now.

>

Masire took his squad down the main road into the city. The road spiraled toward the center. His first objective was Sorrel's home. Sanjuro's reports had described it and its location distinctly, and he figured he would start there.

He could see flames from the city even before they got particularly close. Certainly some of the bombs had hit their targets. The destruction made him feel sick to his stomach. *My god*, he thought: *this is how the human race meets other intelligent species.*

He pushed it aside. He couldn't do his job, thinking that way. Not that he was sure that he should be doing his job. But his training held. He would think about all this later. Right now, he had to do what he could to bring this to an end.

Masire punched into com to raise someone on *Mercator*. "You got some kind of map showing those fires in the city to send me?" he asked the harried-sounded operator who answered.

"I don't know, sir. We're not getting much feed from the pilots. Most of them crashed before we got anything. I'll send you what we've got."

Masire found it almost useless. Even on the edge of town, he could see a lot more fires than were plotted on the map. *We don't even know what we've done down here,* he thought.

An urgent com message from his lieutenant's squad overrode everything else. "Colonel, we're under attack. Can't even see who we're fighting…"

Com went dead. Masire tried unsuccessfully to raise anyone on that squad, then sent Montoya and her people, who were closest, to see what had happened.

*We're fucked,* he thought, and led his squad on into the city.

⤇

"They've figured out how to get to our pilots," Marley told Vargas. "No one in the second crew was able to attack any Cibolans."

"Can we try a new pattern of attack?"

"I don't think it makes any difference to these people, Admiral. They're reading minds and intention, not battle patterns. The only choice we have left are the AI fighters."

Vargas made a face. "I've never seen any good come from using AI."

"Well, at least these people can't hack them."

"I guess we have no choice."

"We could just call the whole thing off," Marley said. *Maybe,* he thought. *If the Cibolans will let us.*

"No," Vargas said quietly.

⤇

"Got it," Masire said. He hit his all-call button. "Everybody pull back as much as you can. We're sending in AI fighters. They're programmed to avoid us, but we don't want to get too close."

He got acknowledgments from the other two squads. Montoya's people still hadn't located the fourth one.

266

One of his people muttered, "They're always programmed to avoid us, but they never do."

Masire let it pass; he felt the same way.

He wondered where Sanjuro was in all this chaos. He thought he'd heard her voice in his head earlier, but maybe he'd just been arguing with himself in her voice. He'd tried punching her up on com. He'd also tried to trace her. She'd probably destroyed her com so she couldn't be found. Which could mean that if she did try to contact him, it would be telepathically. The idea gave him the creeps.

Com buzz. It was Montoya. "We found the lieutenant's squad, Colonel. They're all dead." Her voice conveyed the grimness of combat bad news, but she didn't sound like she was freaking out.

"Any Cibolans about?"

"Not if scan is running right. We've had a couple of incidents, but nothing serious. Not like these people had. They died nasty, Colonel. The looks on their faces."

"Cover them up the best you can, and get out of there. We'll worry about a proper funeral if any of us live through this."

"Yes, sir."

From the vantage point of a hill outside the city, he watched the first fighters come into view. *Don't let them hit us,* he thought. And then he realized he didn't want them to hit their intended targets either.

>➤

A lull had occurred after the second wave of fighters. Those in the weave following the aliens on the ship reported that they were planning something else, but no one could find humans climbing into ships and taking off. This alarmed rather than comforted them, because they could not conceive of what other attacks the aliens might bring.

Sundown looked at Sanjuro. The alien could probably reveal what the humans were doing, if she got into their minds. But the attackers were Sanjuro's people. Sundown didn't think Sanjuro would do it.

They had ventured outside the caves and were watching the sky. Suddenly Sundown saw more flying ships in the sky. Another attack.

A response came back from the weave. We feel nothing up there. No minds in those ships.

>∈

Sanjuro became aware of the growing panic in the weave. No minds up there. Nothing. *Must be AI*, she thought. If we had enough AI, we could fight here. The thought didn't cheer her up.

She felt conflicting urges. The Cibolans couldn't stop the AI unless they went after *Mercator* itself. She wanted to tell them; she didn't want to see them bombed into the ground. But she didn't want to see everyone on *Mercator* destroyed, either. Damn it all to hell. She kept her brain shut down as much as she could.

But the Cibolans were figuring it out. Commands had to come from somewhere, and *Mercator* was the likely choice. Probably they'd picked up a clue from the other humans on planet, the ones who couldn't shield their thoughts. Sanjuro felt the swell of Cibolan minds, blending together to attack the people on *Mercator*. She wanted to scream out a warning. But she'd destroyed her com. And even if Sundown's faction would help her contact their minds—and she doubted that they would—she didn't think any-one on *Mercator* would respond to telepathy.

This was her fault. She hadn't tried hard enough to explain the Cibolan weave to the *Mercator* leadership. She should have trusted Kyo, explained the human capacity for telepathy, and worked with her to get to the others. Maybe Vargas would never have listened, but Captain Marley might have. Or Ari Gervaise. Even Masire might have paid attention if she'd shared her current knowledge with him instead of her old nightmares, if she'd treated him more like a professional colleague instead of taking refuge in him as a lover. And everyone might have been more receptive if she hadn't thrown a public fit back in the earlier meeting. If she'd done things differently, maybe she would have had others at her back, others willing to risk the charge of mutiny to keep Vargas from starting a war.

Or maybe everything would have still gone to hell if she'd done more. Second guessing yourself was hell. She shut everything out and curled up in a corner of the cave. Sundown let her be.

# 8

Kyo had been watching the battle and feeling useless when a piercing scream came through all-call. She tried in vain to raise someone on com, but got no answer. She ran from Sci/Tech head-quarters to the bridge.

At first glance, everything looked normal, if somewhat more tense than usual. Marley was standing next to the pilot, watching over her shoulder. Gervaise sat in a corner, a holoscreen up. She looked nervous; Kyo suspected she'd never seen a battle this close up before. Legal usually advised from a safe distance away. Vargas sat in the command chair, looking calm, if intent.

Then Kyo saw the chief com tech slumped over in his chair. Several other techs were working frantically around him. Kyo touched the com tech, found he was dead, moved him carefully from the chair, and asked the tech next to her what happened.

"The chief used a command override and shut down com. Then he screamed and fell over. We're trying to get back in, but even the Admiral's code doesn't work. You know how to hack com?"

"I used to," Kyo said. She'd run com on Mars, back in her enlisted days.

The crewman gave her a series of protocols, and Kyo tried to work with them. She heard another scream behind her.

"Kuso," the guy who'd succeeded to the chief's job said. "She just undid what we've been working on."

Kyo stole a glance to the right. Two people there were linked to the AI fighters, feeding them info. All of a sudden, one of them screamed, and the other started banging on the platform where there had been a holo keyboard.

Kyo jumped up and grabbed the one who screamed before he fell. His eyes were open wide; saliva dribbled from a corner of his mouth. But he was breathing. Kyo laid him on the floor. Someone else pulled the other crewman off his station and hit him with a tranq gun.

Marley said to the comtech second: "Give it up; we can live without internal com. Put your crew to work on the external. We don't want to lose contact with our people planetside."

Others from the Sci/Tech crew had headed to the bridge when com failed. Marley picked a lieutenant at random. "Organize a crew of runners for internal communications. Anybody you can draft. We've got to stay in touch. And first thing we need up here is a medic." He turned to Kyo: "Think you can fix the AI com? I don't want those things completely out of our control."

"I can try. I ran AI com on Mars."

"Then you know how to handle fucked-up situations," Marley said.

Kyo tried to call up the com, but the damage was extensive. The tech had managed to disconnect the entire system; it was as if someone had pulled all of the wires out, except the system didn't use wires. With wires, you could at least reconnect them with a little tape and a knife. Here, you had to restructure the program. Kyo wrestled with it, thinking all the while, I'll be the next to go.

But Marley was. He passed out, suddenly, after having restored a certain amount of order to the bridge. As he fell, he clipped the back of his head on the edge of the pilot's station. Everybody stopped what they were doing, turned to stare. Vargas reached him first, and laid him out on the floor, as they had done with the others who fell. "He's breathing," Vargas said. "Keep working."

Kyo kept struggling with the com, but stole a glance at Vargas. Clearly the Admiral had decided he should take direct command, rather than using Marley's second, Commander Pham, in the role. Pham didn't seem to mind. She was working with the scan techs, trying to restore images of the fighting. Vargas took over seamlessly, giving a word of encouragement here, a bit of direction there.

A couple of medics showed up. As they started in on the injured, one of the techs running com to the surface gave the by now familiar scream. Now all com was down. Kyo wasn't having any luck getting any of it back online, and no one else was either.

A crew member raced in, panting heavily. "Somebody better go take charge of engineering; all hell is breaking loose down there."

Vargas turned to Pham, who had started out as an engineer. "Get down there, Commander. And take some marines with you."

*It was like a virus outbreak*, Kyo thought. Couldn't tell where it would strike next. Kyo looked at her holoscreen and saw she'd been inputting gibberish. She jumped away from the keypad in horror, staring at it. "Everybody stop what you're doing," she shouted. "We're just making things worse."

"Are you sure?" Vargas said.

The comtech second jumped in, "The Major's right, sir. We're putting the wrong data in."

"Just do what you can," Vargas said quietly. "Do what you can." He stood near the pilot, as Marley had, so that he could watch their direction and still keep an eye on everyone else. His bearing said he was confident that the bridge crew could do its job.

Kyo looked at him and felt her own breathing slow. She tried once again to get com back online.

⇒

The minds of the aliens on the large ship were a muddle of screens and numbers and sounds. And fear. Fear was the strongest feeling.

No one in the weave could figure out what the aliens were doing with those screens, but they could find ways to get the aliens to destroy them. No way to tell if that destruction would stop the mindless fighters overhead.

Others in the weave played with the fear, calming some aliens down so much they did nothing, paralyzing others with fright.

And others, not content with stopping the aliens, put pressure on their minds not unlike a tumor. Some of these aliens collapsed.

Sundown watched the ships coming toward their planet. None of the action in the weave seemed to be stopping them. The large ship was in trouble, but the war was far from over.

Surely the aliens would surrender, though. Their headquarters was damaged, their leaders injured. Surely they would surrender.

Sundown wondered if they knew how.

>

Masire shouted at his com. It still didn't work.

"I think the whole system is down, sir," one of his troopers said.

"They must have got to *Mercator*," the Sergeant said. "You suppose they're okay up there?"

Masire shrugged.

They stood on a small rise, overlooking the Cibolan city. Significant fires burned throughout it. As they watched, a sweep of fighters appeared. The bombs didn't land anywhere close to them, but more fires broke out.

"Think they're still getting orders from *Mercator*, sir?" The Sergeant spoke quietly, for Masire's ear only.

"Not if the com outage is systemwide."

"What will those machines do, without orders?"

Masire said, "They're supposed to be able to think for themselves. So they'll probably think *Mercator*'s been attacked, and keep bombing. I wonder how much information they have about the overall situation."

The Sergeant did the shrugging this time.

Masire sighed. He figured it was unlikely that anybody'd bothered to bring the AI fighters up to speed. No one gave AI fighting equipment as much information as they gave human pilots, afraid they'd really think for themselves. Without com he couldn't coordinate with the fighters, and coordination was vital to keep his troops from being bombed. No way could they move into the city now, not until the fighters pulled back. He hoped his other squads were coming to similar conclusions; without com, he couldn't give them orders.

*They should retreat to the shuttles,* he thought. *Get off the ground, anyway.* Suddenly deeply tired, he sat down on the ground. His troop did the same. No one spoke.

"Take us out of orbit," Vargas said.

"Aye, sir," the pilot said.

A marine corporal on the bridge—one of the many people drafted to handle communications—said, in horrified tones, "Sir, we've got people on the ground."

"I know. But we can't get them back until we get our systems operational, and we can't do that sitting in range." Vargas's voice was calm, assured.

"Admiral, the ship's not responding to my commands," the pilot said. Her voice shook. "I can't get us out of orbit. I can't even change our speed."

Vargas said, "Corporal, get down to engineering and tell them that there's a problem with the pilot's controls." He turned back to the pilot. "Keep trying, Ensign." But she suddenly collapsed. Vargas looked around for someone to take her place.

*No pilots left on the bridge,* Kyo thought. *Maybe none left on the ship.*

Vargas must have reached the same conclusion, because he gently shoved the pilot out of the seat and took the helm himself. He got no more response out of the ship than she had. But he continued working, patiently, calmly.

*He'll get it done,* Kyo thought. *He'll figure out a way.* Vargas had his faults, but the man knew how to lead in a crisis.

And then Vargas screamed. He put his hands over his face, as if that would stop the attack, and kept screaming until he fell over out of the chair. That scream destroyed Kyo's last bit of hope. She wondered whether Vargas was alive or dead, but sat staring, watching Ari Gervaise walk over to the pilot's seat. She moved Vargas carefully to one side and sat down, staring at the controls.

Gervaise didn't have any piloting skills; as far as Kyo knew, she'd never guided anything more complicated than a landcraft. While flying *Mercator* was over her head, Kyo had at least flown some of the flyers and shuttles. She understood the principles. *Get up and go help her, you bakatare,* Kyo thought, but she couldn't move. She watched Gervaise tentatively push one button, then another, as she tried to puzzle out the right sequence.

Kyo doubted she could pull it off. The Cibolans would probably hit her next. They'd nail them all eventually.

➤

Iron wandered, dazed, around the city. The child was back at the lodging house, hiding in the cellar with others, though who knew whether that was really safe. Someone—a healer, probably—had taken Sorrel's body out of Iron's arms. But a healer cannot raise the dead. Sorrel wanted to negotiate with the invaders, but they killed him. Iron wanted to kill aliens. The desire to destroy overpowered even the pain of loss.

But there were no invaders here to kill. The palace was burning, and the market, and the great outdoor arena. Firefighters were pumping precious water on the fires, but the flames seemed almost to thrive on water. Other people stumbled through the streets, some barely able to walk. Iron walked past one damaged home and saw a person lying on a makeshift stretcher. A young one was trying to pull the stretcher, though it could barely move it. Iron picked up the other end of the stretcher, and the two of them carried the person until they found a healer. The young one was sending a confused array of pictures. Iron blocked it all. Iron could not bear the pain of others now, could find no way to comfort, to help in any way except the lifting of a stretcher or the carrying of a body.

Two planes circled overhead. Iron wondered if they would rain down more fire. For a moment, Iron didn't care. What was there to live for? Visions of the child, of the child-to-be, of Sundown, filled Iron's mind. There were reasons to live. Iron ran toward the nearest building. Those inside were making their way below ground. They felt explosions as they closed the trap door.

# 9

Sanjuro had put up the strongest mental block she knew how to create, but now someone was pushing on it, seeking entrance to her mind. It was a gentle push, but a persistent one. She opened her eyes and found Sundown sitting next to her on the floor of the cave, one hand resting on Sanjuro's arm. She let down her block and received a flood of images from the Cibolan, first humans collapsing and dying and then pictures of surrender. Sundown repeated the surrender message, with embellishments. Humans laying down their weapons, kneeling back from them. And then an image of Sanjuro speaking to Masire, to others, interposed with images of people lying dead on the ground.

*We've lost the war*, Sanjuro thought. I have to tell them to surrender or more of us will die. She joined the weave of the peace faction and, with their help, searched for Masire's mind. She couldn't quite reach it. Something—someone—had put a barrier up.

Sanjuro drew on the strength of her Cibolan allies even harder. A few Cibolans from the group that had been monitoring the marines joined in once they understood that the object was surrender, and the additional effort was enough to release his mind.

She only had a few minutes before whoever had been restraining him returned with greater force. She must use words, sharp words. She had to treat mind communication as if it were a com. Masire. This is Sanjuro. You must surrender. Now. Think of this image. She sent it to him. Get your people to do it.

He heard her. She was certain of it. She repeated her message, with greater force.

And he did it. His people physically laid down their arms and backed away. The weave picked up his images. Soon several of his people began projecting a similar picture.

In a corner of her mind Sanjuro could tell that Sundown was sending to others. The surrender gave her credibility. More Cibolans joined the peace weave, allowing Sanjuro to communicate with the humans.

Sanjuro tapped into the larger weave, looking for humans. She found images of a few pilots and some marines, wandering around, dazed. And then she read the chaos on *Mercator*. Kyo came through. And Gervaise. But she could not find Vargas or Marley. Dead, then, or incapacitated. Masire must be in command. He could tell *Mercator* and the rest to surrender, and they would. She spoke into his mind. Contact the ship. Order surrender. You're in charge.

No com. She read it in his mind. Systemwide no com.

It struck her then: without com, no one could call off the AI fighters. Even if all the humans surrendered, the AI would not. She counted four pilots with working fighters on the ground. Briefly, she thought of contacting them, of telling them to shoot down the AI. But even though she had reached Masire, she doubted the pilots would respond to telepathic sending. And if even if they did, likely they wouldn't do something as drastic as firing on their own fighters—even AI—on instructions coming through the weave. Why can't we stop those fighters as we did the others, Sundown sent. Why do their minds not respond?

They are machines, Sanjuro answered. Not a complete explanation, but close enough for now. And that gave Sundown and others an idea: the pilots they had forced to land earlier, the ones sitting in their ships doing nothing, could shoot down these ships. A few minutes passed. Sanjuro picked up images of the pilots pushing buttons and checking readouts in preparation for flight.

It might work. But the pilots left alive were outnumbered by the AI. They might have some surprise factor, but once the AI figured out what was happening, they would have the upper hand.

Had it been treason, telling the Cibolans that the AI were machines? Perhaps. But she couldn't think about that, not now. She went back to Masire, showed him the pilots going after the AI. Then, pulling his mind into the mix, she projected the surrender order to every human she could read on planet. Some reacted in puzzlement, others actively resisted. But they were people worn down with fighting an enemy they couldn't see, couldn't shoot. She saw the images come up, one after another, from all save the pilots, busy on their mission.

Now for *Mercator*.

Kyo sat staring at nothing in particular. Vargas hadn't moved. Gervaise's efforts at piloting had done nothing, and now she sat there, looking dazed, like a zombie. No one on the bridge said anything. Kyo could not tell if the others were alive or dead. Getting up to see felt impossible.

A young man raced into the room and skidded to a stop like a character in a cartoon. Kyo laughed. The young man—a corpsman by his uniform, from the mess hall or some other service job—looked frightened as he glanced around the room, trying to figure out who to speak to.

Kyo said, "What is it?"

"There's nobody left working in engineering, ma'am. Everyone is either dead or passed out, or—" he hesitated—"or kind of like this, ma'am." He gestured around the room at the people sitting zombie-like."

In the part of her mind that was still functioning, Kyo started to inventory people. Vargas is down, Marley. Didn't Commander Pham go to engineering? Is she down? "Where's Pham?"

"She's unconscious, ma'am. But breathing."

Masire is planetside. Rao is in the asteroids. Just me and Gervaise up here. "Who's in command, corpsman?"

The corpsman shrugged.

"You are, Major." It was Gervaise who spoke.

It startled Kyo to hear her voice. She thought, *Oh, kuso. Why me?* and said to Gervaise, "Why not you, Commander. You're Space Corps; I'm Sci/Tech."

"You outrank me. And you've been in combat before. I haven't."

"That was twenty years ago. And I took orders; I didn't give them."

"It's more practical experience than I've got."

Kyo sighed, but knew she was right. "Corpsman, find me everyone who's still moving and get them up here."

"Yes, ma'am." The voice sounded doubtful.

"We've got to figure out how to surrender, son. And it will be easier to do if we're in the same room."

The corpsman raced out.

Kyo felt as if a load had been lifted off her mind—a funny feeling, since the load of being in charge had just been piled on. The Cibolans must be pulling back. She saw Gervaise stand up, as if she had forgotten how. She sat up in her own chair, flexed her fingers.

And then, in her mind, she heard Caty Sanjuro's voice, almost as clearly as if she were standing next to her: Sumi. You have to surrender. Think about this image. Get everyone to do it. The image formed in her mind: the people on *Mercator*, hands empty, standing away from their machines.

She heard Sanjuro again: Good. A pause. And then: The AI are still firing on the Cibolans. Can you stop them?

No com, she thought, wondering if she were really having this crazy conversation.

Sanjuro again: The pilots alive down here are trying to shoot them down. But they're outnumbered.

The remaining people on *Mercator* were stumbling through the door, more than she expected. The bridge fast became crowded.

Someone said, "There are more people in sick bay, but they're trying to tend the injured."

Kyo nodded. "That's reasonable. Anyone here a pilot?"

Two stepped forward: a Space Corps ensign and a junior Sci/Tech lieutenant who'd gotten some of the pilot training on the trip out.

"Grab yourself a flyer, whatever's left down there. We've got to stop our AI fighters, and without com, we can't talk to them. The only thing we can do is shoot them down."

The two pilots stared. Shaken as they were by the events of the day, they were not prepared to be told to shoot down their own ships. The Sci/Tech, who had no combat experience, looked stunned; the Ensign's face reminded Kyo that Sci/Tech wasn't Space Corps.

Because they deserved an explanation, Kyo said, "We're beat, ladies and gentlemen. We've got to surrender or we'll all die here, and everything this mission was about will die with us. We can't call back the AI fighters, and we can't surrender while we're firing on the Cibolans."

The Ensign looked around the room, staring at Vargas and Marley lying on the deck, and then catching Gervaise's eye.

"Major Kyo is in command," she said. "And that was an order, Ensign."

The two pilots gave a fast salute and turned to leave.

"And while you're flying out there," Kyo said, "remember that the Cibolans read minds. Keep an image of shooting down the AI in your head. And try not to think about anything else. The rest of you: we have to think about surrender. In pictures, so the Cibolans can figure out what we mean. If they understand it, the attacks will stop." *I hope*, thought Kyo.

☙

The aliens on the ground were laying down their weapons. The ones on the ship were sending images of surrender. And alien pilots were shooting down the ships with no minds.

The weave resonated with elation, tempered by strong feelings of loss from those who had been with the injured or dead. Others remembered the fires and the destruction of buildings. We have won, but now we must rebuild, someone sent.

A few worried that the ships without minds would come back to bomb them again. It is not over yet, one of them sent. And others wondered, what will we do with these aliens now?

>=

Communication through the Cibolan mind weave did not provide as precise an image of battle as human scan and com did. But picking through the data, Sanjuro could tell that while some of the AI fighters had been shot down, so had some of the people sent out to stop them. Kyo was sending two more fighters down. That would help. But it would take time for them to reach the planet, and at least one AI was starting a flight pattern preparatory to a bombing run.

She wished she could do something else. Cibolans were dying, and she could hear their screams in her mind. More destruction, and the Cibolans would likely kill all the humans. They might anyway, but Sanjuro was hoping the surrender might give them a chance to start over.

Then she remembered: the fighter she'd flown from *Mercator* was close by. It had weapons systems. And she could fly it. She'd never flown in combat, but she could give it a shot. She sent an image of herself taking off to Sundown, and ran all-out to the place where she'd hidden the flyer.

Taking off was easy. And the flyer gave her another advantage, one she hadn't counted on: local scan was working. It ran off the onboard comp and wasn't networked into *Mercator*'s systems. Now she could see what was going on.

One of the original pilots was still in the fray. Five AI fighters remained. Four of them concentrated on their bombing runs, while the fifth handled the attack. The two fighters Kyo had sent from *Mercator* arrived just after Sanjuro. She contacted them through the weave, with help from Sundown's people, and managed to keep them from firing on her.

No way to give orders, though. Not that she had any orders to give. The pilots from *Mercator* were likely as inexperienced as she was, and the AI fighters were well-programmed, highly skilled fighters that registered her as a threat. One turned from a planned bombing run to take care of her. Only quick maneuvering kept its first shot from taking her out.

Target weapons systems, she thought. Or engines. Got to put them out of commission. Nothing else matters. She told her weapons comp to do that. Ideally, the pilot should be jacked into both the piloting and weapons comp; the system was designed to work best with a combination of human mind and AI tech. But Sanjuro had only mastered flying skills. Putting the system on automatic seemed best; the comp could judge firing situations better than she.

Her flyer fired once, missed. Fired again, with the same result. The AI fighter was quicker and integrated; it fired back and Sanjuro barely evaded its fire. She had opted for only minimal shielding because shielding took power she needed for her weapons.

The AI fighter came around again and charged straight for her. She let it come, and then, anticipating that it might be about to fire, dove just under it. Scan showed a blast of fire where she'd just been, as her comp sent a direct attack into the AI ship's belly. She moved rapidly away as the other flyer exploded. *Instinct*, she thought. Combat instinct. Just one step up from pure luck. Had she moved any earlier, the AI would have tracked her. Any later, and she'd have died.

Scan showed three AI left and three human-crewed fighters, counting her. One of the flyers Kyo had sent didn't register, but the remaining skilled pilot had taken out an AI. Two of the AI left had started a bombing run, but now they peeled off to fight the new threat. The third AI was locked in combat with the other fighter Kyo had sent. As Sanjuro watched, that fighter took a hit, and flames broke out in its tail section. The AI came around again to finish it off, and the pilot plowed directly into the AI ship. Both ships exploded into flames and fell toward the planet.

Now they were two and two. One of the AI fighters was coming directly toward Sanjuro. She turned and ran, hoping to lead it away from the populated areas. It followed, firing as it came. She was just out of range; the two ships had about equal flying power. Sanjuro suddenly braked and turned back toward the AI, dropping just below her earlier path. Now she was in range, but the AI fighter hadn't anticipated the drop. It had fired as she turned toward it, but the blast went just above her ship. The ship shuddered, and scan blanked out. Her weapons comp fired, and Sanjuro mentally crossed her fingers. She didn't think she'd get another shot.

The AI exploded, and Sanjuro dove low and forward to get away as debris rained down. Her ship wasn't responding properly. She cut her speed back, way back, and limped back to where the other two had been fighting. Her scan no longer worked, but she felt for the weave and found the human pilot sending signals of relief. His fighter was already on the ground.

She put her own down beside his, wondering as she noted the unevenness of the landing if she could get the ship to take off again. The other pilot stumbled out of his fighter, looking dazed. His mind, released from a combination of controls, was a mass of confusion. Why had he been shooting down his own fighters? Sanjuro sent messages to calm him down as she climbed out of her own fighter.

"Sanjuro," the other pilot said. "What is going on?"

She recognized him as Goran Yurinko, the pilot who had taught her to fly.

"It's okay," she told him. "The battle's over."

He walked toward her, stumbled suddenly.

She read him remembering all the pilots crashing their planes.

"Oh, God," he said, "They're all dead. Everyone's dead but me. And for what? For anything? Did we even win the battle?"

"No," Sanjuro told him. She put her arms around him, pulled him close to comfort him as if he were a child. "No, Goran, we didn't win the battle. But we might still win the peace."

She knew he didn't understand what she meant. Goran sobbed as Sanjuro held him.

☀

No more ships flew over the planet. Alien minds in the weave signaled either surrender or pain. The aliens, too, had, suffered. Conscious of Sanjuro's concerns—concerns she was carefully masking from the weave—Sundown spared some thought for the alien suffering. The war was the aliens' fault, but their people had died and their incredible technology had shown itself to be weak.

But, oh, the damage to Golden Mountain. The aliens had targeted their region because that was where they had first landed. They had never understood the political makeup of the planet. Sanjuro understood it, Sundown knew, but perhaps the others had assumed only one region existed, one government. Unless they could rebuild rapidly, Golden Mountain could find itself at risk from its neighbors as well as from the aliens, especially with Sorrel dead. Fire was strong, but transition times were risky.

Some in the weave were arguing that the aliens must be sent away. Sundown disagreed strongly. We must negotiate with the aliens for help, Sundown sent into the Golden Mountain weave. Our losses will be meaningless if we do not use this surrender to obtain value from the aliens. Agreement came from Fire, among others, but Sundown suspected that Sorrel's heir might have very different ideas about what they should seek from the aliens.

# RESOLUTION

# 1

The Cibolan healer sat at the head of the bed of the ensign who had collapsed on the bridge. It put a hand on either side of her face. The healer was smaller than the average Cibolan, with unusual snow-white fur. Although so much of what the Cibolans could do mentally was done at a distance, healers always touched their patients if they could. Sundown had explained to Sanjuro that some minimal healing could be done without physical contact—enough to help someone trapped a long way from care—but touch improved the process. Sanjuro added the explanation to her running list of things she didn't understand.

She tried to follow what the healer was doing in the ensign's mind, but the images made no sense to her. Most Cibolans could do minor healing—the equivalent of a parent handling a skinned knee or a bout of flu—but only a few developed the powers fully. Many more Cibolans could kill effectively than could heal. *Not unlike humans,* Sanjuro thought.

Since the humans' brain injuries had been caused by Cibolan attacks, a Cibolan healer might have a better idea of how to treat them. While human medicine had developed sophisticated diagnostic and treatment equipment for neurological damage, it was based on physical rather than mental harm. Further, the scanning equipment used to diagnose brain damage was one of the many things out of commission, which had made it impossible for the med staff to determine the extent of injuries or to devise a reasonable treatment plan. The staff were grateful for the Cibolan assistance, despite the fact that they could not understand how it worked.

Sanjuro's inquiries in the weave had shown her a parallel situation: most of the injured Cibolans had suffered significant physical injuries—broken bones, third-degree burns, damage to internal organs—and human medical care, even without the tech normally used in medical treatment, was much more advanced in dealing with those types of injuries. Soon after she and Yurinko shot down the last AI, Sanjuro secured Masire's permission for a medical exchange and had med techs from *Mercator* brought to the makeshift Cibolan hospital set up in the city's big theater before she told Sundown about her idea of a medical exchange. Given the shaky state of the truce, Sanjuro hadn't been sure the Cibolans would agree to help the humans, so she offered their assistance without officially asking for anything in return.

The strategy had paid off. A pair of healers agreed to work among the humans on *Mercator*. So far they had successfully revived several people who had been locked in deep comas. Sanjuro knew the human med techs were scared to go among the Cibolans, but they were military, trained to do what they were ordered. The Cibolans were likely scared as well, though they kept their private thoughts locked away from her. But they were volunteers. She appreciated their courage.

The ensign's eyelids fluttered. The healer took its hands away from her head and stood up. "She'll be awake soon," Sanjuro said to the doctor who ran medical, translating the images the healer had sent. "And she should make a full recovery."

"Gracias a Dios," the doctor said. "That's five people they've brought back. If only we could have had them here earlier, maybe the Admiral would have survived." Vargas had died a few hours after collapsing.

Sanjuro nodded, and didn't say the obvious, that they'd still been at war when Vargas died. The doctor knew that. She wondered whether the war could have been averted if they had invited exchanges with Cibolans from the beginning. Another thing she should have pushed for earlier, another thing to regret. Though she still had no idea how she would have convinced Vargas or Rao of the value of such a project.

"I wish the scan was working," the doctor went on. "I'd love to see what they're doing in there."

"With luck you'll get other opportunities to work with the healers," Sanjuro said.

She went to find Masire. The healers generated enough power so that she could stay in touch with them anywhere on the ship. They were also connected to the weave planetside, and through them, so was she. None of the lifts were working, so Sanjuro climbed several flights of stairs as she worked her way up to the bridge from sick bay. She found Masire in his small office off the bridge—the security office. The door was open. Perhaps it was stuck that way. Commander Pham sat in the office, talking with Masire. Sanjuro waited in the doorway for the conversation to finish.

"We can't do anything further to the engine until we get more of nanotech online," Pham was saying. "Too much hardware damage. We've got to build some pieces to stick in there."

"Why is it taking so long to get nanotech operational?" Masire asked.

"Because I don't have any nanotech engineers. What I've got are a couple of techs and an engineer who took some classes in college. They're having to take apart one of the few systems that didn't go down, to figure out how it works, so they can put together a new one."

"I thought nanotech could rebuild itself."

"It can, if you have the right systems functioning. But the kind that are still working produce simple necessities, not engineering systems. Maybe we can convert them, but it's still going to take a long time. If we can get one of the devices Col. Rao took out to the belt, we can do a lot more. Though even with the right equipment, we'll still be guessing about what parts we need to construct."

Masire sighed. "I'm trying to get hold of Rao. Do what you can, Pham."

"When you talk to Col. Rao, tell her we're going to need some of that Helium-3 they've been capturing out there. The damage to the reactor let a lot of what we had leak out."

Masire nodded.

"Piece by piece, Colonel. Just going to take time." She stood to go, saw Sanjuro in the doorway. "Hello, Captain. Nice to see you."

"Likewise. I'm glad you suffered no ill-effects from the attack. I heard you were injured."

Pham banged her skull with her fist. "Hard-headed." She laughed. "Come to give us a hand in rebuilding the ship?"

Sanjuro detected genuine friendliness in her voice. "No, ma'am. I don't think you'd find me very helpful. I'm no engineer."

"I'd find anyone with half a brain and a low frustration factor helpful right now," she said. "But I suppose you have other things to do. I'll let you know where we've made some progress, Colonel."

Sanjuro didn't offer a salute. Masire didn't seem to notice. After a minute, he waved her to a chair. "Sit down, Sanjuro."

"The Cibolan healer has been successful in healing five people so far."

Masire's face relaxed. "That's the best news I've had all day."

"It is nice to hear something positive."

"Pham's putting most of the engineering resources we've got into keeping the engines operational. I hope some of the people they can heal are engineers, because I really need Pham to run the bridge. I don't have a clue about most of the Space Corps systems. But I know even less about engineering, and Pham started out as an engineer. I guess we don't need to run the bridge until we actually have enough power to go somewhere."

"Have you heard from Rao?"

"No. I suspect once com went dead she decided it would be best to wait and see."

"You'd think she'd send someone over to check on what happened. If *Mercator* is destroyed, she's stuck out here, too. And she's got the big shuttle, so it wouldn't take her long to get here."

"She doesn't have the big shuttle. Vargas had been using it. It took some damage during the attack. But I think we've got it back up and running."

"You made it a priority?"

"In case we lose the engine, I want to be able to get everyone possible planetside."

"Still, Rao should have checked in by now."

"I sent someone over there this morning—found one of the astrobio crew who'd learned rudimentary pilot skills on the trip out." He looked worried. "You don't think the Cibolans got to the geo crew, do you?"

Sanjuro shook her head. "No. I'd have felt them in the weave."

"The weave?"

"That's what I call the Cibolan communication net. It's more than a web; it has so many interlocking parts. Hard to explain."

"More things to learn about them. If they'll let us. Will they let us?"

"I don't know. There's a lot of anger in the weave."

"Not surprising."

"Right now they're much like us: too preoccupied with repairing damage and dealing with the injured. So the truce is still holding. The medical exchange seems to be helping. A lot of people are watching us, though, and if we do anything that can be interpreted as hostile, they'll probably kill us all."

"Fortunately we can't do much of anything, hostile or otherwise." Masire's tone was slightly sarcastic. "We need to negotiate a more stable peace with them. Is it possible?"

"We still have things they want. Our med techs are healing injuries usually considered fatal, proving to the Cibolans that there is real value in our tech. But a lot of Cibolans died, and a lot of homes and other property were destroyed. Winter's not that far off, and from what I understand, winter on Cibola requires solid housing. If we could offer some significant building help—and we could, even in our current situation, with working nanotech—we'd give ourselves a better chance of surviving."

Masire nodded. "I can see that helping them rebuild could work. We're certainly going to need Rao's equipment to do that, though."

"Like the med tech, it shows them that they can get things of value by dealing with us, even after all that's happened. And that may be enough for those who still want to deal with us to win the day."

Masire raised his eyebrows. "May?"

"A significant part of the population is in favor of killing us all, despite the truce. Another large group wants us to go and never return."

Masire shuffled papers around on his desk. "Even if they kill us, others will probably come. Hell, the *Cortez* is only about a year and half away. We may get ETQ back up at some point. But until that happens, we have no capacity for letting anyone know what happened, to tell them to hold off. The System may have already sent off another ship, based on Vargas's last communications. And you know as I do that the System will try again, even if we don't make it."

"Yes, but most Cibolans aren't convinced of that. In the past, killing off invasion forces worked."

He dropped the papers he held. "Dios! They've done this before?"

"A long time ago." Sanjuro waved a hand through the air. "We're not alone in the universe, Masire. Other species developed space travel a long time before we did."

He ran a hand through his hair. "I wish I could get this ship out of their range. I'd shuttle people out to the asteroids, instead of bringing those folks back here, except I can't spare anybody and hope to get the ship operational. So whatever else we do, we have to try to negotiate real peace. And you're the only person who has any chance of doing it."

She had expected something like that. "I'll certainly do my best, Masire. But you're going to have to go down there with me, at least for an initial meeting."

He gave her a puzzled look.

"I've got to show them I have the commander behind me. I've got personal credibility with a few Cibolans, but my lack of clout on *Mercator* is widely known. If you want me to negotiate, you have to prove that I have authority."

"I can do that."

"And you're going to have to give me real authority, Masire. Or else stay down there with me. I'm not going to be able to come up here every time we need to make a decision."

"Understood. I'll try to spend as much time as I can with you, because this is crucial. And I can probably delegate most of the *Mercator* functions. But I can see some potential crises where no one else is going to be able to make the call. Damn. We really need com up and running."

"Or to have developed telepathy."

He let a small smile show through. "I imagine that will take longer than rebuilding the com system." The smile faded. "You have full authority. Your goal will be a negotiation leading to a full relationship. But if you can't get that, at least try to keep us alive until we can rebuild the ship enough to get out of here. I'll try to find some people to help you out. Though I don't know who just yet."

"All right."

"As soon as I get some of the nanotech devices back from the asteroids, we'll put one on the ground and help them rebuild."

"I'd thought of sharing some of our stock of instabuilds. For the present."

"That's not a bad thought. Though we probably don't have too many, except what's down at the astrobio site. That's something else we may have more of in the asteroid belt. They were using a few of them as added shelter to keep the dust down in the hollowed-out asteroid cores."

Quiet, they looked at each other. Then Masire dug into a desk drawer, leaned across the desk, and held out her captain's bars. "Do you want these back?"

She stared at them. "I don't know. I know I can't really resign, but I don't want to give you the impression that I'm still a marine. Or even a Sci/Tech."

He grinned—a real grin, not the bitter humor he'd exhibited so far. "Don't worry. I'm not under the illusion that you're going to follow orders."

She took the bars, held them in her hand. "It's not just that, Masire. My loyalties are all mixed up. I didn't want to see the Cibolans wipe us out. But out of loyalty to what we can develop with them, not out of loyalty to the System, or the marines, or even *Mercator*. And I want to make damn sure that we negotiate something that protects them from us. Not now, but down the road. There are ways we can destroy them."

"An AI fleet, for example," Masire said.

Smart man. "Or development of human telepathy."

He nodded.

"I'm really not a soldier anymore. So I don't know if I should wear these."

"Put them on, Sanjuro. Like you said, you can't quit anyway. No one's going to give you orders that conflict with your purpose."

"Really? I can't see Rao buying into a negotiated settlement with the Cibolans that gives them a major stake in the asteroids as part of reparations."

"Yeah, but you don't report to Rao anymore."

She looked at him.

"You report to me. I'm revoking your delegation to Sci/Tech; I need you elsewhere. When I say you have full authority, I guarantee that no one will undercut it. Even if you give away a colonel's pet project.

"Of course, once we're back in communication with the System, things could change, but it's going to take us some time to get ETQ back online. And if they try to second-guess us in a way that endangers what's left of us...well, I made the mistake of going along with stupid orders once. I won't do it again."

She started to pin the captain's bars onto her lapel. Masire said, "Here, let me do that." He came around the desk. She stood up, to make it easier for him to reach the pin. He left his hand resting lightly on her shoulder as he finished. They didn't speak for maybe a minute. They both knew that the shift in Sanjuro's status meant putting any repairs to their relationship on hold as well.

It was Sanjuro who pulled away, broke the silence. "I'd better check in with the Cibolan healers. And then get back down to the planet, see if I can get some kind of meeting set up. Cibolans may be able to meet through the weave, but we need to be face to face."

"I'll get down there as soon as possible."

>►

"You're making this up to screw with my head," Kyo said. Sanjuro had found the astrobiologist working on a nanotech machine.

"While I admit that it would be fun to lay a line of bullshit on you," Sanjuro said, "this is not the time or place. I would have told you earlier, but things fell apart too fast. I'm not making anything up: The Cibolans have mutable gender. They can be either sex, and when they're having sex for fun, they apparently try all kinds of variations. But when they decide to reproduce—and both parties must agree for that to happen—one party decides to get pregnant and the other to raise the newborn. Those decisions cause hormonal changes in both, thus the pouches in the 'fathers.'"

"I admit it explains why we had so much trouble sexing animals. I guess they don't have sexes either."

"No, though apparently the process is more instinctive for them, just as it is with Earth animals. The ranchers use mental tools on their animals to encourage healthy diversity in mating season or to breed for specific traits, but in the wild it just happens."

"Wow. More to learn, if I can ever get away from trying to rebuild damaged equipment."

"Why are you doing this work, anyway?"

"Because I know how. I was one of those kids who built tech machines over school breaks. Why aren't you working on stuff like this?"

"Because I suck at tech stuff. And because I'm in charge of negotiating peace with the Cibolans."

"I think that's probably more difficult than rebuilding nanotech devices."

"Could be. I'm asking Masire to put you on that project as well."

"Oh, kuso. Come on, Sanjuro. Leave me to machine repair."

"You know the Cibolans better than most. They're more likely to trust you than some stranger."

"Bah. Sounds like an impossible job. And Pham will probably make me keep working on machines in my spare time."

"The joys of a military career," Sanjuro said.

>➤

Neither the ETQ nor the A/ND com system proved easy to fix. "We're fortunate that the entangled particles are still secure," Pham told Masire. "But the system for running ETQ was completely destroyed, along with the AI that ran it. We're going to need to activate one of the stored AIs to get it up and running."

"Do we have to use AI?" Masire had already okay'd use of two other stored AIs to work on the rebuild, but he was still reluctant. The AI bombing runs on Cibola haunted him; he shuddered to think what might have happened if Sanjuro and Yurinko and the others hadn't been able to shoot them down.

"We don't have any humans with the skills. Using quantum entanglement to communicate is complex. It's always been done by AI."

Masire approved it. They needed communication with the System. Pham thought it would be easier to get the ETQ running than A/ND com. They had lost some of their capacity for making negative energy; she preferred to keep what they had in the hope of bringing the shipwide drive online at some point. Given the three-month delay in A/ND com transmissions, it was also less useful.

>➤

Iron walked among the ruined buildings, part of a team of builders taking a first-hand look at the destruction across the city. All were reporting back to a support team within the weave that kept them in contact with each other and remembered the details they each sent back on the scope of the damage and repair priorities.

A few fires still smoldered. The team of builders struggled to control their feelings of despair. Being experienced at their work, they knew they couldn't rebuild the city before winter set in. How would they manage to provide everyone with shelter through the winter? Emotions were running high, and they did not bother to block their hatred from the weave. Iron, picking through the destruction of Sorrel's home—that great structure that stood for generations, only to be destroyed in minutes—was especially angry. Kill them all, Iron sent.

But the healers, working alongside human doctors, watched in wonder as these odd people who could not control their own sendings deftly reconstructed even damaged internal organs, put their thoughts into the weave too. No more killing, they sent. We have seen enough of killing. Others worked their way into the weave. And so, rebuilding their city and its surrounding places, they argued over the best response. Such was the value of the weave.

# 2

The meeting, in the supersized instabuild that had served as the main lab at the astrobio site, hadn't started well. Nothing much was left in the space, except for tables and chairs: all the working equipment had been shipped up to *Mercator* to use in the rebuild. Though highly functional, instabuilds were drab at best. After several months among the colorful buildings on Cibola, Sanjuro found the dullness oppressive. No reason the buildings couldn't be purple, she thought.

Thinking about irrelevant things helped; she was getting tense. Masire hadn't made it down yet. She'd sent him word, with the last transport up to *Mercator*. And the key Cibolans had shown up early. A local weave had been established for this meeting, and Sanjuro was aware that the Cibolans were concerned about the absence of other humans.

Sundown could read her nervousness. Privately, it offered to help Sanjuro reach *Mercator*. But they both knew this couldn't be done without attracting the attention of the leadership.

Although Sundown had an official role, the delegation was led by Sorrel's heir, Fire, not yet officially installed as ruler but widely acknowledged as the one in charge. Fire had opposed dealing with the humans from the beginning, and Sorrel's death made things worse. Sanjuro was starting to understand the Cibolan power structure, and while bits and pieces of it seemed familiar, it didn't exactly correspond to human systems. The old royalty had power but did not rule without consensus. Decision-making within the weave was a complex process. She could watch it unfold, but not follow it completely. Certain individuals had more power in the weave than others, and often it seemed to her that their authority was based on the force of their personalities more than anything else. Fire possessed that force and exuded a charisma that would have been formidable in any culture. Sanjuro could tell that some of the others who had official roles—and she wasn't sure who had appointed any of them—disagreed with Fire, but their thoughts were muted.

Iron was present and angry. She had counted Sundown's spouse a friend, but now she felt unsure. Sundown and Iron did not sit together, even though Iron was visibly pregnant. Sanjuro had learned enough about Cibolans to know that a breach between partners created serious problems, especially when the partners were raising children together. The chemical reaction that allowed conception and triggered the development of milk and nipples in the father only occurred when both persons opened their minds fully to each other. It was one of the factors that kept the birthrate low.

Sanjuro wanted to send Sundown a thought of sympathy or squeeze its hand. But Sundown was maintaining a calm presence, and Sanjuro wasn't sure she was supposed to notice the tension and knew that it wouldn't help the human position if she and Sundown seemed too friendly at this point.

Fire sent Sanjuro an image—Sanjuro, sitting all alone on one side of the table as small ships departed from *Mercator* again.

The implication was clear to Sanjuro: Here we are, talking to you again, when you cannot control what your ship does.

Sanjuro sent back a reply: A senior commander, giving her orders.

Fire's response conveyed skepticism, and Sanjuro started to worry that the meeting might end before it had started. She felt more unrest in the meeting weave. She willed herself to sit at the table, to not go looking for the shuttle.

Sundown suddenly caught her attention: the meeting weave had registered the presence of human minds. Sanjuro, too, felt the jumbled thoughts of Masire, Gervaise, and Kyo; none of them had yet learned enough telepathic communication to block others or even to send intentional messages. She let out a breath she hadn't known she was holding. The Cibolan unrest shifted to curiosity. Within minutes the three officers joined her at the table. "Rao," Masire whispered to her before seating himself.

Sanjuro picked up a hint of the problem from his mind — Rao wasn't accepting his authority. She introduced Masire as the commander of *Mercator* and Kyo and Gervaise as senior officers. A little tricky to do in Cibolan terms, where no mirror of the human hierarchy existed. She used a picture of Masire seated with others at a meeting, presenting the kind of forceful presence Fire did, with Kyo and Gervaise offering advice.

She got back an image of Vargas, landing on the planet, making his speech, the other officers standing at formal attention.

Sanjuro sent back an image of Vargas's funeral. She suspected Fire already knew about his death, but that didn't mean the Cibolan understood how human power shifts worked.

Sanjuro visualized a schematic that showed the military hierarchy. She fuzzed over the differences in the branches of the service — that was hard enough to explain to human civilians, much less to people whose decision-making structure was more fluid. Here was Vargas, in charge of all; Marley second; Masire third. One goes down, another takes the place.

She blocked her worries about Rao.

Next they discussed the medical exchange, judged a success by both sides, which broke some of the tension. Then the Cibolans showed pictures of their damaged cities. What would the humans do to repair that?

Sanjuro offered the few things they had available now: insta-builds, medical supplies. She sent images of damage on *Mercator* and people working to fix it, contrasted with pictures of the ship fully functional and producing food and supplies. A shuttle carried those supplies planetside.

Fire seemed to understand that if they were allowed to fix the ship, they could do more to help the Cibolans.

Sanjuro also offered people, a few now and more later, to help the Cibolans rebuild.

This led to intense debate on the Cibolan side, from which Sanjuro was shut out. The response finally came: humans to help, yes, but none for human purposes.

Given that the astrobio team had all been put to work on *Mercator* repair, this was a moot issue for now, and Sanjuro agreed.

Then Fire sent a picture of the asteroids.

Sanjuro felt Masire stiffen beside her. Better not to promise any deals there—not until all the humans were operating as one again. For now, repair and rebuild, she told Fire. And then we will resolve the asteroids and other matters. They left it at that. *Slowly,* Sanjuro thought. *We must go slowly.*

Sanjuro walked with the three other humans to their shuttle. "What was that about the asteroids?" Masire asked.

"A good sign, I think. They're still interested in some benefit from our work there."

"Yes," Gervaise said. "If they're interested, we have a chance at actually redeeming this expedition."

Masire rubbed his head. "Unless they're thinking of taking over some of us and going out there with us as some kind of puppets."

Kyo raised her eyebrows. Gervaise made a face.

"The Cibolans have highly developed ethics," Sanjuro said. "That kind of behavior would certainly violate them."

"We have highly developed ethics," Masire said. "But what would we do to aliens who bombed our cities?"

Sanjuro cut to the chase: "So what's the problem with Rao?"

"She refuses to bring her people and equipment back in. It's 'too risky,' she says. I think she's very close to challenging my authority."

"What are you going to do?"

"Go out there in person and bring everything we need back. She's not going to deal with anybody else."

"Need some backup?"

He grinned. "I've got Montoya and a few other troopers who can handle it."

"Can you spare a few people for planetside duty?"

"No, but I realize we have to make the gesture, so I'll send some down. Are you going to stay down here?"

"For now. I want to make my place in the weave, get them more comfortable with me."

Masire turned to Kyo. "Can you stay here, too?"

"If you can spare me from *Mercator*."

"Anybody I send anywhere makes me shorthanded somewhere else. But this is important, and I think you can contribute to Sanjuro's friendship mission." He paused. "Look, I realize there's a command structure problem here, but I really need Sanjuro in charge at this point, Major. She's the only one of us the Cibolans trust at all, and probably our main hope that—"

Kyo interrupted him. "Not an issue, Colonel. It's pretty obvious she's the only person who can run a delegation to the Cibolans. No one else can even talk to them."

"Thanks. I'll find you some Space Corps crew and maybe a marine or two, so you can get the rebuilding process underway." He turned to Gervaise. "Commander, I'm afraid you're going to have to shuttle back and forth quite a bit. Sanjuro is going to need legal advice, and I'm going to need you on *Mercator* as well. I hope you won't have a problem with serving in an advisory role here. I know that some would argue that legal should run the negotiations."

"I agree with Major Kyo. Captain Sanjuro is the only person who understands the Cibolans well enough to negotiate. You've got authority to assign people regardless of rank."

"Good. I need you back on *Mercator* now, to help deal with Col. Rao. But I'm afraid you'll have to shuttle back down tomorrow." Masire looked at Sanjuro, sighed quietly, and got on the shuttle along with Gervaise.

Sanjuro and Kyo watched it take off.

Kyo gave her a mock salute. "What shall I do first, ma'am?"

"Just try not to piss anyone off, for starters."

"Seriously."

"Seriously, the most important thing you can do is learn to read minds. We've got to get real communication going. The more of us they know and trust, the less likely we'll be faced with Masire's nightmares."

Kyo nodded. "By the way, I see you were right about the mutability of gender. Iron does appear pregnant."

"Yes."

"Fascinating. Kuso, I hope we can get this situation under control soon so I can re-focus our research. If they let us. Boy, is my cousin on the *Cortez* going to be pissed off when he discovers their big powerful company can't have access to the planet."

"Even when—or if—you can get back to your real work, you may not get much cooperation from Iron. Its anger is so great it's almost physical. I have no idea what's going to happen between Iron and Sundown."

For once Kyo didn't crack a joke. "I hope they can work things out. There have been enough losses among the Cibolans."

Sanjuro raised her eyebrows.

"Just because I suck at relationships doesn't mean I don't want others to be happy."

"Here's another thing that will interest you. Just as we assumed the Cibolans were divided into two sexes, they assumed we were like them: all the same, except during sex and pregnancy. They can't tell men and women apart."

"And we thought we could tell their sexes apart! I don't know what to make of all that, Caty, but assuming we can keep this fragile peace going, someone's going to get a hell of a dissertation out of it."

They began loading the small collection of instabuilds and the other supplies from *Mercator* into the land vehicle. As they shoved in the last box, Kyo said, "You shouldn't have kept secrets from me. I don't just mean the gender facts; I mean everything. Not just because I'm your commanding officer, but because you should have trusted me. I was protecting you, you know."

"I'm sorry, Sumi. I know I fucked up. If had come to you, maybe together we could have prevented the war. I was afraid you'd tell me there was nothing we could do, even if you understood more about the telepathic potential."

"Maybe I would have. Vargas had become unmovable. But I'd like to think I'd have done more, if I'd known."

Sanjuro nodded. "You're the only person who has mentioned that I shouldn't have stayed quiet. Everyone else is praising my ability to work with the Cibolans."

"They're feeling guilty for going along with Vargas when they all knew he was wrong. Besides, you were right. Everyone likes to support the person who was right, so long as they don't have to go out on a limb to do it."

"Right about what I knew; not right about how I handled it."

"No." The load in the landcraft left barely enough room for one. Kyo drove off alone.

Sundown had been waiting for Sanjuro. Together they walked back to the village. It was a long walk, but both of them found it soothing. They walked without sending, as if both were weighing the circumstances until Sanjuro inquired about the anger Iron had shown.

Sundown sent an image of Iron with Sorrel followed by another of Iron carrying Sorrel's body after the bombing, accompanied by a welter of anger, fear, uncertainty. Iron was staying in the city, along with their child; Sundown remained at their home.

Sanjuro took Sundown's hand, squeezed it. She didn't know what else to do.

# 3

Rao's team had hollowed out a section of the largest asteroid as a workspace and dubbed it Sierra Madre. Since asteroid dust could cause havoc in the lab, the team's main lab was located on the small, rotating space station set in geosynchronous orbit around it. The station provided a sterile environment and gravity.

Masire found Rao on the station, along with Case and several other scientists. "Colonel, we're honored by your visit," Rao said. She didn't bother with a salute. Her arms were crossed across her body. "I was given to understand that you were far too busy with repair operations to bother with our little project."

"It appears to be necessary for us to talk in person, Colonel," Masire said. He fought the urge to cross his arms as well.

"You brought so many with you." She glared at the five marines standing a few steps behind him.

"They can help load up the equipment we're taking back to *Mercator*."

"Don't be ridiculous, Colonel. We aren't giving you the equipment. I explained that to that person you sent out here before. We can't spare it. We're about fifty percent through with our survey, but we have a long way to go in determining the most effective way to extract each mineral. There's so much more here than we ever dreamed, so much more than *Copernicus* reported."

"It's not your decision, Colonel." Masire was aware of tension rising in his chest, but he succeeded in keeping his voice calm and firm.

"This is a Sci/Tech operation, not a marine one. You have no authority here."

"I'm making *Mercator* decisions, not marine ones." He let a flash of anger show in his voice. "You know Admiral Vargas and Captain Marley are both dead." He gave her the cold stare he used on new lieutenants when they screwed up something simple. Rao knew the military rules as well as he did; he had no doubt she understood he was in charge. She was probably cursing that few months of difference in their respective promotion dates.

"This is a critical point in our operation."

Masire noticed that the other Sci/Tech officers looked uncomfortable. "Is there some place more private where we can talk?"

"I don't see any need for a private conversation."

*Fine,* Masire thought. *If she wants witnesses, she'll get them.* He waved a hand in front of his face, as if he were clearing away a veil. "I'm reassigning most of your staff, too."

"I certainly can't spare any staff. As I said, this is a critical point in our operation. If we're going to have everything in place before the *Cortez* gets here, we need everyone working at—"

"God damn it. The *Cortez* is irrelevant." Masire had stopped controlling his anger. "Imminent death trumps any amount of political backstabbing."

Rao kept her arms crossed, but she backed up a step.

"We just lost a war back there. I'm not sure how *Mercator* is maintaining orbit, but I couldn't take her out of here if I wanted to. All intrasystem com is down. We still have the particles for the ETQ system, but the interface is completely broken. I can't report the situation back to the System until we get that repaired. I need the nanotech equipment you have out here to get the systems up and operational, and I need your crew to work on the repairs." His voice lost its angry edge as he spoke. "I also need your building equipment and instabuilds to help the Cibolans repair their damage."

"Why are you doing that?" Her eyes widened.

"So they won't kill us all. Maybe we can still negotiate a working relationship. Haven't you understood anything about what happened to us?"

"Frankly I don't understand how such primitives could possibly defeat us. They must have had cooperation from our people." These words were familiar territory to Rao. She stepped forward as she said them, and put her usual sneer into her voice.

But Masire also stepped forward, moving into her space and causing her to cede ground. "Don't be a bakatare, Colonel. You're wasting time with your fantasies about a subject you don't understand. I didn't come out here to debate. I came to get your equipment and most of your crew."

She started to say something else, but he cut her off.

"We will need a small crew out here, working on extracting Helium-3 from the regolith and making it usable in our systems. We lost significant amounts of reactor fuel, and we need to replenish it. Pick a skeleton crew that can work on that project. Other than that, I need everyone, particularly your engineers and enlisted crew. They've got skills we need to repair *Mercator*." He looked at her. "You're welcome to stay, and I'll leave you one shuttle, so you can get back to *Mercator* and move around the belt here. But that's it."

"And if I don't agree, you'll turn those troopers loose on me, is that it, Colonel?" Her attempt to say this sarcastically didn't quite work.

Masire let his voice get very quiet. "Even in Sci/Tech you must understand the consequences of refusing an order, Colonel. Particularly in wartime."

She waved her hand in disgust, but she stepped back again, giving him more room. "Let me assure you that I will not forget how you handled this, Colonel. You may be in charge *technically*, but given the destruction on *Mercator*, you can be sure there will be a full-scale investigation. All of your decisions will be subject to review."

"As will yours, Colonel. As will yours." Masire's voice would have frozen Helium.

Case walked up to Rao and put a hand on her arm. She shook him off, but followed him back toward her tiny private office in a corner of the station.

One of the geo crew members looked at Masire warily. "Should we start packing things up, sir?"

"Yes."

"Some of the stuff you'll want is down on Sierra Madre." The crew member got on com and issued orders.

Case emerged from Rao's office alone. "I'm going to stay up here and handle the Helium problem," he told Masire. "How fast do you need it?"

"According to Pham, we've probably got enough to stay in orbit another month, maybe two. Assuming we've got all the leaks. Plus we're using a lot running the shuttles, since we don't have com."

Case gave a low whistle. "That's fast. You're going to have to leave me at least a couple of crew members. We haven't done much in the way of separating the Helium out to make it usable in the reactor — just a few experiments to make sure we can. I'm going to need people who can set that stuff up."

Masire nodded.

"Other than that, I'll need someone to oversee extraction. And to keep the station running." He paused, and looked over toward Rao's office. "The Colonel is going to stay up here."

"I figured she would."

"How bad is it back there?"

"We lost over a hundred people."

Case looked shocked. "Dios. I had no idea it was that bad."

"Yeah. Every time I turn around, I realize that someone else is no longer there. We had funerals, but they were so rushed that it's hard to remember who's alive and who's dead. And so much to be done. Virtually no ship system is left undamaged."

"How the hell did the Cibolans do all that?"

"It was just like Sanjuro said: we have no defense against their telepathic attacks. When they band together, they can reach

*Mercator* in orbit. They took over people and got them to sabotage systems. And killed some outright."

"It must have been awful."

Masire heard pity in Case's voice. He hardened his own. "What we did to them was terrible; our fighters tore up their city and killed a lot of them. We did them serious hurt, but they could have killed us all."

Case glanced over toward Rao's office again. "You probably ought to take her back with you, just so she can see it for herself."

"I imagine she'll find some way to blame it on me even when she sees it."

"What happens once you get the ship up and running? Do we head home?"

"I'm not sure we're going to get the A/ND back up at all." Masire spoke quietly, hoping the others didn't hear. "Pham's pretty sure she can get the ETQ working if she can get the interface parts rebuilt, but odds are we aren't going home without help from the System."

"Oh." Case spoke in a flat voice.

"So we need peace with the Cibolans. A working peace. If they decide to attack again before we can move out of their range, we're dead." Masire was trying to sound matter of fact, but the actual words sabotaged his effort.

Case shot his eyes over to Rao's office again. She was visible through the glass window, frowning at a piece of paper. "You're going to have to trade some asteroid wealth to get that peace, aren't you?"

"I imagine so," Masire said.

Case gave a small grin. "I won't tell Rao. Not yet."

On the way back to *Mercator*, Montoya sought out Masire. "It's not my place to say anything, sir, but..." She paused.

He'd never lost anything by listening to Montoya. "Go ahead."

"Why didn't you make Col. Rao come back with us? She's defying you. She needs to learn who's in charge." Montoya didn't bother to control the anger in her voice.

"She's not going to accept that I'm in charge, except on a technicality."

"Then throw her in the brig."

Masire grinned. "It's tempting, I admit. But I think she can do less damage out here. If I brought her back against her will, I'd have to fight with her every day."

"She's going to try to undermine you with the System, sir."

"I know. But if she stays out here until after we get ETQ com up and running, they'll get my report first."

Montoya rubbed her chin. "That might be good strategy, sir. But she ought to see what happened to the Admiral and the others, to understand."

"The only way she's going to understand what the Cibolans can do is to be attacked by them, and even then she'll probably find some reason not to believe it. She's so single-minded in her view of reality." He shook his head in resignation.

Fire's team of advisors met in a private home. They shared images of the many things going on: alien healers working with the injured, thousands of people—including aliens—working to rebuild the city, their own healers helping the aliens. But in the room, anger and pain remained strong, and more than one advisor urged ignoring the surrender and finishing the job. Others—Iron among them—pressed Fire to insist upon a share in the asteroids' metals. Fire agreed with this approach. But how, it sent, do we do this? The aliens keep avoiding the issue. We need their ships, and their skills, to obtain these things; we cannot kill to get this. But how do we make them cooperate. Even the angriest were seduced by the idea of getting metals they needed.

But an old one, gone completely gray around the eyes, visualized the aliens coming to their planet in perpetuity. We will never be rid of them, that one sent.

Aliens were not the only concern. The other countries on the planet were watching for weaknesses in Golden Mountain. Two offered supplies and help, which Fire had accepted. But what if their intentions were not merely charitable?

We must press the aliens on the asteroid mining, Fire sent.

>➤

Kyo picked up telepathic skills very quickly.

"I'm jealous," Sanjuro told her, mind to mind. "You're getting this faster than I did."

"I think it's because you're here to help me along. You put it in human terms."

She and Kyo often conversed mentally using words, an activity that greatly surprised Sundown and others they worked with. They couldn't follow the telepathic conversations Sanjuro and Kyo had. This disturbed some of the Cibolans, so they rarely did it when others could eavesdrop. But since it made the learning process faster for the humans, they used it the rest of the time.

When *Mercator* sent them building equipment, Sanjuro asked Kyo to work with Iron. An engineer by trade—though like most Cibolans Iron had more than one skill—it was overseeing most of the rebuilding work in the City. Kyo was the obvious choice, really the only choice. She had developed more telepathy than anyone else—and the crew coming from *Mercator* had none—and she had sufficient rank. Iron's alliance with Fire, coupled with building skills, made it a key player.

But since the breach between Iron and Sundown continued, putting Kyo close to Iron made Sanjuro nervous. "Watch yourself. Iron may have an agenda. And it is certainly going to follow orders from Fire."

"I'll try to ingratiate myself. Do some bonding. Sympathize with the spouse problems—I've had lots of experience with that.

Or maybe a little seduction. I've always wanted to try inter-species sex. Do you suppose Cibolans have sex when they're pregnant?"

Sanjuro was so caught up in her concerns over the job that she took Kyo's comments seriously. "Damn it, Sumi. If you've been paying any attention at all, you certainly know you can't bring up strained relations between spouses. As near as I can tell, no one discusses that sort of thing. And I devoutly hope you're kidding about seductions. We don't have any clue about the extramarital habits of Cibolans. Besides, I don't think humans and Cibolans *can* have any kind of sex."

Kyo put up both hands. "Peace, Caty. I'm joking. I'm not going to do anything stupid. Anyway, I like Iron."

Sanjuro shook her head to clear it. Of course Kyo was joking. Still, Sanjuro gave her a sharp look. "Iron may not like you. It's not feeling very friendly to humans."

"I might feel the same way, if I'd been through what Iron has. If I've got the facts half right, Iron saw Sorrel die."

"You saw Vargas fall," Sanjuro said quietly.

"Yeah, but my feelings about Vargas were a lot more complicated than Iron's were about Sorrel. I get the impression Iron believed in their ruler, thought Sorrel could lead the Cibolans into a new age. And then we betrayed all that."

"If you understand that, then I trust you'll be careful."

"Always am." The imitation of Sanjuro was deadly accurate.

Sanjuro rolled her eyes. "I don't know why someone hasn't had you shot before now."

"I always made the firing squad laugh. Seriously, Caty. I understand the problem. I'll do my best to make Iron trust me. But we both know if Iron decides to do anything to me, I don't stand a chance. Right now I might have enough mental skill to keep a toddler from hurting me; no way I can protect myself against an adult Cibolan. So there's only so much taking care I can do."

"I know," she said quietly. "But do it. Please."

"Yes, ma'am."

Sanjuro spent hours in polite, generally unproductive meetings with Fire. Cibolan diplomacy resembled human diplomacy, involving copious debate over fine points. Would Cibolans or humans be responsible for feeding the *Mercator* troopers working on rebuilding the planet? (Humans.) Who decided which buildings to fix first? (Cibolans.) What was to be done with the crashed fighters? That turned out to be the trickiest question.

On a metal-poor planet, the scrap alone was worth a small fortune. But some of the fighters could be repaired, and *Mercator* needed them. Fire, nervous about the repair of any machine that could again attack them, refused to permit it. Masire remained equally adamant that the humans must get the fighters back and that they must not be damaged. The Cibolans were ostensibly guarding the fighters, but Sanjuro knew that in return some of the metal scavenged from the equipment, the guards looked the other way.

Masire got mad about the pilfering. "Can't they do a better job of protecting the fighters?" he asked Sanjuro on one of her trips up to *Mercator*.

"If they wanted to. I don't think they want to. I'm sure Fire knows about it," Sanjuro said.

They were sitting in his tiny office just off the bridge. The systems on *Mercator* might be chaotic, but Masire's office was tidy. Given that crew couldn't be spared for minor cleaning, Sanjuro suspected Masire cleaned it himself. "Damn it." Masire brought a fist down on his desk, though not loudly. "We're going to need those ships."

Sanjuro kept her voice calm. "Realistically, you don't have anybody to spare for the repair work right now, anyway, do you?"

"No. But we'll get to them eventually, if there's anything left to fix."

"Then give me authority to trade the completely wrecked ones for real protection of the others."

"I want more than protection; I want the ships themselves."

Sanjuro shook her head, firmly. "We aren't going to get that, Masire. Not right now. The hold-up isn't just from Fire. Delegations from the other countries on Cibola are present, and every one of them is afraid we might attack their country like we did Golden Mountain. And when they're not worrying about that, they're looking at how they can get a piece of Golden Mountain. Even if Fire trusted us— and it doesn't—it's not in a position to give us much slack. But if we give them some of the material, we have a chance to preserve the others for repair down the road."

Masire put both hands on his desk and leaned forward. "Do you have any idea how many regulations that would break?"

Sanjuro grinned. "There are regulations that tell you what you can give an enemy that has defeated you?"

He scowled at her. "You know what I mean."

"Yeah, but they don't have to let us have them at all. If we are generous on the one hand, we may get what we need. I don't think we have much else left to bargain with."

Pham knocked on the frame of the open door. Gervaise was with her. "Excuse me, Colonel. I just found out something about our ETQ that you need to know."

"You'll want to hear this, too, Captain," Gervaise said as Sanjuro started to get up.

Pham said, "The AI found something interesting when it reconstructed the ETQ interface: an encrypted file that contained messages from and for the companies behind the *Cortez*. Messages that date back to before we left the System. It was built into the system from the beginning. There was probably one running A/ND communications, too."

"It kept records?" Masire said.

"That's one of the limits built into all AI; they keep a record of everything. It took another AI to find it, though."

"That was our mole," Gervaise said. "That's how people like Sanjuro got private messages from the corporate interests."

Sanjuro said, "So they were planning the *Cortez* expedition all along."

"Looks that way," Pham said. "At the very least, they wanted to know everything we were doing, even if they hadn't yet put together an expedition. I'd venture there's another AI mole built into the ETQ interface on Earth, one that could divert useful data to the *Cortez*."

"We were always meant to be just an advance team for the *Cortez*, weren't we?" Masire said.

"Looks that way," Gervaise said in a bitter tone. Sanjuro had never heard her so angry.

Masire said, "How are the repairs coming?"

Pham said, "We're still a few weeks away from being able to send anything via ETQ. The destruction was so thorough that the AI is having to design replacement parts from scratch—which is the same problem we're having with every other system we're trying to get running. The operational nano machines are running full time, but we've still got a long list of equipment to make."

"You sure this AI isn't a mole, too?" Masire asked.

Pham shrugged. "I'm not sure of anything, Colonel."

"It probably doesn't matter at this point," Gervaise said. "They already know plenty."

# 4

The pressure from the other countries had become more urgent. Sanjuro realized now that three of them had helped Golden Mountain in the war and therefore were entitled to a place at the negotiating table. Fire technically represented that faction, but Sanjuro could tell that they were not all in agreement.

As for the other countries, one was pretending the humans didn't really exist, and the other two were refusing to help while criticizing every decision that was made.

"So much for any idealistic assumptions that a telepathic society might be more rational than ours," Sanjuro sent to Kyo.

"Human nature turns out to be sentient-being nature," Kyo sent back.

Sundown sent messages of puzzlement to them both. The three of them were sitting in a café that had—thankfully—escaped damage. The temperature was almost warm, and sitting in the café indulging in the fermented Cibolan drink felt like a real luxury.

Sanjuro thought about the words they had just sent, and tried to turn them into images. In the end, the best she could do was visualize Cibolans squabbling and humans squabbling, which got across the concept that humans and Cibolans were alike on this point. But she couldn't think of any way to explain the idea that a telepathic culture might be more virtuous than a human one—or that it failed on that score. Abstract comparative terms were difficult to comprehend in a world where one demonstrated differences or similarities by showing the two items in question back to back.

"I need to teach you human language," Sanjuro sent to Sundown in words that she simultaneously translated into images.

Sundown responded with eagerness.

Kyo shook her head.

"Sundown needs to understand how we think," she told Kyo.

"I'm not sure you can do it," she said.

She wasn't sure either. "But I need to try. We can't show everything about humans in telepathic terms; they need some understanding of abstract concepts to fully comprehend us."

Sundown looked lost again.

Kyo said, "Sounds like an impossible job. And you've already got one of those."

Sanjuro made a face in response. She sent an image of Sundown reading and writing.

Sundown responded with the human nod it had already mastered.

Kyo didn't miss it, but said, "Just because Sundown's as nuts as you are doesn't make it a practical thing to do. Sundown's got an impossible job to do, too." She sent them both pictures of themselves climbing steep cliffs, stuck about a third of the way up.

Sanjuro laughed and shrugged. To her delight, Sundown shrugged as well.

"Worry about your own problems," Sanjuro said. "We'll take care of ours."

Sanjuro and Sundown started planning their schedules to meet at some point daily for a language lesson. Since Sanjuro had to be so many places every day, she was using a landcraft to get around, making their meet-ups possible.

The lessons gave them cover for getting together. Sundown had told Fire about studying human communication and had approval. If their discussions sometimes veered into strategy sessions, well, no one was the wiser.

Just as Sundown had taught Sanjuro as if she were a small child, Sanjuro began the language lessons by teaching Sundown a few simple nouns and verbs. Though even that proved difficult.

What did she call herself: Human? Scientist? Woman? Soldier? She was all those things.

What did she call Sundown: Cibolan? Astronomer? Scientist? Mother? And father-to-be. But Cibolan was a made up word, professions defined a limited part of someone's life, and Cibolan parenting was too complicated for easy rendering in human terms.

Names presented another challenge, because human names bore little relationship to their holder's appearance. And humans had so many names, plus titles.

Bioscans showed vocal cords in Cibolans, though Kyo wasn't sure they were developed enough to allow speech. So Sanjuro began with teaching Sundown to respond to hearing spoken words. Cibolans responded to sounds in the environment—the thud that tells you an object has fallen to the floor, the purr that announces that an engine is working—but they never used sound of any kind in communicating with others. If Sundown had not carefully observed the humans talking with each other, the entire concept would have eluded it. Sanjuro found she had to first attract Sundown's attention telepathically and then say the words. She translated mentally at first. As Sundown made progress, Sanjuro blocked out any mental images, making Sundown rely on sound alone. Soon Sundown was responding to such words as "Sanjuro," "ship," "eat," and "drink."

They then took a stab at written words. Sanjuro tried to teach Sundown the alphabet, but that proved too abstract, so they tried whole words instead. Sundown memorized the shape of the words quickly. Cibolans seemed to remember things more easily than humans. Sanjuro speculated that the fact that their culture was the telepathic equivalent of an oral one made memorization easier. She hoped to get a chance to work with other Cibolans to see if her experience with Sundown held true.

"I should probably teach you Japanese or Chinese, instead of English," Sanjuro said to Sundown's puzzled look. Kanji might be easier to remember, at least the symbols that bore some resemblance to the concepts they represented. But they had started with the English that was the human lingua franca of the day. Introducing new languages at this point—outside of the many words adopted into English from other languages—would add confusion. Besides, Sanjuro's Japanese was rudimentary. She knew more swear words than anything else and had only a beginner's grasp of kanji. She knew even less Chinese.

It didn't take Sundown long to master enough words to read a book for small children. But it remained unable to follow words when Sanjuro thought in them. Sanjuro found it necessary to think of each word as if it were printed on a page for Sundown to read her thoughts, whereas Kyo could follow the briefest hint at a word.

If they had more time—but of course they didn't. Both were constantly working, and the lessons were held in brief periods snatched from the long days. Sanjuro railed against the time limitations, but Sundown sent her an image of the coming winter, with long evenings inside.

*If,* thought Sanjuro, *we're all still here.*

In those stolen moments, they embarked on yet another project. Sundown told Sanjuro stories about Cibola, by sending her the images that had been passed down to her from childhood. Sanjuro turned those stories into written ones, by translating the images into words and dictating them into her comp. Then, because the visualization that Sundown had sent gave her the feeling of human folk tales, she did her best to edit them to reflect that type of style. Their first completed tale was of the earlier invasion of Cibola.

Fire's headquarters, in an inn in the city that had escaped damage, was small and used for sleeping as well as for meetings. Whole families now were living in similar rooms. Iron and several others met with Fire to discuss strategy for dealing with the aliens and the asteroid minerals.

Withhold cooperation, someone suggested. But the cooperation is benefiting us as well, another replied. Threaten them? But how well will that work? Take control of their minds and force them to agree? But will they change their minds when they are out of range? Alter their minds permanently to agree to do whatever we want done?

Even the person who made that last suggestion rejected it. There were some boundaries beyond which no one was willing to step. Their history showed them the harm caused by permanent mind control.

We should visit the asteroids, Iron sent. The response was puzzlement, so Iron went on: They have ships that can fly there. We make them take us up there and show us the minerals. They won't agree to fly us, someone sent. We would have to force someone.

Sundown's friend?

No, Iron sent. Sundown's friend is too good at communication. It could block an effort at control. And Sundown would protect it. No, it should be someone weaker. The one helping us rebuild is a good candidate. And Iron sent an image of Sumi Kyo.

Can it operate the ships?

Yes, Iron sent. And we have been working together. It will trust me.

A betrayal, sent Fire in a gentle way that Iron had not expected.

Yes. But sometimes betrayal is necessary, Iron replied.

⤜

Now that they had moved the nanotech equipment from the asteroids, the amount of rebuilding on Cibola done by *Mercator* crew had increased substantially. By winter Golden Mountain would probably be able to house all of those who had lost their homes. Some Cibolans might suffer from a lack of privacy, but they would not freeze.

Fire had taken this progress as an excuse to press the humans about the asteroids, but Masire was still telling Sanjuro to go slow. On his visit to the planet to tour the repair operations, they discussed the asteroid issue.

"I know the Cibolans are entitled to a share of the asteroids. It's their system, and we owe them reparations. But we can't complete any deals without bringing Rao into the discussion, and that has the potential for making the whole relationship go up in smoke. Literally."

They were sitting in the shuttle, huddled around the comp. Both intrasystem com and the Mercator-net were operating, more or less, though delays were frequent, and they were looking at reports from the various repair operations.

Masire went on. "If we can hold off until Case has got us enough Helium-3 ready for the reactor so we can get out of Cibolan mind range, we'll be on safer ground."

"The trouble is," Sanjuro said, "Fire knows I'm stalling. I've been showing the Golden Mountain leaders what is available and how it works—teaching them asteroid geology. They're very interested, but I've exhausted the science lessons, and they're more than ready to see for themselves. Plus Fire is no scientist—doesn't give a damn about theoretical stuff. It just wants to see a nice shipment of iron. I'm running out of things to say to put it off."

"We need to wait," Masire said firmly. "I want to have enough power on hand to protect ourselves while we're negotiating. That way we don't have to give away the store to survive."

Sanjuro stood up. "It could be argued that they're entitled to the whole thing."

"Yeah, but the System won't back us on that, and you know it. And they can't realistically exploit it without our help. Right now, the iron is the only thing they can use on their own, and that's if we bring it to them. Making the rest of that technological jump will take a lot of time; you're talking about something that humans did over a period of 600 years. And we had more technology to begin with when we were at this level. It really is of no value to them unless they work with us." He, too, stood up, and moved toward the pilot's seat.

Sanjuro sighed as she watched him take off. She knew he was right. But convincing Fire of it was another matter, given the lack of trust. She knew, as Masire did, that if they died out here, the System would find a way to take the asteroids while avoiding Cibola. It could be easily done.

The tension increased the next day, when she met with Fire, who demanded a full conference with Masire on the direct subject of the asteroids. Intrasystem com was back up and running, though intermittently, and there were long lag times when *Mercator* was on the other side of the planet. Sometimes she regretted that she had managed to reinstall her own com system and that the intrasystem com was working. Putting Fire off would have been easier if she could plead communication problems. But speedy responses were useful some of the time, so she had not kept the communication repair a secret from the Cibolans.

Sanjuro sent Masire a priority message. He replied immediately, suggesting a date about ten days off. Fire found that unacceptable. They left the matter unresolved, which made Sanjuro very nervous. She composed a long message to Masire after the meeting, urging him to come down more quickly, but the com system decided to cut out again before she could send it.

Sanjuro was in the city with a mixed Cibolan-human crew working on rebuilding Sorrel's home. The choice of that property to repair was both psychological—their leader symbolized a great deal to the Cibolans of Golden Mountain, and the loss of Sorrel had been a major blow—and practical: the building could house many over the winter.

The builders' weave, recognizing that all repairs could not be completed before winter, had chosen to concentrate on larger buildings that could provide services to many people. Factories and other public buildings were the first priority, since they could be used for both living and work.

Sanjuro's bodysuit was cranked up considerably over the settings she had used in the summer. It worried her; the actual onset of winter was unpredictable, according to Sundown. Sanjuro had spent most of her life in environments where weather was controlled and didn't know how people planned without knowing when it might get colder or wetter. But she was learning.

Her personal knowledge of building was limited and theoretical: she had studied the cultural differences in construction in one of her anthropology courses. The Cibolans on the crews knew what they were doing, so long as they were working with Cibolan materials. Watching them work fascinated her; four hands really were more useful than two when wedging pieces of stone into place, for a worker could hold the piece with two hands while adding mortar with the other two.

The humans varied more in their skill levels. Some had spent time building permanent bases on planets, moons, and asteroids in the System, so they knew how to combine local soil and high-tech synthetics derived from nanotech. Most, though, were only useful when told "go there and do that."

Since they were using a combination of materials, the person who understood what needed to be done changed frequently. Although the Cibolans accepted that the humans knew more about the human tech, and the humans acknowledged that the Cibolans had, indeed, been building with native rock and soil for untold centuries, both sides found it hard to cede control to the other, even when it made sense.

The humans were learning some rudimentary telepathy, but among themselves they found it easier to talk. Few Cibolans were as good as Sundown at teaching adults who had no control over their mind skills, so Sanjuro spent most of her time translating and resolving disputes. Smoldering feelings of hate left from the war—there was no one on either side who had not suffered losses—made the situation that much more difficult, Sanjuro thought; she had arrived at the work site just in time to prevent a Space Corps tech from punching out a Cibolan, while simultaneously stopping a second Cibolan from frying the tech's brain.

She watched as a mixed crew managed to set a steel wall in place between two walls of mud bricks. The steel had a greenish tinge, from the use of some native elements in its construction, which made it look more in keeping with the other walls than she might have predicted.

Her com pinged. "Sanjuro." Kyo sounded shaky. "I'm taking the shuttle. With Iron and Fire and a couple of others. To the asteroids."

"What?"

"Can't fight 'em. I could crash it, maybe."

"No. Do what they want. But go slow."

"Right. Oh, baka-na," she swore. "They know…" Com went dead. Sanjuro said, "Sumi?" But she knew it was pointless. The Cibolans must have guessed what she was doing even if she was using subvocalization. She knew she had to go. No way Kyo could handle the situation without help. She explained the situation to Chang, who had learned construction working in his family's business when he was young. She left him in charge on the planet. His telepathy was rudimentary, but the Cibolans had reason to trust his building skills by now. Dios, let no murders occur while she was gone.

She believed there was a fighter at the landing field near Sundown's village. And she wanted Sundown, if possible. She raised Masire on com as she raced for her landcraft. The ship was on this side of the planet, so the lag was mercifully short.

"I can see them on scan. You're sure they're going for the asteroids?"

"Kyo got a message out."

"They're moving slow. We can beat them there. You've got a fighter down there, right? You get there as soon as you can. Better bring Sundown with you."

Sanjuro put a sending for Sundown out into the general weave. She wondered if Sundown would be willing to go. Arriving with Sanjuro would put Sundown in opposition to the official Golden Mountain position.

It didn't take Sanjuro long to reach the village. She found Sundown directing the rebuilding of the marketplace—or rather, announcing their departure. Sundown had also learned of the expedition and reached the same conclusion as Sanjuro and Masire. Sundown's sending showed a whole group of people—Sundown, Iron, Fire, other Cibolans; Sanjuro, Masire, Kyo, other humans—sitting together.

# 5

Fire sat stiffly. The shuttle seat was designed to fit an average alien, making it both too short and too wide. The straps rubbed uncomfortably. Fire could read the others' fear, mirroring its own. The vehicle was too slight and too foreign and was traveling not just in the air— alien enough—but away from the planet. Fire had been forced back into the seat as the shuttle accelerated, increasing its discomfort.

Unlike the others, Fire blocked its feelings. The self shown to the others was calm, serene. A leader must not show fear. The alien piloting the ship was not afraid of the flight, though it feared Fire and many other things. Reading this alien was easy; its blocking was still primitive. Fire held on to the alien's lack of fear about the flight and kept a calm demeanor because of it. The others relaxed.

Iron had put Kyo's mind in the mental equivalent of a come-along, so that any direction but one would cause extreme pain. One advantage—or maybe disadvantage—of a rudimentary understanding of telepathy, she thought, was that you knew what others were doing when they controlled your mind.

The Cibolans were uncomfortable. Take-off had made two of them vomit, and Fire looked increasingly miserable. The resulting chaos had allowed Kyo to send a com message to Sanjuro before Iron had figured out what she was doing and caused her to shut down the com. They didn't know how to fly the ship, though, so they had to leave her mind open for that. Kyo might enter wrong coordinates, fly off toward the gas giant, but what would that do to the shaky peace? Granted, the Cibolans had breached it first, but killing Fire would create new problems. Sanjuro had said to go. She would have to trust that Sanjuro and Masire would come up with something.

Kyo felt Iron's agreement. All that effort to think only in words, wasted. Kyo changed her focus to the asteroid belt. Iron seemed to like that image. But she kept the ship slow, trying to avoid even thinking about choosing a speed. The longer they took to get there, the greater the likelihood someone else could get there.

Unless *Mercator* decided to shoot them down. Well, that was out of their control. Without com they couldn't even argue about it. Kyo felt a mental push from Iron. Had those thoughts been images again? She sighed and kept her mind focused on the asteroids.

⤜

Sanjuro wished they'd been able to take a shuttle. Shuttles came equipped with a small galley and a head; fighters had only catheters built into fight suits and an array of instant foods. Sanjuro managed to jerry-rig one of the flight suits for Sundown and helped the astronomer strap into the copilot's seat. They packed some Cibolan food— instant rations would not provide nourishment for Sundown.

Seats on fighters were a tight fit to begin with—they were stripped-down ships, designed for maneuverability, not comfort, and the average Cibolan was taller than the average human. Sundown held very still as they took off, but stared at the viewscreen and watched the planet slowly shrink in size.

*Sundown can't be comfortable,* Sanjuro thought. *And must be scared.* The short hops they'd done when they'd moved the telescope hadn't prepared Sundown for a flight across the Doradoan System. Plenty of fear to go around. A parade of asteroid belt scenarios strolled through Sanjuro's head, each one more frightening than the last. She could see so many ways for all of them to die out there. What did Fire hope to accomplish?

Unlike the shuttles—which were intended for intrasystem travel—the fighters lacked a second engine for breaking free of gravity. However, given the stripped-down design, and the fighter's high end speeds, it was possible to get loose from the planet through sheer speed. Sanjuro made sure their course would miss *Mercator*, and cranked up the speed to maximum. On the viewscreen the planet shrank rapidly. Feeling Sundown's discomfort, Sanjuro shut the screen down.

Interplanetary travel was nothing new to Sanjuro, but she'd never done it in a vessel this small. *Mercator* traveled much faster, but on a huge ship you didn't feel you were moving. Sanjuro liked the awareness of speed and motion. She wished she was doing more actual flying, instead of simply setting coordinates and letting the ship fly itself. But she contented herself with watching the comp readout, making sure they were actually leaving Cibola behind.

She could tell from the slight change in pressure on her body when they crossed the invisible boundary that broke them out of Cibola's pull, knew before she checked the comp readout that they were on their own. She ran scan and picked up the shuttle at the edge of the range. Comp told her Kyo was keeping it at the low end of the shuttle's speed. Sanjuro cut back her speed to a pace calculated to get them to the asteroid station at about the same time as Kyo and her passengers.

Sundown's face relaxed as they settled into the slower speed. Sanjuro reopened the view screen, and Sundown began to take a great interest in the trip, watching as their relationship to the other planets and stars changed. Sanjuro thought of the telescopes. *Sundown belongs out here,* she thought.

Com pinged, and a message from Masire came through. Sanjuro let it play out loud to avoid any hint of secrets. Sundown looked startled. The image Sanjuro got was one of wonder that voices could travel so far. Masire said, "We're setting a pace that ought to get us there several hours ahead of Kyo. They seem to be going slow, so it's easy for us to outrun them. I'm not going to try to contact them, just in case Kyo's com isn't destroyed. Surprise might give us an edge over the Cibolans."

They had a two-day trip ahead of them. Might as well spend the time working on the language lessons.

>⟶

Masire was feeling grateful for little things. Yurinko had been on *Mercator*, so he'd had both the big shuttle and the best possible pilot available. He'd brought Gervaise and ten marines who weren't working on planet, including Montoya, giving him a solid crew. They were moving at top speed; with any luck at all they'd beat Kyo and the Cibolans by half a day.

Rao was going to be a challenge, probably as great of one as dealing with Fire. He'd managed to back her down before, but he didn't have any illusions that she wouldn't push him to the limit again. He hoped Gervaise could put pressure on Rao. The only edge with Fire was that the Cibolans didn't understand the tech. That didn't seem enough.

They could all die out there, humans and Cibolans. He began composing a detailed message to Rao. She had the right to know what was going on.

>⟶

"What the hell is this?" Rao read the message once more. "I cannot believe it," she said out loud, though no one was there to hear. "That bakamono can't even keep the aliens down on the planet." She punched com. "Case, get up here. I need you."

"Colonel. Can we do this over com? If I shut down now, we'll lose a day's worth of work." The short staff meant Case was running the robots doing the Helium-3 mining.

"No. We've got aliens coming."

"What?"

"Apparently some of the aliens have forced Major Kyo to bring them out here in a shuttle." She wondered how much persuasion Kyo had needed. "Masire's on his way. And I gather Sanjuro is following with even more aliens. Going to be a regular picnic."

"How much time do we have?"

"A day, maybe. Finish up your current job, and then shut down completely. We don't want the aliens messing with the mining."

"I'll be up in about four hours."

Rao punched out. Why the hell hadn't Masire just shot the shuttle down?

>⇒

The shuttle hooked into the asteroid station's landing dock. The marines disembarked. Masire told Yurinko, "Keep your distance. I don't know how far these few Cibolans can project, but I want you to go far enough to be sure you're out of range. I'll leave my com link open. If all goes to hell out here, get back to *Mercator* and report."

"Yes, sir." He looked doubtful.

"If we can't talk our way out of this one, Lieutenant, there won't be anyone left to rescue."

"Sir."

Masire found Rao and Case in the main lab on the station. Rao's mouth was set in a tight line. She gave him a perfunctory salute. She'd never saluted him before.

*I guess we're playing it military,* he thought, and returned the salute.

"So you're bringing the aliens up here for a tour," she said.

Then again, maybe the salute was just another form of sarcasm. "Not by choice, Colonel. This was their idea."

"Are you sure Major Kyo didn't suggest it? Or Captain Sanjuro?"

"Yes, I am." He gave her the voice that brooked no arguments.

She just raised her eyebrows. Command voice wasn't going to work. He said, "We all tried to keep the asteroids out of the peace negotiations until we could get *Mercator* out of range of their mental powers. But the Cibolans pushed the agenda. Now we have to talk."

"Nothing to talk about. The aliens are primitives. They can't do anything with what we've got out here. They can't even reach it without our help. It's not theirs."

Gervaise said, "Colonel, the legal situation is a little more complicated than that."

Rao dismissed her with a wave of her hand. "Oh, please don't waste our time splitting legal hairs."

Gervaise ignored her. "First of all, the Cibolans are intelligent life. To the best of our current knowledge, they are the only intelligent life in this system. Based on our decisions with respect to the Solar System, there is ample legal precedent for recognizing their claim to this system."

"Except that they have no way of exploiting it without help."

Masire said, "We understand that, Colonel. That's giving us substantial room for negotiation we wouldn't have otherwise, given the military situation."

"I see. You lost a battle against these primitives—how I cannot imagine—and now you want to buy peace with what we came out here to get in the first place."

Gervaise crossed her arms across her chest. Montoya stiffened.

Masire said, "Colonel, if you can't imagine how we lost to the Cibolans, you're skipping over important data in reaching your conclusions. Their telepathic power is completely new to us. We're just beginning to understand it."

"Oh, yes. By letting Captain Sanjuro go native."

Masire took a deep breath. Exploding would be useless. Case stepped close to Rao and whispered something. She made a face and turned away from him.

Gervaise said, in a quiet voice, "Colonel, you are isolated out here. Those of us who were in the battle now realize that we should have listened to Sanjuro much earlier. At this point, we're very lucky that the Cibolans are still willing to talk with us. They could have killed us all. They still can."

"You mean they could have killed everyone on *Mercator*. That may be true. But they couldn't get up here. You could have shot them down. We still can."

"And if we do, we sign the death warrant of everyone on *Mercator*. Fire is no fool. I am sure the Golden Mountain people will attack *Mercator* if the Cibolans don't return in a reasonable period of time," Masire said.

"You attribute a lot of strategy to primitives."

Gervaise said, "Nothing primitive about these people, Colonel. They're just different. You'll see."

Rao didn't appear to have an answer. Masire said, "I don't suppose you have any coffee."

"Why don't we move into the lounge, and I'll make some," Case offered. One of the troopers jumped in. "I'll take care of it, sir," he told Case.

The coffee tasted weak to Masire. But the ritual took some of the tension out of the air. He sat with Case, Gervaise, and Rao at the dining table in one corner. Most of the marines had arrayed themselves casually around the room — though a couple had stayed in the lab to monitor scan and com — and Montoya was chatting with Case's engineering techs.

Masire turned to Rao. "Colonel, I don't know how to put this delicately, so I won't. I know you don't like the decisions I'm making. I'm going to have to come up with some kind of deal on the asteroids, and I'm sure you're going to object to it. I will note in my log that my decision was made over your objections, if you want. Commander Gervaise will witness it. I'm sure you'll put your own reports in. That's fine by me. But when the Cibolans get here, we need to present a united front. So I want you to go along with whatever I say, no matter how much you object."

"Colonel, I can't—"

"Yes, you can. And you will. That's an order. If you cross me in front of the Cibolans—if you so much as roll your eyes— I will put you under arrest and send you back to *Mercator*'s brig."

"You can't…" She looked at Gervaise.

Gervaise shook her head slightly.

Masire said, "Yes, I can. Don't be a bakatare. You understand the rules as well as I do. Are we clear?"

"Colonel—"

"Are we clear?"

"We're clear. But I guarantee you my reports are going to show up your incompetence. You'll end up as the baka who gave away a fortune."

"As long as I'm not the baka who got everybody killed."

One of the marines came in. "Sir, scan shows the Cibolan shuttle is about a half hour out. And I've got Captain Sanjuro on com for you."

"Right." He looked hard at Rao before he walked into the other room.

"Sanjuro. You still on their tail?"

"Less than five minutes behind them, Colonel."

"Good. You might as well pull in along with them. The landing zone is cramped, but there's room if you come in carefully. And there are two passenger tubes."

"I promise not to scrape the fenders. How are things there?"

"I think I've got cooperation. But just barely."

Sanjuro laughed. "Hope it holds. You thought about how we play this?"

"I was thinking we pretend Fire asked Kyo to bring them out here, instead of forcing her."

"I was thinking that myself. Might put them off balance. They're probably expecting belligerence. We going to deal?"

"We don't have much choice. I figure if Fire doesn't get back safely in a few days, we can expect an all-out attack on *Mercator*. *Mercator* can't sustain it."

"We're thinking alike. Sundown agrees. That's Fire's kind of strategy. See you in a bit."

# 6

K yo's shuttle was having some trouble with the landing tube. Sanjuro, following coordinates sent over com, realized she was having to eyeball it.

"Send me the shuttle's coordinates, too," she told the tech who was handling docking. "I'll get it over to them."

"Uh, here you go, ma'am." The tech sounded a bit confused— how would she do it if he couldn't—but he didn't waste time arguing.

Sanjuro and Sundown expanded their weave and focused on Kyo. Sanjuro kept it to words. "Howdy, Major. The cavalry's here," and sent her the coordinates. She wondered what Fire would make of all the horses that came to mind when she said cavalry, then guessed that the Cibolan had probably picked up an image of Masire and his marines as well.

Sanjuro and Sundown were already on the station by the time the landing tube opened to admit Kyo, Iron, Fire, and two Cibolans Sanjuro didn't know. Fire showed no surprise. Iron looked toward Sundown, and then away.

Masire spoke official welcoming words. Sanjuro noted that the images in his brain were the ones she had taught him for Cibolan formal meetings. He introduced Rao. Sanjuro played translator, sending images showing Rao in charge of the asteroid operation, but making her subordinate relationship to Masire clear.

Rao nodded civilly at the Cibolans, but Sundown sent Sanjuro a quick message, showing the hostility she was reading off the Sci/Tech Colonel. Fire was picking it up, too. Sanjuro nodded, then shrugged. Sundown had learned enough to know that meant Sanjuro understood but had no answer.

Fire was exercising iron control, and Sanjuro couldn't tell what it was feeling. But Iron and the others were not so well-disciplined in the face of something completely beyond their wildest imaginations. They were mesmerized by the view screen, which showed the large, misshapen asteroid the station orbited. Sanjuro caught both fear and excitement.

"Our main mining operation is over there," Case said. "Helium on the surface, platinums inside."

"Visualize it," Sanjuro told him. "They'll pick it up." She watched as he did, gave him a pointer or two.

Iron lit up. The Cibolan might not have known how to make use of all the materials out there, but could make some guesses. Sundown was looking with similar fascination. Sanjuro had explained it, as much as she could, but seeing it in person clearly gave the Cibolans a thrill.

*Sundown and Iron are so much alike,* Sanjuro thought, careful to block. Both of them want to explore. If we can get past all this, maybe that will bring them back together. She had to admit to herself that the work out here was fascinating. It was easy to pick up on Case's joy in his work. She could even feel Rao's enthusiasm beneath her hostility. Of course the Colonel wanted to protect this work. Who wouldn't?

Fire was focusing on the computers and other equipment the geo staff used to analyze samples. Sanjuro did her best to send explanations, though a lot of the equipment made little sense to her. She was amazed at how calm Fire was, especially compared to the other Cibolans. It had to be conveying calm on purpose, a mental skill Cibolan leaders would have to develop, Sanjuro thought. No one could be that calm faced with experiences so far removed from their ordinary life.

Rao stood near the equipment, arms crossed over her chest, a frown dominating her face. Mentally, she conveyed even more hostility and anger. Sanjuro still felt guilty when she dipped into human brains without notice — it was so different with Cibolans, who were always blocking what they did not want to share. But a lot of things depended on this situation going right, and Sanjuro had to watch Rao.

Fire picked up another object and sent the image that Sanjuro had labeled "quizzical." Sanjuro looked at the object and turned to Rao. She started to ask the Colonel to explain it, but then she read the images coming off of her. All of them telegraphed the concept of "mine." Some of it was words, but some of it was in images so obvious that Fire had to be reading it.

Fire laid the object down and picked up another one. It didn't care about the objects; it was working on reading Rao. And it wasn't bothering to hide that fact from Sanjuro.

Rao said, "Tell it to be careful with those things."

Sanjuro said, "Fire already knows that. You're broadcasting that point loud and clear."

"It's reading my mind?" Rao said.

"It has to. Cibolans don't talk, and the words you say make no sense to them. The only way Fire can understand what's going on is to read the images in your mind. I'm sending supplemental pictures, based on what you're saying, but I suspect it's getting more from you than from me."

"Make it stop," Rao said. Her voice sounded panicky.

"Colonel, you're sending so loud that it's difficult for the Cibolans to block you out. Try doing some deep breathing exercises."

"Make it stop." Rao didn't quite yell.

Sanjuro felt the wave of calmness that Fire projected to Rao. It was like the one Sundown had sent her when they had first gone to the marketplace.

At the time, it had been one shock among many, and after she had figured it out, she had characterized it as benign. Now, though, she knew that Cibolans used a similar calming projection for animals about to be butchered. She didn't trust Fire's purpose.

Sanjuro responded by putting a mental block between Fire and Rao, stepping between them to dramatize it physically: this far and no farther. Behind her she heard Rao gasp as the calmness went away.

"Make it stop," Rao said again, but this time it was almost a whimper.

"I am," Sanjuro said.

Fire's response was the mental equivalent of a shrug and a grin, a reminder to Sanjuro that she was the weaker one here.

Sanjuro was well aware of that, but she didn't move or lift her protection from Rao. Fire focused on Sanjuro; the pressure felt like a drill in her skull. At the edges of her consciousness she could feel Iron and the others join Fire. And then Sundown was there, telling the three of them to back off. Sanjuro caught something about the rules of dueling. The presence of others went away. So this was what a duel felt like.

Now she felt Kyo and Gervaise with her. Gervaise's skills were even more rudimentary than Kyo's, and she staggered a little when she felt Fire's power. "No," Sanjuro said aloud. "This is between Fire and me." They disappeared from the weave.

Sanjuro heard Gervaise sit heavily, and then another sound: the soft click of a weapon being readied. Fire chose that moment to add force to the attack, and now Sanjuro could not speak, only focus on blocking.

Kyo said something, and she heard a short command from Masire. She could still feel readiness from the marines in the room, but no weapons were aimed at anyone.

Rao said, "What is going on here?"

"Sanjuro's protecting you," Gervaise said. "She's keeping Fire out of your head."

Fire bore in again, and this time the force of the attack staggered Sanjuro. She stumbled back. Her head throbbed with pain.

"She's overmatched," Kyo said quietly.

The pain in her head, coupled with Kyo's words, jolted her out of dependence on her block. No way she could hold Fire off forever. Sanjuro took a deep breath and relaxed her body as she exhaled and dropped her block. Fire's attack lessened.

Maybe it was just a brief respite before a renewed attack, but Sanjuro took advantage of it to send an image: everyone in the room dead, except Fire. She followed it with more images of Fire unable to operate the machines, unable to fly the ships.

Fire responded with an image showing a few humans left. In the image, one of the humans flew them back to the planet. Sanjuro came back with that shuttle crashing into an asteroid. Fire's next image showed it standing calmly as a fire raged through the station.

Sanjuro replaced Fire in that image with herself. But then she sent an image of a crew of Cibolans and humans working in a mine on the nearest asteroid. It was cartoonish, showing them working with picks and shovels as miners did on Cibola, but it got the idea across. She showed huge piles of iron on the surface of Cibola, and humans and Cibolans working with that iron.

Then she showed all those things destroyed, and sent an image of the room on the space station, with everyone dead: It's not just our lives at stake here; it's our dreams as well. You can kill me, kill us all, but that won't give you what you want.

For a moment she felt Fire press even harder. Sanjuro rocked on her heels, but took another deep breath and managed to stay upright.

Then Fire backed off. This time it felt permanent.

Sanjuro reached out with her mind and felt everyone in the room. Sundown sent her an image of the two of them hugging. She heard both Kyo and Gervaise exhale. Masire was looking at her. She gave him a nod, and he gave an order. The marines stood down.

Fire turned and picked up another object. But now its question reflected simple curiosity.

"Colonel," Sanjuro said, "if you think in images about that object, it'll be able to figure out what it does."

Rao did so. Sanjuro caught the image of a spectral analysis of a piece of rock, the colors flowing from one to the next.

"Are you okay, Colonel?" Sanjuro asked.

"Yes. I think so. If we keep it to objects, I think I can handle it."

Sanjuro told Fire objects only, and got agreement. She stood back and watched as Fire once again asked about the different tools, prompting Rao for the images. Enthusiasm crept into Rao's explanations. She loved explaining her work.

From across the room, Kyo said in her head, "What the fuck did you just do?"

"Damned if I know," she sent back.

Masire walked over to her and took her arm. She appreciated it; her legs were weak. He said in her ear, "I think Rao is starting to understand what the rest of us went through."

Sanjuro nodded. "And Fire is figuring out how to work with us. We may get something here after all."

They spent the next four hours giving the Cibolans a fast course in asteroid geology. Despite heroic efforts from Case, they couldn't quite explain Helium 3; there were no images that worked. But it was easy to break down the various metallic elements found in the rocks.

All the Cibolans recognized the value of the iron; at the current state of their tech, it was something they could all understand. But Iron and Sundown both grasped the uses of rhenium and some of the other platinums.

The big breakthrough came from the water. Mixed among the asteroids were a number of spent comets. In fact, the asteroid station had been designed to use those comets for its water needs. Some of the water had been shipped down to *Mercator*.

Sundown sent Sanjuro an image of the shuttle towing one of the comets to the planet. Sanjuro turned to Case. "How hard would it be to get a substantial quantity of water down to Cibola?"

"Easier than getting the iron down there," he said.

Sanjuro felt the Cibolans' excitement. The significance of the other things would grow in importance over time, but to a dry, metal-poor planet, water and iron loomed large.

"Water and iron," Rao said. "Plenty of that to share, I guess. At least until the *Cortez* gets here. They probably already have it divided up among the major corporations."

"Well, we've got time to get things established before they get here," Masire said. "They'll have to make some concessions to reality."

Rao said, "Oh, sure," in a sarcastic tone.

Sanjuro privately agreed.

Gervaise said, "Especially if the Cibolans own the rights." The small grin on her face spread into a huge smile.

"What?" Masire said it, but everyone was thinking it.

"If any rights we have out here are based on a treaty with the Cibolans, then the corporations won't be able to change those rights unilaterally."

"Even if the System has given them rights?" Kyo asked.

"We have full authority to negotiate treaties. Any rights the System gave the *Cortez* are necessarily subject to those agreements. If we recognize the Cibolan rights here, both the System and the *Cortez* will have to accept it."

"But didn't the System assume we wouldn't need to negotiate a treaty over the asteroids?" Sanjuro didn't want to put a wet blanket on Gervaise's suggestions, but they sounded too good to be true.

Gervaise was still smiling. She brought her hand up like a lecturer emphasizing a point. "Sure. But that was based on the assumption that the Cibolans had no control over the asteroids. Obviously that isn't true." She waved her hand at Fire.

Sanjuro could read the puzzled reaction of all the Cibolans in the room. None of the images this conversation generated made sense to them. She sent them all a quick "patience" message while she tried to understand the legalities herself. "You mean, since they've come out here, we have to deal with them for the asteroids, despite the other interests involved?"

Gervaise nodded. "Exactly."

Kyo broke in. "But our orders—"

"Our orders cover all contingencies," Gervaise said.

"Of course, we'll still have to deal with these, um, Cibolans," Rao said.

"Yes, ma'am, but we have to do that anyway."

Sanjuro thought back to her duel with Fire. *Yes, we have to*, she thought. *We always had to.*

Gervaise went on. "Assuming we can establish a solid working relationship with the Cibolans, we might even be able to protect ourselves from having the work pulled out from under us by the *Cortez*."

Rao said, "Oh." It didn't take telepathy to see the gears start working in her mind.

"It makes sense," Masire said. "Are you sure we have the authority to negotiate a treaty that broad?"

"Yes, sir. Our mandate gives us the authority to negotiate any treaties necessary to complete our mission. The Cibolans have made it pretty clear that we can't do anything without their consent." She inclined her head toward Fire and the others.

"Well," said Rao. "If we have to deal with them anyway..."

Which was probably as much agreement as they'd ever get from her, Sanjuro thought, as she turned to the difficult task of explaining the concept of treaties to Fire.

>

"Is it going to work?" Masire asked Sanjuro. They were sitting in the galley by themselves. Sleeping facilities had been set up for all the visitors, and most people and Cibolans had taken advantage of them.

"I think so. We're going to have to reduce it to a written contract for our people, and it's going to take some doing to explain the abstract ideas in Cibolan terms. Gervaise's idea of doing a holo of the negotiations, complete with simultaneous translation, makes a lot of sense. Sundown told me that there are Cibolans whose job it is to remember agreements. So we do it with both their formality and ours.

"And, of course, we aren't dealing with all the Cibolans as yet. So we have to get some agreement from Fire to try to bring the others around. But we're going to get much more cooperation than I ever thought we would."

"We probably should have brought Cibolans out here before."

"Yeah. Turns out that what we thought was a complicating factor was the breakthrough factor."

"What *I* thought was the complicating factor," Masire said.

Sanjuro smiled in acknowledgment of the apology. "Well, I didn't think we could work this all out, either. I was just getting a lot of pressure." She yawned. "I have to get some sleep." As she headed for her bunk, she noticed Iron and Sundown were still staring out the view window at the sky around them. She hoped they were making peace.

⁂

Iron and the other Cibolans who had come with Fire were staying on the station for a month to learn everything they could. The baby wasn't due for several months, Sundown explained to Sanjuro; a month would not cause problems. Case and one of the techs had come up with some ideas on how they might modify the skels they used for outside exploration to work for Cibolans, so that they could see up close what the asteroids held.

Several of the marines were also staying behind. The shuttle and fighter were being modified to haul back a load of iron and comet ice to the planet, as a sign of good faith. Everyone else was going back in the large shuttle.

"I'm going to need my crew back," Rao told Masire as they got ready to leave.

"You can have a few," he said. "We still need most of them on *Mercator*."

"This project has to be successful, too, if we're going to keep the peace," she said. "And if I have to waste time on the iron."

"I'll send several people back when we get the iron and water planetside, Colonel. More, as soon as I can spare them. We still need to get *Mercator*'s systems back online."

"Don't take too long. And don't think just because I'm going along with this that I have changed my mind about the way all this was handled. I still think a lot of mistakes were made, and someone's going to have to answer for them."

"I'm sure you're not alone in that assessment, Colonel."

# 7

Iron and water. Over and over, the discussion returned to iron and water. The other countries were suspicious of the aliens; they had seen the destruction. The aliens were easy to fight, but their machines were powerful. Machines could destroy them. Still, all acknowledged that Fire had won the day. And while many wanted to—at best—tell the aliens to leave and never return, iron and water loomed too large to be ignored. They needed the aliens to get those materials.

A powerful image arose, one composed of ideas harvested from alien minds: crowded cities, bustling crowds, vehicles speeding down wide streets, tall buildings rising to the sky, noise. So much noise. Aliens, aliens everywhere, controlling this business, that operation.

Then it shifted as others added their ideas of the future to the weave: their own future, one with aliens on the periphery. The cities were grander and bustled with more commerce, more manufacturing, more art. But the people still moved leisurely, and the vehicles in the streets were fewer and moved at a slow pace. Iron and water. Our iron and water. Our future.

Fire showed the present, the vast spaces unusable, the tools most could not afford due to the cost of metal. The implications were clear: stay here, crippled, or move forward into whatever changes the future might bring. Who can know the future?

Iron and water.

One more image, this one sent by Sundown: a spaceship, on it some of their people, along with the aliens, going farther out into space, finding something new. A few retorted with images of their current life stretching back for generations: what was good enough for my grandparents, their sending implied. But now there were images of other planets, other stars creeping into the debate. Iron and water, yes. And maybe something more.

➢

ETQ was back up and running. Masire sent an initial message notifying the System that they had survived, followed by a short one that explained the war, listed the casualties, and provided the highlights of the treaty with the Cibolans. For transmissions after that, Gervaise provided a detailed follow-up of the treaty, while Sanjuro and Kyo did a summary of Cibolan telepathic power, along with other details of their civilization, to back up the need for the treaty.

They were prepared, but Sanjuro still felt a pit of dread in her stomach when Masire pinged her to say the System had responded. Soon her reports would be going in — reports that made it obvious she had not shared all her discoveries about the Cibolans when she first made them, reports that might anger both the military brass and Bogdosian.

"We got several months' worth of What the Hell Is Going On followed by acknowledgment of our We Are Alive message," Masire explained. "The war summary, casualty, and treaty report is going out with our next transmission at 0800. With luck we'll have a response to that at 2000. The next set of reports goes out tomorrow."

It was early winter now on Cibola, and already so cold that Caty Sanjuro appreciated her occasional trips up to *Mercator*, where the temperature never varied from comfortable now that they had managed to repair the damage to life support.

Stabilizing *Mercator*'s systems had proven no easy task. Neither had the rebuilding effort on Cibola. They had been far from finished when winter hit, but at least everyone planetside had a warm place to stay. And the initial deliveries of iron and water from the asteroids had given the economy a boost.

The initial responses from the System were businesslike. The treaty had been referred to the SSU legal department, military brass were reviewing war reports, and various scientists—including Bogdosian—were looking at Sanjuro's descriptions of Cibolan telepathy. They were expecting the next transmission to include rafts of questions. All the senior staff had come up to *Mercator* to discuss them. Afterwards, Sanjuro and Masire shared a drink in the recently reopened bar, staffed by robots and self-serve, open to all. Distinguishing between enlisted and officers no longer seemed important.

"Do you think they'll accept the treaty?" Sanjuro asked.

He shrugged. "Gervaise thinks so. She says the Secretary General will bring a lot of pressure to bear, just to set a firm precedent. If we're going to send out more long-range missions, we need to establish the authority of those crews to make deals. Could take years, though: all the different nations will want to weigh in. Not to mention lobbyists for the people who put together the *Cortez*. Of course, people can always bend treaties when they want to do something different."

"I hope they have better sense."

"So do I. The Cibolans won't stand for it."

"How about us? Will we stand for it?"

"You mean, will I stand for it. We both know what you'll do."

"All right. What will you do?"

"They aren't on the scene. If they make a bad call, I'll have to reject it. I'm not starting any more wars."

"You think everyone else will go along? It could mean court martial eventually."

"I think so. We may even bring Rao around. Immediate death trumps eventual court martial. Anyway, most people will have a following-orders defense."

"You won't." She gave him a grin this time.

"No. You won't either."

"I guess I am Becca's daughter. They'd have court-martialed her, if she'd lived."

"Maybe not. After all, she was right. They might have given her the medal anyway, and used that to sweep the truth under the rug."

*Like you're doing with me*, Sanjuro thought. "I read your report," she said abruptly. "Your summary of the war, I mean. Particularly the part about how the AI fighters caused a problem."

Masire shrugged. "AI fighters are always trouble. You know that. It's one thing using them in conjunction with humans, another entirely to have them on their own."

"But you never pointed out that the Cibolans couldn't hack them, the way they could human pilots."

"Didn't I? I thought it was obvious."

"Obvious to anyone who's been thinking about fighting telepaths. Probably not to anyone else. They're going to assume AI isn't effective here, when in fact a fleet of AI fighters could destroy Cibolan civilization."

"Somebody's bound to figure it out."

"With any luck at all, by the time they do we'll have an entrenched relationship with the Cibolans, and no one will act on it." Sanjuro grinned. "Though if they figure it out too soon it could be another item for the court martial."

Masire shrugged. "A minor one, probably. We've still got to negotiate the minefield of the *Cortez*. We've got about a year to make sure the treaty is solid before they arrive. Regardless of what kind of orders we get from headquarters, the System will be sending some higher ranks out to look into all this. No telling what might happen in a few years. Can't worry about it too much, though."

"No."

⇒

They couldn't send images via ETQ, much less holos or vid. It was text-only. After months of thinking in images to communicate with Cibolans, Sanjuro was finding it hard to use words to clearly describe things. "That old saw about pictures being worth a thousand words makes more sense now," she grumbled to herself as she tried to describe how the Cibolans worked together to communicate over distance.

Both Bogdosian and Sci/Tech headquarters had sent her hundreds of questions. Dealing with them felt like doing schoolwork, except that a lot more was at stake than just a grade. Sanjuro stretched and sent a telepathic message to Gervaise, who was sitting nearby working on an equally long questionnaire: "I feel like I'm taking a final exam."

"I was thinking it felt more like answering interrogatories in a complicated lawsuit, especially the way the trivial is mixed in with the important," Gervaise sent back. "Except that in most legal departments, responses to this kind of crap are done by smart comps. All the lawyers have to do is look them over." The lawyer was getting good at mind-to-mind communication.

They were not alone in agonizing over piles of questions from the System. Everyone on the mission was doing something similar. For all that she was complaining, Sanjuro was glad to be describing things related to her actual work. Earlier sheafs of questions on the war and the treaty negotiations had been harder to do. Even Pham had had to take time away from making sure things got rebuilt to explain the damage.

At least Bogdosian asked interesting questions, ones that made Sanjuro think carefully about what she had learned from her study of Cibolan culture. Dealing with her questions was like the good parts of school, the situations where you found yourself digging deeper and deeper until you truly understood a subject.

Bogdosian was a great teacher and a great scientist, for all her political machinations. Sanjuro found herself regretting that the professor couldn't meet Sundown and the others, so she did her best to give the her as much detail as possible. Maybe in the future, there might be an opportunity to take a Cibolan delegation to Earth; maybe Bogdosian would live long enough to see that happen. But she couldn't rely on that.

　　　　　　　　　　　　⇒

Two weeks after that first call Masire held a shipwide meeting. Those in remote spots were patched in, audio only; they still didn't have vid working. "System high command has preliminarily accepted our reports, subject to further investigation. They're sending out a high-level team. Obviously, the original shipload of miners and settlers was called off when we went missing. They'll be sending a smaller crew along with the investigating team, since they have accepted that they can't start settlements on Cibola. A/ND flight is down to two years at this point, so that's how long it will be.

"Until they get here, I'm in charge. They've confirmed my appointment of Commander Pham as acting captain of the *Mercator*, and of Sgt. Montoya as an acting lieutenant and marine commandant."

Montoya, sitting with the rest of the marine crew, was heard to say, "Oh, kuso."

"Commander Pham's appointments to fill vacant Space Corps spots and Col. Rao's decisions on Sci/Tech are also approved. And they agreed that Captain Sanjuro should continue as liaison to the Cibolans."

Sanjuro let out a breath she hadn't realized she was holding. If the brass had approved her job, her explanation of her actions had satisfied them, at least for now.

"They should have made you an ambassador," Gervaise sent to Sanjuro, making sure Kyo and Masire could pick up the message.

"It's good enough. I can do my work," she sent back.

"The Security Council has approved the treaty in principle, but it's still subject to country by country debate. Official acceptance will take awhile."

"Meanwhile we're making it a foregone conclusion," Gervaise sent around the same circle.

Masire glared at Gervaise, Sanjuro and Kyo. Sanjuro gave him a grin. He knew as well as any of them that the comments were their way of letting go. Everyone had been worried that high command would try to run the show from the System.

"The *Cortez* has been told of the treaty and informed that anything they do will be subject to it."

"Wonder how many lawyers they have," someone said loudly.

Even Masire joined the laughter. "It's okay. Their lawyers aren't half as good as ours."

That got a bigger laugh.

"You all know what your assignments are. Let's get back to work."

Sanjuro monitored the mental chatter as the meeting broke up. People were discussing the various Cibolan-human projects and their progress in telepathy. *We are weaving a place for humanity in this world,* she thought. *May it be the right one.*

# Epilogue

Sanjuro and Sundown sit in the main room of Sundown's house, warming themselves at a small stove. The stove is new, made of hastily forged steel from asteroid iron. Outside, a sharp wind blows, but the house has thick walls, and the stove is effective.

Iron and Sundown have made peace, but Iron left the day before to join the mining crew in the asteroids. The baby had been born a few weeks earlier and was now comfortably ensconced in Sundown's pouch, nursing greedily. Their older child was off on a month-long educational retreat.

Human astrobio quarters have been set up in the town, and Sanjuro has a room there. But she only goes there when she needs to talk to Kyo or one of the others; she and Sundown are working closely together, and she has found herself adopting the Cibolan habit of spending the winter with the people you need to work with. No one goes out in that wind who can avoid it. The house is well-stocked, and they can go into the weave when they need different information.

A half-empty bottle of human-made wine—marine home brew—sits on a table, along with a crock of the Cibolan fermented drink. Sanjuro and Sundown have been alternating between the two bottles and are both mildly drunk.

Tomorrow both have work to do. Sanjuro is honing her telepathic skills. Taking Sanjuro's own learning as a template for training other humans, they are developing something like a curriculum. Kyo has speculated that telepathy is like languages, easier to master in childhood than as an adult. Sanjuro hopes to prove her wrong. Sundown is learning human language. This is much more difficult than Sanjuro's learning telepathy. Sanjuro frequently wonders whether Sundown really understands the words and whether any other Cibolans will even try to understand how humans think.

But tonight they are not working. Tonight they are telling each other silly stories. While Sanjuro misses the point of some of Sundown's stories, and Sundown clearly doesn't follow all of Sanjuro's, it doesn't really matter. The drinks and the companionship are enough. Sundown communicates feelings of pleasure, and Sanjuro giggles like a girl at a slumber party. Which, it suddenly occurs to her, this is. The idea of a Cibolan/human slumber party makes her giggle all the more.

Sundown sends her a query, and Sanjuro responds with an image of a roomful of young Cibolans and humans, eating and giggling and generally causing an uproar. She's not quite sure Sundown gets the idea—do Cibolan kids have sleepovers, she wonders? Which sends her into another spasm of laughter.

And then there is a noise from Sundown. A snuffling sound, from the nose, more or less. Sanjuro stares at her, trying to figure it out. Sundown seems unable to control it, but the sending Sanjuro receives is one of pleasure.

It's a laugh, Sanjuro realizes. Or maybe more of a giggle. It's the first noise she's ever heard from Sundown, and it's a laugh. She laughs more herself.

"Friend," she says, sending the image of the word to Sundown. They've been working on relationship words today. "Friend." She accompanies the word with an image of the two of them arm in arm.

The image of the word comes back: friend. It's hard to tell with an abstract concept, but Sanjuro thinks that maybe, just maybe, they both mean the same thing.

# Author Biography

Nancy Jane Moore has been writing fiction seriously since the early 1990s. Her short fiction has appeared in numerous anthologies and in magazines ranging from *Lady Churchill's Rosebud Wristlet* to the *National Law Journal.* Her novella *Changeling* was one of the early Aqueduct Press Conversation Pieces and her collection *Conscientious Inconsistencies* was published by PS Publishing in 2008. Two other collections and a novella have been published by Book View Café.

Moore also practiced law for many years, specializing in the organization of food and housing cooperatives. She later worked as a legal editor. She began studying martial arts in 1979 and holds a fourth degree black belt in Aikido.